PRAISE FOR
ANN TONSOR ZEDDIES

"*Typhon's Children* is exciting and visionary science fiction—recommended for those who enjoy their imaginary worlds rich and complex. Fans of *Dune* should find it very satisfying."

—GREG BEAR
New York Times bestselling author
of *Darwin's Radio*

"[She] blends perceptive writing with psychological depth and scientific realism . . . the ideal science-fiction mixture."

—JAMES GUNN
Author of *The Immortals*

"[Ann Tonsor Zeddies] takes the reader into the heart of a world few writers would attempt to imagine let alone achieve with such depth and sensitivity. Her work is some of the most original I have read in a long time."

—KATIE WAITMAN
Author of *The Merro Tree*

"*Riders of Leviathan* is a haunting melody, a stirring and remarkable book. Even better than its predecessor, it combines marvelous scientific speculation with superb storytelling and a deeply human compassion."

—JEFFREY A. CARVER
Author of *The Chaos Chronicles*

By Ann Tonsor Zeddies writing as Toni Anzetti:

TYPHON'S CHILDREN
RIDERS OF LEVIATHAN

STEEL
HELIX

ANN TONSOR ZEDDIES

BALLANTINE BOOKS • NEW YORK

A Del Rey® Book
Published by The Ballantine Publishing Group
Copyright © 2003 by Ann Tonsor Zeddies

www.delreydigital.com

ISBN 0-345-41873-5

Manufactured in the United States of America

First Edition: March 2003

10 9 8 7 6 5 4 3 2 1

I
The Island of Dr. Rameau

My Love is of a birth as rare,
As 'tis for object strange and high:
It was begotten of Despair
Upon Impossibility.
ANDREW MARVELL,
"The Definition of Love"

Then I look about me at my fellow men. And I go in fear. I see faces keen and bright, others dull or dangerous, others unsteady, insincere; none that have the calm authority of a reasonable soul. I feel as though the animal was surging up through them; that presently the degradation of the Islanders will be played over again on a larger scale.
H. G. WELLS,
The Island of Dr. Moreau

1

Rameau knew that something was wrong. He was watching the colors dance. Streaks of many hues drifted past his face—deep red, magenta, and bubbles of frothy pink, as if someone had been washing their hands of the whole mess with a bar of ruby soap.

The bubbles slow-danced, coalescing into faceted clusters, surfing in slow motion to their silent extinction against a ventilation grid. A film of deepening red layers grew against that grid and the wall around it, clotted purple-black in the center, surrounded by a corona of red. As if the walls could bruise.

The colored circle drew his gaze like a mandala. It was the one focal point in a spinning world. For he was spinning slowly with the colors. The brightest ribbon of all trailed past his face as he spun, and the bubbles burst against his face with a soft wet kiss, and a smell—

Blood. It's blood in free fall.

His face intersected with the ribbon of droplets, and he choked. His body twisted in a spasm of agony, retching the choking moisture out of his lungs. He gasped.

Why is there no air?

Because the Dome is holed!

His transient bubble of calm burst. He was fully conscious again, just in time to die.

The trajectory of the blood ribbons showed where the holes were. The blood, the other tumbling bodies like Rameau, and what was left of the air, all aimed inexorably toward the pin-pricks and gashes in the Dome's crystal skin. The fluids and the

air would escape out into space. Solid objects would remain behind, dancing their foolish dance in an empty bubble.

*Dance. I was watching the dance when—I was up on the
light bar—*

He thrashed against the current, trying to change direction.
When he turned his head, his entire body turned in a slow
pirouette, and the stream of red bubbles crossed his face again.
Something red and wet bumped against his side, and he tried to
brush it away, but couldn't move his arm.

My arm!

The limb came into sharp focus. He could view it clinically,
as if he were diagnosing someone else.

*That's my arm. Crushing injury. The bones are smashed. Se-
vere blood loss—*

His chest heaved in involuntary, gasping spasms that he recognized as the precursors to asphyxiation.

Air—where? Emergency suits—

He knew where the suits were. He hadn't been that far from
the locker—perched on the bar that supported the colored
lights, the perfect vantage point to see the dance, to watch over
the dancers. And then—how far had he drifted?

Catch hold of something—

But all was in motion. Smashed and jagged objects waltzed
past him. He might be crushed before he suffocated. Gathering
speed, a clump of debris flashed toward him, and for a moment
he glimpsed arms outspread—an offer, or a plea for help? Then
he saw the face, frozen in pop-eyed, eternal surprise.

He lashed out with both feet, connected with a soggy thump.
The body tumbled away, and Rameau cartwheeled on a new
vector, toward the wall. He scraped along its curve, staring for
a cold moment into the void that lay just beyond the transparent skin. Then he crashed into a projecting bracket and threw
his good arm over it before he could bounce off. He clung, and
gasped, and the spinning in his head slowly stilled.

He shifted his grasp from the bracket to the beam it supported, and kicked himself along the beam, sliding like a bead
on a wire. He reached the utility locker and slapped it open. His
movements were wide and spastic now. He could no longer

coordinate his fingers. His field of vision narrowed to a graying tunnel through which he could barely see the glimmer of helmet stripes.

One-handed, he jammed the helmet onto his head and bit down on the mouthpiece. Oxygen blasted into him like cool fire. His sight returned.

Too bright! Too bright!

The pain came back with it, blazing up in his arm like a blowtorch in his veins.

The suit was full-zip; he could yank it open one-handed. He thrust a leg in to hold it in place. He couldn't get his injured arm into the armhole. Crying aloud with pain, he used his good arm to stuff the mangled mass into place, and hit the differential pressure node on the shoulder. As he struggled into the rest of the suit and zipped it shut, the left sleeve pressurized itself around the injury. It shut off the bleeding like a tourniquet. A good feature—he remembered approving it himself. He let the mouthpiece retract as the suit sealed and filled with air. Automatically, it began to administer medications to ease pain and shock.

He knew what he had to do next. Not get to the clinic and treat himself. Not assess the casualties. The one thing that mattered was to find Dakini.

She was dancing. She was dancing when they—

He found another suit and stuck his good arm through the belt so he wouldn't lose his grip on it. He switched his suit mike to external and launched himself away, calling her name.

Bodies and debris swept past him, still dangerous even now that he was suited up. He aimed himself spinward, going with them but a little faster, passing through the silent herd, looking for the one, singular shape. The dead spared him guilt. Not one showed any twitch of life. They had passed beyond the bounds of Rameau's duty. Someone else would have to serve them now.

But Dakini—if she's—what can I—with one hand—

He pushed that thought away. He could get her into the suit. He could drag her to safety, somewhere.

Then he saw a glint of gold among the pale, the dark, the buff, the ashy drab, the endless sequence of debris. Her long gold limbs spinning slowly, alone, on the far side of the swarm, still glinting in the last splintered light from the spots. Just as he'd seen her first, alone and dancing. He shot toward her through the slow avalanche of corpses.

O Kannon, O Compassionate One—

He was stammering prayers and adjurations he'd abandoned long ago. He tranced out for a moment—not surprising with the suit dripping meds into every vein—then came back into focus, and found himself vainly trying to wrap the suit around Dakini's drifting body. He should have known better. There was no way to fit her impossibly long and slender arms and legs into a suit made for a human. No help there.

He yanked the helmet loose—too sharp a movement; it sent him drifting away from her. He snatched her back only just in time, letting the helmet go. It bobbed away.

Sobbing under his breath, he wrapped his legs around hers to hold her, pulled the helmet back.

He tried to force the mouthpiece between her lips, but her mouth hung slack. The blast of air fanned the blood in streaks across her golden cheeks, but there was no answering gasp. Her head nodded in the current, like a flower too heavy for its stalk.

She was dancing. She was only dancing. And they—

He tried to breathe into her mouth, the old low-tech way he'd learned long before he came to Varuna, to this station that had the best equipment anywhere, the best guards, the most infallible shields, this paradise where the rich and mighty came, because here no one could—

No one could die.

Her throat was crushed. Her chest was crushed. His offered breath could not pass the blood crusted on her lips. He had known. He had known too much about this body not to know.

He had been hidden among the lights, and hadn't seen the first disturbance as the invaders swept though the house, through the patrons in their box seats. He had only seen them when they fell through the Dome itself and smashed the dancers aside like kites in a downdraft. He had known in the first moment, as he saw her flung aside. He had launched himself toward her, as the patrons fled the other way.

But they got there first. The Rukh.

And as the massive, heavy fists descended on him, too, as their bludgeons crushed and tore, he'd known. Just one of those blows would have been enough to shatter her grace forever. They'd killed him, but it would take a while to die. For her, one brutal moment had been enough.

He let the helmet go, and drifted. It didn't matter now.

All that mattered was not letting go of her. Until. But it was hard to be sure his grasp was gentle enough, through the thick gloves of the suit. The micro-g transforms were so fragile, so easily damaged. It was the first thing a genedoc had to learn about them. He had learned. He'd given the transforms the very best of care. Until now.

"I'm sorry," he said.

The last of the air, on its way to the stars, carried them to the inner shell, and Rameau let himself float there, fending off the wall with his back, so Dakini's head was cushioned from any impact. He turned his face to the wall, looking down into the great darkness. He could see the edge of Garuda, the planet they orbited, rising below the station, and the bright reddish spark of Meru, sunward. Dakini had seen this every day, had known every day that she could never go there, never leave the bright bubble that imprisoned her.

And I didn't help her. I helped them keep her here. I thought Varuna was safe.

And now? O Kannon, does her soul fly free?

There was no answer from the Compassionate One. The Reform Mahayana that Rameau's parents had practiced claimed that transforms had no souls. Created by humans, they had no place on the wheel of life. When they died, they simply stopped, and would not be reborn. If Rameau had still believed that any being heard his words, his one prayer would have been to stop with her. He didn't want to be reborn.

A thousand lives of suffering couldn't make up for what I've done. And this one will be over soon.

He tried to focus on her face, but darkness spread into his field of vision. Then a flutter of white caught his attention, and he looked up.

A child floated above him, just out of reach. He thought it was a girl, though he couldn't be sure. She wore only a thin white coverall, and she was very pale. Wisps of hair stirred in the last of the breeze. There couldn't possibly be enough air left for her to breathe. He thought vaguely of the helmet. If she could get to it, she might still be all right. He tried to reach out to her, to say "Don't be frightened," but he could only make a faint choking sound.

She didn't look frightened, though he was. She moved a hand to her face, with a puzzled expression. Dakini's arms floated free of Rameau's grasp, as he tried to reach the child, and the movement appeared to catch the child's eye. As if curious, she stretched out to touch Dakini's hand. There was a sound like a sigh, though the Dome was nearly vacuum by now.

Suddenly Rameau realized that the girl had a massive dark bruise on the cheek she had touched. How had he missed that? It spread over her whole face as he watched. Her fingers, touching Dakini's, turned purple, then black. She slumped inward, and shrank, and her body shriveled and cracked like a puffball, releasing a faint brown mist. For a moment he could see pale bones in a cloud of dark fluid. Then even those turned to powder and drifted away.

This can't be real.

Involuntarily, he clutched Dakini closer. She seemed to crumple in his arms. He looked down. Her face was covered with a dark, sticky substance. He tried to brush it away with his gloved hand. His hand went through her face. There was no face, just a gelid mass that melted away when he touched it. Then there was no body. Just a dark liquid that soaked his suit and ebbed away.

And she was gone.

Staring around him, too shocked to make a sound, he saw the other corpses disintegrating. In a slow wave, spreading outward as if he were ground zero, the bodies twisted in on themselves, and shrank, and a brown mist hovered for an instant before dispersing into the empty Dome. All around him, the dead were dying a second death.

As the bodies dissipated, he saw the massive figures who

had been hovering behind them, in their dun-colored p-suits. He had nowhere to run. He could only watch as they closed in on him.

He expected them to kill him. He took a deep breath for his final moment. But the moment went on. And on. He had to breathe again. Huge hands grasped him, and towed him across the Dome, and then out of it, into a narrow space where he bumped against the walls. Yet his life had not ended. He felt restraints close around him, painfully tight, and then the crushing pressure of hard acceleration. He blacked out.

He regained consciousness knowing there was weight, because someone had dumped him onto a hard, cold surface. The shock brought a moment of agonized clarity. The suit was gone. He was naked and cold, and he couldn't feel his arm at all. A deep voice spoke. The only word he understood was his own name.

"Huh. E go terminate," said another voice, close to his ear, and then laughed cheerfully.

"Cohort, unspecified, is conscious," said another. This voice had the inhumanly calm intonation of an AI monitor. Relief shot through Rameau; he must be in a hospital. He felt no pain. He had air. He was conscious. They must be treating him, whoever they were. He'd be all right.

Don't panic, he thought.

Then he opened his eyes.

The surface he lay on wasn't a bed. It was a moving belt like a conveyor. He scanned the rest of the room, and gasped. He wasn't in a normal hospital room; instead, the belt carried him around the perimeter of a cylindrical space. If this was a hospital, it was in orbit.

Before he could move or speak, something soft but tight wrapped around his legs, and a plastic shield closed down over his chest. A mask descended to cover his nose and mouth. He tried to raise his arms, to get hold of it and tear it loose, but only one of his hands seemed to move. He still couldn't feel the other arm.

Don't panic.

I am *panicking.*

Where's my arm?

He could feel his shoulder. The joint was pulled painfully taut.

Like they're trying to rip my arm off!

Straining against the mask that immobilized his head, he caught a glimpse of something metallic in motion. It flashed downward.

Rameau yelled, and his whole body convulsed in shock. It hadn't hurt. But he knew what had happened. The severing blow resounded through his whole body. Someone had just chopped off his arm.

He could hear himself sobbing, and feel the positive pressure as the mask forced more oxygen into him. In the back of his mind, a frantic voice kept repeating words that might keep him sane.

Automated medicine. It's automated. He heaved in more air and held it, then exhaled slowly and forced himself to pause before he gasped again.

Stop crying. You've watched this happen to other people. They're not torturing you. They're treating you. They used anesthesia.

But—Kali Mat! They cut off my arm! Amputation? We don't do amputation anymore! Why couldn't they regenerate me? Jesus Mohammad, it must have been completely mangled.

He had never realized how terrifying automated medicine was—to the patient.

But he was calming down—or maybe they were giving him something to make him calm down. Whichever it was, it didn't last long as the belt dropped him with a jolt into a vertical position, and he looked down.

Directly below him lay a tank of pinkish-yellow fluid capped with the confinement membrane that would prevent fluids from escaping in micro g. The fluid seethed with movement, and the darting motion of white things shaped like rice grains. Convection currents bumped larger objects to the surface, then pushed them under again. For a moment, Rameau thought it was a soup pot and they were going to cook him.

The reality, when he figured it out, wasn't an improvement.

The rice grains were maggots. The larger objects were severed limbs—arms, legs, hands, feet—trailing red and white cords of vein and tendon.

Kannon. Amitabha. Help me!

The mask snaked a soft plastic tube like a finger down his throat, and he could no longer cry out in protest. Then the belt released him.

The shock of having his arm chopped off was nothing compared to splashdown through the membrane. Every muscle in his body strained in a vain effort to hurl himself back out of the pot. But new restraints held him tight and kept him under. He could feel the nibbling action of a thousand tiny mouths against his skin. *They're going to eat me.* But it didn't hurt. Except his arm. A ring of fire gnawed at the socket where the arm had been. It seemed to bore into his bones. A waxy white, dead hand bumped against his face, maggots sizzling around it.

His senses hit overload. He could feel himself going mad. Fear and loathing filled his whole mind.

And then he was pulled free of the membrane, knowing that time had elapsed, though he didn't remember passing out. Maggots tumbled back into the tank as he ascended. He was dumped on his back onto a moving surface that angled gradually upward until he was in a sitting position. The mask and tube were pulled from his face, leaving his throat raw, as if its inner surface had been torn away.

The restraints snapped free, and then the belt pushed him off. He sprawled on a floor. He was naked. He was trembling. And his two hands were clenched in front of him.

"Treatment complete," the cool artificial voice said.

Immediately after that, another voice said, "Get up. The Commander will speak with you."

He looked up. The man who had spoken towered over him—would have towered, even if Rameau had been able to stand. Everything about him was larger than normal. His arms and legs were longer and more muscular than those of any ordinary man. His features were so clean and regular that his face looked like a mask. His hair was the color of bleached aspen leaves and was precisely cropped. His eyes were the color of river ice on a cold day. His lips moved with crisp precision when he spoke, and the teeth that showed when they parted were perfect. The face was faintly tanned, but in the shadow of his chin, his neck was white, and Rameau could see a blue vein beating, like water flowing under ice.

The man wore a simple gray coverall, decorated at the shoulders by a jumble of colored symbols Rameau could not decipher. Only one sign stood out clearly. It was the same stylized face-symbol that had marked the p-suits of the men who had dragged him off Varuna: an oval, holding two eyes and an m-shaped or wing-shaped line that could have been meant for brows and nose. You could read it as letters, too—OMO. And the big, enclosing oval stood for another O.

Omo Originale.

Original Man.

Despair filled Rameau like icy water. He still did not know where he was, but he knew who was there with him.

"Oh, Kannon," he choked. His stomach twisted.

"Not responsive," the pale man said. He flicked his wrist, and a needle appeared in his hand. He slapped Rameau with it. A burning sensation surged through Rameau, and quelled his nausea. He was able to speak.

"What was that?" he sobbed. "What did you do to me?"

A startled look passed over the pale man's impassive face, as if a lab animal had spoken.

"Regeneration tank," the pale man said. "The damaged arm was removed. Bioforms in the tank reprocess dead flesh. Cloned limb attaches. Treatment is complete. This is standard treatment."

He held out a coverall. "Dress. Hurry."

Rameau's new left arm was still clumsy as he tried to pull the garment on, and his ribs still hurt. The pale man lost patience and tugged the fabric over Rameau's arms and legs, then did up the zips on the sides. The coverall had been made for someone much bigger, but at least he wasn't naked anymore.

"What are you going to do with me?" he said. His voice was pathetic—weak and shaky. It was a mistake to sound so much like a victim.

"The Commander will speak with you," the pale man said again. Rameau saw him straighten just a bit more as he spoke. The Commander must be a person of importance.

He expected to be taken to another place to meet the Commander. But the pale man spoke briefly to his own hand, then pointed and clicked with a mailed finger, and a marked square on the wall in front of them suddenly turned into a three-dimensional space, like a window, showing the torso of a man in uniform.

At first, the face in the display looked to Rameau like a mirrored reflection of the pale man who stood beside him. Then he saw that the coverall was a different color—white instead of gray—and the face was older, defined by lines that expressed a separate personality. It was a personality Rameau had seen before: Kuno Gunnarsson, the human who had created Original Man. The one they called the Founder.

"Gunnarsson," he whispered. It *must* be shock, he thought. Kuno Gunnarsson was dead.

"Error," the man in the window said. "I am not the Founder. I have the honor to continue his lineage. I am Gunnarsson Prime, Commander, Original Man jumpship *Langstaff*. This is both rank and persig. You will address me as Prime, or Commander. You will now state your own rank and persig."

"I don't understand," Rameau said. That statement covered a lot of ground.

"Your *name*," the Commander said.

"I am Piers Rameau," he said. "I have no rank. I'm a civilian. I'm a doctor. I was giving emergency care to victims of the assault on Varuna. They were all civilians. They were defenseless and unarmed. They had no military affiliation. The Sol-Terran Concords demand that you set me free. Put me back. I want you to put me back where I came from."

"That will not be possible," the Commander said remotely. "We are accelerating to jump node." His eyes focused somewhere else, as if he were scanning a heads-up display that remained invisible to Rameau.

"This is kidnapping! I demand you return me to human space!"

As Rameau spoke, he felt a tremor pass through the surface he stood on. For a minute he thought his legs were trembling, but then it came again, more strongly. The structure in which he stood vibrated like a bell, grinding his very bones together. He recognized the signs of sonic bombardment. Wherever he was, the battle continued.

The Commander issued a brief series of orders to unseen personnel. Then his attention returned to Rameau.

"The Founder left instructions regarding the baseline human Piers Rameau," he said. "He ordered that we salvage you. We located you on Varuna and fulfilled this command. The Founder left a personal message for Piers Rameau. The message will be communicated, but not at this time. We are in crisis mode. Your assistance is required. You have medical training. You will affiliate directly to me, and your designation will be Rameau, G-Prime MedSpec. Repeat the designation."

"No," Rameau said. "No! You can't do this. I'm a civilian!"

Gunnarsson's eyes flicked to the pale man beside Rameau.

"Motivate him," Gunnarsson said.

The pale man grasped Rameau's arm, as if to lead him away, but with a slightly different grip. Rameau bent double, gasping.

"Rameau, G-Prime MedSpec!" he cried. At the time, he didn't feel that he was surrendering. It was merely an incantation that he had to recite as fast as possible to stop the unbearable pain.

"Motivation complete," Gunnarsson said. The pale man let Rameau go.

"Your duties begin immediately. Further indoctrination is postponed until normal operations recommence. You treated transforms on Varuna. You will now treat transform casualties on *Langstaff*. The cohort will escort you and will provide you with any necessary information. Dismissed."

2

The cohort dragged Rameau through a tight maze of corridors, ending in a vertical drop tube through which they shot feetfirst. The cohort looked curiously at Rameau when the fall made him cry out again.

"That cohort need enabler installed," he said.

Rameau clung to a handhold, trying to breathe through a chestful of knives.

"Where are we?" he asked despairingly. "Are we anywhere in Garuda system?"

"This cohort affiliates to security, not navigation," the cohort said. "But he heard the Commander say we approach jump. Since this is stated, it is not possible we are still in-system."

He glanced again at Rameau. "That cohort need enabler fit, first opportunity. E no process good, current condition."

An accurate diagnosis, Rameau thought. But whatever an enabler was, he didn't think it would be an improvement.

He staggered after his guide until they came to a set of pressure doors, apparently an air lock. The cohort passed his hand through a scanner to make the doors operate.

A blood key, Rameau thought. He could never deceive such a scan, based on specific markers in the blood—unless he could cut off living flesh from one of the cohorts and pass it through the scanner before the proteins altered too much.

Not much hope of doing that.

They passed through the second door, and all hope vanished.

Rameau had been expecting another rotating steel drum of a room, like the one where he'd been treated. This place was more like a cargo bay. But instead of cargo, it was full of bodies. Half the available floor space was taken up by portable litters, and each litter sagged under the weight of a pinioned Rukh. The Rukh were spread-eagled, their arms and legs locked to the frame by heavy steel fetters. Clamps immobilized their heads.

Heaped on the floor in front of the litters were more bodies—more Rukh. As he watched, a pair of clean-up bots with soft plastic housings, like ambulatory pudding molds, trundled across the floor. They gripped the nearest of the dead Rukh by its boots and dragged the body to a wall grid that opened to suck it in. It left a broad sticky smear behind, but the bots licked that up, too. When all traces of the Rukh's existence were gone, they moved on to the next.

"Kali Mat," Rameau muttered. He had long since ceased to chant to the Compassionate One, but this sight brought the names of the old harsh gods easily to his lips.

I did die, after all, he thought. *I've come back as a demon in one of the hell worlds.*

"Transform triage," the cohort said. "Damage was taken in approaching Varuna."

"I have no equipment," Rameau said. "I can't—" But he took a few steps forward, automatically. Training died hard.

He stopped at the bodies piled on the floor, and knelt by the nearest one. Sounds that were not words bubbled from its mouth, along with a pale foam that had already caked to powder on its cheeks. It stretched out one hand and grasped his sleeve. The hand was huge, the size of his head.

Rameau struck it away and leapt to his feet. He cried out in horror, then in agony as his own cracked ribs gouged at him. As he waited, bent with pain, for the red to clear from his eyes, he added paralyzing shame to his anguish and despair. He had struck a patient, and added to the suffering that he was meant to relieve.

What could I do? How could I help it? he howled within. *That thing is a Rukh. It's not human. It is an abomination. And it touched me.*

He longed to scrub his hands, his whole body, with disinfectant. He retched in spite of the medication, but there was absolutely nothing in his guts.

The cohort took his hand in a warm, firm, perfect grasp. Rameau was startled. Did they know compassion after all? Then the cohort found the pressure points and twisted.

Rameau screamed.

"You require motivation," the cohort said stolidly. He let go, and Rameau fell to his knees again beside the dying Rukh. He saw the massive fist clenched in agony. The eyes were swollen shut, half hidden by the heavy browridges. Cracked, blistered lips writhed in the dark tangle of the mane-like, curly beard.

But inwardly, all Rameau could see were those massive bodies, encased in gleaming armor, moving like a deadly boulder-swarm of meteors, swooping through the Dome in a halo of flame and death.

The Rukh hadn't flamed the dancers. They had merely swept through the space where the dancers hung like crystals on a solstice tree. The Rukh had smashed them with the casual brutality of falling boulders. Smashed them, shattered them, with the blows of fists like that one.

Rameau no longer wished for his medical kit. An iron bar would do—anything heavy and brutal enough to smash the abomination in front of him. His chest was bursting with hatred. He could hardly get the words out.

"I can't. I won't . . . treat that thing."

The cohort glanced at him, puzzled again. He did not seem to grasp Rameau's emotion.

"Correct. Standing orders state no treatment for transforms," he said agreeably. "More efficient to recycle damaged units and resupply. But crisis conditions apply now. MedTeam is ordered to salvage transforms. We need functional units and cannot resupply until crisis ends. You have permission to treat. You are transform doctor."

"I'm not touching it," Rameau choked. "Go ahead and kill me."

This time the cohort found pressure points at his temples and the back of his neck. He clawed at the cohort's hands, but the cohort didn't let go until Rameau was howling like a beaten dog.

"Yes, yes, okay," he panted, dropping to the floor in abject relief.

The cohort bent to peer at him, a faint confusion on the too-large face.

"Not kill Rameau," the cohort said. "Rameau get treatment. E go live."

The cohort's face cleared to its usual blank expression, as if he had assessed the problem and found a satisfactory answer.

"Function impaired," he said. "Enabler go normalize function."

Rameau heard him talking to his hand, and felt relief. The creature couldn't twist his joints while the hand was in use for communication.

In his crouched position, he was face-to-face with the Rukh. Its swollen, oversized lips were still, and the foam on them had dried. It had died while he resisted treating it. He was ashamed, but he was glad. He had won; at least he would not have to touch this one again.

But there were others. Many others.

He turned to the pale man—the cohort.

"You," he said, trying for an authoritative tone. "Does 'this cohort' have a name?"

For a fleeting moment, the cohort looked panicked, as if Rameau had required something beyond his ability to supply.

"MedSpec require this cohort's persig—uhh, this cohort's personal designation?" he said.

"Yes, if it's shorter and more to the point than 'this cohort.' "

"This cohort is Neb. This cohort is Group Nu of his cohort. His sibs are Nor, Nik, and Nuun. No, not Nik no more," he corrected himself. "Nik terminate, this engagement."

"Neb, I can't treat these . . . things. I don't know what's wrong with them."

"This not 'thing.' This a Rukh."

"Exactly. I don't know anything about . . . them. There are too many. Call help. Get your own medical officer to do this. I can't."

"Cohort medical officer busy treat cohorts," Neb said. "Fix transforms is baseline job. Rameau must hurry. Many await treatment."

"You were ordered to provide me with assistance," Rameau said. It was a last-ditch effort to stall.

Neb straightened up, and Rameau flinched, thinking the cohort was about to motivate him again. Instead, Neb pointed.

"Assistance come now," he said. "With enabler."

Half a dozen cohorts approached. The perfect, pale-skinned young man in the lead carried a hard-sided case.

"No! I don't bloody want to be enabled. Leave me alone!" Rameau protested. But the warm, heavy hand descended on the back of his neck, dropping him again to his knees.

Two more cohorts pulled his arms out straight. Their control of his joints was pinpoint-perfect. If he had moved an inch in any direction, his bones would have snapped.

Rameau couldn't see what they were doing to him. He felt them zip away the left arm and side of his coverall. He gasped as something touched his ribs.

For an instant it felt like scalding heat. Then he realized that it was the tingling chill of anesthetic spray. The spray moved along his ribs and up his arm. Something punctured his skin. It didn't hurt, but he could feel it burrowing under the surface, following the path of the spray.

Suddenly, his mouth went dry, with a metallic taste. As quickly as it dried, saliva flooded back in, and he had to swallow hard. His mind seemed to clear and brighten. He recognized the symptoms; he had been given a stimulant.

The pain in his ribs was replaced by a dull ache, accompanied by continual prickling.

An electrical current, to stimulate bone growth, he thought.

"Enabler installed," said one of the cohorts. They let go of his arms.

The outer section of the enabler sheathed his left forearm in a semiflexible shell that looked like a metallic kemplex composite. Noding covered his wrist and the back of his hand, and a set of crystal flash-nodes were still settling themselves into the notches between his knuckles. A flex-screen display lit up along his forearm when he rubbed at the nodes. They itched. A second, bulkier section had closed around his arm above the elbow. Rameau guessed that the visible part of the assembly held a sophisticated medical kenner, with a self-contained medication unit. He didn't know what the interior sections were doing. Narrow tubing—nonreactive plastic, he hoped—had worked its way into his arteries at elbow and neck. He looked in vain for a manual override.

While he was looking, the cohorts put away the case. One of them unslung another device that looked like a gun. Then Rameau recognized its blue-and-white medical markings. It was a subcutaneous injector, but of a larger caliber than any he had seen outside an animal lab.

"You're not pointing that thing at me," he said, trying to crawl away.

But Neb pinned him to the floor with one booted foot, while the other cohort punched the muzzle of the gun into Rameau's arm, between the two sections of the enabler.

"Ow!" The gun injected a button-sized disk deep into the muscles. It felt like being stabbed with a blunt knife—one more insult to his already overloaded system. He began to tremble, then stopped as the enabler took over and plunged him into a warm, fuzzy relaxation.

Neb sprayed his arm with antiseptic and glued shut the breach in his skin.

"Now Rameau locate by shipmind," Neb said. "Ship find that cohort, ship give e message. That cohort affiliate *Langstaff* now."

Rameau felt his flesh creep. The injected pellet moved under his skin as the enabler sent out fine wire tentacles and drew it closer. He guessed the locator was connecting itself to his implanted kenner.

Neb grasped him under the shoulder and hauled him to his feet. Apparently the cohort thought he'd had enough time to get used to his new equipment.

"E function better now," Neb said. "E go work fast."

"I can take a hint," Rameau said. He staggered toward the next patient. As he moved, the stimulants filled him with reckless energy. He knew the symptoms; he was definitely over-amped. If the enabler was calibrated for these oversized super-men, it was overdosing him. He would get through the next twenty-four hours all right. After that he would probably have seizures.

Something to look forward to.

He looked down at the nearest litter.

"Use enabler," Neb said.

Rameau looked stupidly at his kenner screen. Nothing registered. Rameau turned his hand over. The wires were still moving. They were knitting an almost microscopic web across his palm. The ends of the web dived beneath the skin of his fingers as he watched, then were still.

"Touch," Neb said, gesturing to the Rukh.

"No way," Rameau said.

"Diagnostic," Neb insisted. "Must touch to get data."

Impatient, Neb seized Rameau's wrist in that warm, implacable grip, and forced his hand down against the transform's body. Rameau shuddered as his fingers ground against bloody flesh.

The kenner calculated rapidly from the contact, presenting him with data. It wasn't interested in his feelings. The anti-nausea meds wouldn't let him vomit.

He tried to focus on the task, not on the foul taste in his mouth.

According to the kenner, the Rukh's liver function was failing. Rameau could see with his own eyes that its limbs were grossly swollen and discolored.

It looks like snakebite. Or mushroom poisoning. Something with toxins.

Fumbling, he found basic nodes on the kenner and extracted more data. The fluids his enabler had sampled were loaded with virus. The kenner rapidly matched viral fragments to cell proteins until it found the point where the virus locked onto a liver enzyme, causing the liver to dissolve its own tissues. It couldn't hurt humans, because the enzyme that it subverted was an engineered variant, present only in the transforms.

Too bad it's not snakebite. It would be a fitting end for them.

Rameau had seen plenty of deaths from venom in his childhood on Garuda. Not exactly snakes by Sol-Terran standards, but there were plenty of creeping, poisonous things. Death could drag on for agonizing days, or come in an instant. Either way, there was nothing much a doctor could do about it.

Unfortunately, it would be easy to fix the transforms.

"What are you hanging around for? Any second-level viral antagonist can stop the virus. Then you're going to have to put them through a cycle of system cleansing to remove the toxins, and then regenerate their livers. Get them out of here and put them in the tanks."

The cohorts didn't respond.

"Move! The longer they go on metabolizing, the sicker they're going to get!"

Finally Neb spoke. "This cohort regret, obey impossible. Already gave antivirals. But system cleansing not calibrated for Rukh. Rameau must remove damaged tissue from functioning organs and transplant liver tissue to transforms that cannot function." He spoke slowly and formally, as if trying hard to make sure Rameau could understand.

"I can't do that," Rameau said. He felt the enabler pouring artificial energy and alertness into his veins, assuring him that whatever happened, he was going to feel fine. But it couldn't touch whatever part of him felt sick at the sight of those rows of monsters, staked out like lab dogs.

"Team One here to assist," Neb said. "Rameau will instruct them. Then they will perform correct technique. Team Two will observe and then assist. The Commander has ordered that Team One and Team Two salvage transforms and learn technique from the medical officer."

"I can't," Rameau said. He clung to that thought. He couldn't help the Rukh. It was impossible.

At a movement from one of the other cohorts, he flinched, expecting more motivation. He thought it was Neb coming toward him, until another cohort stopped the first one, and he realized *that* was Neb.

Neb put a laser scalpel in his right hand.

"Rameau is ordered to fix transforms," he said.

Rameau looked longingly at the pinioned Rukh, prepped for surgery, abdomen exposed. A laser scalpel wasn't much of a weapon, because it sealed off most bleeders as it sliced through. But if you sliced an artery lengthwise, you could still do damage. If he went down the row, he could probably kill at least a couple of them before the cohorts could stop him.

Even the cohorts—if I hit the carotid just right, then slice off a finger, an ear, get through the blood key—

Before the thought had even finished taking shape, he turned toward them, lashing out with the scalpel.

They moved so fast it seemed as if he were standing still.

The scalpel was twisted from his hand, nearly taking his thumb off with it. One of them pinned both his arms in a grip that forced him to bend over until his head nearly touched the floor, and still it felt as if the arms would be ripped from their sockets.

He was shoved back and forth as if the cohorts were fighting over him. They shouted in hoarse bursts of a language that he couldn't understand. Someone twisted his arms until he screamed. Then they dropped him.

He crashed to the ground, his arms numb, unable to catch himself. His head cracked against the floor, another stunning blow. Even the enabler could only deal with it by making his whole body go numb. His head, his guts, his hands, all were fuzzy cotton.

No more, he thought, as if the kenner could hear him and readjust itself. *No more. I'll die.*

There was a brief, fierce snarling that sounded like a dog-fight. Rameau turned his head, with an effort that felt like cranking some enormous steel cog, and saw that one of the cohorts had seized another, restraining him. That was where the snarling came from. Rameau couldn't tell the combatants apart. Was it Neb who had shaken him, or Neb who had made them let him go? Was Neb the one he'd tried to kill? He couldn't tell.

But one reached down and dragged Rameau to his feet, and put the scalpel back in his hand.

"Rameau fix transforms," he said, as if nothing had happened.

That ended Rameau's brief rebellion. Clearly, killing them had never been a possibility, except for that one brief instant, and only in his own mind. The real question was, would they kill him?

"Wait, e go blood," Neb said.

Rameau flinched violently as the cohort cupped one big hand around the side of his head again, immobilizing him. But Neb had a sterile swab in his other hand. He just wanted to wipe off the blood that was streaming from Rameau's nose.

"All ready you cut," he said. The cohorts stepped forward attentively.

Rameau's hands were still unsteady.

Maybe I'll kill them by accident, he thought.

The Rukh's open eyes were disconcerting. Rameau flipped a corner of the drape across them. He showed the cohorts how to feel for the liver, then confirmed the position with his scanner.

Ugh—they're right. This liver is a mess. Rotted full of holes. Looks as if someone splashed acid on it.

Laseroptic surgery wasn't going to work on this one. An incision was necessary. The cohorts were ready with glue and suction.

Rameau drew the first smooth line with the scalpel, wrinkled his nose at the first wisp of scorched hair and singed skin.

And hell broke loose. The litter rocked and crashed against the floor as the Rukh threw itself from side to side. A stifled bellow rose from the creature, a baying of horror and despair. All around the room, the same smothered howling rose from the Rukh's fellows. Rameau's patient writhed in one more convulsive spasm and overbalanced the litter. Still pinioned, it fell heavily to the floor. The others howled as if in sympathy with its pain.

"Kali Mat!" Rameau said. "The creature's not anesthetized! You said they were ready for surgery!"

"Yes, ready," Neb said. "It is waste to anesthetize transforms. Not needed. They do not have pain like humans."

"What are you talking about?" Rameau shouted. "Look at them! Of course they feel pain. Amitabha, I just cut the damned creature's belly open. I wouldn't treat a dog that way."

Neb approached him, the steely pale fingers raised and menacing. Rameau lifted his scalpel again. Let them knock him down again—or let them try.

They're treating me like a dog, too—not even a dog should suffer this way. I wouldn't do this, even to an animal.

His rage wasn't for the Rukh; it was for himself.

You can force me to be a surgeon, but you can't make me a butcher.

"No!" he shouted. "I am your senior medical officer, and I order you to properly prep these casualties for surgery. If you don't obey me immediately, I will put you on report for insubordination and incompetence."

Neb looked uncertain.

"No affiliate combat," he said.

"What does that have to do with it?" Rameau said.

The other cohorts stared.

"To make them sleep, need control codes for collar. This cohort no have."

"What collar?"

Neb gestured. Rameau stared at the metal rings circling the Rukh's thick necks. For the first time he looked closely, and realized that the collars were embedded in flesh, like his enabler.

"So you don't control the collar. So use normal medicine. Cohort medicine."

"It is waste," Neb said, but he gave in. He dispatched another cohort for nerve-blockers.

"Get it back up on the table," Rameau said. "Make sure it hasn't fractured anything."

Rameau's hands were shaking again. He tried to calm himself as he watched the cohorts lift the Rukh back into position. It took four of them to handle the weight.

He bent over the litter, trying to ignore the thick animal smell.

"That was a mistake," he said. "We don't intend to hurt you. It's not going to hurt anymore. Try to be calm."

"Rukh not have speech," Neb said.

But, though they could not speak, they must have understood, for the howling stilled.

Rameau took refuge in his art. Surgery for him was like the

trance of meditation. It narrowed awareness to a single track, where he could exert all his skills to reassemble the puzzle, to bring order, to re-create perfection. It carried him, even now. It was the last thing he could cling to.

The cohorts followed him closely and soon set up their own sterile field next to his, repeating each movement he made—opening the Rukh's belly, excising the damaged tissue, gluing up wounds and adding growth factors to the livers that could still function, or replacing them from a portable vat full of healthy pink segments. Every technique was perfectly imitated, though mechanical.

Like teaching a monkey to play the piano, Rameau thought.

They finished, finally, and he was still on his feet. There would be no convulsions today, which was good. Convulsions on top of a possible concussion should be avoided. The brain was made of meat and could only take so much abuse—unlike the spirit, which apparently could suffer wounds without limit.

"For god's sake take the restraints off them," he said. Turning away from the bodies, he began to clean up. "Nothing alive can get well in prison."

3

Neb steered him toward the air lock again. A series of electronic tones sounded.

"Eat now," Neb said.

"Not hungry," Rameau said. The idea of food seemed grotesque—something that belonged to another world entirely, the world of living men, which he had left behind.

Again a faint crease appeared in the cohort's smooth brow.

"Bells say MedTeam One eat now," he insisted. Apparently when the bells sounded, it was unthinkable not to obey. "Rameau must come."

The cohorts trotted tirelessly through the ship-maze. Rameau found the corridors completely confusing. All were cylinders of white kemplex, crossed at intervals by connecting tubes slightly smaller in diameter. The curved walls were marked with lines of colored light that presumably had some directional meaning, but not for Rameau. Just as the cohorts all looked alike, their environment seemed sterile, neutral, and homogenous. Rameau wasn't even sure what shape the *Langstaff* was.

Could be built like a giant cheese cube with rat tunnels running through it, for all I know.

He tried to focus, but his battered mind couldn't make any sense of the endless twists and turns. What was obvious to the cohorts seemed beyond his grasp.

Then the walls began to glow with a delicate gold color, gradually intensifying from primrose to saffron. At the same time, there was a scent of coriander in the air. They stepped through another round doorway, into another cylindrical room.

Though the room seemed stationary, Rameau still felt as if

he were spinning. The whole area looked as if it had been designed for use in zero g, with gimbaled seating that had folded against the walls except on one side of the room, the current *down*. The golden glow, from somewhere within the walls, lit the cohorts' alabaster faces to a strange topaz. Rameau didn't find it appetizing, and the persistent spicy scent made him feel queasy.

The cohorts, however, looked happy. They weren't smiling, exactly, but they looked alert and expectant. They formed a line along one wall, where the food was dispensed automatically. Rameau noticed there was no jostling for position; they lined up in perfect order with perfect spacing. He tried to hang back, to the end of the line, but Neb insisted on walking behind him.

He felt himself wobbling a little as he walked.

"What's up with the spin?" he said.

Neb pointed. "There is current up."

"No. I mean, how is the ship producing weight?"

"Ship still experience core control difficulties," Neb said. "Gravity field inoperative. Spin whole ship, provide partial gravity, help repairs."

That explained the persistent, low-level nausea, Rameau thought.

"Doesn't spin make you sick?" he asked Neb.

Neb gave him the already familiar look of mild incredulity.

"No," he said.

Then he seemed to realize that Rameau expected more information.

"Baseline humans are genetically inferior," he explained. "Original Man is incepted without debilitating reactions. Original Man is designed for high function."

"I'm glad to know that," Rameau said solemnly. "Thank you for sharing this information."

The cohort did not react. Evidently, sarcasm wasn't part of his conditioning.

Neb activated the dispenser and handed Rameau a metal dish filled with a large portion of beige mush.

"What is that?" Rameau said.

"Grain-based high-protein food," Neb said. "High fiber."

He added a metal plate that fit neatly over the top rim of the bowl. It was piled with yellow, porous cubes that looked like tofu, except for the color.

"That cohort want veg drink, select flavor blend variety?" Neb said helpfully.

"Uh . . . this cohort will select his own blend," Rameau said. *Damn it. Now they've got me doing it.*

He chose a socket at random and plugged his cup into it. The fluid that came out was a dark red.

Ugh. Should have let Neb pick. Any color but that.

He followed Neb to a table and pulled down a seat. The table was a little too far away, and his feet barely touched the floor. He closed his eyes to shut out the color of the fluid, and sipped at his cup. He felt like a wanderer who had been lost in the desert for a long time, as if his throat must surely have closed up. He wasn't sure he'd be able to swallow.

But to his surprise, the liquid tasted good. He had been hoping for tomato; it was more like beet with a hint of guava. But it did seem to settle his stomach.

When his thirst was satisfied, he ate the mush. It was bland, essentially tasteless. That was all right. He didn't want taste. The yellow cubes were less palatable. Their pale, spongy texture made him feel as if he were eating chunks of skin. After the hours he'd just spent in surgery, he couldn't face anything that reminded him of body parts.

After eating, he felt stronger, more alert. He wasn't sure that was a good thing. Strengthening himself for escape could be good. Increasing his endurance so he could suffer a longer period of torture and slavery wasn't so good. But his body took over the decision, and he found himself scraping the last bite of mush from the bowl.

It wasn't unlike the carefully mixed combination diets the transforms on Varuna had been given. Rameau remembered with aching remorse how many times they'd begged him to let them taste human food. Especially Dakini, and the dwarf brothers who made up the tumbling troupe. They'd watched the elite patrons eating and drinking delicacies in the skyboxes. They couldn't help wondering how those delicacies tasted.

But Rameau, as their doctor, knew better than anyone how delicately their engineered metabolisms had been balanced. During his predecessor's time, a star performer had been killed by a patron's thoughtless gift of chocolate. Rameau had occasionally smuggled in tiny pastilles, scented with rose or lemon, for Dakini. He hadn't dared anything more.

Now it looked as if he'd be eating mush for the rest of his life.

"Where does this food come from?" he asked abruptly.

"This cohort not affiliate to bio—" Neb started to say.

"Never mind where you affiliate," Rameau said. "Just answer the question as well as you can, based on your own knowledge."

"High-protein foods, meat analogs, go be synthesize, make most efficient use of components," Neb said. "Meat animals not efficient. Plant foods from biosupport system."

"I'd like to see that sometime," Rameau said.

Biosupport is important. And I know how to poison things. Give them a taste of their own medicine.

The tones sounded again, a different sequence this time.

"Not now," Neb said. "Now is MedTeam sleep cycle."

The word "sleep" hit Rameau like another drug. To curl up in the dark somewhere—to be alone—it was the only thing in life he could still crave.

Crew quarters weren't far from the mess. It was logical, and fortunate. Rameau would almost have welcomed being towed again, by the time they climbed the ladder-tube that took them to the next ring and through a hatch into the sleeping quarters. He wasn't sure what to expect. Not private cells, certainly, but small-group cubes, perhaps, or at least something like a bunk room.

Instead, he stepped into a single big, curved chamber, a toroidal section wrapped around the ship's axis. He could see slots where pressure doors could slide shut in an emergency, dividing the chamber into separate wedges, but all the barriers were open at the moment.

No beds or bunks were visible, no orderly open spaces. The chamber was filled with scaffolding, soft plastic bars joined at ninety-degree angles. Now, when the ship maintained an appreciable fraction of Terranormal gravity, the cohorts slung their sleep sacks in hammock mode, all oriented to the current version of *down*. In free fall, they would be able to bag themselves at any angle on the scaffolding, which could also serve as a perch, a storage rack, or an easy way to traverse the room in zero g.

Groups of cohorts clung to the bars like birds perched in an aviary, or bees in a hive. It was a logical and adaptive use of space, Rameau thought, but it wasn't a sleeping place.

"I can't sleep here," he said. "Humans need dark, and quiet. And privacy. This is like a huge, bright nightmare."

"No ken nightmare," Neb said.

"Nightmare. Bad dream. You do dream, don't you?"

"Dream not good, not bad. Dream nothing. Nonfunctional. Cohort sleep in blue, no dreams."

Rameau wobbled on his feet. He was reaching the end of his rope. He could hardly stand up.

"What does that mean, sleep in blue?"

Neb pointed. "There is sleep section. Rameau follow."

At the far end of the curve, the walls again glowed with color—not yellow this time, but a deep, soothing blue. The color of twilight shadows. Rameau followed. There was no door, just a terminator of indigo. Inside, it was light enough to see, but the hue smoothed out all shapes and seemed to press on Rameau's eyelids, urging them shut. Cohorts lay in their hammocks, briefly harmless. Rameau stepped cautiously through the boundary of color. Immediately his ears were filled with a soft rustling and murmuring, just at the low end of his hearing.

Some kind of sleep conditioning, white noise to block out stimuli.

His head spun with a strange vertigo, as if he were losing himself in a sea of whispers. He jerked himself back out, into the blank brightness of the big room.

"Rameau must enter. Sleep now," Neb urged. "Sleep in blue is good. Blue make sleep with no dreams. Good that way."

"No. It's not good. Good for cohorts maybe. No good for humans. Humans can't sleep like this."

But his eyes were swimming. It took only a gentle push from Neb to make him stumble back over the line. The blue light with its odd deep sonic undertow dragged him under. He fell to his knees and didn't even feel the rest of the way down.

Sleep without dreams—it's good that way.

4

He woke up hardly knowing where he was. He still had weight. The floor was still *down*, and it was hard and cold. The blue light was gone—apparently moved to another section. He was back in the ship's eternal daylight. He groaned as it all came back to him. He tried to roll over, but his left arm was stiff and unwieldy. He started to massage the life back into it, and encountered the new skin of kemplex and metal.

Ow.

Shading his eyes against the brightness, he looked up. As he expected, a big pale face was looking incuriously down at him.

"Work cycle now," the cohort said.

"Are you the same one who was here before?" Rameau said. "Neb?"

"This cohort has that persig," the pale man said.

"Then tell me what's happening, Neb."

Rameau flexed his fingers and stretched. He wondered if he was going to be put back to work immediately.

"While that cohort—Rameau—in sleep cycle, Commander announce *Langstaff* victorious. Broke free from enemies. Stand down from battle stations. Go make emergency repairs, then jump."

A fresh sense of desolation overwhelmed Rameau.

"Victorious. Broke free." That means we're headed far from human space. There's no chance human forces will catch us now.

As swiftly, he was seized by an inexplicable feeling of elation.

They'll never catch us. Because Langstaff *is the best. The finest, the fastest.*

33

The two thoughts collided like ships on opposite courses.

What am I thinking? Langstaff is a flying prison, a ship of monsters. This is insane!

But the other voice in his mind stubbornly persisted.

If you must be stuck on a jumpfighter, at least it's Langstaff. Langstaff *is the best.*

"Rameau hurry," Neb said. "Commander go speak Rameau, evaluate performance."

Rameau scrambled to his feet, all other thoughts swept away.

The Commander is going to speak to me? Oh, gods. They're not in crisis mode anymore. Maybe they don't need me now. If he'd just turn me loose somewhere—anywhere in human space.

He wondered how far from Garuda they could be. Surely they couldn't have left the system entirely. That would take at least a week at conventional acceleration.

"Rameau ordered, report to Commander now," Neb said.

Rameau ran his fingers through his tangled hair. The cohorts all wore their hair cropped short. No chance of finding a comb in this place.

Worse, now that he was on his feet, he could smell himself: unwashed human, with overtones of blood and disinfectant.

"Can't I wash first?"

"No. Obey order first. Here—you eat. Ration bar."

Neb handed him a chunk of some concentrate, and he chewed as they traveled. Again, Rameau followed the cohort through the ship-maze. He tried hard to memorize their path. It could prove important to know the way to the Commander's station. He assumed it would be near the bridge, or whatever they called the main locus of control.

Along the way, he was distracted by remnants of the battle. The scent of burning and toxic particles of smoke and ash circulated throughout the ship. The air-scrubbing systems hadn't yet caught up with the overload. Ash still crunched underfoot, and trash bots scurried past, still cleaning.

He glanced curiously at the work teams that passed them in the corridors, usually at a brisk trot. They all looked like Neb. They all seemed to be the same size, and the same age. He never saw one who looked as Rameau expected an officer to look—older, more experienced.

"Neb, are you *all* clones?" he asked. "And don't tell me you don't affiliate to reproduction or whatever," he added hastily. "Just answer the question."

"Yes," Neb said.

Rameau realized that he had put the question badly.

"No, I mean, are you all clones of each other? Are all the Omo on this ship identical, or are there some variations within the population?"

"This cohort identical with e sib group," Neb said. "E ken sib group identical within self. E no ken intragroup genetics."

Rameau pondered this as he followed the tireless cohort. If all the Omo were identical, it would make many things possible—like the limb reattachment tank. They wouldn't have any immune reaction to being grafted with cloned limbs. In fact, every aspect of battlefield medicine would be much easier. The Omo could be treated as identical, interchangeable units.

On the other hand, biological diversity existed among humans for a reason. Each individual had a unique array of immune-system defenses. A variable population made it easier for the species to survive microbial assaults. The Omo would risk a killer plague by bringing together a group whose immune systems were too much alike.

Rameau wondered which alternative the Founder had chosen—the potential of diversity or the power of solidarity.

Finally they arrived at a clean, undamaged curve of white kemplex wall. Neb flashed the wall with his noded knuckles. The wall slid into itself in several directions, creating an oval opening. Rameau stepped through. Neb followed, and stood to one side.

Immediately, Rameau's attention was riveted by the display on the far wall. For a minute, it seemed as if he were looking directly out into space. An asteroid or two slipped past, almost close enough to set off proximity alarms. Stars blazed like magnesium flares, and nebulas of glowing multicolored gases moved in majestic, silent procession.

"Fake," he said, before he realized he had spoken aloud.

"You're not impressed?" a voice said.

Rameau turned instantly. The voice was alive with irony, with curiosity, with overtones not present in cohort speech. Its tone was roughened by time and experience. Even the cosmic vision presented to Rameau couldn't compete with a voice that sounded human.

Then he saw who it was.

"Commander," he said.

Oh, merciful Amitabha. Not the best start to winning his favor.

"Why is the baseline not impressed?" the Commander said.

"Of course the display is impressive," Rameau said. "At first I took it for reality. Until I saw the stars in motion relative to the ship. Then I knew it could only be a simulation. And not even Original Man genius would insert a slab of transplex of that size in the hull of a ship, and expose it to the kinds of stresses we've just experienced. Anyway, as far as I can guess, we're nowhere near the periphery of the hull, so we couldn't be seeing a live display even if you have one."

"I, however, am impressed," Gunnarsson said. Now he sounded a little more formal, more as he had when Rameau first encountered him. "You have a reasoning mind, for a baseline."

"What do you know of 'baselines'?" Rameau asked bitterly. "Or, to put it more accurately, what do you know about human beings?"

"I have met others of your kind," Gunnarsson answered. "I was raised in the human way. I met humans during my learning years. I told you, I have the honor to be of the lineage of the Founder himself. He took care that we should have an understanding of the differences between us."

"And why have you honored me with this interview?" Rameau said. Then he reminded himself that his freedom might hinge on the outcome. He knew he should hide his bitterness. But it burst out in spite of his efforts.

"I've seen reports on your treatment of the transforms. Your performance as a medical specialist was acceptable," Gunnarsson said. "I've decided to make your temporary affiliation durable until we reach our destination."

"You can't—" Rameau began. He swallowed his protest and spoke again more temperately.

"Sir, I am a civilian. Under the Sol-Terran Concords, it is illegal to enlist me in a military cause against my will. In addition, the Metta Laws of the Republic of Vaharanesi on Garuda, which govern the former station of Varuna, require that physicians giving assistance to the helpless must remain unmolested by all factions. Therefore, I must respectfully ask that you provide me with transit to an inhabited planet as close to Garuda as possible, and allow me to return to my home."

Gunnarsson listened without interrupting. He waited until Rameau finished, then shook his head.

"I told you that was impossible. Even if I could consent to return you there. Garuda is no longer inhabitable. Perhaps at the poles, a few baselines remain. It will not be suitable for resettlement for another ten years, planetary."

Even in such plain language, Rameau could barely grasp the enormity of this statement.

"What do you mean, not inhabitable?" he said.

"You can look up the specs on your own time," Gunnarsson said, showing the first signs of impatience. "The planet was seeded with toxicants bearing a fast-spreading viral agent that will clear within five years. The extra time is a margin required by the baselines who plan to reestablish there. It will also allow recovery from some of the damage on a macrolevel."

He extended a hand toward the majestic display on the wall behind him.

"See for yourself," he said.

The display changed to a low-orbit view of a world. At first Rameau couldn't recognize the planet. Normally, Garuda bore the colors of life: blue, green, and white. Now its surface was hidden beneath roiling cells of sullen vapor, pouring up from fires of unimaginable size.

The picture shifted to a jerkier transmission, probably footage from a drone. Now Rameau could see the surface itself, a blackened wasteland scarred with pits of fire. The drone moved lower still, but Rameau covered his face. The destruction of

Varuna had seemed to him the worst that could happen. His mind couldn't encompass the destruction of an entire planet.

"You killed the world," he said. "The whole world."

He remembered the child he had seen, and the bodies shriveling, blowing away like dust in the wind.

"You sent toxicants? Like the one you put on Varuna?"

"They were bred in the same batch."

"On Garuda they call it a death child," Rameau said. "I saw it. I thought it was a true child. One of the casualties."

"You may be the only man alive who can say that," Gunnarsson said. "Normally, those who come so close to an active toxicant are dead within minutes. Of course, my troops gave you antidotes, and put you in one of our protective suits."

"Put me down in any system," Rameau said. "Anywhere. There are laws. I demand that you let me go."

"There were human laws, baseline laws, that applied to the man Rameau," Gunnarsson said. "But that man was last seen in a habitat that has been reduced to ash and fragments. When we found him, he was contaminated with enough lysers to powder him within an hour, even if his heart had continued to beat. The man was dead.

"The man Rameau had rights on the world Garuda. Neither one exists anymore. The baseline I see before me is G-Prime MedSpec Rameau. He exists on the ship *Langstaff*, and he has no rights."

"I won't serve you," Rameau said. "I refuse to perform military duties. I will not help those who murdered my world. You can 'motivate' me till you drop dead."

He had expected to provoke the Commander to rage, but Gunnarsson gave him a curious glance, and then returned to indifference.

"No, baseline—until *you* drop dead. But I doubt that will be necessary. No military duties will be required of you for the duration of our journey. You will perform routine transform maintenance until we reach our destination and acquire replacement personnel."

Rameau changed tactics.

"But, sir—if I'm no longer essential, why not dismiss me

now? Rid yourself of the inconvenience. Put me in a rescue pod. Drop me anywhere in the vicinity of human space with a beacon. I ask only that much."

For a moment, he thought he could read a trace of surprise in Gunnarsson's expression.

"Did you think we salvaged you to fix transforms? Baseline, you are in error. You are essential for other purposes. You must continue with us to our destination, where you will receive permanent assignment. You will not be dismissed, now or at any time. You will never return to human space. And when I deem it necessary for you to obey, you will obey."

Lights blinked on Gunnarsson's kenner, and he seemed to listen to something that Rameau could not hear.

"This interview must end," the Commander said. "We will speak again when you have assimilated to the ship. You have your ID/locator. When you have duties, you will be summoned."

He seemed to be about to dismiss Rameau, but then he turned back toward him.

"Recall that I possess personal message cubes addressed to you. I judge that at this time it is best for me to withhold them from you. Baseline psychology dictates that control of desired items will ensure cooperation. When your continued performance is judged satisfactory, you shall have them."

"I don't give a damn about a message from the Founder," Rameau said. "You think you can use that as a bribe? You know nothing about humans."

"I have given you far too much of my time," Gunnarsson said. He ran a finger over the ebony surface of his desk. A translucent prism rose, and Gunnarsson lifted a message cube from it. He held it out on his palm. A golden figure, no larger than the Original Man's long pale hand, arose from the cube and danced silently, with the constellations as a backdrop.

Dakini. He has a message cube made by Dakini.

"Give me that," Rameau said. His voice caught in his throat. "Give it to me *now*."

The Commander closed his fist over the image and slapped

the clear prism back into the seamless black surface. The figure vanished as if it had never been.

"Later," the Commander said. "You have a long time ahead of you in which to earn it. You are dismissed."

He turned his attention back to the unseen voices.

"You can't dismiss me," Rameau said. "You can't do this and just turn your back!"

The enabler sensed the surge of hormones and gave him a boost; it was like being kicked in the seat of the pants. Before he was even sure that he wanted to, he dived over the desk and straight toward the Commander's form. But there was no one there. He crashed into the floor instead.

"A damn holo," he choked.

"That is correct," the Commander said. "At present, there is no need for you to know my location."

He vanished.

Rameau would have continued to search the room, but Neb's powerful hands were irresistible.

5

"Rameau is dismissed. Must go now," the cohort said in a soft, worried voice. He dragged Rameau back into the corridor as the wall sealed shut again behind them.

Rameau sank to the floor, hands over his face. All he wanted was a place to hide.

If he just had time to think, to understand what was happening—but as fast as his despair flooded into him, the enabler was smoothing it away.

Damn this thing. I'm marked and branded like a slave, and it won't even let me give up. They're running me like a machine.

He tore savagely at the nodes buried in his skin. He pried out one corner of one crystal, leaving a pit where blood welled up. It hurt, but not enough. The enabler was still blunting the pain. He ripped at the loosened node, and pulled free one of the wires connected to it, tearing a furrow in his skin. But as soon as he let go, the node sank itself back into his flesh, and the wire reburied itself. Bloodied knuckles were the only trace of his effort.

Neb seized his wrist.

"Not damage enabler," the cohort said. "Enabler essential e function."

Rameau groaned. "Not for baselines. Baselines don't function like this."

"Rameau function good," Neb said. "Affiliate to *Langstaff* now. Get used to it."

Something buzzed, bone-deep inside his arm. It was like an electrical shock. At the same time, the kenner blinked at him. Was this a punishment for tampering with the equipment?

"What is it?" he said. "How do I make this stop?"

"Rameau affiliate to *Langstaff* now," Neb repeated, as if that explained it. "Kenner buzz when e got message."

Neb took his arm and touched the kenner screen.

"See? Location and message ID. Repair team in cargo bay four call Rameau come fix transform. Touch here, say 'Discobey.' "

"Say what?"

"Say 'This . . . cohort . . . obeys,' " Neb said with awkward precision.

"No. I can't say that."

The buzzing continued, a grating electric surge that vibrated all the way to his elbow. He could see that it would be impossible to ignore.

"I'm on my way," he said to the kenner. That seemed to be good enough. His arm stopped buzzing.

Location.

He experimented, and got the location grid back on-screen. He found a dot that represented his position and that moved across the map as he moved.

They know where I am at all times, it seems. But at least I'll know where I am.

A cargo bay sounded like a promising destination. It would be on the periphery, closer to ways of getting out.

I have to escape before we jump. A life pod, a shuttle—those I could steal, and maybe even pilot. At the very least I know how to get away from the ship and trigger the beacon. But once we jump, I'll never find my way back without a jumpship. And I could no more steal and pilot a jumpship than I could fly through vacuum without a suit.

"Great. Let's go to the cargo bay," he said, bouncing to his feet.

Oh, yeah. Rameau function good. Let them think so.

As he followed the dot on the screen, he finally began to grasp the basic structure of the ship. *Langstaff* was like a spindle, its central circumference tapering to a needle point at each end. A ring of engines and docking ports circled each tip. Travel corridors were arranged in concentric circles around the ship's axis, connected by cross-corridors between coreward and hullward circles. Straight drop tubes ran parallel to the axis, intersecting the circular passages.

Rameau lost count of how many steps he'd taken, and couldn't estimate how far they had gone, but he knew the ship was big.

Langstaff *is big.* Langstaff *is the best,* that smug voice in his mind said.

Rameau knew they had reached the outer ring when the white kemplex walls turned to metallic gray, studded with hazard markings and locked hatches sealed by blast irises. He saw the numeral 4 stenciled in orange at the next cargo lock.

Neb raised his palm to signal the lock, but Rameau got there first. He wanted to see if his kenner gave him any freedom of access. He flashed "open," and the lock let them in.

Not all the doors are blood-keyed, he noted. *At least the exit opens for me.*

The air inside was cold, and Rameau thought the pressure was lower than Terranormal. Cohorts were at work in the bay, wearing only gauntlets and welder's helmets—no pressure suits or oxygen gear. One group was engaged in ordinary cutting and scavenging of damaged parts. The others clustered around a lighted screen.

As Rameau approached, the cohort who seemed to be the squad leader looked up and pointed to the screen. One of his team stood in front of it. He wore a sim helmet and waldo gloves, and moved his arms and head in odd, trancelike gestures. Looking over the cohort's shoulder, Rameau saw a chunky shape like a trash bot on-screen, crawling over a dark surface. The bot, apparently a repair drone, zigzagged back and forth in time with the cohort's motions.

A second member of the team flashed the screen, and it split focus. The feed from the drone shrank into one corner, while the rest of the screen showed a view of the stars Outside.

Rameau's fist clenched as he restrained himself from trying to seize the controls. He wanted so badly to see any hint of a familiar sky. But the segment in view was too small to show any distinctive features.

The cohort redirected the screen. For a moment, the view

swung through an arc of stars, as if to grant Rameau's wish, but then it steadied hullward, and a dark figure blocked most of the sky.

Kannon, there's a man out there! Rameau thought. He assumed it was a man. He saw two arms and two legs, and boots fixed to the hull. The figure's skin appeared blackened and leathery, as if it had already been Outside a long time. The face no longer appeared human. It, too, was black, apparently earless and noseless, as if the features had burned or withered away. A masklike bump concealed part of the face, but Rameau couldn't see any other protective gear.

Don't they realize it's too late? he thought. *Poor bastard— must have gone Outside without a suit, or maybe he got caught in the battle somehow. Either way, he's been a long time dead.*

Then the figure moved.

Rameau jumped—higher than he meant to, in the diminished g. By the time he reached the floor again, the figure filled the whole screen. It bent toward the hull, and picked up some device that floated at the end of a long tether.

"What is that thing?" Rameau said. "What's going on?"

"Vacuum jock," Neb said. "It malfunction. Controller try to bring it in, vacuum jock no go. They think maybe Rameau fix."

"I've never had a chance to examine a vacuum jock," Rameau said. "I worked with entertainment transforms, not the technical side."

Vacuum jocks were rare, extreme variations from human stock, on the cutting edge of transform design. They were never seen, except on jumpships and occasionally on a deep-space station. Varuna hadn't used work transforms. Hull maintenance had been performed by imported human workers from Garuda, who lived in their own module, tethered off the station where their presence wouldn't impinge on the wealthy patrons. Vacuum jocks were used where there was vacuum and hard radiation, where humans became disoriented or proved too fragile. Even while Rameau disclaimed any expertise, he longed to get his hands on this one.

He caught himself, and felt deeply ashamed. Vacuum jocks were created with monstrous attributes for intolerable conditions. If it was wrong to enslave entertainers, who only had to dance, how wrong was it to condition a living being to go out on the ship's hull and move irradiated metal with its bare hands?

But he still wanted to see the vacuum jock up close.

The drone moved forward again, toward the vacuum jock. It carried a shieldlike panel in its grippers. On-screen, the panel appeared flat black, as if it absorbed visible radiation. The dark figure of the vacuum jock took the panel from the drone and moved awkwardly around the curve of the hull. A glow sprang up at the edge of the curve, bright enough to be painful even in remote viewing. The operator dimmed the screen to compensate.

Now the dark figure was only a partial silhouette, mostly invisible where it crouched behind the light-absorbing panel. It stopped moving and drew in its limbs until it was completely hidden. The screen operator abruptly increased the brightness. At the same time, the crouching figure jerked violently, its thin limbs spasming like a spider's legs.

The convulsive movement seemed familiar, but Rameau was too intent on the scene to recall where he had seen it before. The figure jerked again, then stretched its arms over its head—in surrender? In protest? It crept forward again, carrying the shield and dragging the tool behind it.

It dropped the shield and pointed the laser tool at the bright area. The beam couldn't be seen from their vantage point, but a readout next to the screen showed that a pulse had been fired. The bright area swelled. A searing, incandescent blob detached itself and floated toward the screen's eye. The screen went black.

The sim runner performed a frenzied little dance, but the screen stayed black. The screen operator switched back to the drone camera. There was a momentary image of the laser tool pointed directly at the camera. Then the drone camera blanked out too.

At that moment, the scene came into focus for Rameau. Finally it made sense to him.

They're shocking the jock, he realized. *They condition it with electrodes, so they can steer it by remote.*

But it looked as if the jock had turned its weapon against the camera. That would mean that even an extreme transform could retain some capacity for independent reasoning.

"It thinks," he said to Neb. "It knocked out the drone on purpose."

The other cohorts heard him. The one who had been running the drone was shaking his head to clear it of the shock.

"Error," he said. "Vacuum jock no have speech. No ken nothing."

Rameau noticed that this cohort and the rest of his team were an inch or two taller than Neb, and broader across the shoulders. The bones of their faces were heavier.

A soft, insistent tone began to sound, and the lighting strip above the pressure lock glowed orange. All the cohorts looked alertly toward the door. They reminded Rameau of a pack of dogs sighting a rabbit.

"Jump warning," Neb said. "Team must pull jocks inside before jump. Must hurry."

This is my chance.

"Let's suit up," Rameau said. He tried to sound casual, though the cohorts might not know the difference.

"No," Neb said. "Rameau not good to go EVA. E stay."

The work team scrambled into pressure suits. They were the same full-zip style as the suits on Varuna, but helmet and torso were light-armor composite.

No built-in weapons.

There were two outer locks: a big cargo dock and a personnel door next to it. The cohorts crowded into the cargo lock and left together. They carried tools—poles with wire loops and staff-length shock rods, the standard tools for controlling untrained transforms.

Barbarians.

Rameau had seen such devices, but never used them himself. His charges had been far too valuable. They had been carefully trained with behavioral mods from their inception. Crude force was never needed.

Neb put on the sim runner's gear. Rameau watched him run through the diagnostics to reset its sensors and raise another drone. The screen came on again, as the drone followed the repair team in their hull-walk. Neb worked the gear with practiced ease, completely absorbed in tracking his fellow cohorts.

Now or never.

Rameau stepped into the suit locker and dragged a suit on.

Maximum speed—no time for the checklist—just make sure it's tight and there's air.

The suit was much too big for him. The neck joint was at lip level. His feet clunked heavily as he walked with agonizing slowness to the small air lock. He was terrified Neb would notice and stop him before he could start the cycle.

But the lock opened.

Then he was Outside.

His stomach dropped into his oversized boots as he realized that he had no tether and didn't know which helmet switch turned on the boot magnets. He stood frozen, panting, fearing that the smallest misstep, even a sudden breath, might give him the tiny push that would send him spinning off into the void. Suddenly it didn't seem like such a bold solution, to cast off with nothing but a suit beacon. His breathing sounded very loud inside his helmet.

With the utmost caution, he moved one hand sideways until it just brushed the air-lock frame. He found the switch for the boot magnets. Then he clamped his gloved fingers around the rim of the door. Delicately, he tried to lift one foot. It wouldn't come off the hull. He pulled harder. And harder. Now he feared the opposite—maybe his human muscles weren't strong enough to pry the boot magnets off the hull.

One final tug, and he was able to move his foot a few inches forward. He could see the drone off to one side. As long as he angled away from it, Neb wouldn't see him on-screen.

He wasn't sure he had the guts to do this after all.

Okay, I'm not going to throw myself overboard.

But maybe he could find an emergency pod. Maybe he could find one of the tools the jocks had been using, and break something. Maybe shoot up the jump engines and stop them from going anywhere.

He knew nothing about jump engines, but that was enough of an objective to allow him to take another step. Three steps out of the doorway, he suddenly realized he was hanging by his feet over a hole ten million light-years deep. He gasped and shut his eyes.

Don't look down. Or up—wherever. Look at the hull. Find one of those lasers.

He crept forward. Eyes on the hull, he almost missed the tool he was looking for, as it floated at the end of its tether. Carefully, hand over hand, he pulled it down. He clipped the tether to his belt and hugged the tool to his chest.

He looked for a target. He could see a ring of gleaming metal shapes that might be the engines. But they were still so far away, across an endless expanse of hull metal.

Must be a distance-viewing option in here somewhere.

Stretching on tiptoe, he located the helmet switch and activated it with his tongue. The shapes sprang into view in his visor. He could see all their complex detail. He still didn't know what they were, but anything that complicated must be breakable. One shuffling step at a time, he trudged painfully toward his goal. He knew that it was much farther away than it looked, but he left the magnification on, to give him hope.

Suddenly there was a face-shaped object in front of him, hugely magnified. It seemed close enough to touch. He tried to step back and lost his balance. Only the boots remained planted as he fell over backward and recovered, flailing. He tongued the magnification switch, and the face receded to a less threatening distance, three or four meters off.

It was a vacuum jock, and it was aware of his presence. He was sure of that, by the way it had frozen in an attentive position. Its head wove back and forth, but remained oriented toward him. He stared, but didn't know if it was staring back. It had no eyes, just sunken pits covered with the same leathery, rhinolike hide that enclosed its whole body. A mask covered the lower part of the face. Where the ears should have been, there was a thick flap clamped tight to the skull. One side of the head had been smashed, or burned, or both, and the creature was seamed and blackened all over, but Rameau couldn't tell if those were burns or frostbite or its natural state.

It feinted toward him with its long, dark arms. Rameau couldn't run in the boots. Clunking along at a lung-bursting crawl, he zigzagged around the creature, still heading for the distant engines. He turned around once, expecting it to seize him, but it was only following, in a strange, troll-like, crouching gait, its barrel-shaped torso carried close to the hull on thick, misshapen legs.

Then he heard voices.

No sound out here. They must be on my suit radio.

Cohorts.

In a moment, they came around the hull horizon. The whole team was there. He'd never be able to fend them all off. They moved easily, the heavy boots hardly slowing them from their normal pace. He could click off his magnets, use thrust to jet away, and hope they wouldn't bother to follow him—overboard in deep space.

Or he could use his remaining moments of freedom to shoot up something. He was as close to the engines as he would ever get.

He aimed the laser tool and fired. His visor darkened as the bright line sprang out. He saw sparks flashing at the end of the beam. He hit something.

Then something hit him. The vacuum jock's long, cable-like arm whipped around from behind and struck him in the chest. He lost his grip and almost dropped the laser tool. The beam died. He had a brief vision of spidery, leather hands, or gauntlets—he wasn't sure which—as the vacuum jock wrested the tool away from him. Its appendages seemed to be equipped with suction cups that made its grasp irresistible.

The cohorts closed in on him. Desperation gave him the strength to do the unthinkable. Before they could seize him and take the choice away from him, he slapped the failsafe for the boot magnets and launched himself into the starry well. There was a moment of terror and exhilaration as the bright sparks spun around him, and he thought he'd made it off *Langstaff.*

Off the wheel.

Then two cohorts matched speed with him, each catching one of his elbows. They performed a synchronized somersault, and reimpacted the hull. Rameau could feel the impact, though he couldn't hear it. They had performed his capture like a dance move. He could hear them in his suit radio, and they weren't even breathing hard.

He kept struggling in their grasp, trying to see what had happened to the vacuum jock. Had it tried to fire on them? Was that why it wanted the laser? He would never know.

The cohorts stuffed him through an emergency air lock. Once inside, they yanked him out of the suit.

After the silence of the Outside, the ship seemed cramped and noisy. The orange glow had deepened to red, and the insistent tone had changed to an intolerable clanging. Rameau was actually relieved to see Neb—a cohort who would at least speak comprehensibly to him.

"Neb?"

"Correct. Rameau must hurry. We jump soon. Rameau make team late."

Neb took charge of him again. Rameau was dragged along, barely touching his toes to the ground, like a child dragged by an angry parent. They hit a long drop tube, and Neb went down it by bracing his boots against either side and sliding. The walls were too far apart for Rameau to do the same. He dangled from the cohort's arm until they touched down.

Rameau thought they were headed for cohort quarters, but they stopped long before they had gone that far. They tumbled through another blood-keyed lock into a gleaming, sterile medical bay lined with rows of tubes like the cells in a honeycomb. Most of the tubes were already filled with unconscious cohorts. The walls were a delicate shade of pink in the red light. Rameau guessed they would have been bright white if the light had been off.

"Prepare for jump," Neb said. It was the first time Rameau had heard a cohort breathing even slightly faster than normal.

"What is this place? What are you doing?" Rameau demanded. The tubes looked like stasis pods. He didn't want to be in stasis.

"Go jump in semistasis," Neb said. "Best jump way. You sleep. Like in blue, no dreams."

"No," Rameau said. But no one was listening. Neb injected himself, and then Rameau, with a dose of some transcutaneous aerosol, then casually pried Rameau's mouth open and pushed in a tablet that dissolved immediately, coating his mouth and throat with a thin film that felt like plastic. The cohorts were dumping their coveralls on the floor and swinging themselves up and into the tubes, which closed behind them.

The bell stopped ringing, and the red light abruptly switched off. Neb moved faster. He zipped off Rameau's coverall with one pull, lifted Rameau by his knees and shoulders, and stuffed him into the tube feetfirst. Rameau had an upside-down glimpse of Neb wrestling with his own bootlocks before fluid bubbled into the tube and he had to close his eyes.

The cold, pale blue gel surged up and over his face. For an agonized moment he tried to resist.

I'm drowning, I'm drowning—

Then he thought, *What's the big deal? I just tried to jump off a spaceship.* And inhaled. The initial choking sensation passed as the gel did his breathing for him.

I'm tired of things that crawl down my throat, he thought. *I'm angry and I'm going to do something about it. Just as soon as I wake up.*

He knew he was supposed to be asleep. He dived deeper and deeper, pursuing sleep.

"Life is a dream; death is a dream. Through realization, we awake." It was his mother's voice he heard, lecturing him about the nature of reality, as she always had. But he didn't want to listen to her; he didn't want to awake. He wanted to keep dreaming. Dakini was there; he was sure of it. If only he could dream deep enough.

"Go, then!" That was his father. His father wasn't happy that he was going to take his expensive medical training and leave Garuda. "Go live with rich degenerates who are enslaved by their bellies! All this training you've attained—you could win merit by good deeds. Instead you're wasting it."

"You didn't pay for my training anyway," Rameau had said then. His lips moved faintly in the blue gel as he remembered. "You said I could learn all I'd ever need to know by watching you. I didn't want to spend my whole life bandaging the same damn sores and giving the same injections, in the same endless shantytowns. It's like being a cattle vet."

"Better that than to spend your life taking care of the false believers and their toys. Better you should be a veterinarian. At least animals have souls. They are fellow travelers on the wheel. You can win merit by helping them. But you—you're no doctor! A cattle vet, did you say? You won't even be that. You'll never be more than a circus veterinarian. You're like those people who used to torture elephants."

"Go, then." His mother always spoke calmly. She believed she had extinguished the deluding passions. "When you leave this world for Varuna, our parental obligations will be ended. You must choose your own fate."

"Thanks, Mother, Father," he'd said sarcastically. They hated it when he called them that.

"We are all fellow travelers, spiritually," his mother always said. "Some more advanced on the Way, others less so. The forms of parent and child are impermanent."

Clearly they had considered him at a low level of advancement. They did not believe in attachment, and had never been attached to him. He was an obligation they had been forced to assume, as a result of some sin they'd committed in a past existence. By putting up with him for eighteen years, they had rectified their karma.

Now they were through with him.

Through with me, he thought, watching himself inside the dream. *They're through with me now. If Garuda's dead, they're gone, too. But where? To rebirth? To enlightenment? Into emptiness.*

I can never surprise them now—never return to work in their clinic, never save my pay and give them a really big donation,

*never turn out to be enlightened after all. They died thinking me
a failure. Or not thinking of me at all.*

"Go, then, Piers. Good-bye."

He wanted to go. He'd go anywhere—death, the hell worlds,
nonexistence—if only Dakini would be there. But she was
nowhere.

"I want to go." He could hear her whispering. She was looking out into the starry night beyond the Dome. "I want to go out
there. I want to go somewhere. Anywhere but here."

He was the doctor. He tried to tell her. He showed her films
of her own bones and how they'd been created. How she'd been
incepted in orbit and brought to Varuna as an infant, cradled in
aerogels, under the lightest possible acceleration. She was born
to dance weightless, in the Dome. Weight would kill her. She
could never leave.

She shrank her wishes, as the world shrank around her. First
she wanted to visit a world, then a moon, then some other station, then just the recreation facilities on the other side of
Varuna. When even that was denied, she said she wanted to see
where Rameau lived, what it was like to be a human.

I had to show her.

He'd wrapped her in foam and put her in a power chair, sitting up so she could see. He'd warned her that even the half-g
in his personal quarters would be too much for her, that they'd
probably never get that far. But she hadn't believed him.

Just a few meters past the clinic, she'd started to feel it. She
started to twist and writhe, to try to rise and fly, away from this
invisible attack, this alien force.

"What is it? Make it stop!"

She was gasping for breath, and there was blood on her lips.
He hurried her back as fast as possible, but one of her ribs had
already fractured, puncturing a lung. Small bones in her feet
had fractured when she tried to push away from the weight.
Nothing he couldn't fix, then.

Mr. Chunder, executive director of the station, called him in.
How dare he risk such a valuable asset?

And he'd tried to explain. "I wanted her to see for herself, so
she'd never try it again. A demonstration."

He couldn't explain the truth to Mr. Chunder.

Her spirit was so strong. She wanted so much to go. I almost believed she would make it, on will alone. That she'd rise and fly. I wanted her to win.

But she didn't rise. She'd never rise again.

Rameau twisted and turned. He wanted to fly free and find her, but he was caught in the blue space where the cohorts were sleeping. He could feel huge, invisible masses passing him in the dark, slowly spinning, dragging him in their wake. He was carried on the wheel. He tried to throw himself overboard, but he couldn't leave.

6

Then he was sitting on the floor, convulsively retching blue gel out of his lungs. There was gel all over him, all over the floor, all over the cohorts, who were also coughing and wheezing. Lukewarm water pelted them from all directions, washing them clean. A blast of warm air dried them as the liquid soaked into the floor and disappeared. They put on new coveralls, and in less than five minutes, the cohorts were fully operational. Rameau wasn't so sure about himself.

The hatch opened, and the cohorts swaggered out into the corridor in identical clusters, leaving Rameau and Neb at the end of the line.

"Rameau dream in pod," Neb said.

How would he know that?

"So? Is there a regulation against that?"

"Neb dream, too."

For a moment, Rameau felt that the cohort was looking *at* him, instead of past or through him, as if he had become more than just a baseline. He waited for Neb to explain or elaborate, but Neb said nothing more.

"Now what?" Rameau asked, following behind as usual.

"Now normal," Neb said. "Ship in jump, repairs made. Back to standard orders. Neb go train with sibs."

The cohort slowed his steps so he wouldn't outdistance Rameau, but his eyes were on his retreating fellows. His face bore an expression Rameau recognized, because he had seen it on the face of a dog, left behind when others were going for a walk.

He wants to go back to the group, Rameau thought. *They don't like to be alone.*

"How do you and your sibs train?" he said.

"All normal physical conditioning. But only basic combat. Group Nu has noncombat specialty."

"Emergency medicine, right? I can do that, too."

Neb's brow crinkled. Another error statement from the baseline.

"No. MedTeam is secondary specialty, for crisis situation. Group Nu is pilot sib."

You see? the smug voice in his brain said. *Langstaff is the best. Here you get to work with pilots.*

The rest of his mind was astonished. Pilots were another form of engineered life that Rameau had never seen up close. Pilots were legendary. Those rare minds with the ability to pilot a jumpship were the foundation of all human trade and travel. They were so much in demand that normal humans never saw them.

When humans first learned to enter jump space, pilots had been humans, too, sifted from a population of tens of billions by complex tests. Many were lost in training, often taking other lives with them. Kuno Gunnarsson had amassed his huge fortune through producing and marketing a steady though limited flow of consistently successful, genetically engineered pilots. Reliable pilots had been his first great success, providing him with the resources to create Original Man. Pilots were still a mystery to the rest of the world. And now Rameau was looking at one of them.

Or so he says. He doesn't seem very remarkable, as clones go.

When Rameau followed Neb back to cohort quarters, he learned that in fact there was no group for Neb to train with. Neb had two sibs left: Nor and Nuun. Nuun was currently piloting *Langstaff* though jump space. Nor and Neb took turns watching over the pilot through some kind of link. Neb described the watcher's position as "pilot jock."

This meant that neither of the sibs spent time with a group of their own. Later, Rameau watched them hang around on the edge of other clone groups, performing solitary calisthenics in the back row or picking up an occasional partner from a group with an odd number of sibs. When they worked on other tasks familiar to Rameau, like checking inventory in the medical units, or repairing medical equipment, Rameau served as the partner, and learned as he worked. Soon he knew exactly where to find chemicals that would poison the biosphere. Now all he needed was to locate the biosphere.

Neb and Nor were identical. He could tell them apart only because Nor spoke less often, and had a tendency to notify Rameau of their destination by dragging him there rather than stating its location. Rameau often hinted that he could be of some help to them in their shifts as pilot jock, but they never offered to take him along.

His fascination grew, and his curiosity gnawed at him until he convinced himself he could postpone his search for the biosphere. He wasn't even sure that destroying the biomass would kill a significant number of cohorts. They might have an emergency plan he didn't know about. And even if he killed the entire crew, he guessed Original Man would salvage the *Langstaff* itself and use the ship again to spread more ruin.

Crew may die, but Langstaff *will never die.* Langstaff *is the best.*

Rameau shook his head, as if to clear away an irritating insect.

Anyway—if only I could get a clue to how navigation works. It would be so much more satisfying to destroy the whole ship. I don't need to know how to fly it. I only need to know how to crash it.

But Neb and Nor, while they insisted he accompany them everywhere else, never took him to the pilot cube. If he tried to tag after the one on duty, the other would seize his belt and drag him away. He particularly disliked the silent hours with the noncommunicative Nor, and gradually slept through more and more of Nor's off-duty cycles, so he could spend most of his waking time with Neb. But when he tried to pry information about piloting from Neb, the cohort would only say "Pilot ken pilot," and fall silent.

He slept in blue, with the cohorts, and came to welcome it

like a drug. In sleep he forgot everything. It dulled his grief better than alcohol, which wasn't available on *Langstaff*. If he were planning to live on board for long, he could probably devise some way to produce alcohol. But he wasn't planning to live.

He was startled when his kenner buzzed again, bringing him a summons from Gunnarsson Prime. He had lost track of how much time had passed since they entered jump.

By this time, he was ship-wise enough to know roughly where he should go. The place was coreward from cohort quarters, but Rameau knew better than to think he would actually see the Commander at the *Langstaff*'s command nexus. He guessed he'd find himself in another holo-space. Still, he hurried to the appointment.

He might tell me where we're going. And he might give me my recording, at last.

He went alone this time; Neb was in the pilot link, and Nor was sleeping.

When the wall opened to admit him into the assigned space, he didn't see a star display. The Commander floated above his head in a swing-out console seat apparently attached to nothing, against walls of a cobalt color that masked any irregularities or clues about the size of the room. Rameau tried to give the impression that his eyes were on the Commander, while staring past him into the space beyond.

Gradually, he made out other Omo shapes, and the lines of other seats and equipment. He guessed that the Commander was transmitting from the command nexus itself, but that electronic privacy curtains concealed the rest of the room. The cobalt walls were probably designed to give maximum contrast for projected displays that Rameau couldn't see. And indeed, the Commander kept moving his head from side to side as if he maintained 180 degrees of invisible input.

The Commander waited for a few seconds.

Probably expecting some kind of salute. Which he wouldn't get, even if I knew how.

"Baseline!" the Commander said, without quite making eye contact. "I have a few moments to speak with you. In less than a week, subjective, we reach our destination and end jump."

"I want my message cube," Rameau said.

There's no point in trying to be tactful with Original Man.

"I think not," Gunnarsson said. "Satisfactory performance does not include going Outside when ordered to stay. You nearly caused a repair team to be caught Outside during jump. No reward."

"It's mine," Rameau said.

"Error," Gunnarsson said. "The MedSpec has no personal possessions. You are lucky we let you use our air. And I have no time for irrelevancies. You are here to receive orders. You work well with the pilots. I am extending your duties to include supervision of the pilot team. You will observe the final phase of jump and oversee their welfare in the link."

Rameau was stunned. And wary.

"Why?" he said.

Why would he give me exactly what I want?

"Because it is so ordered."

"Sorry," Rameau said. "That may be enough reason for one of your clones, but not for this baseline. I'm not preprogrammed. I need a reason to cooperate."

Gunnarsson's fingers stopped their ceaseless fidgeting on his console.

"Pilots are essential to our function," he said. "We are down to the redline. One pilot in the tank, two to monitor. We cannot afford further mishaps. I want full-time medical supervision of the pilots in this crucial phase of jump. You have worked well with them, and other medical personnel are otherwise occupied. Hence, Rameau is the logical choice. In addition, your duties as pilot medical officer will keep you fully occupied. Should you choose not to perform your duties, or to enter unauthorized areas of the ship, you will be locked in a confinement cubicle for the rest of the journey. Is this clear?"

"Yes," Rameau said.

"State your compliance," Gunnarsson said. "I have observed that in baselines, comprehension and submission are not the same thing."

I was hoping he wouldn't notice that.

"I understand and will comply," Rameau said.

I understand and will do what I damn well please.

Rameau turned to go.

"Baseline! One more thing: your ill-targeted laser tool damaged a refuse vent. Seldom used, since Original Man is not wasteful; we recycle everything. And the damage will be easy to repair. Original Man are incepted as warriors. Rameau is not. It is advised you conduct yourself accordingly. Dismissed."

Rameau found himself in the corridor again.

I shot up a garbage dump. That's it. All that fear and sweat to ping a trash bin. They killed my world, and this is the best I can do.

I will find a way to do something they can't ignore. I owe that to Dakini and all the others.

He was ready to charge off to the pilot space, but after taking three steps, he remembered that he still had no idea where it was.

His kenner buzzed. The screen held a text-only message: *Update kenner.*

How am I supposed to do that?

He remembered seeing the cohorts flash the wall at certain points, apparently receiving data. When he'd tried that, the shipmind hadn't recognized him as a valid user. He searched along the corridor for one of the communications nodes, and found a roughly circular cluster of crystals embedded in the kemplex.

The flash codes he knew so far were rudimentary: hardly more than "open" and "close." He flashed a simple recognition code. Most nodes refused him, with "unknown," "unauthorized," or no response at all. This time, however, the wall flashed him back. The nodes embedded between his knuckles winked, and the kenner screen read "Update complete."

"Locate pilot pod relative to this location," he told the kenner. Promptly and obediently, it pulled up a map.

Hey. There's something to be said for Original Man efficiency after all.

He followed the map coreward, confirming his guess that important command functions would be close to the ship's axis. When the dot on the map stopped moving, he faced a blank wall. He couldn't see a door. But he flashed the wall, and it opened for him. He stepped through, and it closed behind him.

It took a minute to adjust to the semidarkness inside. When he did, there was nothing to see. He was in some kind of entry space, function unknown. Groping forward, he saw another glowing wall node. He didn't even flash it; he touched his palm to it, and a pressure hatch opened just ahead of him. Again, he stepped through.

He found himself in an indigo light that he remembered. That had been the color of Gunnarsson's command nexus. Did it mean there were holos and screen displays here? He moved his head back and forth, saw nothing. It was dark. He wondered if cohorts had ultrasensitive vision. He caught a gleam of moving light on pale hair, and realized he was looking down on a seated cohort's head.

He sank into a crouch so he'd be at the same level. That placed him at the correct angle to see an array of holos that nearly covered the curved wall in front of him. Their flickering light illuminated the rest of the room, so he could see the cohort sitting beside him in a support chair. The cohort wore sync gear, and his masked face moved back and forth in little twitches, responding to whatever it was he saw through his link.

He wasn't sure the cohort was Neb, but thought it might be a bad idea to rouse him and ask his persig.

I don't know what he's doing. Or what happens if he stops.

He looked more closely at the cohort, and found cables that linked the Omo to an object beside the chair. It resembled a stasis pod that only enclosed the inhabitant from the chest down. The chest was partially covered by a monitoring and support breastplate, connected to sensors and inputs. Blue fluid pumped in and out through tubes embedded in the breastplate. It looked blue, anyway; it could have been some other color, but in the indigo light it could be nothing but blue. A padded collar around the neck held permanent shunts. Rameau recognized an elbow; the arm protruded from a carapace of kemplex and wire, and disappeared again at the wrist into an oversized sim gauntlet.

Rameau followed the line of the arm to where the head should be. For a minute he thought the pilot had been transformed into something with a snout—derived from a cow, or maybe a bear. But the head-shape was smooth and light-colored all over, probably white if the illumination had been different. It was an artificial hood that covered what was probably a normal cohort head. If the cohort in sync was Neb, this would be Nuun. But they were both unrecognizable in their gear.

Rameau stared at the readouts and holos, trying to figure out what they revealed. He could see that the pilot was being carried in a state of semistasis, much like what he'd experienced when the ship had entered jump.

They're running him very lean.

Rameau thought that if he were running this cohort as a patient, he'd enrich the nutrient mix and let the heart rate come up. The organism in the pod lay very still, not even breathing for himself, but judging by the diagnostic array, he was working under severe and extended stress.

I shouldn't be thinking about how to lengthen his working life. I should be thinking about how to ruin him.

He wondered what would happen if he just ripped out the chest tubes now, turned the pilot off.

Would we fall out of jump? Would we stay in, but become lost?

Then he remembered that they still had one pilot left—Nor, who presumably was off somewhere sleeping or working out. Even if Rameau could disable both of the silent cohorts in this room, the others would catch him, and then they'd bring in Nor and install him. It wasn't too likely that Rameau could dismantle the pod with his bare hands, either.

Everything else in here is built like tank armor. Better not to waste my chances on a random attack. Better to find out, for sure, how this works, and then *strike. I'll only get one try.*

The cohort's right hand trembled in continual motion. Rameau thought it was some kind of seizure, but when he looked more closely, he recognized the delicate, patterned digital movement of a sim runner hooked up to a demanding process in need of constant adjustment. It was the only part of the cohort's body that showed any sign of life.

The wall displays were harder to figure out. Unlike the pod

diagnostics, they didn't fall anywhere near Rameau's areas of expertise. Most of them seemed to show different sectors of the hull, and some showed interior views. Nothing happened on any of those screens.

Of course not. Nobody can go out on the hull in jump.

The major screens showed schematics. Each schematic was accompanied by a numerical readout, but Rameau didn't know what the numbers stood for, or what scales they registered. He guessed that one of the screens showed a vector plotted against star maps in normal space, and one showed proximity to mass concentrations—presumably stars, but he couldn't be sure.

No wonder Gunnarsson thought it would be safe to send me here. He probably thinks a baseline could never figure it out. He may be right.

The proximity screen display fluctuated in a constantly changing rhythm that never quite made a pattern. As Rameau stared at it, he experienced an oddly hypnotic effect. It was like watching a moving mandala. He couldn't take his eyes off it, because it always seemed as if it would make sense in just one more minute, if he kept watching just a little longer. His breathing steadied automatically into the slow, soothing pattern he'd been taught as a child.

A touch on his shoulder snapped his concentration. Heart pounding, he jumped up, realizing he'd been tranced out for an unknown amount of time. He faced a cohort who had just entered the pilot space.

"Nor?"

The cohort had been poised to grab him, but checked at the sound of his persig.

"Why MedSpec in pilot space?" Nor demanded.

"Update your kenner. The Commander changed my orders. MedSpec Rameau now monitors pilots."

Nor glanced at his kenner, then turned away from Rameau and began to remove the sync gear from the cohort who sat in the chair. Rameau tried to memorize the sequence Nor used for shutting down the inputs, but the cohort moved too fast. Rameau lost track after the first three moves.

When Nor lifted the mask away, revealing Neb's face, Rameau

thought he looked tranced, too. His face was slack, his eyes rolled up so only the whites showed beneath his half-closed lids. Neb tried to move, and then jerked in an uncoordinated spasm that looked like a brief seizure. Rameau checked his heart rate and found it elevated, but rapidly returning to normal.

I wish I could monitor his brain functions. That's where the interesting things are happening.

Unconcerned, Nor brushed Rameau out of the way to pull Neb out of the chair. Neb stood swaying for a minute, then regained his equilibrium. He picked up the gear and checked it over, getting ready to help Nor into it.

"Wait," Rameau said. "Before Nor starts his shift, I want to check that out."

"Gear operational, Rameau. This cohort just checked."

"No—I mean, I want you to put me in the link. I want to see what you see."

The brief pause, the exchange of glances between the cohorts, counted as consternation by Original Man standards.

"No, Rameau," Neb said. "Only pilot ken pilot. MedSpec not pilot."

"But I am your MedSpec," Rameau persisted. "I must have full awareness of all your functions, so I can fulfill my orders to monitor you. I insist. Put me in the link."

Nor shook his head emphatically. "No can. Put in link, e go nonfunctional. E no pilot."

"Is it going to kill me?" Rameau said.

Nor spoke rapidly in the ship language of cohorts. Obviously, he was telling Neb this was a bad idea, but Rameau couldn't catch the full meaning.

"Wait!" Rameau interrupted. "Use speech I can understand when you're talking about me."

"Rameau no ken ship jo," Neb said.

"What is jip cho?"

"Ship jo. All cohorts affiliate one ship, talk ship jo. Faster than Formal."

Nor spoke again.

"E say, Rameau affiliate *Langstaff* now, e ken ship jo soon."

Neb resumed the discussion with his sib, but spoke more slowly.

"Rameau dream in stasis," Neb said, as if that were a counter to Nor's argument. "Maybe e see link okay."

"Look, just put me in," Rameau said. The more they hesitated, the more curious he became. "If you see any danger, I authorize you to pull me out at your discretion. Understand?"

"Discobey," Neb said. Nor stepped back as if to say "I wash my hands of this."

Rameau found it hard to let Neb close the mask over his face, even though he'd ordered him to do it. He'd been locked into so many restraining devices lately; his body rebelled, even though his mind stayed calm. He squeezed his eyes shut reflexively as the mask descended.

When he opened them, cautiously, he found it wasn't like being blindfolded. Though he knew it was just an illusion, he felt as if he were staring into a deep, spacious night. Things moved in the night. Dots and contrails of light flicked at his peripheral vision, vanishing when he tried to pin them down with a direct look. Gradually, the lights expanded to fill the whole visual field. He could feel them moving in three dimensions. They glowed; they acquired halos in colors on the far side of blue-white. The glow hurt his eyes. It became so intense that he was afraid it would damage his sight. He tried to close his eyes, but he couldn't shut out the light.

He reminded himself again that it wasn't real. He should be able to control the intensity with his gauntlets, but he had no idea how to use them. His gloved hands hung at his sides, too heavy to raise. The sensations that came through the mask were overwhelming.

He tried to scream for help. He cried out endlessly, it seemed, until his throat closed up and he could only utter a faint nightmare moan.

The unbearable brightness dimmed slightly. Something like dust, an infinite multitude of tiny particles, seemed to be sifting down on him. It was like iron filings, clinging, dark, smelling metallic to his altered senses. It stuck to every surface and weighed him down until he couldn't move or see.

Then came a wrenching, tearing sensation. The sky split around him. He was dragged through a sickening swirl of dimensions. Totally disoriented, he heard a voice—not the roaring and snarling of white fires, but a small immediate voice built from blood and breath.

"Rameau! Come out! E got come out! No more link. E no got jump sense."

The voice was familiar, though Rameau couldn't immediately recall the name that went with it. The sky hadn't been torn apart; someone had taken the link helmet from his head, that was all. They had released the restraints and were dragging him from the chair. He tried to help by moving his arms and legs, but it felt as if he no longer knew how to make his body work.

They let him lie still for a minute. Even when flat on the floor, he felt as if worlds were spinning around him. He heard them talking over his head. Then the cohort dragged him out into some other place where there was light—a plain, ordinary brightness that came in through his eyes, not through his skull.

Large blue eyes peered down into his.

"Rameau function good?" Neb said.

"Neb. Whuh . . . what . . ." Forming speech was difficult. His tongue twitched with motions of its own. "What . . . took you so long? I call . . . help. Hours . . . Tol' you, take me out, ri' away . . ."

"Hours?" Neb's forehead crinkled—strong emotion, for a cohort. "No. Error! Neb see Rameau's life signs, break link next minute. In hours, Rameau maybe dead. Permanent dead."

"Minutes. Is that all?"

So much for my fantasy that I could learn about piloting.

"Minutes long time, in link. Long time for baseline. Rameau did good."

Rameau looked around. He lay in the chamber just outside the pilot space. It had seemed dark when he entered. Compared to the darkness in the link, it seemed bright now.

"Is this a recovery room for the pilots when they come out of the link?"

"Yes," Neb said.

Rameau made an effort and got to his feet.

"I think I'm okay now. Take me back to crew quarters. I think I need to sleep."

He didn't mind that Neb occasionally grabbed his coverall to keep him from falling as they headed hullward again.

"Is Nor going to be all right in there? Is that normal functioning for the link?"

"Yes. Nor is well trained. E ken link."

If I had time, I could get them to train me, too, Rameau thought. *No, stop it; that's a crazy idea. Jump isn't something I could learn to control. I can see that now.*

"Tell me, what happens if the pilot loses the link? Or if something happens to the pilot jock?"

Neb looked very serious. "We fall out of jump."

"Is that bad?"

"Can be. If we fall out too close to big mass, like star. But mostly okay for ship—can accelerate to jump speed, try again. Just bad for pilot."

"But if we fall out of jump, it doesn't destroy the ship or anything?"

"Ship okay if not too close to mass. Then gravitational forces go deform ship. Or could get lost, if ship fall out of jump too far from node, end up in unknown space. Mostly okay though."

"What happens if you lose all the pilots, and there's no one to fly the ship in jump?"

"Not so good. *Langstaff* fly only normal space. Omo command send rescue ship, supply new pilot so we can move through jump again."

Damn them. There's no way to kill this monster ship.

"Is there anything that could go wrong in piloting that would destroy the ship?"

Rameau wondered if the pause before Neb spoke was unusually long.

"Sometime," he said. "Sometime, pilot . . . get lost. In mind, not in map. Twist ship through jump space. Shape too wrong, can't get back. Ship go."

"Go where?"

"Away." Yes, Neb was definitely speaking in a lowered voice. "So e say. Pilot hear pilot say. This cohort never see."

So I could make the ship go away, if I knew how to make a pilot crazy, Rameau thought. *But that would take more time than I have. I don't even understand them when they're normal.*

Inexplicably, he felt happy, rather than distressed. *Langstaff will never die. Langstaff is the best.*

"This pilot talk," Neb said. "Rameau understand? Only pilot ken pilot."

"Oh. Yeah, sure. I understand. Don't worry—who would I talk to?"

Interesting. That was the first hint Rameau had seen of any crack, however tiny, in cohort solidarity.

"Neb, do the other cohorts ever treat pilots badly? Talk bad about you?"

Grunts always resent the special teams. GPs resent neurosurgeons, too. Like my parents resented me.

"Original Man is one," Neb said with reflexive pride. But then he added, "Sometime, combat sibs say pilot weak. Pilot always get pinned in Five Minutes drill, because no combat training."

He smiled faintly. "Sometime, pilot ask combat sibs, e try pilot training. E get lost in link. Come out, e fall down, e throw up. Worse than Rameau. Much worse. Then, few cycles, no more talk about pilot weak. Till e forget again."

His face returned to its normal impassive expression. "Bad thing, put combat sib in pilot link. Reduce group functionality. Get punish. Bad thing."

7

They reached the hatch to cohort quarters and separated. Neb wanted to eat and work out. Rameau wanted only to sleep.

Less than five minutes, and I'm exhausted. He's been in for hours and isn't even tired.

Rameau longed for the oblivion of blue sleep. His mind felt bruised. He wanted to forget the jump-space invasion of his senses, and think of nothing.

But when he stepped across the twilight border into the blue section and sank to the floor, something was wrong. He slipped under, as if in trance again, but the soft, hushing, subvocal roar that had lulled him like the rush and retreat of surf held voices now. They invaded his mind like the assault of jump sense.

Insistent, penetrating, they wouldn't let him rest. They told him things he didn't want to hear: about the greatness of Original Man; the strength, the glory, of cohorts; the immortality of *Langstaff*, the greatest ship of Original Man.

Original Man is one. Original Man is All. Outside the will of Original Man, there is no life. And the constant, happy whisper under the grand voices of the greater themes: Langstaff *is the best.* Langstaff *is the greatest.* Langstaff *will never die.*

He groaned and tried to cry out for help, as he had in the link. The word-waves crushed him, forcing him into a world that wasn't his, a space where he couldn't survive. *You are the soldiers of the future. You are Original Man.*

Not me, not my reality! Help me!

No one came to help him. But he felt himself being shaken and rolled and pushed out. He woke up outside the blue, with white light crashing into his aching eyes. The cohort who had shoved him across the borderline gave him a final boot in the ribs.

"Stupid baseline! Go sleep far away! Keep silent!"

He couldn't do more than wheeze anyway; the kick had knocked the breath out of him. When he could move, he dragged himself toward the hatch.

Out in the corridor, he considered his options.

I can't sleep there. I'll never sleep there again, he swore to himself. "Langstaff *is the best." Indeed. My body is full of their drugs, and now they're mainlining their thoughts into my head. I can't trust my own mind. If I found a way to kill them, would I be able to do it? Or have they already installed some program that would stop me?*

Equally disturbing was the knowledge that his brief exposure to jump had changed him already. Only his altered awareness had made him able to hear and understand the messages in blue sleep.

"Biosphere," he said to the kenner. The map appeared, and he followed it.

I have to get away. He longed for somewhere green. Everyone and everything on *Langstaff* was manufactured for a purpose. He needed other genuine living things, however low on the scale.

Ribs aching, he staggered through corridors and laboriously climbed through drop tubes until he reached the final ring, and there were no more cross-corridors. He faced a cylinder of kemplex that stretched from one end of the ship to the other. Green arrows pointed to a circle where a door might be, but there was no visible entry.

Rameau held his palm to the wall node in a gesture that looked like praying.

"Open," he flashed. "Open, open."

The hatch that opened for him looked as if it could be configured as an air lock, but the inner door was in open mode. He dragged himself through, and fell over the baffle on the inside, to sprawl in a narrow aisle that lay between rows of green.

He found himself in a room shaped like a tunnel. The ends

curved away from him, so he couldn't see where they terminated. In the other direction, though, the cylindrical room was only four or five body lengths across.

A light tube stretched down the center of the cylinder, emitting a blindingly bright light with a faintly purple aura. With his feet planted on the floor, he couldn't stretch out far enough to touch the tube with his hand. He thought the air felt a little warmer as he raised his hand, but the light seemed mainly for illumination, not for heat.

A current of air, almost strong enough to be called a breeze, flowed from fore to aft. It felt deliciously damp, and carried with it the distinctive smell of a shipboard biosphere, mingled from nutrient chemicals and the organic perfumes of leaf and sap.

Every possible inch of floor space was covered with hydroponic tanks. Green stems pierced the confinement membranes that kept the fluids from splashing out during weight changes. Narrow paths left only enough space between tanks for maintenance personnel—or possibly bots—to squeeze through. Rameau had to push through thick, overhanging green foliage.

He didn't recognize all the plants immediately. He was sure that all were edible in some way, but their most important function, no doubt, was to suck up the carbon dioxide produced by the cohorts, and breathe forth oxygen in turn. The cohorts would have used state-of-the-art bioengineered plants that could purify significant amounts of wastewater while still producing uncontaminated, edible roots and leaves.

Still, the floor under his feet was mere kemplex.

That's a waste, he thought. *They could have used tiers, and grown moss and lichens even on the undermost story.*

He waded through leaves until he came to the aftward end of the room and had to stop. There, a large vine had overgrown the flat, circular wall that marked the end of the biosphere. Its dark green leaves nodded in a thick clump that partially blocked the eye-piercing light.

Rameau curled up under the leaves and tried to fall asleep again. He knew right away that it wasn't going to work. The dreams came back. And it was worse this time, because the voices in his mind whispered and roared at him, too. As soon as he closed his eyes, his head spun with vertigo, no matter how tightly he hugged his knees to his chest.

Ever since he'd tried the link, everything seemed in motion. He could feel the garden spinning.

He groaned. *You know what you have to do.*

The breathing. He wanted to leave it behind, but he couldn't stay sane without it. Every time he took the long cleansing breath, he saw his mother's face, and smelled the fragrant leaves of the scrawny phoenix tree that had grown behind the house they'd had in Vaharanesi, when he was five. He'd banished the chanting, the mantras, and the meditation, and the brightly painted faces of the little regional gods. But the hook was set in his body and breath. He had to have air, and as long as that was so, he could never truly leave Garuda behind.

Meditation tortured him.

The focused breathing was supposed to help him let go of all thought and attachment, so the soul could taste freedom, dissolving in the light of the divine spark that lay within. For all good practitioners of Reform Mahayana, it was so. Or so they said. But not for Rameau. For him, the focus only brought sharp clarity to his fears and regrets. But he knew he'd have to face them again, before he could sleep.

He let the outer world fall away, knowing what he would see, as soon as his inner sight cleared.

Dakini. Seven feet of polished copper, seven feet of gilded gingerbread, of gold-brushed sandalwood. A gazelle, a giraffe, a sun-kissed puma. A swaying tree with limbs of gold, a vine, a lily whose curled petals sent forth a perfume of grace. A silk scarf dancing on the wind, or a plume of eddying incense smoke. Eyes of agate and amber, lips of cinnabar.

A dancer whose very existence was barely possible—built with limbs that delighted the eyes, but were too fragile to support her anywhere but in the Dome where she had been forced to dance. A thinking mind in the body of an expensive toy.

Even in a dream, she wouldn't let him remember her without challenge. She had never accepted her role as a delight for other's eyes, as entertainment. To herself, she had always been real.

When she was mending from her attempt to leave the Dome, she had demanded that he bring her things to look at—things she might have seen, had she gone to his quarters. There wasn't much that he could bring. His possessions were few, and his prize, the bonsai sequoia, was too precious to move. But he had brought her his mother's silver medallion, thinking she would like it because it was an ornament.

He had been wrong as usual.

"Jewelry," she had said, instantly losing interest. "This is a human thing. Why do patrons bring me jewelry? It has no value."

"No, no, this belonged to my mother. She didn't care about appearance either. This holds spiritual meaning. And pictures."

He had floated the medallion toward her. It flipped lazily over and over, the dull, antique-silver surface catching an occasional gleam of soft light. She extended one long, slender arm and caught it.

"Show me the pictures," she demanded.

"It's a picture of the world," Rameau said, taking advantage of the opportunity to drift closer, bend over her shoulder. "Or one way of thinking about the world. See, it's round, like a world, or like a wheel, always turning. Around the edges, those are the jaws of the god of death. He's always waiting to swallow everything up. Because everything that lives must die.

"It's divided into six parts, to show six different kinds of lives. Down here at the bottom are the hell realm, the ghost realm, and the realm of animals. Hell is where we suffer endless pain caused by our bad choices.

"In the realm of ghosts, the inhabitants are always hungry and craving, but they can never be satisfied. Their food and drink turns to fire and ashes when they try to swallow. That's what comes of greedy attachment to material things.

"And in the world of animals, they live in constant fear of pain and slaughter. See the hungry ghosts, with their mouths always open?"

Dakini had withdrawn her fingers from the carving.

"I don't like it. It's ugly."

"But look, up at the top here. You can see the realm of humans. Being born and dying, trying to prosper, falling in love. That's what we do.

"And the land of demons, who are tremendously strong and powerful. They live in violence. It's their choice and their punishment. They're impressive in their own way. But cruel.

"And here, the most beautiful place, is the land of the gods. They live in endless happiness, with every pleasure and beauty gathered around them. Just like the patrons on Varuna. We're living in the land of the gods up here. But even the gods eventually must leave and return to the wheel.

"So that's the spiritual meaning—that life is a wheel and you're always passing through one of these realms. Even if you get to live like a god, it won't last. Life goes round and round, through all the realms. Forever."

"Isn't there any way to stop?"

"Ah, that's what the Compassionate One discovered. Supposedly. So my parents believed. That's the meaning of the writing on the other side."

"Read it to me."

In theory, entertainment transforms could be taught to read. Dakini was intelligent, but Rameau didn't think she had ever had a chance to study. They'd been too busy drilling her in physical perfection.

"Okay, here's what it says." He paused.

He knew he was stalling. The words made him feel a little edgy, as if they had some power to compel him, even if he didn't believe them.

"The deluding passions are inexhaustible.
I vow to extinguish them all.
Sentient beings are numberless.
I vow to save them all.
The truth is impossible to expound.
I vow to expound it.
The way of the Compassionate One is unattainable.
I vow to attain it."

Dakini looked puzzled. "But he says it is impossible," she said. "Why do humans say they will do impossible things?"

"I don't know," Rameau answered. "Maybe they say impossible things because they want to make them true. Wishing to be something we are not, or wanting not to be something we are—those are among the deepest human things."

"Then in this way I am like humans," Dakini said. "For I wish that I were something I am not. And what about you? Did you wish to attain this impossible goal?"

Rameau laughed. "Not me, no! I have a skill. I want to use it. I didn't want to live in the world of poverty and suffering all my life, like my parents. It's like hell down there; you don't know. I wanted to be here, seeing beautiful and wonderful things, like you."

Dakini had turned the medallion over in her hand, thoughtfully.

"Transforms cannot have a religion," she said.

"Why not?"

"Because, unlike humans, we already know who made us, and why we are here," she said. "You made us. But it is not possible to worship humans."

I showed her the wheel to amuse her, Rameau thought, breathing smoothly, deep in physical stillness, though his mind still ran on. *She found her own meaning in it. I think it should have been a helix. That steel helix within her that defined her being and made her fate unchangeable.*

The memory blurred till all he could see were the changing lights glinting on her face as she bent over the silver circle. His head drooped under the nodding leaves, and finally he slept.

8

A nagging pain in his arm woke him. He had been dreaming that he was hooked like a fish, by the elbow, and was being dragged out of his sleep. His kenner was buzzing. As he stared at it, the sensation kept growing until it felt like a red-hot needle driven through his elbow joint.

No such thing as not returning your messages. Not on this ship.

He was being summoned to return to his duties with the pilot team.

"Rameau hears and obeys," he yawned, hoping that would be good enough to shut off the pain.

He opened his eyes wider when a tiny, digitized version of Gunnarsson's face appeared on the kenner screen.

"Explain your presence in the biosphere," the Commander's voice said. "You were ordered not to leave the authorized areas."

No small talk here, Rameau thought, and then had to repress laughter when he realized that the voice was, indeed, very small.

Focus! he ordered himself.

"I was kicked out of blue sector. Some cohort said I was talking in my sleep. I slept in the biosphere because there are no cohorts in here."

To his relief, Gunnarsson actually looked amused.

"Blue is for cohorts, not baselines," he said. "Sleeping in blue may have done the baseline good, but if you are disturbing my crew, you have permission to sleep in the biosphere. Remember, however, that you are constantly under surveillance. I will assign an observer to monitor the biosphere during sleep cycle. Any unauthorized behavior will be stopped."

"Thank you so very much for that kind thought," Rameau mumbled. But the Commander had already vanished.

It was morning for the biosphere, too, Rameau thought as he brushed through the leaves, looking for the hatch where he'd come in. He nearly tripped over a bot that scurried between rows. Here and there he could see other bots moving beneath the foliage like small animals. He could hear the trickle of automated watering systems topping off the trays. He left reluctantly, tearing off one leaf to roll between his fingers just for the sake of the green smell.

Laying waste the biosphere isn't an option—not if they're watching me. And it would take time. Takes time to learn about piloting, too. I don't have time.

They watched him even more closely after that. He spent his work cycles in the pilot space, and Neb or Nor escorted him to the biosphere at each sleep cycle. He was given no opportunity to explore the ship.

It was frustrating to sit with the silent pilots in the darkened room, able to follow their work only through half-understood readouts.

"Neb, is there a spare set of link gear?" he asked as they headed back to the mess cube after another work cycle.

"Yes."

I always forget how specific the question has to be.

"Okay. . . . Can I access it?"

Neb considered this. "No. Rameau not pilot trained. Can't be pilot jock."

"Well, how do they train you to become a pilot jock? Could I run in tandem with one of you?"

"No. One pilot jock only. Minds in link must work together. No good put in extra baseline."

Rameau suppressed his exasperation.

"But how do you train, the first time you try it? They don't just put you in the pod and let you sink or swim, do they? That would be too expensive, I would think. Too many ships down the drain."

"Rameau, no water in pilot space."

Rameau paused to bang his head against the wall. Neb waited until he was finished.

"Rameau enabler need refit?" he inquired.

"No, my enabler is fine." He hadn't hit himself hard enough to make the enabler dose him with painkillers. "Baselines do this when we fail to access needed data. It's called 'frustration.' "

"Rameau ask again. Neb try."

"Neb, I'm the MedSpec for the pilots. Right?"

"True. No error."

"I need to understand all pilot functions, to monitor pilots correctly and assess their functioning. I can't do this because I don't know what you're doing in the link. I'm trying to think of a way to learn about link. Can you help me?"

"Yes. This cohort understand and comply. Rameau need level-three sim gear. Take feed from pilot jock. Link already edit jump data down so pilot jock can read. Sim gear feed data edit through shipmind, skim and digitize. No good for pilot—not enough data. But good to monitor pilot. This cohort remember, trainers use sim gear to monitor e sib in first-stage training. Understand?"

"I think so. How soon can you get me sim gear?"

"This cohort requisition, get for next work cycle."

The level-three gear reminded Rameau of the equipment he'd used in medical school for learning gene surgery. In much the same way, it revealed the processes that in reality were not accessible to the human eye. The difference was that, as a gene surgeon, he'd maintained effective real-time contact with the object of his observations. While monitoring the link, though, he was only an observer.

So it was that he was watching as the *Langstaff* came down out of jump. He had been dreading the end of jump, thinking he'd be stuffed back into the stasis pod. But Neb explained to him that going from jump to normal space wasn't as hard on the humanoid body as the other way. He didn't understand why. It was something to do with different energy states; he had never studied enough about the physics of jump to know exactly what. Neb seemed puzzled by his ignorance.

Rameau watched the pilot's readouts intently when the moment came. He wanted to know exactly how they did this. He already knew from asking questions that the moment of transfer, whether in or out of jump, was a window of vulnerability. He wanted to know if there was a way to take advantage of that.

Even through his highly filtered feed, he could see that lines of force were coming together into a tight node where they all curved around each other. One of those lines was the vector and speed of the *Langstaff*. Others, terrifyingly powerful, represented starry masses and swirls of star material. And some were forces visible in jump that weren't embodied in normal space, though their shadows could be seen, if one looked in the right way. Rameau did not have the mathematical ability to symbolize these lines of force more accurately; he could only see them as three-dimensional representations.

Without blinking, Rameau followed the line that was the *Langstaff* as it bored into the heart of the node. Space was a gossamer substance folding rapidly inward on itself, as a billowing scarf crumples and compresses to pass through a narrow ring. But at the very moment when he thought he would witness how it was done, time paused. The pilot's breath and heartbeat ceased, distracting him in alarm.

Then he realized that he wasn't breathing, either. The last surge of his own heartbeat whispered past his ears, like a waterfall spilled into an infinite chasm, and ceased. There was an instant of silence like the end of the world.

Then life poured back into its noisy, normal course. The gravity lurched and returned, in a subtly different direction. On-screen readings simplified and slowed down, and the star charts of normal space reappeared.

Rameau clicked off his mask and removed it. He helped Neb remove the sync helmet and close down the link.

"What about him?" Rameau said, nodding toward the pilot, who still lay motionless in his pod.

"Nuun stay," Neb said. "Ship need pilot always ready.

Maybe need jump fast, escape enemy. Normal space like sleep. E rest."

Rameau remembered that most ships came out of jump still at some distance from their destinations and had to slow down. They were still going as fast as they had been when they left normal space.

Retained velocity? Something like that.

"Who's flying the ship now?"

"Helm crew control in normal space. This cohort affiliate to pilot, not helm."

"Where is the helm crew?"

"Command nexus, with Commander."

Rameau's kenner still wouldn't lead him to the command nexus.

"Can you take me there?"

"Rameau no affiliate to command."

They have grenades that could destroy the pilot space beyond all repair. I've seen them in use.

He flinched from that memory.

If I could get hold of even one of those—

"Neb, Original Man are incepted as warriors, right?"

"Correct, Rameau. No error."

"But I don't see any weapons. How can you be warriors without any weapons? Where do you great warriors keep your weapons?"

He's giving me that 'you aren't normal' look again.

"No need weapons inside ship. All here are Original Man. Combat teams get weapons when attack comes. No need now."

But they were carrying weapons when they came to get him, several shifts later. The kenner summoned him from his hiding place, in the biosphere, and as soon as he emerged into the corridor, four full-sized combat cohorts with sidearms and bandoliers surrounded him.

"What's going on?" he demanded. "Where are you taking me?"

Apparently, they weren't programmed to answer questions.

He looked desperately for a chance to bolt as they escorted

him, but each ring they passed through was doorless and blank. They were going hullward.

They reached the outer ring, near the cargo bay where he had been before. A hatch stood open. Two of his escorts grasped his arms above the elbow and levitated him through the open air lock, into the landing bay beyond.

There he finally saw Gunnarsson in the flesh. The Commander stood next to a small shuttle craft, accompanied by one other officer. He barely glanced at Rameau.

"Put him inside," Gunnarsson ordered.

Rameau's mind raced.

We're leaving the ship. Is he setting me down on a planet after all? Even if he isn't, maybe there's somewhere else I can go, somewhere I can escape.

At the same time, he noticed the size of the craft. It held eight narrow seats, all but one occupied by Rameau and the six Original Man. The engines looked more like maneuvering thrusters.

This thing's no bigger than one of the supply bugs that used to fly from Varuna to the shuttles. There's no way it could go from orbit to surface. We might be able to land on a small moon—but more likely it's a ship-to-ship or ship-to-station transfer.

The craft backed out of the bay and launched into space. There wasn't much acceleration—just a rocking motion as the steersman made course corrections, and the intermittent hiss of the attitude thrusters.

Desperation flared in Rameau.

I'm not going to be dropped off like a package, delivered like a spare part to another gang of faceless clones. No! *If there's nowhere for me to go, I'll turn this thing around and ram the* Langstaff. *At the very least, I know how to totally ruin their garbage chute.*

These cohorts carried weapons.

Their mistake.

He took a deep breath, unlatched his seat belt, and snatched the sidearm from the cohort sitting in front of him. He pushed off from the seat and rose into the narrow headspace to take aim at Gunnarsson.

"You first, you son of a bottle," he shouted, squeezing both fists tight around the firing studs. A bright line sliced the air, and sparks exploded from Gunnarsson's chest. Rameau swung the gun toward the steersman. That was all he had time for before he was tackled and hurled backward.

He made no attempt to save himself; all he cared about was keeping his grip on the gun and continuing to fire. He heard shouts, and an explosive hissing, before his head hit the rear wall and the sparks burst inside his own skull.

The next thing he heard was the Commander shouting "Hold your fire! Don't shoot!" He was wrapped from behind in a grip that held his ribs and throat so tightly that he couldn't breathe, and he was looking down the muzzle of another cohort's gun. His right hand hurt as if all the fingers were broken. He couldn't move it.

He wasn't holding a gun anymore.

The interior of the shuttle was crowded with cohorts floating at random angles. They had all unstrapped to take part in the struggle.

"Strap down for docking," Gunnarsson ordered. "Strap down the baseline and restrain him. Set his enabler for light sedation."

The cohort who had been strangling Rameau pushed him back into his seat and locked him down. The cohort pulled Rameau's arms behind him and whipped a self-tightening memory cord around his wrists. As the cord tightened, the "light sedation" hit him.

It took all his concentration to turn and see what had happened to the Commander. But when he did, his heart sank. The breast of Gunnarsson's white uniform was scorched and pocked. The body armor beneath it was hardly marked.

One cohort still floated on the port side, fitting an emergency sticky-patch to the wall.

Gunnarsson seated himself next to Rameau.

"Baseline, your aim was adequate," the Commander said, baring his teeth in an expression that wasn't friendly enough to be a smile. "And the setting you chose was appropriate—for target practice. You caused no significant damage.

"Know this: as long as I have use for you, you will continue to exist. These feeble efforts to have yourself terminated are pointless."

Rameau felt a mild lurch of deceleration, followed by a couple of jolts and a clanking noise. It sounded like the usual docking routine, but it was an uncanny sensation in deep space. There was no way to know what object they'd contacted. He felt a puff of pressurized air from the other side of the docking tube, and then the cohorts dragged him out of his seat.

The other side of the hatch held nothing more exciting than a landing bay like the one they'd left, though much larger, and clean as a surgery. Beyond it lay more corridors, made of the same smooth white kemplex as those on *Langstaff*, but much wider. Rameau expected weight, but there was none. Perhaps gravity was considered a baseline thing.

A double rank of cohorts greeted them, standing at attention like an honor guard, and fixed to the floor as if they did have weight. They were uniformly tall, and their faces had the same perfect symmetry as those on *Langstaff*.

But where the cohorts from *Langstaff* were identically pale, the new group were identically dark, their features carved from basalt, not alabaster. Their uniforms were mahogany and gleaming black, rather than silver-gray and white. But they wore the same Omo insignia.

The guards saluted, then bent and fixed discs to the soles of the visitors' boots. Suddenly Rameau had traction again. When he tried to move forward, his feet stayed fixed to the deck, and he nearly fell. Watching the cohorts, he tried to imitate the small twist at the end of each step that freed their boots from whatever was creating the friction. When he staggered, the *Langstaff* cohorts caught him by the elbows and boosted him onward.

Moving lights in the floor and walls guided them toward their destination. The corridor curved and widened, and was decorated with colored insignia and symbols that Rameau did not recognize. On *Langstaff*, everything had been designed for utility. Here, everything seemed bigger and brighter than necessary, as if it had been made for display.

An arch opened in front of them, and they passed into a spherical space, bigger than the Dome on Varuna. Troops of cohorts filled the entire space. Rameau wondered how they held their stations so perfectly till he saw the thin, transparent rods of transplex spaced throughout the volume of the dome. The cohorts aligned along those handholds. The small group from *Langstaff* found a place along one such line.

Some kind of ceremony was in progress. Half a dozen officers in white, bearing many colored chest patches, occupied a floating platform in the center of the dome. Representatives from each troop of cohorts flew forward to salute those in the center, to exchange kenner flashes, and to receive in turn some kind of token. After each exchange, a chant went up from the assembled groups, but Rameau couldn't understand it. The constant chanting, in the deep voices of Original Man, had a hypnotic effect on him. It reminded him of sleeping in blue.

If I were Original Man, he thought, *maybe I'd feel absorbed, united with all the others. As a human, I feel more alone than ever.*

He looked in vain for any sign of other humans. But he was alone. This was a space designed solely for Original Man. He saw no signs of female presence, either.

Gunnarsson was one of the last to receive his token. Rameau caught a glimpse of it as the Commander tucked it into an inner pocket. It looked more like a memory crystal than a medal. Then the ceremony seemed to be over.

But something else was happening.

What had seemed to be the solid floor turned transparent, and they were looking down from a great height, into a maze of winding paths. Rameau didn't know if this was a real place, or a projection of something happening elsewhere. He chose to believe it was a projection. When he thought of it as real, he was overwhelmed with vertigo.

A voice boomed out from the center.

"The Five Minutes," it said.

A wild cheer went up.

Five minutes? What does that mean?

The cohorts understood. They yelled, grabbed each other's shoulders, punched each other's arms like humans at a football match.

An alarm sounded, and troops of cohorts poured from separate entrances into the maze below, shouting happily. It was the first time Rameau had ever seen color on the cohorts. They weren't wearing uniforms or coveralls, but tight workout skinsuits, each troop in a different color.

They bounded through the maze to crash together like waves meeting. It was unarmed combat, but it was combat, brutal and swift. The constant, joyous yelling assaulted Rameau's ears. Below him, the combatants piled up in thrashing heaps, and the scarlet of blood streaked all the colors with a common stain. All around him, even the officers were breaking ranks to assault each other.

Rameau felt a tug at his coverall.

"We go," the Commander said. Without questioning, Gunnarsson's other officer took hold of Rameau and towed him after the Commander.

"What are they doing?" Rameau asked as they reached the edge of the crowd, and speech became possible again.

"It is the Five Minutes," Gunnarsson said, his face impassive.

"What for?" Rameau said. He couldn't seem to get his mind, or his mouth, around more complicated statements.

"These cohorts are incepted as warriors. Their hormone systems are designed to function at peak efficiency under combat conditions. During periods of inactivity, they require hormone balancing. The Five Minutes provides an alternative method of regulation and release.

"And it is for decision making," he continued. "Baselines decide by vote, by chatter, like monkeys. Original Man makes decisions based on strength. The will of Original Man is forged in combat. Outside the will of Original Man, there is no life."

9

The officer hustled Rameau along. They entered a small room with only one door. Though there was no sense of motion, the door opened again on a completely different area. Corridors were once again narrow and crowded with hatches and markings.

They entered one hatchway and passed a series of observation windows, each opening onto a large, brightly lit bay. Rameau had been dragging himself along in a kind of stupor, able to focus only on the increasing pain of his pinioned arms. But here he stared.

He saw hundreds of infants and young children, all apparently male, working on row after row of treadmills. The babies wore support harnesses that held them in a crawling position. The bay was soundproofed, but Rameau saw their faces crinkled in howls of protest. The older children also wore harnesses, but only to catch them and dangle their feet back over the treadmill if they fell or tried to get off. Screens in front of them flickered and flashed. Rameau guessed they were being flash-taught as they exercised their bodies, but the material on-screen blinked past too fast for him to absorb.

"This—this is wrong," Rameau croaked. "Those are children."

"Not children," Gunnarsson said. "These are Original Man juveniles. They receive speed-training, to mature rapidly. This is standard training, for our present situation."

Abomination, Rameau thought.

"Why show me?" he said out loud.

"That will become clear very soon." It seemed to him that

86

the Commander sounded grimmer than usual, but it was hard to tell.

They returned to the decorative, spacious part of the facility, and proceeded to a ring with a small circumference. Rameau guessed that, like the area where the pilot space was located on *Langstaff*, this place was near the inner axis, so it must be considered important and worth protecting.

"Does this structure have a name?" Rameau said.

"The Founder called it 'Eyrie,' " the Commander said. "He envisioned it, but never came here. We are far from human space."

Probably not a ship, then, Rameau thought. *It sounds more like a permanent station.*

Their destination was marked by wall nodes like those on *Langstaff*. Gunnarsson passed his hand across the nodes, and the wall opened for them. Inside, three Original Man awaited them, floating in console chairs like the one Gunnarsson had used on *Langstaff*. The officer who towed Rameau fixed his own feet back to the floor, and tugged Rameau down so that his boot soles also made contact. This placed them a foot or two lower than the three figures who sat in front of them. Since Rameau was already a head shorter than a normal cohort, he found himself looking up, like a child before adults, or a dwarf in the presence of giants.

The Commander saluted them and remained at attention.

"High Command," he said. "Gunnarsson Prime of *Langstaff* reports."

High Command implied considerable rank. All three wore uniforms richly decorated with bright patches, and their kenners were elaborately noded and jeweled. Their faces bore no wrinkles, only a few lines of habitual expression. But there was a hardness to their bearing, an aura of authority about them, that contrasted with the average cohort's blank mien. These were men who had exercised power for years, for long enough that it had become second nature to them.

Rameau had seen human beings with that expression. He had never liked them. Seeing the same look on Original Man evoked his unbridled hatred. He wanted to smash those arrogant faces.

One of those who faced him now looked very much like Gunnarsson and all the others on *Langstaff*: smooth white skin like faintly veined marble, ice-blue eyes, white-gold hair cropped short. The man on the far right was equally perfect, but in a different mold. His skin was like polished ebony; his eyes pure, glittering black like onyx; his full lips cut in perfect curves. Leonine muscle swelled with every breath against the perfectly pressed black uniform.

The third man stood in the center, a little ahead of the others, as if, among equals, he held a slightly greater share of power. He wasn't as tall as they were; in fact, Rameau thought that if they stood on equal ground, this man would outstrip a tall baseline like himself by only a few inches. His legs were shorter in proportion to his torso. Yet, he did not seem in any way diminished. He radiated a sense of perfect equilibrium, a dynamic balance that seemed as if it could explode with exquisite accuracy in any direction, and that made the others seem overgrown. His skin was a pale gold that seemed the perfect mean between light and dark. His straight-lidded eyes glowed with rich depths, like dark amber. His hair was blue-black, thick, and straight.

Jade Clan, Rameau thought. He had seen pilots and vacuum jocks, and now he was seeing something even more elusive. Kuno Gunnarsson's prime creations had appeared in all the media—Diamond Clan and Obsidian Clan, the light and the dark, balancing each other as if to repel any suggestion that a crude racism had motivated his search for the "perfect man." They were to have been the pinnacle of human strength and skill: perfect pilots, soldiers, engineers, architects, construction teams.

Only rumor spoke of a third group, the seldom-seen Jade Clan, said to be the perfect strategists, scientists, and supreme commanders—an elite within an elite.

"Ras," the Obsidian officer said.

"Ingve," the Diamond commander said.

"Tan Gun," the Jade Clan representative said.

Their persigs were more individualized than those of most cohorts, Rameau noticed.

Gunnarsson started to give his own, but he was interrupted.

"It is understood that you bear the name and lineage of the Founder," Tan Gun said. "But we find it inappropriate that the Founder's name be used as a persig here. You will answer to 'commander.' "

"This officer obeys," Gunnarsson said in a stifled voice.

The High Command turned their gaze on Rameau with an almost tangible force, like probes sinking into his weak human flesh. He stared back defiantly, surprised by how hard it was not to lower his eyes.

"Is this the baseline in question?" Tan Gun said.

"Yes, High Commander. This is Rameau, the baseline mentioned in the Founder's final commands. *Langstaff* salvaged him and brought him here to continue the Founder's plan."

I'm not going to work for you! Never! Rameau thought. Even in his sedated state, he was shocked into shouting it aloud. But he got no farther than "I'm not—" before the officer twisted his bound arms so hard that the pain prevented him from speaking.

"Control the baseline," Ingve said.

"Let him go," Gunnarsson said. Before the High Command could chastise him for contradicting them, he reached into a pocket and held out a message cube.

"I received specific orders from the Founder to keep this baseline unhurt. He was important to the Founder's plan. I intercepted this message sent to him by the Founder. I brought it here to show it to High Command."

Ras reached down for the cube and set it on the console. Tan Gun activated it.

That's my *message*, Rameau thought.

Kuno Gunnarsson's face and upper body appeared. Rameau glanced from the human in the message cube to Gunnarsson Prime, comparing the two faces. The human original appeared old and tired. His lined face and gaunt cheeks differentiated him from the Commander, as did slight asymmetries and irregularities in his bone structure. Yet, overall, the two were a close match.

"Dr. Rameau," the holo began.

Strange to hear my name spoken by a human again. Strange to be called "doctor" once more. This could be the last time.

"We meet again," the Founder said, "in a manner of speaking. I can no longer see you, but be assured that when I made this cube, you were vividly in my memory.

"When we last spoke, you rejected my offer of employment. I regret your decision. I would like to think that, by this time, you may regret it, too. Original Man is still in the process of being born—a delicate process, and one that will require care and attention for some years to come.

"I was impressed by your work on Varuna. You showed surpassing talent in dealing with transform genetics. Your technical facility is of the highest level, but it is something more that makes you essential to my purposes. You have the instinct of an artist for creating and maintaining functional organic systems. If technical perfection alone were required, my Original Man would soon surpass you. But to learn artistry requires a long apprenticeship.

"If human politics take the course I fear, Original Man will not have the time they need to grow to their full stature. This is why I have ordered that you, and a few others like you, be brought into association with them, and kept in a safe environment where they can maintain continual access to your knowledge. I regret the disruption this may cause to you, but I point out that your current employment involves at least as much moral ambiguity as any service you might render to my children.

"For that is how I think of them, Dr. Rameau. My children, and the children of all mankind, whether they are a welcome birth or not. I hope that you will come to see them in the same light. Think of them as children, waiting to be born, and help guide their passage into this world. Or if you cannot find that clear a vision, think of them as cripples, and assist their steps. Compared to them, of course, it is we who are cripples. We are like test molds, flawed in our creation. Yet in your flawed humanity, I must place my hope."

His face disappeared into the clouded crystal of the cube.

Rameau twisted in his bonds. He wished he could seize the cube and shatter that solemn, self-intoxicated face.

The Commander spoke. "As you see, the Founder knew of this baseline, and considered his services valuable."

"Baseline!" Tan Gun said. "How did you know the Founder? Speak."

Memories surged over Rameau like surf, breaking and then vanishing, sinking away from his grasp.

Kuno Gunnarsson in the flesh had not seemed so grandiose as the voice in the cube. He had been brilliant, witty, warm— and persuasive as only the holder of great power and wealth can be.

Not that he'd promised Rameau wealth or power.

He offered me the kingdom and the glory. Not money—just access to data. Knowledge of what makes us what we are. Knowledge of how to shape our own fate. He wanted me to work for him, and I was tempted.

"Speak!" Tan Gun ordered him again.

"He came to Varuna when I was working there," Rameau said. His voice came out slurred and halting. The words were flattened by the enabler's power to dull feeling. "He observed me in my duties. He offered me a job. I turned him down. As he said."

He had the pleasure of seeing a hint of surprise flicker across the faces of the Original Man High Command.

Score one point for the human.

The Founder had understood why Rameau had refused.

Not only did he understand, but he respected my choice. He could have forced me. He could have had me fired. But he left it up to me. Or so it seemed at the time.

I guess he changed his mind later. Maybe he knew he was dying and decided to foreclose on everyone else's choices, too.

The Founder had seen Dakini, and admired her design— publicly, in front of Mr. Chunder, Varuna's manager. When alone with Rameau, he had smiled, indulgently. It hadn't been necessary to say more.

"I understand your attachment to Varuna," he had said. "This place is a treasury of many marvels. You are one of a rare breed, Dr. Rameau. Like myself, you are a human who is able to see value in something beyond your own humanity. I shall not press you further at this time.

"I must remind you of one thing, however—transforms have short life spans. Surely you are aware of that. You may outlive your work here. And what then?"

He had held up one hand to still Rameau's protests. In that hand, a silver oval had gleamed.

"All I ask is that you let me leave this with you. It is a highly sophisticated messaging device, not yet available on the open market. At any time, if you wish to discuss this further, trigger the device and I will contact you. It does not reach me directly, you understand. I may be at some distance, and 'nothing moves faster than jump,' as they say. But it will reach a relay station from which I will be contacted as fast as possible. You need not have changed your mind to use the device. You are an interesting man, Dr. Rameau, and I would be pleased to speak with you about any matter which may come to seem urgent to you, in the future."

Rameau had taken the device. How could he have refused such a marvel, offered with such persuasion, by such a man? But he'd never used it.

"The baseline states that he refused the Founder." Ingve was speaking. He seemed angry. Something about Rameau's answer had displeased him. "But the *Langstaff* Commander says he was sent by the Founder to salvage the baseline. The baseline must be lying. Why would he refuse the Founder's offer?"

"Baseline!" the Commander said. "Explain your statement." *Why did I refuse? How could I explain that to them?*

"You'll go now," Dakini had said. "Genedocs all go, after a while. They say they care for us, but they leave."

"Dakini, I am not going to leave," he had said. "I told him to go away. I said no."

"He gave you the magic egg so you could change your mind. I saw that. Humans say many things, but they lie."

He had tossed the device across the space between them.

"You keep it. Then I can't change."

The silver ovoid had spun in a wobbly rotation, over and over and over, flashing as it spun. Dakini had moved to catch it, gleaming golden as she whirled.

Rameau tried to blink away the sparks that flashed behind his eyes. Dazed by the enabler drugs, the ache of his bound arms, the constant effort to breathe, he felt himself sinking into confusion. He wanted to let go and fall away into his memories, fall away like Dakini. But he couldn't. Not as long as her killers stood in front of him, arrogant and whole.

"Not lying," he mumbled. "I said no. Founder was no god. Just one of us. Just a man." He could say no more, but his thoughts continued.

And now that I've seen what his "children" have become, it sickens me that I ever talked to him. Such lofty ideals. Such a noble goal—and all tossed on the ash heap with the countless billions his children have destroyed. Dakini's life burned on that pyre. And they're about to do the same with mine.

The High Command argued above his head. Their words were heavy and stern, weighted with logic. Gunnarsson Prime's voice reasoned, pleaded, offered. Rameau couldn't catch all the words, but by the music of the voices, he guessed that the *Langstaff* Commander was losing his battle.

Tan Gun glanced at his console.

"The words of a baseline are of no importance," he said. "*Langstaff* Commander, know that the Five Minutes have concluded, and the contest has decided against your proposal. Those who supported the proposal are defeated. This concurs with my own belief, and that of the High Command."

"But the Founder—" Gunnarsson began.

"The Founder is dead," Tan Gun said. "Our allegiance to him ends here. He was our Founder, and we honor his memory. Nevertheless, he was not Original Man. The judgment of the High Command is that Original Man has gone beyond the Founder. We must follow our own vision now."

"At least take the baseline under protection of the High Command and use his skills," the Commander said. "We need him. The Founder has said it."

Rage boiled over Rameau as he heard them discuss him like an obsolete tool.

He put all his effort into making his speech clearly understandable.

"Go to hell.

"I'm not working for any of you," he said. "Damn you, and damn your Founder. May he rot in the hell of incessant suffering where he belongs."

This time the officer forced him into a crouching position.

Don't show fear, Rameau thought. But he lowered his head to evade the High Command's blistering stare, in spite of himself.

Yet no further motivation followed.

"Waste no more time on the baseline," Tan Gun said. "He is ordered to be terminated. Original Man will survive without the assistance of baselines.

"It is time for the *Langstaff* commander to receive orders. High Command has determined that he made an error in choosing to obey the Founder, rather than the orders of High Command. This error in command judgment requires that the officer be reassigned for training.

"*Langstaff* will not be refitted. It will be broken up and reused among other ships affiliated to Diamond Clan. *Langstaff*'s crew and transform complement will be assigned to other ships of Diamond Clan.

"The commander of *Langstaff* will return to the ship and issue such orders, then accompany his crew members to Replacement Quarters pending reassignment."

"This officer obeys," Gunnarsson said. He, too, seemed to shrink under the glare of the three officers. Rameau finally understood that this must be something like a court-martial. He had played a part in it, but now it was over.

"Dismissed," Tan Gun said.

10

The officer towed Rameau out. He couldn't walk, let alone make any attempt at a daring escape. His overactive enabler cast a warm haze over his shock and apprehension. He hoped they would terminate him quickly and not break him down for spare parts like Gunnarsson's hapless ship.

I needn't have tried so hard to find a way to destroy Langstaff. *They're going to do it for me.*

The wall closed behind them. They flew a short distance down the corridor. Rameau could still hear the sound of chanting and thought they must be near the open door to the dome, but he didn't see any other cohorts nearby.

They were alone.

The Commander held up his hand for a stop. Their boot soles clicked down onto the floor again. The Commander gestured for the officer to move ahead with Rameau. Without question, the cohort moved on.

Rameau heard something snap. The grip on his arm tightened convulsively, and then slipped away. Rameau twisted to look over his shoulder, but couldn't see the officer who had been holding him. He turned around, and no one stopped him. The cohort sprawled awkwardly, his body bent backward, parallel to the floor, his boot soles still stuck down. One hand floated high, gradually subsiding toward the floor. The Commander stood over him, his hands still flexed, his face unreadable.

At first Rameau thought that the officer had tripped or something. Then he saw how the officer's mouth was frozen, half-open, strangely awry, and how the eyes were fixed and unblinking.

"You killed him," Rameau said.

He's probably going to do me next.

Rameau strained at his bonds, but they didn't give.

"Silence," the Commander said. "We rejoin *Langstaff*, as ordered. Come."

He seized Rameau's right arm, nearly tearing it from its socket, as he took flight before Rameau could unstick his boots from the deck. The Commander flew like an arrow, not pausing at turnings or bothering with handholds, but kicking both of them through careening flip turns. The walls flashed by. Just as the guards at the landing bay came in sight, the Commander turned to hit the wall with both feet, absorbing the full shock of their velocity with his powerful legs.

Gunnarsson threw Rameau away from him, headfirst. As Rameau somersaulted in the air, he caught glimpses of the flash from Gunnarsson's handgun. Cohorts in body armor tumbled past him. Then he crashed into the wall, his arms still tied, unable to save himself. He avoided a skull-crushing impact by twisting to hit the wall sideways.

He slid off the wall, half paralyzed by the shock. He saw Gunnarsson push off toward two guards who were still moving. It was free-fall combat, arms and legs equally useful. Gunnarsson locked his ankles in a scissor hold around one cohort's neck and flipped him like a rag doll. The Commander used his momentum as he twirled to strike the other guard two knifelike blows with his bare hands. Both of the cohorts turned slow cartwheels down the corridor. Their movements were random, no longer volitional. Gunnarsson hit the wall at a precise angle, grabbed Rameau by the belt as he rebounded, and shot both of them through the hatchway and into the landing bay.

Gunnarsson took time to belt Rameau in before he took the controls of the shuttle. The other cohorts who had come over with them had all been left behind on the station. Rameau sat in the seat just behind Gunnarsson, and caught a glimpse onscreen of the place they were leaving. It was huge. He could see only a section of a massive arc. The light of some nearby star sparkled off swarms of ships in parking orbits.

He still wants me alive. He belted me in. It didn't make any sense.

"You killed them," he said. "You killed your own first officer. You broke his neck with your bare hands, and you left him for dead. Why?"

"Doubtful that he is permanently dead," Gunnarsson said, intent on piloting the shuttle. "There is a high probability that he will be found in time for salvage. They planned to reassign him, so I think he will be salvaged. It would be waste to terminate him due to a few broken vertebrae. He had a long and extensive training."

Only the last sentence seemed to hold a hint of regret.

"Kannon! You talk about him like a sandwich you left in the freezer," Rameau said.

"Emotional reactions are waste," Gunnarsson said. "Learn from this. Under normal conditions, the officer would have been of much higher value to me than you, an undisciplined baseline. But he did not rank above the mission."

"You killed the guards," Rameau persisted. "They'll punish you for that."

"Try to focus," Gunnarsson said. "Do not let your baseline monkey mind jump around. The officer had to be neutralized because he heard the orders of the High Command. Those orders could not be obeyed. The officer would not understand that. Dissension could not be tolerated."

"You could have saved yourself the trouble," Rameau said. "If you did this to keep me alive, you wasted your time. You already destroyed my life. You killed my world. I'll never work for you."

The shuttled lurched. Gunnarsson was going for speed, overcorrecting in his haste. He rocked the little craft with another thruster burn, then turned his attention to Rameau.

"Baseline, understand this: *Langstaff* did not take part in the subjection of Garuda. We did not destroy Varuna. *Langstaff* came to salvage Rameau, and for that reason only. The High Command decided to take pay from humans on Meru in return for the destruction of Garuda. *Langstaff* was ordered to join in this action, but I chose to follow the wishes of the Founder rather than the orders of the High Command. For this we have been condemned. We will be hunted by our own clan because we did not destroy you.

"Vengeance is a baseline concept. It is waste. But if you persist in this wasteful desire, seek vengeance on the baselines of Meru—it is they who sent Original Man against their fellow humans on Garuda. Seek vengeance on High Command—it is they who took pay and did the job. *Langstaff* is not guilty. If you act against us, you serve the destroyers of Garuda."

Rameau felt as if he'd been punched in the stomach yet again. Each time he found some certainty to cling to, it crumbled.

"I don't believe you," he said. "Anyway, it's all the same. 'Original Man is one,' right? You're all the same."

Gunnarsson slammed his fist into the console. It cracked beneath the blow.

"Wrong!" he said. "Try to understand. There is little time. The Founder had one vision for Original Man. High Command has chosen another. He is dead now; to them his words are no longer relevant. I am Original Man. But I cannot follow them.

"I carry the Founder's lineage in my cells. He kept me with him as a juvenile; he shared his memories with me; he trained me. I see as he saw. My mind was shaped by him, and therefore I cannot turn my thoughts to agree with the Council. I would prefer to follow the High Command. I would prefer to be one with my clan. But I *cannot*.

"We will be hunted. There will be no resupply. Therefore, you must continue as a medical officer. You will obey and serve, or you will be confined and isolated for the duration of the journey. But be warned—the journey will be long."

"Why should I believe you?" Rameau said. "And even if I did—what makes the Founder's vision better? He betrayed humanity. To hell with his plan."

Gunnarsson raised his fist as if to strike some obstacle, but restrained himself at the last minute.

"Words prove nothing," he said. "Reasoning with a baseline is useless. You come; you see. The destination will prove it to you. *Langstaff* approaches. I have other concerns. Agree to serve, or be confined when we dock. Your choice."

He needs me that much—

"Give me my message cube," Rameau said.

The Commander struck the console again, and the craft wobbled as the blow triggered the yaw thrusters.

"Baselines are monkeys," he said. "True, no error. At a time of crisis you focus on toys. Possessions. Stupid baseline monkey."

He reached inside his uniform blouse and extracted the message cube.

"Take it."

"You'll have to untie me first," Rameau said.

The Commander spared a hand from the controls to unlatch the memory cord. It loosened itself and fell away. Rameau's arms were so numbed that at first he couldn't grasp the cube. He put out his hands palms up and let the Commander drop the cube into them. Then he pressed it against his chest while he tried to rub some flexibility back into his fingers.

He focused his full attention on the cube. He had to see it before he died. There might not be a future beyond the next five minutes. The only thing that mattered, in the time they had left, was to see her face again.

He managed to bend his fingers enough to press "play."

He was startled and disappointed when the Founder's face appeared instead. But a glowing line of characters below the image told him that this was a framing message, in which the original had been embedded for transmission.

"This message is for Piers Rameau," the Founder said. "The message originator requested Original Man to preserve it and transmit it to Rameau at the earliest opportunity. Pursuant to our agreement with the originator, in return for services to Original Man, we have done so."

The face disappeared. For a moment, only wisps of golden cloud swirled above the cube, and then—

Dakini.

Her face, too, was golden, as if she had coalesced out of the delicate mist, and her handlers had artfully dusted her cheeks with a glimmer of the true metal. Diamond dust gleamed in the eddies of her hair, and a single diamond shimmered on the flared curve of her nostril like diamond dew on a perfect lotus petal. Her eyes shone like forest pools that reflected the rising moon. Now and forever, her eager look sought beyond the clouded crystal of the message cube. She was not seeking him, he knew, but the world beyond—that world she had longed to touch and had been forever forbidden.

His hand paused the cube as soon as she appeared, as if in a futile attempt to stem his pain.

Why cling to the blade when the point has already entered your heart?

He pressed again and let the message continue.

"Rameau, this is to explain," she said. The audio wasn't perfect. Even the visual flickered slightly at times, as if the transmission had traveled a great distance. "I used the magic egg. I want to leave this place. You said I could never leave. I remember that day, when you took me from the Dome and brought me back broken. That day I thought that nothing I do would ever matter. I have no choice to make. I must do what I am made to do.

"But now I have a choice. I have used this egg to speak with the Founder myself. You said there was nowhere I could go. He says they have a place for me, a haven for transforms, where humans will never touch us. I hope that is true. But even if they lie, I prefer their lies to this reality.

"I have called Original Man here, and given them the location of the shields. You think I am a transform who knows nothing. But patrons are always so kind. They give me things. Like giving me this message egg. You said you would give me freedom, if you could. So I hope you will understand that I have taken it for myself.

"The Founder himself promised me that he would save your life, when they come. He said they had a use for you, and they would keep you alive. Just like me, remember? Mr. Chunder had a use for me. And you kept me alive.

"This was your doing, Piers. Because you treated me in some ways like a human, my eyes were opened and I saw that I am not a human. The Original Man say they are more than human. But as long as I stay here, I am so much less. Less, even, than an animal, for animals are part of the world, and have their own places where they can go if they are free. But for me, there is no place on any world where I belong. Even when I die, I go nowhere. Transforms have no souls. So I have to do something that matters now.

"By the time you see this, it will be done. They promised to give this to you when it is over, so you can understand. I know that is important to you, to understand. The other thing that is important to you, I cannot do. I was not made to care for a human. I was made to dance. And that, at least, I have shared with you."

And then she turned away from him and danced. She danced as he had never seen her dance before. She danced for herself alone, as if by one act of will, she had escaped the owners' eyes and seized her freedom. She danced like the starry night around the poles, in a pattern preordained, but one she had freely chosen. Tears streamed down Rameau's face as he watched, but he never knew he was weeping.

She died free, he thought. *If she could dance like that, she died free.*

And she had so nearly won. Maybe it was true—maybe the Founder knew of a way to move her safely. No one had directly intended her death. She had died because she was a pawn in a game she did not understand. She had died by accident—because the wrong Omo got there first, because the war machines were too stupid to know foe from prize. And he, Rameau, who deserved to die for his crimes if anyone did, had survived.

I'm here because of her, he thought. *The Founder wanted me, and she told them how to get in.*

Had she hated him that much? Had she wanted him to know the suffering he had inflicted on her, by helping her to survive as a toy, a slave, an object? Or had she done it because she thought that was what he truly wanted?

Whatever she had meant to do, her final gift would torment him as long as he lived.

"The message proves I spoke the truth. You will agree to serve now," Gunnarsson said.

Rameau could feel the shuttle decelerating. They had almost reached *Langstaff*.

The message proves nothing, Rameau thought. *But it does sound likely. Gunnarsson might have come to Varuna on a "salvage" mission, to pick me up—and maybe Dakini as well—before the others got there. But he failed. That could explain what happened.*

My only chance to punish the High Command is by sticking with this ship.

"Yes, okay," he muttered. "I serve. For now."

It was too late for the Commander to demand more. The shuttle grounded.

11

The Commander opened the hatch and jumped out as soon as the pressure in the landing bay would permit it.

"Bring him," Gunnarsson said to yet another blank-faced cohort. Then he took off down the corridor at a bounding, low-g run. Rameau was seized by the belt and dragged along. He managed to curl his fingers around the message cube and stuff it down the front of his coverall before it could be jolted from his grasp.

Gunnarsson spoke orders into his kenner as they ran. They came to a halt a few minutes later. A wall opened, and Rameau saw the command nexus within.

"Stay with the pilots," Gunnarsson ordered Rameau. Then the Commander vanished into the nexus, his guards with him. Rameau found his way to pilot space. As he guessed, the command center lay along the same ring.

He entered the familiar dusk. Nuun still lay silent and motionless in his pod. There was no one in the pilot jock's support chair. Neb and Nor must still be en route from crew quarters, he guessed. Rameau sat down in the chair. It cradled his body, which seemed to be always aching and sore from blows and strain.

Then he realized there was nothing to prevent him from putting on the helmet. He remembered what had happened the one time he tried the link. Still, he wasn't afraid. He had so little left to lose.

This could kill two Omo with one stone. Get Gunnarsson and the High Command. Smash the ship into their station, blow it up—it's probably impossible, but I won't know till I try.

He hurried, fumbling in his haste. It would be unbearable to be stopped now. As the helmet closed around his head, he experienced a moment of suffocating panic. But the air inside was fresh and pure, certainly better than the ship's atmosphere.

He remembered to open his eyes, and once again the feeling of confinement gave way to a sense of freedom. The stars came back, and with them the nodes and vortices of light he'd seen before—more of them, this time.

Then he felt himself beginning to move. He no longer had weight. He couldn't feel the chair cradling him. He was flying at a tremendous velocity, in constantly changing relationships to huge, invisible masses that brushed him with senses other than sight. The lights that filled his vision no longer appeared as points and lines, but as planes of energy. They shifted and locked around him in crystalline forms of folded light. And as he moved, the sounds began. The light roared and shrieked, too high or too low for human hearing.

Too *big*.

It could have been beautiful, he thought. But it was *wrong*. It hurt. Outwardly he was cocooned in perfect comfort, but his perceptions stabbed at him. They no longer felt like his own senses. It felt as if something massive had forced its way into his mind, until his skull was about to split open. He felt as if he had been plunged into molten heat, or absolute cold, flung into a blast furnace or a sea of liquid nitrogen, with only nanoseconds to appreciate the beauty he perceived there, before his fragile senses were annihilated.

It was a killing, crushing glory, and he had no defense against it. He hurtled into it, like a man thrown from a cliff.

He tried to extend his perceptions as the pilots did, to will a direction, to surf the waves of sensation roaring over him. But another consciousness was there beside him, gathering up the lines of force and hurling him aside with casual power. He felt himself spinning into a bright, thundering oblivion.

He screamed as his senses were torn away—and regained awareness sprawled on the floor of the pilot space, with Neb and Nor standing over him. Neb had pulled the link helmet from his head. Nor took his place in the chair, and Neb settled helmet and gauntlets on his sib.

Rameau could only moan and try to hug the floor as a deadly sickness swirled within him. He felt as if he were Outside, on the hull again, hanging over the great void. Raising his eyes to the holo-screens, he saw scenes of ruin and destruction. He could see the hull. It was under attack from a swarm of modules shaped like blunt-nosed, parasitic larvae, all trying to burrow into *Langstaff*'s skin. Two of the modules exploded into slag, and the screens blacked out. Rameau felt the shudder that rang through the ship.

Another screen, internal this time, showed a chamber bursting into a boiling mass of fire. Rameau stared at it in brief horror before that screen winked out. He heard a high, insistent tone sounding, as if at a great distance. Beyond the bulkheads that protected him, it was probably deafening.

An all-stations alarm, he thought. *It looks as if we've been breached.*

Another viewer came online. It showed molten blobs and hot gases venting around the module that was still embedded in the hull. More of the bullet-shaped objects clustered like flies around a gaping wound. Clanging and rumbling vibrated through the hull.

Finished with Nor, Neb bent and tried to pull Rameau to his feet.

"We jump soon," Neb said. "Have to get out. Back to quarters. Come."

But Rameau couldn't. He could move his arms and legs, but not coordinate them. He flailed like a baby. Neb grasped the back of Rameau's coverall and dragged him out of pilot space, into the corridor—from dusk and stillness into bright light and the insistent shrilling of the alarm.

"Back to quarters," Neb repeated. The cohort seemed agitated, even frightened.

"Why?" Rameau said. "What's happening?"

Before Neb could answer, Rameau heard another panic sound—not a mechanical warning this time, but a shriek torn from a human throat. The screaming did not end. But Neb took off at top speed, dragging Rameau down the corridor with him, until Rameau couldn't hear it anymore.

No one would scream that way unless something terrible was about to happen. And Rameau knew that no matter how fast Neb ran, they would not reach the cohort quarters before catastrophe arrived. Neb towed him, with one hand at his belt and the other twisted into the front of his coverall. With great difficulty, Rameau pulled his own hand upward, like a dead weight at the end of a cord, and grasped Neb's wrist.

"Quarters," he gasped out. "Why?"

"Secure for jump," Neb said over his shoulder.

"Can't," Rameau said. "Stop! Can't make it."

Rounding a curve, Neb leaned into the wall and slowed down. He pulled Rameau level with his face. He looked more frightened than ever.

"Try drop tube," Rameau said. "Can we brace in there?"

He watched the idea sink slowly into the cohort's mind, and reappear on Neb's face.

"Possible." Neb was already running toward the nearest raised sign.

"Flash it," he said, shaking Rameau's arm impatiently. Rameau fumbled with his kenner. It seemed a long time until the wall folded itself out of the way. Neb dragged him inside, and the wall closed behind them. A hideous keening shook the whole ship, as if the hull itself screamed in pain.

In the dim glow of the wall lights, Rameau saw Neb bracing his back against one wall of the tube, his legs extended so the soles of his feet pushed against the opposite wall. Neb thrust Rameau away from him so Rameau felt the wall behind him. Neb's feet were on either side of him. Rameau extended his legs. He couldn't put his feet flat against the wall, but by stretching, he could push against it with his toes. His legs crossed over Neb's. The cohort interlaced his arms with Rameau's. They braced each other within the tube. Rameau could hear the harsh sound of Neb's breath coming and going near his ear, echoed by his own smaller breathing.

"Not good, not good," Neb panted. "We should—"

But at that moment the world turned inside out. Rameau felt

as if he were simultaneously slammed against the wall and sucked away from it. Either he was vomiting, or his guts were being pulled through his skin to change places with the outside. He tried to push Neb away, but instead found himself crushed against the cohort. They spun faster and faster, as if in a centrifuge, to the sound of strangled howling. The lights blinked out. Rameau lost consciousness, but even in that blackness, somehow he could still feel himself falling at infinite speed.

12

He was paralyzed, and still falling, but it was no longer completely dark. He regained control of his eyelids and opened his eyes. The wall lights were on again. He floated with Neb in the drop tube, still enmeshed with the cohort, but no longer braced against the wall.

"How did we get back here?" he said. His voice was rough, and hurt his throat. His question sounded stupid to him as soon as he said it. Of course they were in the drop tube; so why did he feel as if he had been hurled out into some alien abyss?

It smells awful in here. Oh, shit. I've pissed myself.

Rameau touched his own face. Blood and vomit crusted his nose and mouth. Neb still drifted, twitching randomly. Rameau struggled to pull free from Neb's unconscious grip. Neb's eyes snapped open, aware again.

"Ship in jump—we go find group!" he said urgently. "Find crew quarters!"

Rameau followed him shakily, clinging to the grips inside the tube rather than launching himself down its length like Neb. They were in zero g, as far as he could tell. Malodorous bubbles of body fluids splatted against them. Fortunately, most of the ejected liquid had impacted against the walls, forming a slimy film that was unpleasant, but couldn't asphyxiate them.

As soon as they emerged into the corridor, Rameau had to duck a corpse drifting toward his head. They passed more floating bodies. Neb's lips moved; Rameau heard what he was muttering: "Neb, Nor, Nuun, Nik . . ." The names of his sibs.

Neb's hand, towing Rameau, was slick with sweat. The air in the corridor grew steadily hotter. Rameau rubbed at his face.

Sweat had loosened the noxious crust around his mouth. He scraped at it with his sleeve in furious disgust, and watched it trail away in a spiral of crumbs.

They turned hullward three levels, and the heat increased. Neb looked worried. He went several compartments' width clockwise around the axis, and tried another hullward corridor, but the heat was still intolerable. They continued clockwise. Suddenly they were looking through a crater in the floor, the pale kemplex edges melted smooth, like a freeze-frame of a drop of milk at splashdown.

Heat smote them through the hole. Glancing quickly through, and pulling back before his skin could crisp, Rameau saw a distant, molten glow. He wondered if he was seeing all the way to the hull. A cluster of trash bots hovered several decks down the hole, as if they had been ordered to repair the damage, but couldn't get close enough.

"Hot," Neb said. "Hot is bad. E got no place to go in jump."

"What happened?" Rameau said.

"This cohort no ken," Neb said. "Ship different now. Everything different now."

Sweat poured down Neb's face. Rameau wiped a sleeve across his own stinging eyes. He craved water. He tried to call up a possible route to crew quarters on his kenner. The kenner's memory hadn't yet registered the devastation around them. Rameau needed a ship node that could give him fresh data.

He flashed a summons toward a bot that clung to the wall, closer to them than the others. It trundled slowly toward them, navigating the crumpled kemplex of the decks between. Rameau reached out to it, but snatched his hand back quickly. The bot's metal skin was hot enough to scorch. Rameau wondered how much hotter it could get and still function.

"Bot," he ordered, "transmit command to repair bots within range—pull back to nonlethal temperatures."

"Awaiting confirmation," the bot said in its small, droning voice. It waited, the little red dots of its scanners blinking like eyes.

Rameau flashed his identity code. That seemed to satisfy the bot. It turned and messaged the others. The little cluster of bots moved away from the fire, and Rameau felt a small tug of satisfaction. He had salvaged something.

"Bot," he said again, "find ship node for data download."

It skirted the edge of the hole, and headed away from them, on the opposite side of the damaged area.

"Come on," Rameau said. "I lead now."

He covered his face with his arms and pushed off. A blast of heat crisped the fine hairs around his forehead as he crossed over the hole, but then he was past it into comparative cool. Neb followed.

The bot found three nodes before they came to one that still functioned. The data, when it came, was chaotic, but the flickering screens finally settled. The maps that remained were riddled with red, a maze with no clear solution. It took the kenner several seconds, an eternity, to propose a possible route to crew quarters.

Neb bumped Rameau with his shoulder to get his attention. It hurt.

"Check location of sibs," he said. His hand hovered over the kenner as if he wanted to snatch control. Rameau jerked his arm away.

"Don't touch that!" he said. "Check it yourself. Use your own kenner."

Neb reached over Rameau's warding hand and pressed nodes.

"Emergency situation. Rameau is officer. E can authorize."

The text-only message glowed. "Emergency designation: MedSpec Rameau now chief medical officer, jumpship *Langstaff*."

"That's not possible."

"Yes, possible," Neb said. "All cohort medical officers terminate."

Son of a bitch, Rameau thought. *You can't do this to me.*

"Check sibs," Neb repeated. Two designations registered as tiny points of light, still in the pilot space.

"Still functional," Rameau said. Neb didn't smile or say thank you, but he nodded.

"Functional is good," he said.

They followed the kenner route slowly, letting the bot set the pace. Every turn to hullward brought them to increasing heat and damage. Yet an uncanny silence reigned. All sounds, even their own brief exchanges, were muted.

"Why is it so quiet?" Rameau said. "What's wrong?"

"In jump," he muttered. "Sound go different. Ghost sound, e say. Quiet. But not good."

Humans never performed the leaps through unknown space that jumpfighters dared. Humans traveled established routes, with trained pilots who guided the ship through jump space while the passengers slept, sedated and cocooned. Passenger ships never experienced the kind of disjunction from normal space that *Langstaff* had just been through. Rameau had only heard stories of exploration ships that passed through extended jump routes. "Ghosting," they had called it.

"How long do we stay in jump?" he asked. "When do we come out?"

Neb only shook his head. "This cohort no affiliate command," he said.

The quiet made Rameau's skin crawl. But soon it was broken. He heard sounds of muffled tumult, and then a crew of cohorts broke through a gash in the wall and dived past them. A wall of heat surged through behind them, drying the sweat instantly on Rameau's face. More teams in radiation suits swarmed through the corridor. Another crater had melted through multiple decks, and beyond the tangle of damaged infrastructures, the last intact deck was a scar tissue of charred pockmarks and glowing craters. The teams didn't even try to fix the mangled structure; they worked feverishly to block the gaping hole with insulated panels. Rameau and Neb were bumped and jostled as if the busy teams didn't even recognize their presence. Neb called out to the suited figures in ship jo, but received no answer.

"Hurry—quarters that way," Neb said.

They ducked around the cohorts, Neb leading again, to a stretch of corridor that seemed vaguely familiar and largely undamaged. Rameau thought this must be the area outside the big room where the cohorts lived. The guiding lights that marked function areas of the ship had died, adding to the confusion.

A cluster of bobbing corpses blocked the way. They were truncated and contorted till they no longer looked human. Some were not—they were Rukh and the strange leathery creatures Rameau had seen Outside, on the hull.

A massive, dark lump struck Rameau, and its momentum carried him helplessly along. His face inches away, he could see features in the mass—a face here, blackened fingers protruding there. Half a dozen bodies had been fused into one tangle, along with kemplex slag and something like twisted metal rods. He kicked it away, but it rebounded off the opposite wall and struck him again, crushing him against the wall.

He thrashed, screaming, and somehow caught a hold that kept him in place while the grotesque satellite floated past.

Neb caught his arm and dragged him into what was left of the crew quarters.

"Water," Rameau choked. The word caught in his throat and made him gag.

"Here." Neb towed him to a spigot and held the drinking tube to his mouth. The water was warm, but it was still wet. He drank and drank, then wet his sleeve and scrubbed at his face and hands until the skin was raw but clean. He couldn't do anything to improve the damp stink of his filthy coverall.

"Oh, Kannon," he sighed at last. "What was that?"

Neb shrugged. Back in somewhat familiar surroundings, he seemed calmer.

"They have terminated," he said. "Nothing to do for them. Medical officer needed here."

Rameau looked around.

Not again.

He was back to zero—the eternal starting place. Bodies on the floor, bodies on the ceiling, wherever there were still sleeping straps to secure them. Bodies clinging to brackets, bodies dead and alive, floating aimlessly around the toroidal space. It wasn't safe for the living to fall free; the room was a tangle of projecting stubs and edges, not all of them melted smooth. The drifting wounded risked more burns and cuts.

He'd seen it all before: full-thickness burns, gashes from hot shrapnel, amputations, inhalation burns . . .

O Kannon, O Compassionate One!

In his despair, he hoped they would all be dead before he examined them. But he knew that many still clung to life. He didn't have to treat them. He could let them die. Hunted by the High Command, the chances were they'd die soon anyway. But if he let them die, he'd be helping the faction that killed Dakini. Or so Gunnarsson said. The Commander had given him an impossible choice.

Whose side are you on? Will you side with your enemies, here on this ship? Or with the enemies of all humankind, in close pursuit? No friends to run to, either way.

But even while he rebelled, he knew his choice was already made. He saw Death's jaws gaping to swallow the world, and knew he couldn't let Death win. Without help, without supplies, he still had to do something. He had to try.

He had started sweating again. He could tell without checking the kenner that the temperature was still rising, to a point that was nearly intolerable. If this kept up, it would soon be lethal. The casualties had to be moved.

With his kenner, he opened access nodes, laying in symbols in the search for needed supplies. He watched as the diagrams flowed into each other. Colored lines that marked possible routes were blocked again and again as they dead-ended in forbidden areas. If only they could get to the regeneration tanks, flayed and burned skin could be regrown, quickly and easily. But the tanks had gone up in flames on Kilo Deck. That site was redlined. The kenner reported that fire-fighting teams had occupied auxiliary medical, too, and that the area was contaminated with the by-products of the fire suppressants.

Rameau felt fear, like the distant shuddering of the abused hull, at the thought of the whole ship ceasing to function. It was cold and dark out there. All to the good, really, if the whole boatload of gene-distorted organisms got freeze-dried like banana chips. Even if he had to go with them. But the fear became irrelevant as he focused on the problem.

As he knelt in this ship of the soon-to-be-dead, he found

himself thinking—not quite irrelevantly—about soup. The shuffling of maps on-screen slowed, and gradually came to a stop.

"Stupid machine," he said. "Neb! What area does this show? I'm still confused by your deck designations."

Neb looked over his shoulder. "Biosupport," he said.

"The kitchen?" Rameau said. "Of course! Soup!"

The picture of the regeneration tank—looking much like a soup pot—appeared clearly in his mind.

"Neb, this is the only place in the ship we can produce more skin grafts," Rameau said. "Can you reprogram nutrient tanks?"

"This cohort affiliates to medical, not biosupport," Neb said.

"Oh, come on!" Rameau said. "It's not that hard. Nutrient tanks and regeneration tanks are almost identical. Use the medical programming to get the specs for growing sheets of dermis and epidermis. Then give the tanks new templates. Change the mix on the feeder. If you can grow chicken steak, you can grow skin."

Neb appeared to be working slowly through this strange concept.

"This cohort no got authority use biosupport resources," he said.

"I'm giving you authority!" Rameau said. "Can you perform what I just described?"

Neb looked hunted, but he answered.

"Yes."

"Then do it. Find cohorts to drag the bodies. Sterilize the food-preparation area and set up an emergency field surgery. I know you ken that because I saw you do it for the—" He still couldn't say *Rukh*. "For the others."

"This cohort obeys. But—"

Just adding the qualifier seemed too much for the cohort. He stuck there and could not proceed.

"But what?" Rameau said impatiently. "Spit it out!"

Neb opened his mouth and then shut it again.

"This cohort has nothing to spit."

"Forget it. It's baseline ship jo—means say what you need to say. Quickly."

"Rameau, this cohort tries to obey. But so few cohorts not hurt, not working. Take long time to move all these."

Rameau looked around reflexively, and saw the bot, still watching patiently from its perch halfway up the wall.

"Bot," he said, "accept revised command priority: affiliate to medical officer—uh—G-Prime MedSpec Rameau."

"Awaiting confirmation," came the flat, mechanical play.

Rameau flashed his ID.

"New affiliation confirmed," the bot said. "Awaiting orders."

It worked.

"Bot, accept orders from—what's your designation, Neb?"

"SigmaCGN-Seven."

"From SigmaCGN-Seven. Neb, use the bot to collect other bots to help you. They can cross dangerous areas to collect more cohorts, and they can help you transport casualties. Start work while I check out these bodies."

As Neb moved to comply, Rameau finished examining and triaging the rest of the wounded on his own. About a third of the bodies in the room were already dead. If they had been in an elite hospital on Garuda, the condition might have been temporary, but here in the dying ship, they were simply dead, and would stay that way.

Even with his kenner upgrade, Rameau needed Neb's help to figure out how to reach the food-preparation area. Neb set out with confidence, but had to retrace his steps several times, and Rameau could see frustration and something like fear growing in the cohort as his own ship grew strange around him. Blast doors and air locks sealed them off from the damaged and contested areas. They passed through corridors where the walls were hot to the touch, or where the aircon had broken down under the onslaught of heat and combustion beyond the bulkheads.

Once Neb backtracked quickly, and Rameau followed as a vague stinging in his nose and throat escalated into spasms of coughing. He could feel the fluids seeping into his lungs as tears poured from his eyes. He groped forward, barely able to see, and when his hand met the back of the cohort's coverall, he clung to it. Neb guided himself with one hand touching the curve of the steel wall. When the cohort encountered a crosshatched panel in that wall, he keyed it open and snatched out emergency ventilators. They caught their breath and tried again to pass through the corridor. In those few minutes, it had become unbearably hot. They had to descend two levels and seek another route.

Once Rameau thought he heard screaming in the distance. And the ominous groaning and shuddering of the ship continued, as if they were trapped inside a temple bell that was being struck by a giant's hammer.

Finally Neb established a clear route, and the bots and cohorts brought the wounded to the makeshift surgery. Through the twists and turns of the corridors, they had formed a kind of bucket brigade, stationing themselves at intervals on the route and passing the wounded along.

Rameau told them to strip and sterilize the wounded, then strap them down in rows on the steel counters and tabletops of the food-prep area. He was glad they weren't human. It would have been harder to treat true humans so ruthlessly.

They adapted the food-preparation vats to produce synthetic skin, and before long it was coming down the conveyors in sheets. Rameau sliced it and body-glued it to the wounds. He didn't know how much they would be able to produce, or how much they would need, so he saved every scrap. He patchworked the pieces into useful segments and trimmed off damaged tissue as he worked.

Neb gave the wounded blood replacements and antibiotics as Rameau finished with them.

"You'll have to monitor them by hand," Rameau said. "Obviously we're not in sick bay, and can't hook them to the medikenner."

He hoped Neb could handle that much responsibility. The cohort's technique seemed flawless; only his judgment was questionable.

After hours of work, Rameau could feel fatigue coming over him, approaching in waves. The endless chain of bodies blurred in his sight. But each wave of exhaustion was quickly followed by the tingling heat of enabler drugs flooding into his system. His heart beat faster, more strongly, and his vision cleared again. Along with the renewed, drug-induced strength came a cotton-dry mouth, and a prickly feeling in his head that made him wish he could scratch behind his eyeballs.

"You're lucky I worked in Vaharanesi, where the people are poor," he said to Neb. Talking helped him to stay focused. "Otherwise I would never be able to cope with this low-tech a setup. You know, it's going to take these guys a lot longer to recover than it would in a regeneration tank. With this kind of cut-and-paste repair, the tissues have to regrow on their own."

He motioned for Neb to wipe the sweat off his face, and waited impatiently while the cohort grasped the idea and complied.

He may be a good tech, but it doesn't look as if he's ever assisted in surgery before, Rameau thought. *Under normal circumstances, it's all automated.*

"Get me a big sipper bulb full of something cold with lots of glucose," he said. "Fruit juice, or just water with sugar if that's all you've got. Put it there where I can reach it."

He ran out of body glue, and ordered Neb to have the synthesizers spin out thin strands of sinewlike filament. With these he actually stitched muscle fibers together. He had learned this primitive technique from his parents, in the clinic they had run in a plastic tent. He had never expected to use it on metahumans, in deep space.

He paused to drink. The sipper wasn't cold; it was hot as soup. The temperature around them was still rising. Soon the makeshift surgery would be uninhabitable.

Where can we go? He had trouble thinking. It had to be a place with access to water. *Where is it cooler?*

"Neb! We have to move them again. Pass the word to your team: as I finish up with these guys, start moving them inward, to the biosphere. Find the safest route you can, but get it done quickly. If we stay here, we're toast. Got it?"

"This cohort obeys."

Rameau turned back to his work. It seemed there was no end

to the line of bodies. He felt as if he were sewing up the same wounds over and over. The room spun, as if they were all in an endless loop.

"Isn't this where I came in?" he mumbled to Neb, but the cohort didn't understand.

A low intermittent thunder rumbled through the walls and the floor at his feet. The vibration made his instruments clatter in their trays. Sudden gravity fluctuations made everything lurch upward before dropping back into place with unpredictable force. Rameau was splattered with stray fluids.

Like the ship, his hands sometimes trembled uncontrollably. Things flew from his fingers as if they were suddenly self-propelled. Neb handed them back to him, but for long numb pauses, he couldn't grasp the objects.

"Data delay," he mumbled, but his speech, too, was punctuated with tremors. It was because his mind was in orbit, flying out through the Oort on a long loop that might never return. He could look down and see his body, very far away. The bright thing down there in his hand wasn't sterile anymore. He had to tell Neb that, but the words never came.

Instead, the room became very still and bright. A faint fringe of rainbows haloed each object, even his own trembling fingers. *What's happening to me?* Then he understood. *I told you so,* he thought. *I told you so.*

13

He gasped, and woke up shaking. The instant he moved, he found stabs of pain in all his limbs. His fingers felt swollen and splayed like bunches of sausages. He gulped in air, and smelled blood and bile and stale disinfectant. He jerked his head away from the nauseating odor, but it was him; he stank.

The sudden movement made him retch. His empty stomach cramped in a painful spasm that seemed to go on forever. He thought he'd never be able to get another breath. But he must have made some kind of noise, because the light came on, and stabbed his eyes, and he screamed.

He moved his tongue and found that he had bitten himself several times. Then he remembered. Just as he had predicted when they'd enabled him, the massive overdose of stimulants had finally overloaded his nervous system. He'd had a seizure.

He had to pull his arm up close to his nose to read the kenner screen. Bracing his other arm against his chest, he stilled the trembling of his fingers enough to press the nodes and access his own condition. He needed to perform an override before the enabler decided to hit him with another dose. He winced at the readout.

This thing thinks I'm just another expendable superman. It'll keep me running on uppers until I spontaneously combust.

He ordered a minimal dose of antispasmodics and something to bring his blood pressure down. Almost immediately, he started to feel calmer. But he didn't smell any better, and he was deeply sick and sore. He needed a shower, and a cold drink.

What he got was another bulb of room-temperature electrolyte solution, handed to him by Neb.

He looked around. He was in the biosphere, along with dozens of casualties. They lay beneath the leaves like ugly, overgrown marrows, strapped down with improvised restraints to keep them from being jerked and jostled by the g fluctuations. Those who were still alert maintained a stoic silence, but the semiconscious moaned and cried in pain.

"No more wounded go fit in here," Neb said. "We store overflow in corridor outside."

"Good job," Rameau said. "Now—painkillers. Collect all we have in one place. Use your judgment in administering them."

"This cohort no ken," Neb said annoyingly.

Rameau swore. "Give them to the wounded who seem most in pain! You ken pain, no? Major burns and gut wounds—very painful. That only covers about ninety percent of everyone here. Another hint: if they're screaming, shoot them up. Got that?"

"This cohort obeys."

"Next, reprogram the plant hoses. Cut out the nutrients, and use them to give plain water to everyone who's conscious.

"Then get big containers that aren't too dirty—no chemicals or body residues—fill them with water and take them to hot areas until the water is hot. Not hot enough to burn. Test with your own hand. Bring them back here and use the hot water to clean wounds."

"Use water?" Neb said uncertainly.

"It's what they used before antiseptics. Also mild soap, if you have any. Nothing caustic. Soap. Cleanser. Cleaning fluid."

"Soap." Neb didn't seem to recognize the word, so Rameau wasn't hopeful.

"Go!"

Rameau crouched among the plant trays. He had brought the smell of blood and fire into this green place. He pinched a fragment of leaf from a vine and rolled it between his palms, breathing the crushed green scent like life-giving oxygen.

What am I going to do with them?

People in the shantytowns on Garuda had used teas and infusions of plants when they couldn't obtain medicines. He had looked down on those things when he had worked there, concentrating instead on getting the pharmaceuticals by any means necessary. He'd left the old women to fiddle with what he thought of as herbal placebos.

But here he was in the same situation. In a ship built by the most advanced technology human-derived organisms had ever achieved, he had nothing to offer the wounded but hot water.

He tried to think of something to use for sterile dressings. The poorest colonists on Garuda had access to resources not available on a jumpship: paper, fabric, even bark.

No willow bark here. His eyes blurred, and he blinked the stinging sweat away.

Bleeding! While I'm sitting here thinking about bark, they're bleeding to death!

He scrambled out of his refuge and shouted for assistance. He still had some of the sterile filament from the synthesizers. He could tie off bleeders with that. If all else failed, he could cauterize them. The one thing they had plenty of was hot metal.

Hours later, he was still toiling over those bodies, those tormenting puzzles he couldn't solve but had to keep working on. Sweat blurred his vision, and he no longer tried to wipe it away. Breath no longer cooled him. The heat lay heavy on his head like a smothering blanket. He longed for sleep. He wanted to lie down among the green leaves, unaware when the green began to crisp and smolder like the charred flesh under his hands.

He shook his head and sent a cloud of droplets flying. The room was a stew of vaporized fluids and flecks of tissue swirling crazily in the random air currents. Rameau had two cohorts constantly sweeping with emergency scrubbers, but they couldn't keep up with the particles. Every few minutes, Rameau inhaled a fragment large enough to trigger a coughing spasm.

Only the enabler kept him going. He no longer cared if it burned out his neurons. Let them burn; everything would be burning soon.

He came to the end of one row and paused. The face below him, upside down in his sight, was massive and hairy. It wasn't just his blurred sight—this thing he had been washing and mending like a torn shirt was a Rukh. He hated the Rukh. Still, the sounds it made gave him no pleasure. They were faint sounds, but full of infinite pain. Pleading, like a hurt dog.

"I'm sorry," he muttered. "We have no more painkillers. We have pain. We have killers. But the pain kills us, not the other way around."

He felt a strange prickling sensation on the back of his neck, and thought the seizures might be about to start again. But then he turned, and saw another Rukh, staring at him with those huge, bloodshot, animal eyes. He moved on to the next patient.

I hate the Rukh.

The second Rukh dragged itself slowly toward its fellow and curled beside it, clutching at it with its one unwounded, pawlike hand. Rameau could feel its gaze still on him as he worked his way through the next row of casualties. More of them were dead now; so the work went faster.

Then the lights went out.

The dazzling white bar of light that speared the core of the garden faded to violet for a long minute in which their skins were bruise-colored and teeth and eyes glowed eerily. Then it flickered and vanished. Darkness descended like a shroud. The faint whir of the ventilators ceased.

Slowly and uncertainly, emergency lights began to glow, but the sun-bar did not return. By the reddish illumination, Rameau could make out a cohort curled nearby, hugging his own head in his arms as if he were terrified.

It was Neb.

"We burned the pilot," Neb said. "We burned the pilot."

His voice was low, but full of horror. Rameau barely had time to notice before the world turned inside out again. He was jerked loose from the wall and went soaring across the cylindrical garden in a storm of torn leaves.

When he came to, he was sprawled across something massive and lumpy. His own body was heavy. The weight had come on again, but in a crazy direction. The current floor slanted steeply. The plant trays were bolted down, or he would have been crushed. Everything that wasn't nailed down had piled up at one end of the room. Luckily, he had ended up at the top of the pile.

Oh, Kannon, it's the wounded. The casualties are all on top of each other. They'll suffocate!

He hauled frantically at the bodies, shouting for Neb. His voice blared in his own ears; sound was no longer muffled. They were out of jump.

He dragged away the top layer of wounded and pushed them behind plant stands, vine trunks—anything to keep them from sliding back into the heap. His lungs were bursting with effort. His head, too, felt as if it would burst. He wondered if the ship was running low on oxygen.

"Neb! In the name of the Compassionate One!"

He began to weep with frustration. He shook his own arm impatiently.

"Come on, enabler! Wake up!"

The supply lights on the enabler showed red across the screen. He had outlasted the drugs. Maybe that was why he felt so sick.

A groan from the next layer down resolved into words.

"Help me."

"Neb?"

He burrowed between arms and legs, dragged off one of the Rukh. With its superdense bones and massive muscles, it was like moving a small mountain. At last he grasped a feebly struggling arm. He pulled, and Neb emerged, kicking the still forms of his comrades out of the way.

"You all right?"

"Yes. Functional."

"You help me now," Rameau panted. "Straighten out this mess. Get them laid out where they can breathe."

"This cohort think most have terminated," Neb said. But he helped. When they found another cohort who was still conscious and undamaged, the task went faster.

The ship jumped and lurched.

I'd piss myself again if I weren't completely dehydrated.

"Engine damage," Neb said fearfully. "Ship no go that way, never. Not good."

Rameau only half heard, as he searched for signs of life. In the dim light, he could do little more than feel, with an ear to the chest or a finger to the throat. He ordered the dead ones left in a heap at the end of the room, then crawled up the curved, slanting wall until he found the water tap, and made one more round, giving drink to anyone who could still swallow. The water pressure was very low. He was worried about the air, too.

Not much left to run out of.

"Stay here with them," he said. "I have to go find out what's happening."

"We burned the pilot," Neb repeated. "We fell out of jump. We're lost."

No "This cohort no ken" now, Rameau thought. *He acts as if he knows what he's talking about.*

Rameau opened the hatchway to the drop tube and felt his way cautiously, wary of fire at the other end. When he opened the wall and crawled out, the corridor was intensely hot, but survivable. He found a data node and tried to get an update, but the node was fried. He used his kenner to flash Gunnarsson. There was no answer.

"Hello!" he shouted. "Anyone! Is there anyone here?"

He tried to reach another deck, moving outward from the hub. A gust of hot, black smoke billowed up to meet him. He dropped to the floor to find breathable air.

Idiot! Why didn't you look for a respirator first?

Choking, he tried desperately to think of someone who could help him.

The bot. It was the last order I gave. The address is still in the kenner.

He couldn't see, but he found the nodes with his fingers and sent out a summons. Then he tried to crawl away from the smoke, but the curved walls were disorienting. In the midst of the confusion, his kenner buzzed urgently. He pressed "respond," but the smoke was so thick he couldn't see the message or who had sent it. A voice spoke out of the air.

"G-Prime MedSpec Rameau, stay where you are. You will be sent for."

"Oh, thanks," Rameau said sarcastically. A fit of coughing stopped him short. He disobeyed the order and kept crawling as fast as he could.

I'll be dead before they find me.

A blocky, blackened shape appeared out of the cloud and resolved into a trash bot with a respirator clamped in its grippers. The hoses hung down on either side as if it were wearing a wig. Rameau clasped the mask to his face and inhaled deep breaths of pure canned air. His head cleared, but his eyes were watering so much that he still couldn't see. He felt for the bot and hung on with one arm as it began to move again, through the smoke.

They emerged into clear air, though it was still hot. The sweat pouring from Rameau's face left sooty blotches where it dripped onto the floor. He tore off the mask and knelt, coughing until he gasped and there were bright spots behind his eyes. He couldn't seem to get the smoke out of his lungs.

He looked up. Two cohorts stood over him.

"Medical officer to the Commander," they said. "You come." They pulled him up and half dragged him along. He hung on to the respirator and concentrated on breathing.

When they stopped, they were back at the command nexus. It looked different now. When they'd been in micro g, the Commander and his officers had been throned in the middle of the room, free to use the whole space with all its controls and inputs. Now they were huddled on the current floor, occupying a small, uncomfortable portion of what had been a wall.

Gunnarsson was crouched over a console, but he rose to his full height when he saw Rameau. He was as intimidating as ever, untouched by the chaos around him. Thanks to his scorched lungs, Rameau could no longer smell himself, but he could see disgust in the Commander's eyes.

"My MedSpec—still functional," the Commander said. Rameau almost thought he looked relieved. "You were in the pilot link during prejump maneuvers. Do not try this again. You would have terminated."

"Can we discuss that later?" Rameau said. "If there is a later?

Right now, what's left of your crew is parked in the biosphere, and we have no medical supplies. No grafts, no transplant organs, no nutrients, no surgical anesthetics. And did I mention that we're running out of water?"

"The monitors reported your presence in the biosphere," the Commander said. "And I am informed of the status of our consumables. You were summoned here for another, more urgent matter."

"What could possibly be more urgent than saving your crew?" Rameau said. "Isn't that what you brought me here to do?"

"You were summoned for duty, and your medtech-one reported that you were absent," Gunnarsson said, as if Rameau hadn't spoken.

Rage swept over Rameau like black smoke spewing from a molten crater.

"Yeah, I was absent from my so-called duty—I was out here getting fried because I couldn't go on doing my *duty* with no supplies, no data, no nothing. If you want my help, you can goddamn well tell me what the hell is happening."

The last words came out in a strangled croak; he put the respirator to his face and gasped for air.

Gunnarsson gave his officers a look as if to say "You see what I have to deal with here."

"The pilot is more urgent," he said to Rameau, as if it should be obvious. "You are wasting time. If you want information, follow me."

Knowing that if he didn't follow, he'd be dragged, Rameau obeyed. Gunnarsson led him to the pilot space.

The pilot still sat in his chair, but the constant movement of his fingers had stopped. His body was limp, almost invisible in the grasp of his support machinery.

Rameau reached to feel for a pulse, but suddenly realized that something was missing.

"Wait," he said. "Where's Nor—the pilot jock?"

Gunnarsson pointed. Nor huddled on the floor, as far from the pilot as he could get.

"Nor? Are you all right?" Rameau said. "Did you see what happened?"

Nor moaned.

"Answer!" Gunnarsson commanded in a voice that stung like a whip.

"This cohort . . . fell out of sync," Nor said haltingly. "Could not control." His voice rose to a cry of anguish. "Lost him! Lost him!"

Rameau moved to go to his side, but Gunnarsson restrained him.

"He will recover. He left the link before it was too late. It is the pilot you must attend. His monitor is there." He gestured to one of the wall screens.

But Rameau unlatched one of the gloves first, to feel for a living pulse. The pilot's hand seemed very pale. When Rameau let go, the arm dropped and dangled limp.

Then he tried to make sense of the monitors. Obviously, the patient was in shock. Heart action was weak and irregular, blood chemistry skewed, and chemical analysis showed drugs he had never seen, present in large quantities. The brain scan showed fitful, minimal activity.

"He's in a coma," Rameau said. "If he were human, I'd say the damage was irreversible."

Gunnarsson shook his head.

"I had hoped you might have learned of some new treatment. Since you have not—this is irreversible for Original Man, too."

"Sometimes the 'irreversibly' comatose make surprising recoveries," Rameau said. "There must be something you could try."

Gunnarsson gestured dismissively.

"He will not recover," he said. "Summon a cohort and have him converted."

It took Rameau a minute to figure out what he meant.

"He's still breathing! You can't just . . . recycle him."

"His utility is terminated. And we need all the mass we can get."

"*I'm* the medical officer," Rameau said furiously. "*I* decide when he's terminated."

Gunnarsson gave Rameau a look that made him flinch in

spite of himself, but then the Commander seemed to decide that the point wasn't worth pursuing.

"Then he can be converted when he stops breathing. It will be soon. Brain function of a jump-traumatized pilot is not well understood. It is possible that he would prefer immediate conversion."

"Neb—the other pilot sib—said you 'burned the pilot,'" Rameau said. "What does that mean? What have you done to him?"

When Gunnarsson didn't answer, he pressed on. "I'm the medical officer. You must inform me of conditions affecting my patients. I refuse to take the risk of causing more pointless suffering."

He knew he was bluffing. He had been forced to accept the cohorts as patients, but now that they were his patients, he couldn't give up, no matter how pointless his efforts might be. But he hoped Gunnarsson hadn't yet realized that.

The Commander stared at him with a look of impenetrable ice.

"Come," he said abruptly. "You can leave that one here for now. His condition will not change."

He took Rameau back to the command nexus and gestured for him to enter.

"You wanted to know where we are," he said. "Look."

He touched his console, and the walls disappeared.

Again, Rameau was surrounded by the image of space. Stars burned steadily, with plenty of distance between them. The heat and cramped conditions within *Langstaff* contrasted sharply with the vastness, the cold, the emptiness through which he was falling, embedded in this tiny chip of metal.

"Turn around," the Commander said, behind him.

He turned, and the depths retreated. From this angle, he saw a star that was close at hand, by cosmic standards. Behind the star, bands of translucent color, like filmy scarves, glowed and dimmed.

"What is that? Where are we?"

"Its baseline name would mean nothing to you," Gunnarsson

said. "Its technical designation still less. It is a white dwarf star that still has planets.

"Your MedTech was right. We attempted a maneuver that would deform our jump field in such a way that part of the ship could be excluded—the part where excess heat was concentrated. The complexity of the maneuver exceeded the pilot's capacity. He lost all awareness of his place within the schema, and became unable to maneuver. The effect on the pilot's central nervous system is what cohorts call 'burning the pilot.'

"As a result, we fell out of jump. We were already within the nebula that surrounds this star. We retained the acceleration gained prior to jump, and we are now burning all available mass to fire the conventional engines, in an attempt to slow our acceleration before we are carried away from this solar system.

"Our jump generators are too severely damaged for immediate reuse. We must stop here where repair materials should be available, or we will enter a long cometary path through empty space, and die. This star is our last refuge."

"But—there's nothing here," Rameau said. He tried hard to remember what little he had learned about astronomy. "Any planets left would be nothing but cinders. And it would take weeks to find one and set up an orbit. Even then, how would we get to the surface and obtain materials?"

Maybe the Original Man have better conventional engines than we know of, Rameau thought. *Maybe they have some kind of device for mining and refining materials. . . . Oh, hell, maybe they have magic. There's nothing else that could save us now.*

Gunnarsson's cold gaze bored straight into him. He had always felt the Commander was hiding data from him. Oddly, he now felt as if Gunnarsson was trying to tell him something. But he wasn't getting it.

"I assure you that we can and will perform repairs to the ship," he said. "What we seek is not a planet. If it exists, we should reach it within a week—at optimum, in three days. At that time, we will need every cohort. You must continue to treat casualties."

"What is this place we're going?" In spite of exhaustion, Rameau's curiosity was set on edge.

"The Founder called it Vega. A haven. I cannot tell you more; I have not seen it. You will see it—if it still exists."

He stepped closer.

"But before we reach Vega, I must have your full cooperation. It is not enough that you obey when forced."

"Why? What difference does it make?"

The Commander seemed to be at a loss for words.

"I find myself in a difficult situation. It is difficult to explain these things to a baseline.

"So many of my officers have terminated. I no longer have any associates who were . . . baseline-raised. *Human*-raised."

"Is this a problem?" Rameau said drily. "Baselines are inferior."

"True. And yet . . ." He paced back and forth, as if looking for something to attack.

"I was not trained in the way that has become common for Original Man. See this." He extracted a message cube from his console, and a holo appeared in bright miniature above the smooth black surface.

A group of identical fair-haired boys played in a large, bright room. They tumbled over each other like puppies, scrambling to catch a ball thrown to them by a tall man in uniform. Rameau recognized Kuno Gunnarsson.

"That is me and my sibs, with the Founder. He trained us himself. We had 'socialization.' We had 'play.' Human things. We learned about things baselines do. We acquired a knowledge of baseline behavior. He explained it was necessary to have some predictive ability, so we could understand what baselines might do next. We acquired flexible responses through being placed in ambiguous situations. This was sometimes painful, but the Founder explained it was necessary for survival."

"Which one is you?" Rameau said.

The yearning, distracted look on the Commander's face vanished, and he shut off the recording.

"That is not relevant."

"You don't know!" Rameau said. "You actually don't know which one was you."

He laughed, and was sorry a moment later. The Commander whirled on him, naked rage appearing on his face.

"It is not relevant!" he said fiercely. "Baselines will never understand. It doesn't matter which one was me. They are all me. My sibs. Myself. Original Man is one."

He regained control. "Relevant point: other cohorts are not trained in this way. You saw the methods of crisis training when we were on Eyrie. Have you heard the word 'zippies'?"

"No."

"Ship language for the crisis-bred. They are exercised in utero. They receive growth factors to force rapid development, and continual physical training to control brain-body coordination. Maturity is achieved in five to ten years."

"Wait—what are you saying?" Rameau said. "You're telling me those cohorts are only ten years old?"

The Commander briefly closed his eyes: frustration at having to disclose this information to a baseline, Rameau thought.

"Merciful Kannon," Rameau said. "Ten years old. No wonder." He shook his head in amazement. "What about my Medtechs? Neb and the rest? Are they ten years old, too?" Suddenly Neb's behavior made more sense. His lack of judgment, his panic at unexpected developments, his violence when frustrated—all defects, in a genetically engineered metahuman, but typical in a juvenile primate.

"Yes," Gunnarsson said. "All cohorts currently on *Langstaff* have been speed-trained. None remain who have experienced a full maturation period, except myself. My remaining officers have been functional for more years than their cohort affiliates, but all were originally zippies.

"I have no advisers with full maturity. I need experience to combat *Langstaff*'s enemies. Even baseline experience is better than none. Until *Langstaff* can resupply, it is to your advantage to assist us. Without maximum use of resources, *Langstaff* will be terminated."

"I see your point," Rameau said. *A crew of ten-year-olds! No wonder he's worried.* "But I still don't see how I can help you out."

"You seized the gun on the shuttle," Gunnarsson said. "You

attempted to take control of the pilot link. Both available data and ordinary reason should have informed you these actions would prove worse than useless. Yet you made the attempt. A cohort would not have done so unless ordered.

"Original Man is incepted with superior intelligence. Yet the baseline still possesses a type of knowledge that reflects exposure to widely varying circumstances. This sometimes leads to unorthodox solutions. Your new rank reflects this ability to improvise. The Founder called it craftiness. It is your baseline craftiness I wish to utilize for *Langstaff*, as well as your medical skills."

"If this baseline is so crafty," Rameau said, "don't you think I would turn on you?"

The Commander looked at him thoughtfully.

"Baselines weigh profit and loss," he said. "Bargaining is also a baseline characteristic. At this time I believe you have found it a better 'deal' to keep the enemies of your enemies alive. Later there may be additional reasons to continue the bargain. I cannot share those reasons with you now. I must judge you more carefully, as you are judging me. But until the judgment is complete, I offer you a truce."

"And what would I get in return for my agreement?"

"I will continue to treat you as an officer and give you free access to relevant data."

"Oh, no." Rameau knew he was in no position to bargain, but he wasn't going to give in that easily. "I want to be treated better than an officer. You treat your officers like bots: go here; do this; shut up. I want you to personally answer my questions to the best of your ability. Whether *you* think they are relevant or not."

Gunnarsson seemed to think it over.

"Your highest performance in return for my best data," he said. "Such an exchange is possible. But with one exception: clearly, I cannot share knowledge that could pose a threat to *Langstaff*'s survival."

And clearly, I'll serve you only as long as it serves my own best interests, Rameau thought.

"Done," he said.

"Baseline idiom for the agreement to a bargain," Gunnarsson said. "Then I will continue your upgraded status, and you will continue to treat the cohorts."

He started to turn away, as if the meeting had ended.

"Wait a minute," Rameau said. "You're sending me back to the core? But I still don't know the status of our supplies and consumables. We were down to warm water, and not much of that."

"You may attend the officers' meeting on the next watch," Gunnarsson said. "You will be informed with the other officers."

"And I still don't know how to get around," Rameau said. "I nearly killed myself on the trip here."

"The bot will guide you," the Commander said. "It appears you've slaved it to your command already; you might as well keep it."

The bot sat waiting—though, of course, its state couldn't be called "waiting," since the bot had no idea that anything should happen next. One side was dented, causing its top grippers to extend at a slight angle, like cocked ears.

"It has received the same upgrade as your kenner," Gunnarsson said.

"Okay, then," Rameau said as he turned to leave.

" 'This officer obeys,' is the proper response," Gunnarsson said.

Already in the corridor, Rameau looked back. "Oh, I forgot to mention that. One more condition of the deal—you have to exempt me from military protocols. I never learned them. And my capacity as a baseline is so limited . . ."

He held his breath, but the wall closed behind him. The Commander had not chastised him.

Once outside, he found his legs wouldn't hold him anymore, and he slid down the curved wall to sprawl on the floor, exhausted.

"Wait," he said to the bot. He was trembling.

He wished they were weightless again, so he could float back to the core.

"I suppose you could drag me back now, but it would not be

a dignified picture," he said to it. "And there's still the pilot. I guess Nor could help me carry him, but Nor doesn't look too good himself."

He considered his orders carefully.

"Bot: summon the four bots nearest to this location. Use MedSpec Rameau's emergency command codes. Join with the other bots to find and bring flat, smooth material no less than one-half meter by two and a half meters. Bring bots and material to the pilot space."

Then he recalled the bot's apparent lack of time sense. It could not be aware this was a crisis.

"Wait—duration of search not to exceed fifteen minutes. If no materials found within that time limit, return to pilot space."

The bot blinked assent and trundled away as Rameau limped back to the burned pilot's side.

"Nor? Can you help me with this?"

The cohort didn't move. Rameau raised his voice.

"Nor! I order you to help extract Nuun from the pod!"

Finally, Nor tried to respond, though Rameau had to help him to his feet. Together, they released the helmet, the chest shield, and the pod that enclosed the lower abdomen and legs. The support equipment retracted, and the pilot lay naked on the pod's inner surface: a wan, emaciated shadow of a cohort, with scaly patches on his skin where inputs had been attached.

So this is how a pilot's career ends, Rameau thought.

The other bots returned, carrying a folded strip of composite insulation cloth.

"Each take one corner," Rameau said. Confusion followed as they all tried to grasp the same corner. Finally they reoriented themselves, and formed the fabric into a narrow sling long enough for a cohort.

Together, Rameau and Nor lifted the pilot onto the improvised stretcher. Rameau turned Nuun's head sideways to keep his own tongue from choking him. Then they started for the core. Both Rameau and Nor were so weakened that they limped along with hands braced against the wall for support.

Even before they reached the core, they found the surrounding corridors choked with bodies, laid out in rows. Rameau stepped carefully around them, but the bots crawled straight on, over motionless limbs and faces.

At the far curve of the corridor, a cohort was giving drinks, and wetting casualties down with a hose to cool them. Rameau thought it was Neb, but at this distance he couldn't see the symbols on his coverall to make sure. The cohort turned to them.

"Those have terminated," he said. "Only these are still alive."

Then he saw Nor, and the litter. His face did not change, but he dropped the hose, and left it running. Water trickled across the floor. Neb looked back and forth, from one sib to the other, as if he couldn't decide which to approach first. Then Nor sank to his knees beside the litter, and together they bent over Nuun.

"I don't know what to do for him," Rameau said. "I'm sorry. Gunnarsson wanted him terminated, but he's still breathing. So I brought him back here."

"Nuun, Nuun . . ." Neb touched the pilot's face, crooning his name, but there was no response.

"My sib," Neb said. "E go terminate. E no go mo. Pilot no never come back."

Rising, he made one bound to seize the hose, and another back to the litter. Carefully, he poured warm water over his sib's forehead and chest. He tried to nurse a little water between the pilot's lips, but the cohort didn't swallow.

"Don't do that," Rameau said. "He'll aspirate. We'll try to hook him up with an IV, as soon as I can find some tubing and a needle."

Neb grasped Rameau's ankle with one large hand.

"This cohort see my sib. Rameau e good," he said.

But Rameau was in no condition to appreciate his homage.

"Yeah . . . Neb . . . I can't do any more for him right now. Rameau is very tired. You ken? Disco e go fall down. I'm going into the core to rest.

"You and Nor . . . and whoever . . . you just keep doing what you're doing. Buzz if you need me. You can keep the bots. Send them for what you need. Okay?"

Neb let him go. "This cohort obeys."

He woke up only when his buzzer reached painful intensity. He staggered up, tripped over someone, and in catching himself, put his hand through the membrane into one of the algae tanks. He pulled his hand out hastily and wiped green sludge onto his coveralls. Finally he found the "respond" node, and the buzzing stopped.

He tried to read the message, but his eyes were swollen almost shut.

The smoke—and I didn't even wash them out. Idiot. In the absence of other treatment, irrigate with sterile saline.

He felt for the "voice" button.

You have to see to find the "voice" button—genius Omo again.

"Reminder: officers' meeting," the little voice said at last.

Oh . . . crap . . . did I sleep all the way into the next watch? And what is that smell*?*

Oh yeah . . . it's me.

He felt as sick and dizzy as if he had a massive hangover, and he could feel fluids gurgling in his lungs. He tried to resist coughing; he had a feeling that it was going to hurt.

When he stumbled out into the corridor, he found Neb and Nor at work already. One had placed a makeshift pillow under the pilot's head, and had set up a saline drip, with the bag propped on a lump of slag. The other was running more IVs for other casualties. When he saw Rameau, he hastily completed his task and came to greet him.

"Neb found cleansing booth," the cohort said, grabbing his wrist. "You come."

Rameau was about to step into the booth fully clothed, but Neb insisted on stripping off his coverall so it could be given a more thorough cleansing. Rameau stood in the alcove, and felt the usual pain in one back tooth, and a new tingle under the skin where the enabler web had been installed. When the tone sounded, Neb handed him the clean coverall.

A miracle! It even smells okay.

Neb scrubbed his palm over Rameau's head, trying to make the hair flatter.

"Rameau need haircut."

"I need a drink of water. Please."

He kept forgetting to ask them how they cleaned their teeth. Maybe cohorts were incepted with perfect, self-cleaning teeth.

Not as crazy as it sounds. Maybe they're inoculated with benign bacteria. Maybe I could catch some. Kiss a cohort, get clean teeth. Ugh.

14

Deceleration continued. More than half the crew were dead, and many of the survivors lay helpless. The remaining cohorts worked watch-and-watch. First they collected all the debris of battle and converted the mass to more power. Then they tore out any fittings and equipment that could be spared. Now that he was included in officers' meetings, Rameau knew that they were balancing the need to keep enough materials to maintain and repair the ship against the need to slow it. If they missed their destination, they were dead. But if they arrived having stripped the ship of every usable resource, they might die even faster.

Rameau didn't have to make those decisions. He spent his time in the core with the wounded. The rest of the crew crowded into the first few rings around the core. Nonessential areas of the ship had been locked off, to focus life support at the core. Even the lights had been cut to a minimum. They still had enough water, but their food supply was reduced to pressed algae wafers with a lingering flavor of pond scum.

They suffered from a combination of low pressure and high g that made Rameau feel suffocated and crushed at the same time—the weight of ocean deeps combined with the oxygen scarcity of high altitude. As well, the core was crowded and stuffy. Even the Rukh had been jammed in with the rest of the crew. Rameau wondered where the other transforms were. Perhaps they had already been treated as excess mass.

Defying Gunnarsson's prediction, the pilot was still breathing. Neb and Nor slept head to head with him, and kept him hydrated with a saline and glucose drip, but even Rameau did not expect him to survive long with such primitive life support.

Rameau and his assistants made the rounds during each watch, giving water to the wounded, checking IVs, and changing makeshift dressings. Once the rounds were done, there was nothing to do but wait. Air, light, and water were running short. If *Langstaff* couldn't reach a haven soon, it would become a tomb.

In the cold and the dark, Rameau took the message cube from his coverall and turned it over in his fingers again. He had been waiting for privacy to view it one more time, but he thought that he might never be alone again in this life. With trembling fingers, he activated the cube.

A sound of indrawn breath went through the room. All heads turned toward the golden figure. The Rukh's dark eyes reflected her. Rameau hunched his shoulder to try to block their vision. They had no right to look at her. If he half closed his eyes, he could make it seem as if she danced again in the Dome on Varuna, while he watched from his hidden viewpoint in the superstructure, high above the rich and famous guests. The lights that gleamed on her form were amber and tarnished silver, softened by mist, as if she were dancing in practice mode with the brilliant performance lights turned down.

He muted the sound and let her dance. They watched her in hushed silence.

"That cohort who?" someone said finally.

"That's not a cohort," Rameau said. "That is the most beautiful dancer in the world."

He hesitated. *If this is the end, it would be good to say it once, out loud. The cohorts won't understand or care.*

"That was the woman I loved."

"Woman? E go human?" said the voice. Or maybe it was another voice. He couldn't see where it was coming from.

"No . . . not a human. She was a transform. She's dead now."

"Terminated?"

"Humans call it dying."

"But e no go human."

"But I loved her, so I give her human words."

A silence.

"How e go terminate? Baselines go terminate e?"

"No. The Rukh killed her. Rukh belonging to Original Man."

"What did she do to get terminate?" He thought that was Neb; some cohort who spoke baseline a little better than most.

"Nothing. It was an accident. She was just . . . in the way."

They watched her without speaking. Then two of the cohorts near Rameau nudged each other. "Look, e got water eye."

"What for? You sorry for e no dance for you no mo?"

"No, I'm not sad because she doesn't dance for me."

"Then why? E a transform. Transforms don't matter."

"This one did," Rameau said. "She mattered to me."

But not enough. Not enough, not soon enough.

He was going to stop playing the holo then, but when he reached out to it, they stirred in protest. He paused it, but left it gleaming.

"Talk more, baseline," someone said in the dark.

Ten years old, he thought. *A light in the dark, a voice in the dark, still helped, when you were ten years old.* Maybe it would help him, too.

"I used to tell her stories," he said.

"Story? What is that?"

"A story is . . . an alternate hypothesis. Something that could be true."

He thought about the story he had told her while she healed from their disastrous attempt to leave the Dome—the one about the Little Seachild who wanted feet to walk on land. That story had moved Rameau to tears when he was a child. He'd had sentimental tears in his eyes when he told it to Dakini. To him it was a story about love and longing.

But she had registered only impatience.

"That is not a story for transforms. That is just another story about how humans are better. She suffers endless pain just to be near the human. If the human prince had gone down into the ocean to be with her, if they swam away together, that would be love. For her to suffer until she blows away in the wind—this is not a good story. Your prince is a very stupid human. All he cares about is having feet."

No, not that one.

He needed a story the cohorts could understand. There was one called "Brother and Sister" that involved being lost in the woods—in the dark, as they were lost. They'd get that. As he tried to work out how he might translate for them, it took his mind off the waiting. He warmed to the idea.

"Two sibs got lost in a big facility," he began. "Some of the corridors were dark, and they were still in training. They didn't have a locator.

"They walked around for a long time and couldn't find their way back to cohort quarters. They started to get really thirsty, and they heard the sound of water in the dark, but they couldn't find it."

There was a collective sigh. Everyone was thirsty. They were on severe water rations.

"Pretty soon they found where the water was running. There was a—a tank in the corridor. But when they came to it, there was a sign on it. It said 'Do not drink. This tank contains gene-altering substances. Whoever drinks from this tank will become—uh—a pilot!'

"One sib wanted to drink anyway, because he was so thirsty. But the other sib said, 'No! If you drink, you will become a pilot and, and—they'll put you in the pilot pod. Then I will be alone.' So the first sib said he would wait a little longer.

"They came to another tank, and again the first sib wanted to drink. But the sign on the tank said 'Do not drink. This tank contains gene-altering substances. Whoever drinks from this tank will become a vacuum jock.'

"Then the other sib said, 'No! If you drink, you will become a vacuum jock and go work Outside on the hull. And I will be alone.' So the first sib said he would wait a little longer.

"But when they came to the third tank, the first sib could not wait anymore. The sign said—"

"Do not drink!" called one of the voices.

"Yeah, that's right. It said 'Do not drink. This tank contains gene-altering substances. Whoever drinks from this tank will become . . . a baseline.'

"So the other sib said, 'No! If you drink, you will become a baseline, and I will have no sib.' But the first sib said, 'A baseline? That's not so bad. Anyway, I have to drink or I will die of thirst.' So he drank the water. And they found their way back to a lighted corridor, but by the time they got there, the sib who drank had transformed into a baseline.

"Well . . . they came back to the wrong part of the facility. They were in another clan's area."

He waited, but that seemed to make sense to them.

"So, that clan decided to assimilate the singleton, but they didn't have any use for the baseline. Still, the sib didn't want to lose his only sib, even if he was a baseline now. So he said, 'I need this baseline. I was ordered never to let him leave my side.'"

There was a stirring in the dark.

"E go lie to officer!" someone called out. Other voices joined in.

"E go lie!"

"E go get terminate!"

Rameau suddenly felt alert again, in spite of the thin, stale air. He had disturbed the cohorts, perhaps even contaminated their training. This was worth doing, even at the point of death.

"You can lie to an officer," he said calmly. "Just don't let them find out. Then they can't terminate you."

There was a buzz of ship jo and cohorts shoving each other.

"I've lied to officers often," he said. "I never got caught. Sometimes you have to lie, to protect a cohort. To keep something you need. Sometimes officers don't understand, and you don't have time to explain to them."

That shocked them into stillness. He continued.

"So, they let the baseline stay. They found an assignment for him, and they incepted two new sibs for the one who was now a singleton. They put him in charge of training them. So that was good, right?

"But . . . there was one cohort who didn't accept the new sib. He didn't want him in the clan group. So at night he stole one of the new sibs, and hid him away. Then he blamed the single-ton. He reported that the singleton had experienced a—a mal-function, and put his own sib down the trash hatch. They gave the singleton retraining and put him back on the job. But they said that the next time he malfunctioned, they were going to terminate him."

Rameau paused. He was afraid he had dug himself in too deep on this one. There was supposed to be a king, a step-mother, a ghost, and all kinds of stuff. None of it would make sense here.

On the other hand, they'd never heard a story before. So he continued.

"But nobody was paying any attention to the baseline. So he followed the bad cohort, and he rescued the immature sib just when it was about to fall down the trash hatch. Then he hid the sib in a dark corridor and waited.

"Pretty soon, the bad cohort stole the other immature sib, and again he blamed the singleton. Again, the baseline rescued the little sib just in time, but the officer came to get the single-ton and terminate him. The bad cohort said, 'Sir, this cohort see e kill sib!' The singleton said, 'No, sir! This cohort no kill sib!' But the officer didn't believe him, because the bad cohort was from his own clan.

"They were taking the singleton to be converted when the baseline came in. He said, 'Sir, I can prove he's telling the truth.' And the bad cohort said, 'E go baseline! E no ken noth-ing!' Then the baseline went into the dark corridor and brought out the two immature sibs, and they told the truth about the bad cohort. So *he* got converted, and the other sibs lived happily ever after."

His mouth was dry. Talking so much made him want a drink worse than ever. He turned off the message cube and stuffed it into his coverall, where it would stay with him until they found whatever fate they were headed for.

"Well, that's all," he said. "End of story."

All around him, subdued talking sprang up, and went on for a long time. Rameau was just starting to fall asleep when he woke up with a jerk to find a cohort leaning over him.

"Story, e go lie or true?" the cohort said.

"Uh . . . that depends. Some are all true. Some can become true. Some can never be true."

Rameau was already beginning to regret telling the cohorts that it could be a good thing to lie. If lying could cause them to be terminated, telling them to lie might be even worse. He wondered what the official Omo policy was on informing.

But the cohort's question wasn't about lying.

"Baseline can help you—lie or true?"

"Ah. Definitely true," Rameau said. "Sometimes true," he amended. "You go watch and see."

"Baseline bring back sib," the cohort said thoughtfully. He faded back into the shadows.

II
The Pilot's Boy

The many men, so beautiful!
And they all dead did lie:
And a thousand thousand slimy things
Lived on; and so did I.

. . . .

The other was a softer voice,
As soft as honey-dew:
Quoth he, 'The man hath penance done,
And penance more will do.'
SAMUEL TAYLOR COLERIDGE,
"The Rime of the Ancient Mariner"

15

Rameau woke up in a panic. He kept hoping his weary body would just forget to panic anymore, but it didn't seem to happen. He was falling, surrounded by heavy objects that kept bumping into him. He shoved and kicked to get them out of his way, but they were all doing the same thing. His hip smashed against a metal corner, and the sickening pain kept him motionless for a minute, in which he figured out what was happening.

"Calm down!" he shouted over the din. "We're there! The weight is off! Stop it!"

His authoritative voice, giving orders, calmed them. He watched, amazed, as they moved together, even though they were still half asleep, creating an orderly formation.

The able-bodied all floated, oriented in the same direction, each with one hand on the shoulder of the cohort to his left. Those who started out wrong-side up quickly somersaulted. When they had all lined up, the cohorts at the end of each row detached themselves to dog down the unconscious companions who had floated away from their places on the former floor.

Rameau waited with his tongue between his teeth. Either they had reached their goal and established orbit, or they had run out of mass and were drifting in space. He didn't know what orders to give.

"Just . . . stay alert," he said. "I'm going to find out what's happening."

He burst out into the adjacent corridor, and found the cohorts there awake and lining themselves up, too, like a field of sunflowers at dawn.

He was about to buzz the Commander when the general alert sounded.

"All cohorts, prepare for docking," the ship voice said. "Security teams, report to docking bays four and seventeen. Environment techs, report to docking bays four and seventeen."

Rameau ducked back into the core.

"Prepare for docking," he repeated.

Docking! With what?

It was difficult to imagine a ship the size of *Langstaff* docking with anything—except an Original Man orbital facility, like the one they'd been chased away from. Could this be the refuge Gunnarsson had claimed he could find? True, it would be full of cohorts—but that no longer seemed so important. Not when compared with the promise of air, light, food.

The cohorts stared at him as if they believed he had helped to create this miracle.

"I don't know what's happening," he said to them. "Don't look at me like that!"

They hung in formation, motionless, as the ship shuddered and moved almost imperceptibly. All heads turned together, as they listened for hull sounds. Plainly, it was agony for them not to know what was happening.

Rameau's kenner buzzed.

"Medical officer, report to docking bay four," it said. He jumped to respond, creating a ripple all through the line of cohorts.

Wait. I don't know where docking bay four is.

He called the bot and had it tow him there. As he approached the bay, he could smell something different in the air. It wasn't a good smell. It was dank, stale, perhaps with a hint of mold.

But it came from outside. There was a *place* outside.

Gunnarsson and the other officers were gathered near the air lock, where a group of cohorts had already suited up. Without a word, a pair of Omo came over and stuffed him into a suit, tightening all its fittings to the utmost so he wouldn't swim in it. The boot toes stuck out awkwardly beyond his feet, the stiff neck cuff was still too high for him, and his head stuck out only part of the way into the helmet. They left the faceplate open, like their own.

There must be air where we're going.

He could see out, but he had to crane his neck to access the in-helmet controls. He was about to complain, but it occurred to him that they might keep him from going.

I'd rather go outside in a body bag than be kept in here anymore.

"We realize you haven't been properly trained on the suit," Gunnarsson's voice said in his ear, startling him. "Remain with other cohorts at all times. You will be monitored."

"Do you have any other orders for me, or am I just going along to carry the picnic basket?" Rameau asked sarcastically.

"You are being sent as medical officer, to check the safety of the new facility and to find emergency quarters for the wounded," Gunnarsson said. "It is not necessary for you to carry a basket at this time."

Then it was Rameau's turn to pull himself into the air lock. He waited for what seemed a long time, until the indicator showed the door was opening. And then . . . it was still dark. Moving forward, he tumbled, and steadied himself against the cohort ahead of him. Of course there was no weight on the other side of the air lock, either.

He emerged from the docking tube, and found himself blinking in the glow of portable lamps the cohorts were tethering in place. The air that brushed against his face wasn't stale ship air, nor the sterile air of a well-kept facility. It had that dark taste he had sensed back in *Langstaff*. It held a hint of dampness, a hint of something uncontrolled and organic. A far-off memory stirred.

It smells like a cave.

Ignored by the cohorts, Rameau moved to the edge of the circle of light. He shone his own hand light on the nearest wall. It was smooth and regular, kemplex or metal composite, the same kind of material used in ships. This wasn't a cave. It was manufactured, and modern, not prejump metal technology.

The air was above freezing. This far from the shrunken sun, that meant there must be a power source. Nevertheless, it was cold, and dark, and there was still no weight. No one came to welcome them—no rush of helpful humanoids with food and supplies. Rameau was surprised by his own disappointment.

The cohorts moved ahead in leapfrog fashion, one group setting up floodlights as the next group moved past them with hand lights, weapons ready. The leading group found a sealed door, and sent back an order to close up helmets as a precaution. The heavy pressure door opened slowly and reluctantly. But it did open, and there was air on the other side, too.

When Rameau moved through and opened his faceplate again, he caught a brief scent of something sharp, an ammoniac smell. But it was gone before he could run a test.

"Did anyone smell that?" he said. But the cohorts weren't listening.

"Baseline, report," said Gunnarsson's voice inside his helmet. "Use the private link. Helmet controls, to your left, second row, blue."

Rameau stretched to make contact with the control.

"Commander?" he said.

"Go ahead."

"Nothing to report so far—except that I thought I smelled something odd. It could have been out-gassing from our equipment, I suppose. *Do* these suits out-gas?"

"No," the Commander said, rather dogmatically, Rameau thought. *Of course, Original Man suits are superior in every way.* "Continue to report any sensory anomalies on the private channel."

"You mean I might notice something the Omo miss?" The Commander seemed less intimidating when he was several bulkheads away. Rameau couldn't resist needling him.

"Ship-raised cohorts are less attuned to biological stimuli," Gunnarsson said. "Baselines retain more animal sensitivities."

The cohorts in charge seemed to have some idea where they were going. Without hesitation, they turned to the right. As they busied themselves with securing the new area, Rameau dared a question.

"This isn't what you expected, is it?" he said.

Silence at the other end of the link.

"You thought we could resupply here. But something went wrong, didn't it?"

Still Gunnarsson didn't answer the question directly.

"The resources we need are still available here. We'll find them. That is your priority now."

The cohorts in charge had apparently chosen a direction to explore. One turned back to tug Rameau into line.

"Commander!" he called, in a last effort to provoke some useful response. "Remember our agreement! I expect an answer."

Then he was dragged after the cohorts, into a narrow tunnel, much smaller than the corridors in *Langstaff*. It might have been an access tube for utilities and repairs. There wasn't enough space to stand upright, and the walls were lined with cables and connectors that would have been hard to crawl over. In micro g, though, they could swim along like fish in a narrow channel.

Pushing himself along, head to toe with a long line of cohorts, Rameau felt trapped. If anything went wrong, they wouldn't be able to turn around. He tightened his grip on his hand light and concentrated on breathing steadily.

What *was* that smell? Here in this tube, the moldy organic flavor of the air was layered with the scent of plastic, and a scorched smell, possibly burnt insulation. Still, there was something maddeningly in the background, something that made him nervous.

What have you gotten us into, Gunnarsson? What dangers are we risking?

The line stopped moving.

Were they stuck? He could hear noises from up ahead, but as usual no one bothered to explain what was happening. The other cohorts just waited stolidly.

Then he was tugged forward again, and there was light ahead.

He somersaulted through a small round hatchway and floated out, spread-eagled in amazement. They were in a dome, striped with transplex panels. Some of the panels glowed with concentrated light, others were shuttered, and a few showed a matte surface that was neither light nor dark.

The light panels started about halfway up the dome. The

lower portions were fuzzed with an indistinct, dark material. Spinning slowly, Rameau couldn't figure out what it was— shredded insulation? Then he drifted closer and realized what he was looking at. *Leaves.*

He flailed, trying to get closer, then remembered that his suit had minithrusters. In his excitement, he gave himself too long a shot of thrust, and crashed into the wall of foliage. He grabbed convulsively, trying to stop himself from bouncing back out again, and finally came to rest at the end of a long strand of uncoiled vine, with leaf fragments swirling around him. He sneezed and spat, trying to bat the cloud of green bits away from his face, but the more he thrashed, the faster they swirled. Finally he held still, breathing carefully out of the corner of his mouth, until they settled into a floating clump, and then moved himself very slowly out of the cloud.

"Baseline, report!" the Commander's voice said in his ear. "Your life signs register agitation. What is the cause?"

"We're not in danger," he replied. "Just startled. We've found a living area. It's some kind of biosphere, much bigger than the one in *Langstaff*. It contains living organisms, but it's not fully functional."

"Assist the cohort team in making it functional," the Commander ordered. "Immediately. The next contingent is en route."

"Wait! You can't send them here," Rameau protested. "The place looks abandoned. We have no idea what danger it may hold."

"But the dangers of remaining in *Langstaff* are clear," the Commander said. "Life support is failing rapidly. Prepare to take charge of casualties."

"The wounded?" Rameau said. "You can't take them through that tunnel!"

"We have opened and secured a larger corridor," the Commander said. "I recommend you focus on securing your own area. Cease to inform me of what I can and cannot do."

Moments later, the Commander's voice sounded loudly on the general command link.

"Cohorts, secure this area and its approach."

The cohorts sprang into action. They dug beneath the leaves

and uncovered the substrate and the drip fibers. They traced the drip back to a water outlet, and went to work on the wall, to locate the source.

Leaves rustled as they worked—maybe a little bit too much, Rameau thought. And there was a rustling sound farther along the curve, where no cohort was working. He saw nothing—and yet, he was certain that something moved under the vegetation.

He used the smallest possible thrust, enough to barely drift him in that direction, and watched the leafy wall as he slowly, silently soared over it.

"Yah!" he shouted, startled and vindicated at the same time. All the cohorts spun in his direction as he jetted suddenly downward, like a striking hawk. He came up triumphantly clutching his prey.

"Ow!" he cried, a moment later. He wished he had talons like a hawk. The fat, fist-sized lump he clutched sank small but needle-sharp teeth through his suit glove and into his hand. He hit the thruster stud by accident and zigzagged across the room until one of the cohorts served as a bumper and stopped him.

With difficulty, he extricated his bleeding finger from the thing's mouth, and got a better grip on his writhing captive.

At his command, a cohort brought him a biological sample case big enough to hold his find. Another cohort uncuffed Rameau's glove, stuck an antiseptic patch on his finger, and a patch of another kind on his glove.

Rameau stared at the creature through the transparent case.

"Bring the camera over here," he said. "Look, Commander. We found something alive. An animal. It was living among the plants. Maybe this was the source of that odd biological odor I thought I smelled. If there's one, there must be more."

Then another thought struck him, and the hairs rose on his neck.

"Where there is prey, there must be a predator, Commander."

"Secure the area," the Commander said, and the cohorts returned to their tasks. Privately, to Rameau, he added, "Your observations are valuable. But Original Man do not think of themselves as prey."

16

Rustlings continued in the undergrowth, but the cohorts showed no special interest in the flying hamsters. They concentrated, instead, on locating and opening the main door, in preparation for the arrival of the rest of the crew.

Six cohorts stayed behind in the biosphere while the rest of the team picked up weapons and lights and headed into the darkness of the corridor beyond.

"Wait!" Rameau shouted. "The medical officer is coming, too."

He scrambled to find a biosample pack among their supplies, then hurried after the departing team. On Vega, the wounded might be exposed to infection by molds or bacteria that had grown unchecked. It would be important to identify those dangers as early as possible.

But the cohorts moved so swiftly that they met up with the incoming crew before Rameau had time to take any samples. They carried the wounded on floating litters, or bundled in sleep sacks and clipped to tow lines. Rameau considered demanding that they stop, to allow him to examine the casualties, but decided against it.

There's nothing I can do for them till we reach the secure area, anyway. Best to keep moving.

He hovered over them, checking on them as they moved past, and found himself at the end of the line with the rear guard. Looking ahead into the halo of their lights, he could see that the air was thick with bits of detritus that would normally have been cleared by the ventilation system.

Defective circulation? Blocked vents?

Blackened scraps of what could have been betacloth or

metal foil floated past him, along with bits of organic grime. One fragment gleamed white like a tiny bone, but an air current whirled it away before he could catch it. He fell behind the group as he paused to capture some of the material in his sample box.

When he looked ahead again, the line had stopped. He thought for a moment that they might have halted to let him catch up, but he noticed that they were thrashing around, waving their arms strangely. Then they started screaming.

Halfway there, he started running into drops of blood. He was going too fast to turn around. He crashed into the back of the line, and sent one of the floating litters careening into the wall.

The cohorts were slapping and clawing at their heads, spinning themselves out of control.

Rameau saw a small furry body flash by.

"Stop it!" he shouted. "They're just plant-eaters! They can't hurt you!"

But then—why the blood? What—

Then he screamed, too. Something seized him by the hair and bored into his neck. He struck blindly at it. The small, furry body squashed under the impact of his hand. He tore it loose. It felt as if he had torn his own throat out, along with it.

These weren't plant-eaters. They were roughly the same size and shape as the rodentlike creatures in the biosphere, but their tiny faces were puggy and mean. And fanged. As he felt for the rip in his neck, another flying body crash-landed in his hair. He smashed it with his fist.

Ugh!

Dozens of the flying rats piled up on the heads and faces of the cohorts, who began to fire at the tormenting creatures. Projectiles smashed into the walls or ricocheted through the enclosed space. The recoil sent the shooters off into more collisions with each other. Wounded cohorts strapped to stretchers sailed helplessly into walls and each other, trailing eager flocks of biting rodents.

"Cease firing!" Rameau screamed. "I order you to cease firing!"

He ripped another biter off his ear. His collar was soaked in blood now.

There has to be something I can use—maybe in the medical supplies—

He opened the biosample pack and shook out the contents, pawing through the objects as they floated in an agitated cluster in front of him.

Anything that looks like a knife—

The first weaponlike object he found was a needle-tipped probe. Rameau got a foot against the wall and pushed himself into a trajectory around the main mass of cohorts, to the front of the line. He beat back as many of the creatures as he could. Stabbing them with the needle helped to loosen their grip, so they wouldn't do more damage as he tore them loose. Slowly some of the cohorts' faces reappeared, masked in blood stringing out from cuts to the scalp, ears, or neck. In zero g, the blood wouldn't clear itself out of the way by trickling or running.

The convoy came to a halt again as some cohorts battled the attacking swarm, and others struggled to clear the bubbles of blood away from their eyes and mouths so they could breathe.

We don't have time for this! Rameau thought. *They're so conditioned to fight that they don't know when it's time to run!*

He grabbed the lead cohort's collar and smacked his face to get his attention.

"Run!" he shouted. "We can outfly anything they're using for propulsion! We need to get out of this corridor! *Run!*"

Comprehension dawned. Once they started to move, Rameau was nearly left behind. He hung on to a litter, stabbing at rats as they hurtled past.

They burst through the doorway into the plant chamber. Astonished cohorts scattered from their work on the lights and water.

"Close the door!" Rameau screamed. "Close the door!"

He tumbled across the room on an uncontrolled trajectory and ended up in the vines again.

As soon as the cohorts in the room understood what was happening, they leapt for the door controls. Then it was just a matter of picking off the biters that had already entered the room.

"Save those for me; I want to examine them," Rameau ordered, untangling himself.

This time he had nothing at all to treat the freshly bleeding wounds—not even hot water.

"Has anyone found medical supplies?" he asked hopelessly. "Antiseptics? Body glue? Any type of fabric at all?"

But no one had found those things.

Belatedly, he remembered Gunnarsson and called the Commander's private link to warn him of the infestation.

"My cohorts have reported this," Gunnarsson said. "The next team will wear full armor and carry flame weapons. Give orders for the team in the dome to stay inside until the reinforcements clear the corridor."

"Sir, I have more injuries, and still no supplies," Rameau said. "I need a team to make medical treatment a priority!"

"You must wait," the Commander said. "There are other priorities."

He signed off before Rameau could protest.

"Wait, he says. I don't even have blankets! It's cold in here."

Rameau raised his voice to reach the cohorts working on the shutters.

"I want them all open full!" he said. "Get as much solar in here as possible. Move the wounded where they'll be in line for maximum light."

That would probably disturb the plants' metabolism, he thought, but he couldn't stop to worry about the plants right now. Leaves and bits of stem still floated lazily toward the vents. The cohorts were definitely creating a disruption in this miniature ecology.

Rameau tucked his legs into meditation posture and floated that way, thinking.

Somewhere in this structure, there must be a database of what plants they chose to cultivate, their names, and hopefully something *about their origins and uses. We used the plants on* Langstaff. *There must be a lot more material here.*

The cohorts working on the com nodes had obtained only

limited access to the shipmind—enough to find some collections of read-only storage. It was a start. They showed Rameau how to link his kenner to the node.

The plant catalogs were cross-referenced to listings of their composition, down to the average amounts of all trace elements. The people who had built this place originally had put in place all the protocols needed to maintain a careful ecological balance. Obviously, something had gone very wrong.

Other listings, more immediately useful, cataloged each plant according to its possible uses. In these files, Rameau found more complex substances—tannic acid in leaves, analgesic compounds in bark.

"If only I had weight and pressure, I could build a fire on the floor and brew my own medicine," he muttered. "But I can't even boil water here."

The com cohorts hadn't been able to access maps. They couldn't tell him where to find a food-preparation area. Anyway, he was stuck inside the dome until the exterminator crews had swept the corridor.

"This is a garden," he said. "There must be a plant-preparation area somewhere nearby. I've never seen a garden without a shed."

Rameau floated over to the inner curve of the dome and searched along the meridian. Leaves had spread out, seeking the windows that still gave light. An understory of lichenous growth was invading the transplex itself.

That should be trimmed back, scraped clean, Rameau thought.

Digging into the mat of roots, his fingers found a double set of grooves. Those were tracks. He found two more sets of tracks, spaced a few feet apart. That wasn't what he was looking for. Those slots might once have held plant racks, moving automatically as they grew and were harvested. It would make a lot more sense than leaving the dome open in the center as it was now, wasting valuable production space.

But between the racks . . . He clung to a thick stem with one hand and scraped vigorously at the vegetation with the other. He could only make one or two sweeps with his hand before he spun around to face the other way. There was nothing to brace his feet against. He finally got the whole mat of vegetation loose and peeled off a long strip. Underneath was metal, corrosion-resistant, still as bright as it had been when first installed. And in the center of the panel, a pair of handles. He turned them in unison, one in each hand. The panel lifted away and floated at the end of an elastic tether.

I suppose the cohorts would have found this, eventually. Or maybe not. They're not used to vegetation. They don't know how it hides things.

Rameau pulled himself into the opening and looked around with his hand light. He couldn't see much, but the area inside seemed to be packed with infrastructure of some kind.

"Hey, can I get some lights on here?" he called to the cohorts.

When the engineers got the lights turned on, Rameau hung half in and half out of the space, waiting impatiently while a cohort examined the equipment inside. Even the engineers couldn't identify all of it.

"I affiliate to medical, not to biosphere construction," he told them sarcastically when they turned to him for help. But he couldn't resist the chance to push in next to them. His claustrophobia vanished when he had something interesting to do.

"Okay, look," he said, shoving the engineer farther down the tube to make room. The cohort had to twist his head around to obey the order. "See, here, if you fold this down, it's a prep area. There's a chopper and blender for crushing up plants. This is for measuring . . . and here—ah! This is just what I need."

Built into the space were a microwave oven, a steam immersion heater—something like an enclosed pressure cooker—and another heating device that looked as if it worked by clipping a metal container between two heated plates so the heat would radiate into the container.

"This is a testing facility for the plant room. Obviously, it's not a food-preparation area. This was designed for small-scale extraction and measuring the chemical and mineral content of the plants, and so forth. I'm going to use it now to prepare some plant-based medicines for the wounded. But I still need medical supplies. So report immediately if anyone finds any of the materials I listed for you earlier, right?

"And now—kindly get out of my way so I can work."

He used his emergency rank to order the cohorts to collect the foliage they'd torn loose in their explorations. Then he sorted out the materials he had chosen from the database. He decided to concentrate his efforts on a painkiller that could be prepared from the bark of the most prolific vines. He passed out the results to the cohorts as he finished each batch, then started another. When they saw that his efforts were producing results, they brought him more plants.

He wasn't sure he was helping them very much, but he had to try something. The wounded were a little quieter after receiving the medicine. What he needed was an opiate. Such compounds had been all too common on Garuda, but so far it seemed that the station builders hadn't brought any poppies or sleep root with them.

He felt a tug at his boot, and looked back to see Neb trying to get his attention.

While he'd been absorbed in his work, the remaining casualties, plus teams from engineering and biosupport, had been convoyed down the corridor, and were now crowded into the biosphere. He told himself he was glad to see Neb and Nor only because they would supply extra hands for his work.

He wriggled out of the narrow shed and pushed himself off into the center of the dome space, where he could stretch his limbs in a slow cartwheel. He was surprised to see how much of the excess vegetation he'd already used. To make another batch of painkillers would require another harvest. Right now, food was a more pressing need.

"What did they do with those flying rats I told them to save?" he asked. Nor held up a baggie full of squashed and bloody bodies.

Disgusting, Rameau thought. *But it is meat, and I'm starving.*

"Come up here, Neb," he said. "I'm going to teach you about dissection."

The shed contained a small waldo box. Rameau put one of the creatures into it and clamped it down.

"Neb, take the stylus and sketch on your kenner as I take this critter apart," he said. The stylus looked ridiculously small in Neb's hands.

"This cohort no ken," Neb said awkwardly.

"Well, that cohort go learn, then," Rameau said. "Reproduce what you see—schematically, of course. I mean, don't put in every single detail. Just the important ones."

"This cohort no ken 'important,' " Neb said.

"Just draw what I tell you, then. And write what I say."

It had been a long time since Rameau had worked in an animal lab. As far as he could recall, this creature looked a lot like a lab rat.

It was a mammal. Its dentition, stomach, and intestines seemed to indicate that it was an omnivore. The legs were definitely rotated in such a way that they would have been of little use in normal gravity. The creature would have had to crawl on its belly. But in micro g, it could use them to grasp or to push itself along and fend off from walls.

The most interesting thing about it was the extra pouch he found attached to the intestines, venting to the outside. It was similar in size to a swim bladder in a fish.

"It uses intestinal gas for thrust," Rameau said. "Write that down. No wonder they caught up with us so fast."

He had learned as much as he thought he could from this specimen. And his empty belly was rumbling.

"End of dissection lesson," he said. "Time for micro-g cooking lesson."

He showed Neb how to skin the carcasses and remove the head and paws. There were limits to the amount of scavenging he was willing to do. It was a time-consuming process, because each tiny body had to be placed in the waldo box before it could be cut. Even with the utmost care, bits of blood and tissue floated out of the bag as they removed the remains. Rameau set some of the cohorts to work catching the detritus with damp filter paper.

Then he packed the containers for each heating unit with the dead tunnel rats.

"We'll try them broiled, baked, and microwaved," he said.

Soon the whole dome smelled like cooked meat. Rameau had been a vegetarian for a long time, so the smell was disquieting. But at the same time, it made his mouth water.

He lined the cohorts up, each with a big leaf for a plate, and portioned out the meat.

"Watch out for bones," he said.

Most of the cohorts accepted the meal without question. Neb, who had helped in the preparation, looked down at his share with an unmistakable expression of distaste.

"Dead things not good food," he said.

"On the contrary. Dead things *are* food. They tried to eat us. Now we eat them. Even my karma-obsessed parents couldn't argue with that. Just remember two things: First, food must be freshly dead. If there's a bad smell, don't eat. Second, apply heat to food, if possible. It helps to kill bacteria."

"There is a bad smell," Neb said.

"No, there isn't. That's just the smell of, well, of cooking. Normal."

He took a leg and sucked off the flesh.

"See? It's good. Tastes like . . . rat. Yum."

I hope I haven't just poisoned the entire contingent.

When the cohorts saw that he suffered no ill effects, they followed his example, and it seemed that they had iron stomachs. They ate their former adversaries with apparent relish.

17

As the cohorts finished the last of the meat, Rameau floated to the outer curve of the dome to stretch and look Outside. On the outer surface of the biosphere, curving away from his view, he saw what he expected—strips of adjustable lenses, like those used on Varuna. They collected solar energy, focused and fractionated the light for use in the interior.

Beyond that . . . He averted his eyes, at first, from the plunge into space, and concentrated on the structure to which the biosphere was attached. The shape of the station was a sheaf of cylindrical tubing, like a huge bundle of steel pasta. The sheaf was bound together by a thick cufflike segment that contained the docking bay. Close against the cuff, Rameau could see the battered hulk of *Langstaff*. The bulk of the station made the ship look small. The biosphere was a bubble on the end of that massive cylinder, like a knob on the end of a walking stick.

The cylindrical bundle stretched down, or away, from him, extending far enough that it seemed to taper. At the far end, Rameau could see another dome that reflected back the sun. The cylinder was symmetrical, like a baton with a knob on each end. Three concentric rings encircled it, apparently linked to a central girdle.

The fat concentric rings were mostly smooth, but through one arc of their circle, they had either been damaged or had never been finished. A jumble of debris floated around that part of the circle. Beyond the edge of the structure, sunlight glinted off a group of dark objects herded together like rotund beasts.

At last Rameau raised his eyes from Vega to the space that

surrounded it. The sun seemed far away, because it was so tiny—barely a disc at all. But it was bright enough to cast shadows. Behind its blaze, the nebula shimmered faintly. Four more bright objects sparkled in the same plane. Even with his limited knowledge, Rameau could tell that these must be planets.

There was no planet nearby, though. No friendly, resource-rich bulk. Nor even a grim, cindered hulk. It looked as if someone had been building a space station here, in the middle of nowhere, in a system that was stable but would be very low on anyone's priority list for colonization.

But whoever they had been, they were no longer here. He was about to turn away from the vast emptiness, to return to his own problems.

Wait—what is that?

Far off down the long cylinder, figures moved.

Rameau triggered the private link.

"Commander! I see people out on the hull!"

His heart beat faster in the long pause before Gunnarsson answered.

Who are they?

Sunlight winked off reflective surfaces; the figures must be wearing suits. As he watched, two of them jaunted out from Vega's surface to one of the lumps of rock floating nearby. Bright flashes made a pattern as they moved methodically across the rock.

"Do not be alarmed," the Commander's distant voice said. "They are cohorts of *Langstaff*."

Relieved of his fear that they were being invaded, Rameau grew angry.

"What the hell are they doing out there?"

"They are tethering mass for primary acceleration," Gunnarsson said. "At my order."

Rameau ignored the warning implied in the last phrase.

"Tethering mass? What for? We need every functional cohort in here, *now*, working for our survival. Work Outside can wait."

"Understand this," Gunnarsson said coldly. "High Command has not forgotten us. A ship will come. And when it

comes, we must not be here. High Command will not wait
while you establish living quarters. Moving Vega is the first
priority."

"You can't—" Rameau began. Then he checked himself.
How could he know what Original Man could do? If Gunnarsson said they would move Vega, it must be possible.

"Nevertheless—sir," he said, lowering his voice respectfully
for the sake of his patients. "Nevertheless, I must have assistance here. The casualty convoys got here all right, but we can't
explore the station until we're sure the rats are gone. Meanwhile, we're trapped in the biosphere without resources."

"I will send exterminators as soon as I can spare the able-
bodied personnel," Gunnarsson said. "Until then, you must
continue to improvise."

He clicked off the link decisively.

"Improvise!" Rameau said. He hurled himself angrily across
the dome, ripping out a long swath of leaves in his wake, and
then regretted it. *Leaves—they're all I have.* He took a long,
calming breath, and descended to watch the medtechs at work.

"How is he doing?" he asked Neb, when they came to the
pilot. But he could see for himself. Nuun was fading—thinner
and paler every hour.

"No food for Nuun," Neb said. His eyes never left his sib's
face.

Rameau had been feeling pleased with himself for providing
a meal in this impossible situation; now he was ashamed.

*Yeah, you're pretty smart, getting the cohorts to eat rat
meat—but meanwhile, the wounded are dying.*

He was haunted by the look in Neb's eyes. He tried to banish his sense of failure. *It's not as if he's human.*

It didn't work.

"He needs nourishment," he said out loud. "They all do.
We'll try to find some sugar, and a needle. That can be our next
priority."

I was hoping to sleep. Oh well.

He got the attention of the squad leader in charge of the
engineers.

"Can your team help me search the area for medical supplies?

If we wait till security clears the corridor, some of the wounded will die. I'm the medical officer. I can't sit here and let that happen."

The cohort looked at him impassively for a moment. Then, to Rameau's astonishment, he grinned.

"Meat officer," he said. "Yes, this cohort can help. What orders?"

Rameau showed him. The main corridor was too dangerous, but the access tube they'd used when they first entered had seemed clear of rodent infestation. The squad leader peered cautiously through the hatch, then held a long, partially comprehensible conversation with his team.

"Team can do," he reported back to Rameau. "Commander say, secure biosphere area, make function good. Access tube part of area. Rameau can assist. But this cohort command. This cohort say go, we go. Rameau ken?"

"Yes! I get it. Uh—this cohort obeys. And thanks."

He'd thought their communication was going so well—but suddenly the squad leader stopped and stared at him.

"This cohort no ken."

"No ken what?" Rameau was puzzled—what incomprehensible baseline thing had he done now?

"No ken what say—tanks? Medical officer needs tanks?"

"Oh! Not tanks. *Thanks.* Means Rameau is happy that you help him. He appreciates, he remembers, and gets ready to help you someday if needed.

"Tanks would be good, too. But different."

"Tanks . . . thanks." The team leader tried the words slowly. "Thanks for meat."

The cohorts crawled back into the access tube clad only in coveralls and boots, discarding the cumbersome suits. Their guns were clipped to their belts, but they also carried screwdrivers and probes from the tool kits. If the rats did show up, these stabbing weapons would be more effective in close quarters than guns. No one offered to arm Rameau; he was not qualified.

Again they squeezed through the utility tunnel crammed with piping and wiring. This time they moved slowly, searching for other exits. Soon they found more hatches, circles of metal closed flush with the wall. Rameau dug at the stubborn circles with the scraper from his biosample kit, but without results.

Of course not. The seal is airtight. Nobody's going to open it with a scraper, or a crowbar for that matter—even if we had one.

The team leader used his kenner to speak to the cohorts at work on the com nodes in the biosphere, hoping they'd found some access codes.

Rameau continued to scrape at the wall. He couldn't see a keypad, or any other clue to show how the hatch could be opened. Yet there was something strange about this part of the wall, something unlike the rest of the corridor. He brought his hand light closer.

Like the other corridors, the walls held a matte surface of built-up grime. Perhaps it had started as dust or soot, but Rameau suspected that fungi and bacteria had found a hold and were surviving as a thin film of organic matter. When he had time to analyze his samples, he'd know for sure.

Yet the area around each hatch looked shiny in the glow of his hand light—rubbed smooth, as if by continual touching. That could mean that it had been used repeatedly, even after the station became a dark and grimy place. After whatever catastrophe had caused Vega to be abandoned.

Means nothing, Rameau told himself. *So, maybe there were a few late survivors. A few people passed through this area, even after the station had started to fall apart. That could still have been a long time ago.*

Rameau rubbed his own fingers over the smooth area, and found two points, on opposite sides of the circular door, that had clearly received the most use. When he placed a hand on either side of the door, his thumbs slid naturally into the shiniest spaces.

The team leader's conversation with the biosphere had ceased. "No access codes," he said. "Shipmind still locked."

"Look at this," Rameau said. "What do you think that is?"

The cohort looked over Rameau's shoulder, and then shoved

him unceremoniously out of the way, taking his place next to the hatch.

"Thumblock," the Omo said. He set his thumbs in place and pressed. At first, nothing happened. Then a yellow light came on in the center of the closed hatch. After a few seconds, it blinked out, to be replaced by green. A warning beep sounded. The hatch slid open.

Peering past the cohort's bulk, Rameau saw pale shapes drifting in and out of the hand light's beam. The cohorts ahead of Rameau swarmed through the hatch. He floundered after them, impelled by the guards behind him. Before he could look around, he heard an indistinct cry from one of the team.

"Sticky—ahh!"

And immediately, Rameau, too, was surrounded by the sticky something. Clammy blobs stuck to the bare skin on his neck and scalp. He could feel them clinging to the arms and legs of his coverall, where their increasing mass impeded his movements.

A damp flap adhered to his face, and suddenly he couldn't see. He ripped it loose and held it in front of him as he rotated into the beam of a cohort's hand light.

"It's just a fungus," he shouted. "Keep calm! Peel them away from your faces, and try not to thrash around until we find out where we are."

They bunched together, facing outward, scanning for any other threat that might hide behind the blizzard of floppy white shapes. But the walls held nothing but row on row of metal trays, each one overgrown by a flabby gray substance. As they watched, a few more pale blobs separated from the wall and floated out into the room.

At last Rameau recognized the set-up.

"Food factory!" he said. "This room was meant to grow some kind of edible material. It's overgrown the trays, and it's budding out into the room."

He stuck his enabled fingers into one of the trays. He felt moisture on his hand, and then the sensors did their work.

"There's still a trickle of nutrient substrate in there. The balance is way off, but it's enough to feed these things."

He caught one as it went by, and stuffed it into a sample net.

"Recycle this," Rameau said. "Find conversion tanks and nutrient feeders, then recycle."

The team leader was already communicating with the engineers back in the biosphere.

Shortly, an engineering team arrived and took over. They swarmed over the fungus area, deconstructed wall panels, and found feeder tanks and converters packed into a cubby behind the room with the racks. All but one of the feeders had run dry, but there was nothing wrong that routine maintenance couldn't fix.

The cohorts attacked the machinery like bees gathering up spilled honey. They disassembled it, cleaned it, and put it back together in working order. Meanwhile, other teams entered the rack room, harvested the floating fungus, and fed it through the repaired converters. Soon, fresh nutrient fluids, seeded with protein assemblers, pumped through the newly sterilized racks.

"How long until you can harvest and process edible product?" Rameau asked.

"Three to five days," the team leader said. "Have to get lights up, adjust spectrum."

"I need glucose solution for the wounded right away," Rameau said.

The cohort pointed to one of the feeder tanks.

"That fill to marker, you go take what you need."

Problem solved, Rameau thought. *Put them in surroundings they understand, give them the raw materials, and they work like one smooth machine. Set free in human space, they'd overgrow us like that fungus on the substrate. Lucky for us they aren't that great with improvisation—yet.*

He found a case of squeeze bags and tubing, designed for food packaging, but usable for IV fluids. He cannibalized the hollow needles from a machine meant to pack wet food into the squeezes. He returned triumphantly to the biosphere with a backpack full of supplies, and the promise of as much glucose as he could use.

As he emerged from the access tube, the cohort at the com node greeted him and offered him a kenner update. For the first time, he'd been included in a successful operation, as a recognized member of the team. He knew he should be keeping his distance, that it was crazy to try to assimilate into Original Man. Nevertheless, he felt good.

It's in my genes, he thought. *Just like them, I'm incepted with the urge to affiliate. Anyway, I need to know so much more about this place before I can learn how to destroy it—or if I should even try.*

Rameau mobilized the techs to set up IVs for the wounded who were too sick to swallow. They complied with swift efficiency. Then, as he watched the bags and tubes twisting randomly in the air, it hit him—there wasn't going to be any slow, steady, gravity-powered drip. There still wasn't any gravity. Nor could he hang the bags from anything.

"Damn it. Micro-g emergency isn't my specialty."

"No cohort ken all stations," Neb said.

Whoa. Is he actually trying to be sympathetic? Rameau wondered.

He settled for taping the bags of saline and glucose solution to the floating litters. Then he calculated what the normal drip rate per hour would be, and ordered the techs to circulate among the wounded, squeezing the bags into the veins a few drops at a time, at measured intervals. Something that was simple in gravity had become a labor-intensive and chancy process.

"No more than that—if you try to squeeze it all in at once, you'll hurt them," he said.

At least we don't have to worry about bedsores, he thought.

He was taking a break to drink some glucose warmed in the microwave when the light over the main door blinked a request for access. As the door opened, a wave of heated air swept in, with the smell of hot metal. The cohorts who entered wore reflective battle suits and helmets, and carried projectile weapons and a pair of thermal cannons. They had gone through the main corridor from *Langstaff*'s air lock to the biosphere, burning off the rats and every suspicious patch of potential fungus on the walls. It looked sterile and safe now.

But Rameau knew it took more than one burnoff to alter an

ecology. He suspected that the rats had entrenched themselves elsewhere in the deserted station and would be back sooner or later.

Meanwhile, the cohorts moved confidently into the dead station, like warm blood pumping out into half-frozen limbs, or oxygen diffusing into starved lungs. They turned on lights, set fluids flowing again in blocked conduits, restarted cycles that had come to a halt. They brought life back into the corpse of the machine.

But are they really restoring Vega to life? Rameau wondered. *Maybe they're more like microbes colonizing a dead body— converting it to their own purposes.*

He suggested to the Commander that instead of flame-cleaning the corridors, the cohorts should diligently collect any disseminated wastes from the walls or the air. They brought back a surprising amount of dingy crud. Rameau sampled it and found that it contained much organic material, in the form of live bacteria as well as dead waste, and various kinds of chemical contamination.

But contamination in one place is useful material in another.

The residue was sorted in the conversion chambers and stored for later use.

They still hadn't found regeneration tanks, but at least Rameau located some pump-action IV units so that Neb and Nor no longer had to tend their sib and the other unconscious casualties around the clock.

Rameau showed Neb and Nor how to massage and bend the pilot's limbs, to stave off atrophy as long as possible. He had learned these techniques from civilians as a child on Garuda, where electronic muscle stimulation hadn't been possible. The massage hadn't cured anyone, but the patients had seemed less anxious, less in pain, when other humans had tried to ease them. And the living sibs seemed to feel better when there was something they could do.

Rameau invented many such tasks to keep their minds off their hunger as they waited for the food processors to complete their cycle. For three days, they had nothing but glucose solution and scraps of fungus to ease their cramped stomachs.

The hungry cohorts slowed down to conserve energy. They acted subdued around their injured crewmates, and uncertain in the strange surroundings. They seemed less intimidating. Rameau's visceral aversion to them began to fade.

18

After three days, food production came on-line again. The nutrient trays were covered with a dense blue-green mat of life. The core of the once-dark and fungoid room was bright with nuanced-spectrum light bars, adjusted to pour forth the exact exact frequencies the algae population required. The trays orbited the central light, lifting up each slice of green for a fair share of the life-giving rays. New air pumped into the room. The atmosphere lost its stale, sour smell and grew spicy with the fresh, slightly chemical tang of the hydroponics.

Before long, the growth was thick enough to skim and process. Without the usual array of flavor generators seeded into the mix, the result wasn't tasty, but it was bland, not disgusting. The cohorts lined up eagerly for their servings of protein crackers and carbo mush. After pressed rat and boiled fungus, this was reliable, familiar food. Even Rameau ate it gratefully.

The cohorts themselves straightened up like wilting plants that had been watered. They seemed bigger; they moved faster; their voices were loud again. Their mindless vitality again assaulted Rameau and made him want to creep into a corner to get away from them. Slow, careful exploration and repairs no longer kept them busy. Everywhere he went—except in the plant room—he found them hooked to brackets, doing bungee calisthenics, or hurtling down the corridors enmeshed in free-fall sparring drills.

And on the tenth day, Gunnarsson announced free-for-all Five Minutes. They gathered in the cylinder where the rat attack

had occurred, a place officially designated "Corridor One."
Rameau, in his own mind, called it Rat's Alley.

Neb was on his way out the door to join the celebration when
he stopped and looked back.

"Rameau no go Five Minutes?" he said.

"No. Rameau definitely no go."

Neb measured Rameau with his eyes, speculatively. Then,
too suddenly for Rameau to dodge, he drew Rameau against
him, tight enough for Rameau to feel Neb's powerful heartbeat,
already pounding faster in anticipation. They spun slowly in the
air as Neb stretched his own arms and legs against Rameau's,
put his forehead against Rameau's, and matched faces. For a
moment Rameau was eye to eye with Neb, staring into that pellucid, empty blue.

Neb let go, and Rameau spun off on his own.

"Rameau no go," Neb agreed. "Too small. Rameau is immature. Maybe e go later."

"I don't think so," Rameau muttered. He wanted nothing to
do with this Original Man madness. Yet something about the
exchange with Neb left him bitter.

He had started to feel like one of the crew. Now, as if a door
had been slammed in his face, he was reminded that he was alone.

His heart was pounding now, too. He wrapped his arms
around his chest, as if to calm it, and felt how scrawny he had
become, how his ribs stuck out.

He had been scared. He hadn't known what Neb would do to
him. But it was human contact. Now that it was gone, he almost
wanted it back.

He had intended to close the door between himself and the
cohorts as soon as Neb left, but in a gesture of defiance, decided to keep watching. The cohorts shed their coveralls, but no
collector picked them up for disposal, so the garments spun
around the corridor like headless, handless fabric ghosts while
the cohorts in their gleaming flesh grappled one another.

They no longer looked human to Rameau. They were alien
again, more alien than dogs or cattle. This version of the Five
Minutes was less structured than the stylized combat on Eyrie
had been, and less brutal.

It was combat nonetheless, and it was violent—combat combined with, or followed by, what appeared to be nonreproductive copulation. The whole thing looked artificial to him, like another one of their elaborate free-fall drills.

Rameau felt lonelier than ever.

He tried to think about women.

I used to have relationships.

But the only one who occupied that part of his mind was Dakini. *Dakini.* He saw himself with her, spinning softly in the ever-changing lights of the practice dome, through mists and constellations that were virtual, but sweeter than reality. Limb to limb, but not like the cohorts in the corridor. With her it was like dancing.

He had taken her silence, her lips always curved in a half smile, for consent. He had taken her pliancy, her sighs, for pleasure equal to his own. She was so nearly naked already that he had put off brushing aside the wisps of silk, letting the moment ripen to the perfection he imagined.

Then he had stripped them away and let them float into the mist. And he had stopped, frozen in shock—though the golden mists kept drifting, and the soft music kept playing.

She felt nothing. Nothing at all. He realized that she had been letting him do this. Now that she understood what he intended, she was refusing.

"Why? Why didn't you say something before?"

She had only looked at him, with those golden eyes, too big for a human. Unlike a true woman, she didn't say the obvious: *You didn't ask me.* He was the human; he was the one in charge. She let him experience the full flavor of his own stupidity, drink the bitterness to the last drop. She had spoken only when he understood completely how wrong he had been.

"I am not human, Piers. I cannot give you what you want. I am not made that way."

He'd let go of her, let her drift. But she had righted herself and waited.

"I am made to dance. Reproductive systems were unnecessary,

and would have wasted energy I need for dancing. You knew this, respected doctor."

That had been true. He *had* known it. He had examined her. He had studied her design in detail. But he had always assumed that something could be done. People made accommodations, if they loved each other.

If.

But it hadn't been anything on the exterior that was lacking; it had been what lay inside. Some people wouldn't have cared, he supposed. A compliant partner, without the burden of human feelings, would have suited them very well. But that wasn't what he had been dreaming of.

"It's all right if you touch me," she had said. "Mr. Chunder allows it."

He hadn't thought that he could feel worse, but that had made him burn inside.

"Who?" he had said. "Who touches you?" The words had tasted vile.

"No one, now," she had answered. "A patron thought he wanted to, but when he learned what you learned, he was angry, and he held too hard. He broke an arm and a rib, and I was in rehab for two weeks. I missed many scheduled events. Mr. Chunder allows touching, but not damage. I am for dancing. Other transforms are for other purposes."

She had waited for him to say something, but he had forgotten the question.

"Do you wish to touch me more?" she had said patiently.

"No. Not now."

She hadn't looked relieved, exactly, but her lips had curved very slightly, and her pose had become lighter, more alert, like a bird about to fly.

"Then, would you like me to dance?" she had said.

"Please."

Her dance had expressed no regret. It had been joyful, as if she had been able to put him completely out of her mind. He had retired to his favorite perch, on the transparent bar that held the auxiliary lights. He could crouch behind the lights, invisible, in the only shadowed place in the dome.

He had felt like one of the fat, perspiring businessmen who came to the markets in Vaharanesi, offering to hire young girls, supposedly as housemaids to help their wives. He had felt like someone who had tried to steal from a child. He had imposed his fantasy on a transform, stamping her with his tinsel seal as if she were a blank bit of paper. Everyone had done it, on Varuna. That's why the entertainers had been there.

But Rameau had imagined himself as something better. He had seen himself as the doctor who really cared, a human who wouldn't treat the transforms as toys. He had really loved her, or so he thought. And therefore, he had assumed, she would love him in return.

The hormones triggered in the cohorts must be thick in the air, Rameau thought, leaking into the plant room through the open door. He felt desperate and wild. He knew that he should close that door.

There must be some other memories to turn to. Other women. Real women. I know I was in love, sometime or other.

But he couldn't remember anyone. There had been colleagues. There had been friends. But no more than that. His fellow students had worn the symbolic head scarves of respectable Vaharanesi women, even with their white medic's coveralls. Strictly professional. And he had been glad to leave it that way.

There had been no one else—not since he'd reached Varuna. Though the one Chunder had referred to as "that Sariputra woman" had tried. She was one of the patrons, come to consult him about a favorite transform that wasn't thriving in its new home. She herself had been tweaked to the point where she looked less like a human than like a deva out of legend. She had perfectly shaped, hemispheric breasts, waist like a bamboo stem, rounded hips, and tiny delicate hands and feet, gilded and hennaed. But to Rameau's eyes, her skin had the subtle signs of being resurfaced too often—a kind of hectic pseudo-youth that breathed "age" as surely as wrinkles would have.

Her intentions had been clear. He had tried, respectfully, to evade them.

"Madam, if the least breath of this should come to Mr. Chunder's ears . . . I'd be exiled, banished. Nor would I ever work on the surface again. My career would be finished. My contract is very specific."

In fact his contract very specifically said nothing about this situation.

"I'm sure that representations could be made to Mr. Chunder," she purred, standing next to him so that her cinnamon-scented bosom breathed directly toward his nostrils. "Entertainments are always available to guests who are willing to pay. That's what it says in *my* contract."

"But, madam, that's just the trouble. You see, I have been brought here expressly for the purpose of attending to the entertainers. My services are not dispensable. And I'm sure that to devote myself adequately to your interests, I would have to neglect those duties for which I have contracted."

"You're so right," she said. She traced the line of his chin while he stood there like a potted plant. Like entertainment. Like a transform.

"You have a Noreuropan look to you," she said. "Unusual these days. Perhaps a little old-fashioned. But nice . . ."

"My *parents* were Swedish," he said, emphasizing the word just a little, trying to point out that he was her equal. A naturally conceived man with ancestry and heritage, not an epiphenomenon incepted for her benefit.

"With a little tweaking, you could almost pass for Original Man," she said. "That excites me," she breathed, fluttering her tiny, ringed fingers over his broad, high cheekbones and fair eyebrows.

Her last comment was superfluous; the musk fragrance intensified in response to a rise in skin temperature. He could feel it tickling him like an importunate hand. It evoked desire of a kind, but no warmth.

"Yes, just a bit more *here*," she said, kneading his biceps, "and a couple of weeks of grafting and traction to lengthen *here*," and she squeezed his thigh. "Nice," she repeated. "One can tell you've just come up. You'll have to work to maintain that muscle tone in micro g."

She sighed, suddenly practical again. "Believe me, I know! Such hours in the gym. And for what? Damn it. I'm a true woman. Skilled. Powerful. Beautiful."

She looked at him with doe's eyes, swimming in pellucid tears. Rameau felt as if some comment was called for.

"Indeed, madam."

"So you say! But here I am on Varuna, the pleasure center of the universe, and I can't even *buy* love."

Perhaps more under the influence of the musk than he realized, he began to feel sorry for her. Then he realized what she was saying.

"Then again, what would you know about it?" she said. She raised her head higher, and the tears vanished as if reabsorbed. "True man! An idiot like all the rest of them."

She had turned to leave, and he had just begun to feel relief when she turned her head and gave him a pouting look over her shoulder.

"I might just talk to Mr. Chunder about you anyway, Sven, or Lars, or whatever your name is," she said gaily.

"Madam, I implore you!" But then she was gone.

Later, Chunder had approached him in a casual moment.

"By the way, you handled that episode with the Sariputra woman perfectly," he said.

"I begged her not to speak to you," Rameau said.

"Oh, indeed," Chunder replied neutrally.

Suddenly, Rameau realized that, of course, he had been on record the whole time.

"By the way, sir, is there anywhere on board that I'm not being overseen?"

"It's entirely for your own protection," Chunder said.

"Oh, indeed," Rameau responded.

"You know, she's quite impossible—oh, with all due respect of course. But I had to laugh when she said that you could be tweaked to resemble Original Man."

"Really," Rameau said. "That's what Kuno Gunnarsson said to me, too. I suppose his motives weren't the same, though."

Chunder stared. "Gunnarsson? *The* Gunnarsson?"

"The same," Rameau said. A resentful impulse had moved

him, a desire to assert himself, but he was already sorry he had spoken.

"Curiosity overwhelms me," Chunder said. "Where did you meet the Founder?"

"Just before I met you," Rameau said. "He tried to recruit me. I turned him down."

"Then I have hired an asset who is even more valuable than I knew," Chunder said, beaming.

So much for the Sariputra woman, Rameau thought, curling up tighter in the plant dome. *I can't even keep my mind on her. I end up thinking about Mr. Chunder, of all people.*

Tweaked to perfection—yet still she had seemed like an animal to him, her proportions squat, earthbound. She had been too late.

After he had seen Dakini.

He had touched Dakini. He had learned to dance holding her gently, so gently he could scarcely feel her against him. He had learned to brush her thick black hair lightly enough that it put no pressure on her long, delicate neck. She had learned to like it, he thought. Sometimes he could not help kissing her. She had allowed it, much as a pet will let a child kiss it and hug it just a little too tightly.

He had been ashamed of himself. And so he had cast himself in another role: a servant devoted to a noble rani, too noble to be touched, like the veiled women in the Vaharanesi tales. A servant devoted to a queen who could grant him nothing but to allow his service. But that had assumed Dakini wanted something from him, and he had known all along that she wanted nothing more than to be left alone.

Rameau in the present groaned out loud. Not that anyone could hear him.

"Merciful Kannon, this must be the longest five minutes in history," he said aloud. Things had gotten to the point where he really didn't want to watch anymore. He turned away, and sat by the silent pilot. Experimentally, he touched the cohort's shoulder. The pilot was emaciated and pale, but still his skin was hot, his bones dense and heavy as stone.

Rameau wondered if nonreproductive copulation with a cohort would really be so bad. The alternative seemed to be a lifetime of celibacy. Surely it was no worse than his dreams of Dakini. They weren't really men, any more than she had really been a woman. But he'd be fragile, easily crushed—as Dakini had been to him.

The cohorts were finished, evidently. The sounds of relaxed conversation and horseplay reached him. Neb tumbled through the doorway, fastening the zips on his coverall. He glowed with health and vigor. He was still breathing hard.

Rameau suddenly felt that he couldn't bear to be in the same space with the cohorts. He had to find a place to be alone.

"I'm going out—I have something to take care of," he muttered, darting from the room before Neb could stop him.

He made it through Rat's Alley, dodging a few other cohorts. He passed the big hatch that led to the landing bay, through which they had first entered. For a few meters beyond that, lights were still strung up, and the walls had been cleaned.

Then he was into the unexplored area, into the dark, where the walls felt rough and damp. He corkscrewed in the air and looked back. He could still see the lighted enclave behind him.

"Can't get lost by going in a straight line," he said to himself. He checked his kenner. It was still on. He could call for help anytime. He let his momentum carry him on into the dark.

Then he was completely alone. The darkness was absolute, almost palpable. He felt as if he were standing still, wrapped in black velvet, though he knew he was still sailing onward. He kept his hands out in front, to protect his head in case he ran into anything.

This is crazy.

He turned on his hand light, and saw the walls flicking past. He wanted the light, but he knew that beyond the bright circle, there might be unseen watchers for whom the moving hemisphere of light would make a perfect target, with Rameau dead center.

His half-formed idea had been to go all the way to the other end of this gigantic cylinder. He might find something marvelous. Even if he didn't find anything, he'd be one up on the cohorts. He would have gone somewhere they hadn't been.

But he wasn't sure he wanted to keep on going into the darkness. Maybe he had been alone long enough. Maybe it was time to turn back.

Then he heard a sound. It was a rustle, a scraping—the kind of sound that would bring out a cold sweat on anyone who had spent time in Garuda's jungles. He swept the light around in a panic, and saw nothing, and then snapped the light off just as hastily. It was the only way to hide. He couldn't tell how far away the sound was. It was soft, insidious.

Then someone shrieked—a brief, high-pitched cry. Definitely not a cohort. It could have been a small animal. In fact it had to be a small animal, because there were no other human beings on this station. Unless . . .

Rameau's curiosity pressed the thruster stud before good sense could interfere.

Oh, crap! What am I doing! He didn't have a weapon of any kind. *Unless I could use my enabler to inject the thing with some feel-good substance.*

In truth, he was feeling pretty good himself. The enabler was still calibrated for cohorts, and at the first sign of panic, it had started pumping in a thrilling mixture of inspiring drugs.

He slowed himself, and cautiously edged sideways toward the wall. He pulled himself along it, grasping at any protrusion he could find. The sounds he was hearing now didn't make any sense at all. There were more high-pitched squeaks, but they seemed to be coming from many different directions. The scraping noise continued, as if something were thrashing against the sides of the corridor.

His hand slipped into emptiness. He had come to an open cross-corridor. The darkness ahead was ominously silent. He took a deep breath and flashed his hand light on.

There was a tunnel rat coming straight at his face, its limbs splayed out and clawing the air, its mouth wide open. As he ducked, something huge and dark came at him, behind the tiny rodent. All he could see clearly was a pair of red eyes, reflecting his light.

He yelled, shut off the light, and ducked into the crosscorridor, faster than he would have thought possible. He fired his thrusters before he realized that this corridor might be closed at the other end. Could he open a hatch in the dark? Or—

He did not have time to complete the thought before he collided with the closed hatch as he had feared. All that saved him was that he'd had his hands out in front of him like a diver. But he rebounded, stunned, and only stopped his tumbling by jamming his legs against the walls.

Ow! God!

Bright flashes of light danced in the dark, but they illuminated nothing because they were only happening inside his head. He could still hear that scraping noise, something thumping against the wall.

Let it be outside the corridor, let it be outside *the corridor . . .*

His thoughts scrambled around his mind as frantically as his fingers scraped against the circumference of the hatch, seeking locks that would let him out. He found the twin oval depressions and jammed his thumbs into them.

Suddenly there was a bright circle of light directly in front of him. The hatch opened, and the light shone from beyond it. He dragged himself through so fast that he scraped his skin on the edges, turned, and stabbed the locks on the other side. He hit them so hard that he bounced himself off the wall and was floating helplessly farther away. The hatch closed, and nothing had come through it.

Rameau curled into a fetal position, shuddering with terror and relief.

He floated with his head clasped in his arms until he bumped gently against the far wall. Then he uncurled and blinked.

He was in a small, enclosed space, which at this point was a welcome haven. It was office-sized, a little smaller than the cube he had occupied on Varuna. Tube lights glowed around its perimeter. He was so grateful for the light that he felt as if he could drink it like water.

How am I going to get back?

As soon as his mind started working again, he realized that the corridor was the only way. He decided to postpone the question for a little longer.

I should explore this place before I leave, anyway.

The lights were clean and bright, reassuring. But something was wrong in here—

The smell.

He felt a jolt of fear. But this wasn't the strange, frightening stink from the corridor. It was a smell he remembered from an older time, one that definitely didn't belong here in this world of steel. It reminded him of a lost world, of old times on Garuda. It smelled like an animal pen where people kept the pets they would one day eat. It smelled like the shacks where people lived and grew familiar with their own dirt, because they no longer had the dignity of baths and clean clothes. Nothing in the world of Original Man could ever smell this way. It was a sad smell, really, yet it held a comfort and kindliness for Rameau because it came from the human world.

Wake up and use your head. What is it?

The smell seemed out of place with the rest of the room. Rameau saw lockers, pullouts that probably became desks and keyboards, wall space for data screens and holos. It wasn't only the same size as his old office, it *was* an office. Or maybe a lab of some kind, hooked into the shipmind.

There was only one large item in the room, and it looked vaguely familiar. He pushed over to it and hung above it, looking down. It was a big, white, rectangular block, thick-walled, but with an opening in the top. It was lined with ragged-looking, dark-colored bundles that spilled over the sides. Rameau had seen so many unusual organics lately that he immediately thought of fungus. The smell was strongest near the dark stuff, too.

Rameau touched it gingerly, and was surprised to feel a dry, rough surface, not a clammy one. He pulled, and a piece came free.

It wasn't fungus, but fabric. He pulled out the rest of the material. There were scraps that might have been used for clothing, mingled with waterproof squares and bits of fireproof insulating cloth. He couldn't see any droppings, or other signs of animals nesting. He could think of only one explanation: a human was here, or had been here recently.

That thought was replaced by one that startled him even more. After removing the nest of fabric, he could see the inside of the box, and its fittings. It was a stasis pod. Not the ultranew version he'd seen stacked in rows on *Langstaff*, but an older model he remembered from the trip to Garuda.

Why is there a stasis pod in an office cube, hidden this deep inside the station?

Rameau pressed the pod's controls, but the lid didn't close, though a caution light blinked. Did it require a password he didn't know? Pod diagnostics were beyond him. Then he remembered the kenner, and set it to scan the pod controls. The machine was in working order; he could have set the controls and climbed in, but its fluid levels were too low. The life-support gel had been used up by the last occupant, and had not been replenished.

Rameau sucked in a quick breath, feeling a stir of hope. Some being had survived an unknown time in stasis, and was, presumably, still around. It could have been an Original Man, but it also could have been a human. The room had a human feel to it.

And if one human, possibly more than one. Rameau's imagination quickly sketched the possibility that a whole group of humans might be hidden on the station. The Original Man might still be able to pinpoint Rameau by his locator, but maybe not. Maybe he had slipped off their grid. If they couldn't find him, and if he had a chance to link up with fellow humans who knew something of the workings of this structure, he might have a chance to get away.

The hatch slid open again. Rameau was lucky to catch the movement from the corner of his eye. The approach of the one who entered was completely silent, until the intruder saw Rameau floating above the empty pod, and uttered again that brief, high-pitched shriek. And that brought Rameau a crushing disappointment.

19

It was only a child. As it entered the room and saw him, it tucked itself into a ball to flee. Rameau forgot about using his thrusters; he powered himself with a strong kick to the wall, and shot across the room just in time to grasp a single bare foot before the creature could vanish back into the corridor.

They tumbled together around the room, bouncing off walls and fixtures as the child struggled and writhed. It kept up a continual snarling as it thrashed its head around, trying to find a place to bite. When Rameau finally came to rest, he was holding on to a wall bracket with one hand and letting the child stretch out at arm's length, tugging and kicking. Rameau shifted his grip to a grimy ankle.

"Calm down. I'm not going to hurt you," he said.

He felt that he would very much like to hurt the child, though. His thumb was black and blue and oozing blood where the creature had mangled it with all-too-human teeth. The child looked human in its proportions, but as it panted and snarled at him from within its thicket of snarled, greasy hair, he was beginning to wonder.

"No more biting, you understand?" he said. It showed its teeth at him.

"Damn it. Listen, I want to be friends. Understand?"

Maybe it didn't speak English. He tried the variant of Gujarati that had been prevalent on Garuda, and got no response. He tried Afro-Francais and the bits of Japanese he remembered. Still nothing. Finally he tried the Svedenorsk that had been his mother's tongue.

"Little one, who are you? What's your name?"

The child burst into incoherent sobbing and struggling.

"Lemme go!" it screamed finally. It was garbled but understandable Basic English. "Lemme go!"

But it wasn't strong enough to put up continued resistance, and he cautiously reeled it in. He hooked his leg over the bracket and got a two-handed grip on the child. It didn't smell any better as it came closer. Under a film of dirt, its skin was as pale as Rameau's, and the filthy, twisted hair would probably have been fair if it had been clean. The eyes that darted wildly about, seeking a way to escape, were not the startling blue of Original Man, but they were a light gray that went with the rest of the child's coloring. It could have been one of Rameau's cousins.

The nails on hands and feet had not been cut in a long time. Some of them were broken, but most curved, talonlike. The foot Rameau had been holding on to was soft and flexible. The child's limbs were long and bony. There wasn't an ounce of extra flesh on them, or on the gaunt little face, yet the body had the flabby feel that muscles acquired after a long time in micro g. Rameau wondered if the child remembered how to walk. It had been adrift for a long time.

And alone, he guessed with bitter disappointment. If there were other adults around, they wouldn't have let this young one go feral.

"Hey," he said. "Do you have a mother or father? Is there anyone else here like you?"

The child contorted its face into a grimace, as if it took a big effort to remember.

"Last one," it said in a voice husky with disuse.

"What do you mean? Do you mean there's another person? One last adult?"

"Last one," the child said. It smacked itself on the chest abruptly. "Last one!"

"But where are the adults?" Rameau pressed him, still hoping for something. "Where are the big people?"

"Big people!" The child's face lit up. Finally Rameau had said something it could understand. The child tugged urgently toward the opposite wall, where the screens were.

"There!" When Rameau wouldn't let go, it snarled. "Damn it! Turn on big people. Son of a bitch!"

It cursed Rameau fluently until he let go his hold on the bracket and let the child tug him toward the wall screens. It knew at least several words of each language he had tried, but not the ones he had used. The kid reached the wall with its free hand and slapped the panel.

The screen came to life. Tall blond people in coveralls appeared, their faces smooth and perfectly symmetrical. But they couldn't be Original Man, Rameau thought, because one of them was female. Seemed to be female, he corrected himself. He should have learned by now that one couldn't really tell.

Rameau hoped for a minute that these people had left a message, perhaps one that contained important information, clues to where they had gone, or secret knowledge about the station. Clearly this wasn't the start of a message; they had picked up in the middle.

"—and draining of the secondary water filtration unit," the voice said. "Disassembly procedure follows. Observe step one."

The child had stopped struggling and was staring, rapt.

It's a damn training film.

Rameau slapped it off. The child began to struggle again.

"Who are those people?" Rameau said. "What are their names?"

The child glared at him. "No names. Just big people."

"Are those the only big people you see?"

The child was getting tired. It kicked at Rameau's grasping hand and then floated limp.

"There were . . . some," it said jerkily. "Some. Before. But I don't remember names."

It flapped one hand as if to dismiss them.

"They went away."

"What's your name?" Rameau said.

"Last one," the child said vaguely.

"That's what they called you?"

"They said 'last one.' That's when they put me in there. Said hide."

"They put you in the stasis pod?" Rameau said.

"In there." The child nodded affirmatively toward the white box. "I woke up; they were gone. They said hide. I hid a long time. They never found me. God damn son of bitches."

"Merciful Kannon," Rameau muttered. He must have loosened his grip on the scrawny ankle. The child lashed out with its other foot, kicking Rameau on the point of the chin with stunning impact, got loose, and was halfway out the hatch before Rameau could grab its leg again.

Rameau hauled the child forcefully back into the room. That kick had slammed his teeth together and made him bite his tongue. This time he was the one who swore as he clutched the child's dreadlocked hair with one hand and twisted its arm with the other.

"Jesus Mohammad! What's the matter with you!"

The child screamed and gnashed its teeth and tried to kick him again. At first it just made him mad, and he twisted its arm tighter to stop it from hurting him. Then he realized that it was terrified. The screaming contained occasional words.

"No! No! Don't! Not eat me!"

Rameau loosened his grip, but cautiously.

"Hey. I'm sorry. I didn't mean to scare you. Stop screaming and listen! I'm not going to eat you. What are you, crazy? Who said they would eat you?"

He shook the child, causing himself to bob up and down.

"They said," the child cried. "They said hide. Come out of box, they gonna come eat you. I had to come out. The box stopped. It opened; I can't get it to shut again."

"Settle down. I will not eat you. Got that? Not eat. What's your name? You must have a name."

And if you don't, you must be Original Man.

The child plucked at its lips with its free hand, as if to pull out a word that couldn't be found.

"P-p-" it said. "Puh—"

It can't be. That would be a ridiculous coincidence.

"Piers?" he said.

The child frowned, shrugged.

"Peh . . . uh . . ."

"Per."

The child's eyes widened.

"Per!" it said. "Last one. Last one—Per! They said that."

So it does have a name. But it could equally well be an Original Man persig. Per, Pik, Pot . . .

"They said 'last one,' " he said. "Does that mean there used to be more like you? People who were not big?"

There was no look of recognition in the child's eyes.

"Only big," it said. "And me. Last one."

The name was male, in Noreuropa. But that wasn't necessarily where the child came from. Rameau had embarrassed himself before, in Garuda's polyglot culture, by making assumptions based on names. The child wore a couple of squares of dingy fabric wrapped and tied around its torso.

"Do you have a sex?" Rameau asked. "Male or female?"

The child didn't seem to understand him.

Rameau tugged at the fabric until he could make a guess. The child appeared to be a boy. It would take a more detailed examination to tell if the child really was a male human. Or if he was a child, for that matter. It suddenly occurred to Rameau that Per could have been tweaked to reach adulthood with short stature and immature appearance. He hoped not; if this was an adult, it wasn't very bright.

Rameau grew tired of holding on to Per, even though the boy had quit fighting. He wanted to further explore the office.

"Listen carefully," he said. "My name is Rameau. I am not the same as those other big people. They're gone. Now other people have come here in a ship. We are trying to fix this station. I don't want to hurt you. If you wait quietly, I will take you where you can get some food. If you try to leave the room again, I will tie your foot to the wall so you have to stay. Now, will you hold still, or should I tie you up?"

"I stay," the boy said. "Hurry up and give me food. I'm hungry."

"In a minute. I want to look at your screens first."

The boy collected the pieces of his nest and stuffed them back into the stasis pod. He burrowed into the heap and pulled a strap across the pod to keep himself in place. From that safe

space, he watched Rameau. Only his eyes showed from under a
fold of fabric.

Rameau turned the screen on again. The instruction manuals
might be useful later, but that wasn't his primary interest now.
He turned them off and switched to a communications channel,
trying to hook into the shipmind. Maybe he could find a different route to return.

Like the cohorts, he was able to access basic maintenance
schematics and peripheral information, but core areas were denied him. The interactive screen scanned him and rejected him.

"Per—come here for a minute," he said. The boy approached
cautiously.

Rameau made his request for access again.

"Just hold on to that bar in front of the screen," he said to the
boy. Per complied.

"Look at the light in the screen," Rameau said. The screen
flashed the boy's retina, and collected his prints from the bar he
was gripping.

"Access granted," the voice of the shipmind said.

"Thank you," Rameau said. "You can go back to your nest
now."

He was jubilant. Finally he had gained something the Original Man didn't possess. He could hardly master his excitement
enough to find the correct protocol for registering himself as a
legitimate operator, known to the shipmind. When he was finished, he turned off the screen, then turned it on again. It accepted his directions without question.

"Yes!"

"Food now," the boy said.

"In a minute."

Rameau shifted from the wall screen to the holo tank. A console unfolded from the wall. Rameau's fingers played over its
nodes. He felt a rich sensual pleasure, a leaping freedom, like a
musician reunited with his instrument. As he chose combinations of nodes, he built a pattern in the holo tank. It started with
a single thread and spun itself into a form that held paths to
sites within the shipmind that would give him what he wanted
to know. The same skills that let him build a body from basic

molecular chains made him very good at enfleshing data in a comprehensible pattern.

He had forgotten the boy; he sat with his back to the door.

"Eeeeee!" Per shrieked again. At the same time, Rameau heard the sounds in the corridor. He shot upward from the console, slapping the switch in reflex fear.

"Using assembly tool number seventeen from your omnikit, unbolt and remove cover bearing serial number RK1477 . . . ," the instructive voice of the training film droned.

The hatch opened again, and four armed cohorts entered, one after the other. They filled up the office space almost completely. Rameau glanced at the old stasis pod. Per was no longer in it. Only then did Rameau figure out that the mass clinging to his legs was the boy. His heart sank. Already the kid was looking to him for protection. Yet he had no protection to give, even if he had wanted to take the responsibility.

It might have been better for him if I'd never found him.

"Medical Officer Rameau is ordered to report to the Commander immediately," the leading cohort said.

"Is there a problem?" Rameau said, as calmly as he could. "Just a minute—I'll shut this down." He turned to the console, making sure that nothing of his previous work remained visible, as he shut down the training film.

"Rameau is absent without leave," the cohort said. "He is ordered to return to duty."

"I'll be happy to report to the Commander," Rameau said. "But I have been on duty. Since I couldn't participate in the Five Minutes, I took the opportunity to do some further exploring. As you can see, I've made some interesting discoveries that I'm sure the Commander will want to hear about."

He tried to move toward the cohorts, to show them that he was cooperating. The boy crawled up his back like a monkey, clinging to him with arms and legs and screaming "No! No!"

The team leader tried to point his weapon at the child, but ended up pointing it at Rameau's head, as Per ducked.

The boy screamed.

The cohorts poised on grim alert.

Rameau sighed.

"Why is everything such a production with you people?" he said. "Let me explain this to you in simple terms. This is a child. He's unarmed. He has essential information about this station. We are going to go see the Commander, and you are going to escort us. We are not the enemy. Now, point that weapon away from me. What are you thinking? I'm an officer of *Langstaff*! You are not to threaten either me or the child. *That* is an order."

The cohort leader looked confused. The idea of a baseline who could give them orders, especially one who was accompanied by a screaming, half-naked life-form, was hard for him to grasp. But Rameau's coveralls were those of an officer.

The cohorts lowered the weapons and moved aside to let Rameau take the lead.

Now his only problem was the boy. Per still screamed and clawed at his neck. Rameau pried his fingers loose, and the boy tried again to kick him and bite him. The presence of the cohorts evidently terrified the child.

Rameau crushed the boy's wrists in a painfully tight grip, to get his attention.

"Shut up, or I'll let them have you!" he shouted. The boy stopped kicking, and his screams died away to a whimper.

"Now you listen to me," Rameau said. "If you're good, I won't let them take you. We're going where we can get some food. No one will eat you. But don't try to get away once we're outside, or you'll be sorry."

He pointed to the fabric scraps.

"Bring me that," he ordered one of the cohorts.

He took a chance and let go of Per for a minute. The boy was too much afraid of the cohorts to move. Rameau twisted the fabric into a rope and knotted one end around Per's ankle, the other to his own belt.

"Okay, team leader—lead on," he said. "Be aware that there may be something out there. I saw tunnel rats, and I heard something larger. Be alert."

The corridor wasn't nearly as frightening when Rameau was surrounded by armed cohorts with powerful lights. It lost its mystery, and became just another part of the machine. He felt stupid, both for being afraid of the dark and for thinking he had gone far enough to get away from Original Man. They must have known where he was the whole time.

"How did you locate me?" he asked.

"Silence" was the discouraging reply.

What are they listening for?

Rameau got nervous again. The cohorts wore helmets and gauntlets. Rameau and the boy were unprotected.

If the tunnel rats swarm us again, guess who will be the prime target?

He listened. Nothing. But—

"Do you smell that?" he said.

They silenced him again, with an emphatic hand gesture this time. The boy didn't break silence at first, but he writhed in fear, and clutched Rameau's wrist. He gave a suppressed whimper, and finally screamed again.

"Get away! Get away! It's coming!"

By now the smell was very strong. The cohorts drifted in formation, forming a cube with weapons pointing all ways. There was an unmistakable noise behind them, a scraping sound, as of something long being dragged along the corridor.

Then an enormous head burst into the bubble of light that surrounded them. It blocked the whole passage. A long, lipless mouth gaped open, revealing row on row of fangs that gleamed in the light, and behind them a greenish flexing tube of muscle, large enough to swallow them whole. Above the mouth two tiny red eyes shone balefully. The grotesque head reared back as if the light had struck it like a blow, and there was a whistling hiss like a huge vapor leak. The foul smell was all around them— ammoniac, fetid, gut-clenching.

Rameau saw it in a single instant, and had fired all his thrusters before he had time to blink. His arms and legs were extended at different angles, so he shot away down the corridor, tumbling wildly, with the boy's extra mass throwing him off when he tried to straighten out.

The cohorts' resolve lasted only an instant longer. They fled, too, gaining quickly on Rameau. They fired intermittently over their shoulders, but the creature came on. Soon they would pass

Rameau, and there would be nothing between him and the monster.

The boy had pulled himself up the tether to cling to Rameau's chest. That helped Rameau to control their trajectory, but still the monster was gaining on them. The boy pulled up his knees, then crouched with his feet against Rameau's ribs, his hands still clutching at Rameau's coverall.

Suddenly Rameau felt a powerful kick as the boy pushed off from his body and leapt for the wall that was flashing past. There was a jolt that made Rameau's head whiplash around, as the boy caught hold of something in the wall and stopped himself. The tether pulled tight. Rameau bounced at the end of it. He had just enough sense to kill his momentum with reverse thrusters before he sent both of them into another uncontrollable tumble.

The slithering horror was nearly upon them. Rameau looked to see what was stuck. He thought of tearing the tether loose, leaving the boy to his fate. But he didn't. Instead, he saw that Per was clinging by the tips of his fingers to a bracket on the wall above Rameau's head. Next to the bracket there was a round, dark opening. Rameau braced his hands against the boy's skinny rump.

"Go!" he yelled. He had just time to fire his leg thrusters before the creature caught up with them. Per popped through the circle of black, with Rameau right behind him. Inches away from them, just beyond the opening of their refuge, an endless body slid past—a rubbery, stinking pelt, textured like eel hide.

They were in a cul-de-sac with no other outlet. They could be trapped, but at least the hole was not large enough for that fearful head to enter.

It's not big enough. The thing can't get in, Rameau assured himself. It was more like a prayer.

"It can't get in," the boy said hoarsely. He held Rameau's arm so tightly that his fingers sank painfully into the flesh. He was shivering.

Seconds later, the screaming started.

In spite of his fear, Rameau stuck his head out and looked. He saw the too-familiar blobs of crimson jelly streaking past.

But the monster's bulk was in the way. He couldn't see around it to find out what was happening to the cohorts. The pitted gray tail lashed against the wall. He pulled his head back just in time to escape having his neck broken.

The hissing rose to a roar. It broke into sounds of tearing and crunching, then a gulping noise that was worse. The screaming stopped.

Then the long, ugly body moved past again, going backward. The cohorts' lights drifted in the corridor, still illuminating the carnage. Rameau had a brief glimpse of one red eye, a fanged mouth smeared with a deeper red. He shrank back from that eye as if it could see him and understand who he was. After it departed, he heard the futile pop and slam of the cohorts' projectile weapons. They hadn't stopped it; they hadn't killed it.

As soon as the firing ceased, Rameau stuck his arm out. No one shot him. He leaned out farther and looked away, down the corridor. At the far end there was darkness again. He couldn't see the monster. He tugged at the boy, who was curled into a tight ball.

"Come on," he said urgently. He didn't want to go out there either, but he refused to be left behind in the dark. He dragged the protesting Per out of the hole and kicked off, toward the sound of the retreating cohorts. He had used too much of his thrust already, in panic and because he was pulling the boy's mass, too. He wanted to conserve what was left.

Yeah—in case of emergency, he thought sarcastically.

Bloodballs splattered them as they emerged. The boy cried in a quiet, hopeless tone. Rameau had to trigger the last of his thrust after all. The cohorts were already retreating, towing some kind of pack or bundle behind them. Rameau's stomach twisted as he caught up and saw that it was most of a torso. A contrail of blood fanned out behind them. The monster had left because he'd had his meal.

Rameau caught hold of a cohort's leg before his thrusters died. The cohort kicked, hard enough to hurt, but not seriously. If he'd meant to get rid of them, he could have broken Rameau's neck.

"Damn it! I order you to return us to the Commander!"

Rameau shouted. "That was your mission! Remember? Don't kick me or—or I'll have you motivated!"

They were towed next to the remains of the cohort who had become lunch. Per moaned and buried his face against Rameau's ribs.

"The things that bite are gonna come," he said. "They like blood."

The flying rats converged on them just before they reached the door to the plant dome. Rameau let go of the cohort who was towing him and coasted through the door, shouting "Neb! Get ready to close the door! Incoming rats!" The fleeing cohorts turned at bay and fired on the rodents. Projectile weapons worked better on the rats than they had on the monster, but the rats were harder to hit.

Cohorts from inside the plant dome rushed out to assist. When the air was thick with a blizzard of dead creatures, the others finally retreated. From a safe vantage point behind the cohorts, Rameau noticed that many of the rats carried off their dead cousins, fixing their sharp teeth in the bleeding bodies.

They're cannibals. That makes sense. In an area of scarce resources, they have to eat anything.

Now that they had the food processors back on-line, the cohorts didn't feel a need to eat the dead rats. They collected the bodies and recycled them. Two cohorts shrink-wrapped what was left of the dead Omo, and took it away in another direction. Rameau didn't know what happened to that body.

The rest of the escort group stayed with Rameau, arrayed in micro-g attention posture even though Rameau himself curled up in a convenient clump of foliage, the boy at his side.

Oh, right. They haven't completed their mission yet. They have to guard me until the Commander shows up.

He felt sorry for them. A human would have been terrified by what they had just seen. They were still bloody and disheveled. He wondered if seeing one of their number being eaten really bothered them, or if they were as indifferent as they seemed.

20

Per, on the other hand, was not indifferent. He was still shivering and sobbing, trying to retreat behind Rameau and bury himself in the scanty leaf cover.

"I told you it would come," he whispered, almost inaudibly. "The thing that eats. We should have stayed hiding. It can even eat the pirates."

"Pirates?" Rameau said. "What do you mean? You mean cohorts, like that one the monster got today?"

Per squirmed away from him, as if afraid to answer.

"I'm just trying to find out who was on the ship with you," Rameau coaxed.

"Things that eat you," the boy said. "And *them*—the big hairy ones. I saw *them* kill a cohort once, too. They tore his arms off. There was blood. Like today. They said they'd send the big hairy ones to tear me apart, if I didn't hide."

Two more cohorts entered the dome, with the Commander following close behind. Rameau tried to align himself with the Commander, the zero-g version of standing up, but was restrained by Per, who was once again clinging to his back and screaming like a monkey. A pair of Rukh followed in the Commander's wake.

"The big hairy ones"—that must be what's terrifying him this time.

As the boy continued to scream, the Commander made an irritated gesture to his guards, and one of the cohorts approached Rameau.

"Commander!" Rameau shouted, to be heard above the boy's

shrill cries. "Stop that cohort! You can't motivate this boy. You need to hear his story. Call off the cohort before you scare the wits out of him."

Gunnarsson stopped the cohort with another flick of the hand.

"Keep him quiet, then," he said. "My time is limited."

"Send the Rukh out," Rameau said. "He thinks they'll kill him."

At a gesture, the Rukh withdrew beyond the doorway. Rameau pried the boy loose from his back and gripped him by the elbows.

"If you want to live, stop that," he said tautly. "This is the cohort Commander. He can tell the Rukh to kill you, or he can make them go away. Don't make him angry! He wants you to be quiet."

Per bit his lip in a hideous grimace. His skinny shoulders heaved as he tried to gulp air without screaming again.

"Good boy," Rameau whispered. "Just answer a few questions, and then I'll get you some food." He tugged the boy forward.

"I found him hiding in an office cube, down the axis of Corridor One," Rameau said.

"Tell me what ate my cohort," Gunnarsson said to Per. Rameau could see dangerous anger in his eyes.

Unexpected threat—that's what makes them angry.

"A thing," the boy said. "Monster. The one with the big mouth that comes in the dark."

Gunnarsson looked at Rameau. "Is he mentally damaged?" he said.

Rameau shrugged. "I can't tell. I have to do some tests first, find out how old he is, and so forth. He's so afraid of you that he can't think. And he's been alone on the station for an undetermined length of time. I don't know about Original Man, but baselines don't tolerate solitude well, especially as juveniles."

"Is he a baseline?"

"Again, I won't know until I can run a gene scan on him. I think so, because he has the exterior male characteristics of a baseline juvenile. But I suppose he could have been tweaked in some way."

His eyes moved. He's thinking something that he's not telling me. Maybe this kid is more than he seems.

"Boy," Gunnarsson addressed Per directly. "Describe the monster."

Per flinched when the Commander looked at him.

" 'S long," he said hoarsely. "Very long and fat. Fills up the whole corridor, almost. Has two red eyes. Big mouth like the zip on a bag." He drew the mouth across his own face, from ear to ear. "When he opens, you see all the way down." He shuddered involuntarily. "Has little tiny hands in the wrong place. Tiny, but sharp. He can grab you."

The Commander made a sudden, fisted gesture. He bobbed in the air, and Per retreated behind Rameau again with a squeak.

"The sinué!" Gunnarsson said.

"What is a sinué?" The word raised a chill on Rameau's neck.

I must have heard it before. But where?

"You'll have a chance to examine one," Gunnarsson said. Again there was that look in his eye, as if he meant more than he intended to say.

"Food now," a small voice behind Rameau said.

"Commander, can you send for something to eat? The boy is hungry."

"Give him something yourself. Send one of your useless medtechs."

"Commander," Rameau said patiently, "there's a *thing* out there. Your boys have armor and beam weapons."

Gunnarsson relented, and let him send away the cohorts who had been guarding him. Rameau thought they could probably use something to eat, too.

Anyway, it was getting overcrowded with all the armed Omo in here.

"Food," Per whispered.

"Quiet. They'll be back in a minute."

"What do you find so important about this very dirty little life-form?" Gunnarsson asked.

"I told you—he's been here since it was built. Or for a long time, anyway. I think he can tell us about the people who were here before, with a little encouragement."

"That's not important," Gunnarsson said.

"What do you mean, it's not important?" Rameau protested. Suddenly, he realized why.

"Ohhh . . . I get it. It's not important because you already know. You just weren't ready to tell us yet. Of course. How could I be so stupid. I guess I was just distracted by one or the other of those lovely near-death experiences I've been having lately."

"Silence!"

Rameau looked around. There were still quite a few cohorts in the room.

"Oh, yeah. They may be kind of dumb, but they do have ears. And here I am, about to blow your carefully crafted, secret—"

Suddenly, Rameau found himself thrust backward with Gunnarsson's thumb in the hollow of his throat. He hadn't finished his sentence because he couldn't. He could still breathe, a little.

He hadn't even seen the Commander begin to move.

"Silence," the Commander repeated.

He unwrapped Per from Rameau's leg with one hand and held the boy out at arm's length, by the back of his neck. Per's mouth gaped, but either he was too frightened to scream, or he couldn't breathe either.

"Okay, okay," Rameau mouthed.

The Commander removed his hands from both of them. Somehow Per managed to reach Rameau and latch on again.

I wonder why he keeps doing that. It isn't helping, Rameau thought as he rubbed his throat. *Hiding behind me is like using an aluminum umbrella in a thunderstorm.*

"Amazing. Motivated by the Commander himself," he croaked. "I have learned such an excellent lesson. I will most certainly be quiet now."

Per finally let go of Rameau when the cohorts came back with a squeeze of glucose and vitamins and a stack of protein crackers. Nothing was heard from the boy but the sound of crunching. The crackers were supposed to be noncrumbling, for use in micro g, but fragments soon formed a nebula around his perch.

"Won't you step into my office?" Rameau said to Gunnarsson. "We could talk more freely in private." With a sweep of his arm, he indicated the plant shed at the zenith of the dome. His voice was very soft now. He couldn't speak above a whisper, even if he had wanted to.

Reluctantly, the Commander followed him. They floated with their upper bodies tucked inside the shed room.

"Okay, I'm just going to tell you exactly what's important about the boy, before you do anything rash," Rameau said. He explained how the shipmind had accepted Per's bioscan.

"I assumed that you could use him as a shortcut to get in and reconfigure the shipmind's security protocols so you can use the whole mind." He didn't explain how he had already done that on his own behalf. "Therefore, you want to preserve him undamaged at least until I can finish examining him."

"Very well," Gunnarsson said. "He remains your responsibility until his utility has been exhausted. It is your mission to keep him under control. No further disruptions will be tolerated."

"Oh, fine. In that case, why don't you just terminate him now? I have enough to do already," Rameau said. "And I have a feeling the little monkey is one big floating disruption."

Gunnarsson shrugged. "As you point out, we can use him to break into the shipmind. After that, bring me your report on him, and I will reconsider a request to terminate him."

I'm not winning this game. But I mustn't make it seem as if I want the boy alive. If I do that, I might as well just put a gun to his head.

His sigh of frustration was exaggerated for the Commander's benefit, but it was sincere.

"I suppose I can put up with him that long. I really want to examine him. He may be useful in other ways.

"As for your connection to Vega's former inhabitants, I can see that you don't want that exposed, and I'll respect that."

Not that I'm about to stop prying . . .

"But you agreed to share information with me. And I know you're holding out. That wasn't the deal.

"I kept your casualties alive. I fed them. Now I've found you a way to get into the shipmind. I've kept my part of the bargain. But today, I was nearly killed by a monster I didn't know was there. If you want me to keep helping you, I need more information about this place."

"We do not yet know why Vega was not in functional condition," Gunnarsson said. "Any discussion would only yield guesses and rumors, and harm morale.

"The communications engineers will work with the 'boy' after the next sleep cycle. If we achieve access to the shipmind, you will be notified."

Rameau noted the disdain the Commander put into the word "boy." Original Man didn't start out as boys or girls; they were considered juveniles until they were fully trained, and then they became cohorts. Even if they were only ten years old.

Per might be older than Neb.

After the Commander left, Rameau turned to the problem of getting Per cleaned up. Wherever he went, he carried his own debris field around with him. Now that more of the production systems had been returned to working order, Rameau had access to some basic medical and maintenance supplies, as well as to food. He requested a stack of disinfectant-soaked cleansing pads. Per had gone beyond the limits of sonic dry-cleaning.

The cohorts watched with interest as Rameau hung Per on a rack and started cleaning him, beginning at the feet. His nails were like claws, and had to be trimmed with plant clippers from the garden shed.

The hair was another problem. Rameau secured a portable waldo bag to Per's head. Then he reset the clippers and used them to trim Per's matted tangle down to the scalp. Even though the hair was already snarled into clumps, stray bits escaped when Rameau removed the bag, and caused an outbreak of sneezing among the watching cohorts.

By the time he finished, Rameau had assembled a big pile of trash to be recycled. The boy looked younger, more vulnerable, with his hair and nails gone. His skin was a pinkish color, not the patchy gray it had been. He hung from the rack like a skinned rabbit.

"I guess he should have some clothes," Rameau said. All they could bring him was a spare coverall that would have held several sibs Per's size. Rameau chopped off the sleeves and legs with the clippers, and slashed the sides so he could roughly overlap the slits and glue the extra fabric into place. Per was not grateful for the result.

"Itches," he said, twisting irritably inside the makeshift garment.

"You wear that anyway," Rameau said. "And from now on, you use the cleansing booths like the cohorts."

He finished off the boy's outfit by punching extra holes in a cohort's gear belt and strapping it around Per's waist, not for Per's convenience, but for extra ease in keeping hold of him.

By the time the job was done, Rameau was exhausted.

"Okay, everybody in this section is on sleep cycle," he said. "So let's sleep."

The plants were still drinking in the concentrated sunlight from the lenses, so there could be no darkness. But the tired cohorts tethered themselves in the section where the foliage was thickest. Rameau found a place to sleep alone, higher up the dome.

He was shaken by his confrontation with Gunnarsson, as well as by the sinué's attack.

Every time I think I've made a truce with him, I say something that sets him off again. Today I provoked him deliberately. That's dangerous.

But he didn't regret his action.

I have to keep challenging him, keep him off balance. It's worth it to know that something on Vega is a secret, even from his own crew.

But that didn't make it any easier to sleep. And as soon as he closed his eyes, he felt something bumping against his back.

"Get away," he said sternly. "Go sleep over there."

Per curled himself into a tight ball, from which a piteous keening emerged. Rameau pushed him away. The boy instantly uncurled and caught a handhold that brought him back to Rameau's side.

"Take me back," he said. "I want to go back to my place."

"That's not your place anymore," Rameau said. "The cohorts are in charge now. We obey their orders. You have to stay here."

The boy cried louder, wiping snot across his recently cleaned face.

"I want the big people," he said. "I want to see them."

As exasperated as he was, Rameau was curious.

"You mean the ones on the screen?"

"Yes. Every sleep I see them. They talk to me. I want them now!"

"Oh, merciful Kannon," Rameau said wearily.

He goes to sleep watching instruction tapes, Rameau thought. *That's the only human contact he's had in—how long?*

Per watched Rameau narrowly. "You talk," he suggested. "Tell about tool kit number seventeen!"

The discussion had drawn Neb's attention.

"Rameau has more stories?" he asked, edging nearer.

"What's stories?" Per said.

"A story is like . . . it's like an instruction tape," Rameau said, thinking it through as he spoke. "It shows you pictures in your mind. It tells you about things you haven't seen. And it's like a sim, too. In a story you can try a different way of seeing, a different way of doing things, and think about how it might work out."

He wondered if he was making any sense to them.

"Tell," Per said simply.

But Rameau felt resistance rising inside. It had been all right to tell a story on *Langstaff*, when he thought he was going to die. He hadn't intended to make a habit of it.

I told her stories. They were personal—between us.

But Per and Neb drew closer, their eyes pleading. He'd told Dakini stories to take her mind off her imprisonment. Here on Vega, they were all prisoners of their situation.

"Okay, if I can think of one." He cast around for something that would interest them.

"What kind of picture do you have in your mind right now?"

"Monster," the boy said succinctly.

"Of course. The sinué. Well . . . in Noreuropa, on Sol-Terra, where my parents are from—where I was incepted—they had stories about a monster that was very much like a sinué. It was huge and long and very old, and its mouth was wide and deep. They called it a *dragon*. It was worse than the sinué, because it could pour out fire from its jaws and burn you to a cinder, even while you were trying to fly away.

"The dragon would come to all the places where humans were living and burn them up, and take all their treasures—all the things made of bright metal, all the valuable tools and weapons. But this was on a planet, not in a ship or a station. So instead of living in the corridor, the dragon lived in a cave—a dark place inside the planet. It only came out in the dark, and fell on the humans and burned them up."

Neb looked apprehensive. He and Nor floated together, hugging their knees.

"Well, there was an old transform called Reg. He was the kind of transform called a *dwarf*. They were strong and hairy like the Rukh, but short. Dwarves were the repair crew of the gods. They worked in dark places, fixing things and making tools. But this one had run away from his job somehow, and lived in a cube on his own. He wanted the metal things that the dragon had stolen. But he was afraid of the dragon.

"So he stole this boy named Sig. Or maybe it was an immature cohort. No one was sure. He ordered Sig to kill the dragon for him."

"Transform e no give order to cohort!" Neb interrupted indignantly. "Transform, e stupid!"

The other cohorts had gathered around to hear. They chorused agreement.

"That transform e give orders to cohort, e no go mo," one of them said. "That cohort e terminate transform."

"Just hang on," Rameau said. "Listen. You'll see why Sig did what he was told. You see, Sig was incepted as a fighter, but he had no weapons. If he killed the dragon, he knew he would get some fine weapons from the dragon's corridor. So he agreed to kill the dragon, if Reg could tell him how. Sig knew Reg had to be smart, so he would know how to fix things on the repair crew.

"Reg told Sig to find the corridor in the earth where the dragon came when he was hungry. He helped Sig dig a small pit right next to the corridor, and then Sig hid in it and waited."

"Like me," Per shouted. "I did that!"

"Well, there was one more thing that Sig did. He took a long, sharp knife that Reg had given him. When the dragon came down the corridor, Sig held his breath so the bad smell didn't choke him. He was scared, really terrified, but waited and waited until the dragon was right in the middle of the corridor, and his guts were right next to Sig's sharp knife. Then Sig pushed the knife through the skin and into the middle of the dragon.

"The dragon lashed around in the corridor, and his own mass pushed the knife farther in. The dragon's blood came boiling out and boiling out until he was dead! Then Sig jumped up out of the pit and told the transform that the dragon was dead.

"Reg was very happy. He said that Sig could have all the weapons and anything else that he wanted from the dragon's cube. But there was one thing Reg said he really wanted, and that was something to eat. He wanted to eat the dragon's heart. But it was time for his sleep cycle, so he asked Sig to cook the heart for him while he slept.

"Sig took the dragon's heart and lit a fire to heat it, just like we heated up those rats we ate.

"Now, he was sitting under a tree—kind of like these vines, but a lot bigger. Big enough to fill the whole dome. And in the tree, there were small life-forms, living there the way the leaf rats live here in the dome. They were called birds. They live on planets, where there's gravity, and they're the only life-forms that can fly there. All the other life-forms are stuck to the ground—the deck—but the birds can fly through the air. They can sing, too, but most of the time, humans can't understand what they're saying."

The cohorts were all staring.

"Error," one of them said. "This cohort e no ken what Rameau say."

"Yeah, I know you no ken," Rameau said. "But that's because you've never seen a planet. If you ever went to a planet's surface, you'd see hundreds of new life-forms.

"Anyway, the dragon heart got hot, and some of the juice popped out and burned Sig's hand. He put his finger in his mouth and licked off the juice, and all of a sudden he could understand what the birds were saying. There must have been a smart-virus in the juice, or something. Whatever the reason, he was very excited, and began to listen.

"And what do you think they were saying?"

Rameau paused to let them answer.

"Don't eat monster heart," Per said.

"No—just the opposite. The birds said that if Sig were to eat the dragon heart, it would make him able to understand the speech of birds and all the other life-forms. Then he would listen to their words, and know that Reg was planning to kill him before he could get any of the weapons.

"So he listened. And then, while Reg was sleeping, Sig took the long sharp knife and cut the transform with it, so he died. Then he took the metal things from the dragon's hoard."

"That cohort, e got weapons?" Neb said.

"Yes, he got outstanding weapons. Advanced, state-of-the-art weapons. He got a ring with a mind-control device in it, and a stealth helmet to make him invisible to scanners."

"Sig come out good," one of the cohorts said. "E terminate monster and bad transform. Story good for that cohort."

"Well, not entirely," Rameau said. "It was good then, but not so good later on. He ended up getting killed by his own sib."

"Story come out bad?" the cohort asked, puzzled.

"Sometimes it's hard to tell if a story is good or bad," Rameau said. "Sig was in a bad story from the word go. He was sent on a mission with no good ending. Sometimes that happens."

"It was a good story," Per insisted.

"Why?" Rameau asked, amused.

"Because he killed the monster," the boy said. "My monster is still alive. I like the dead monster better. Boy kills monster. Not monster kills boy."

Neb seemed to be thinking hard.

"In that other story, Rameau tells about lying to the officer," he said slowly.

Rameau winced inwardly. *I was hoping they'd forgotten that one.*

"What if birds lie to Sig?" Neb said. "Transform tries to help. Birds lie. Sig kills transform. Then this no story about cohort and monster. This story about listening to birds that lie.

"Birds tell story to cohort," he continued, the effort plain on his face. "They make story that lies. Before story, no lies. After story, always lying in the mind. And one dead transform. Too late to ask him which story is true."

Rameau's eyebrows rose. *This is getting out of control.* But he was fascinated, and couldn't leave it alone.

"You're right," he said. "Stories create things that weren't there before. This story about Sig put a new picture in Per's mind—one where the monster is dead—and that made him feel better. But it put another picture in your head, too."

"What?" Per said suspiciously, putting his hand to his head as if he could feel it there.

"Before the story, there was only one monster," Rameau said. "The sinué was in the ship, and the sinué was in your mind. Now the dragon is in your mind, too. There are two monsters. And while the sinué can die, the dragon can never die. He'll always be there."

"But the boy is there, too," Per said. "And he has the sharp knife. When the dragon comes, the boy will always be there to kill him."

"That's good," Rameau said. "Then you can go to sleep now. Let Sig stay up to watch for the dragon."

Reluctantly, the cohorts let the discussion die and found their way to comfortable sleeping stations. Rameau withdrew from them to find his own comfort zone.

But in his mind, there was no little hero to stand guard.

A story is a sharp knife, he thought. *I'm scrabbling for a weapon in the dragon's hoard, and it could all end badly. Humans have made monsters and set them roaming the corridors of the mind. We've made stories that can eat us. Stories that consume a world.*

He thought about the Original Man, now sleeping the sleep of the innocent, all around him.

Original Man were monsters, created by the minds of others. They never asked to play that role.

Blame it on the Founder and his wish for the perfect man. But what if it went further back than that? What if it was me and my kind who began to tell that story? Gunnarsson did the buying—but we were the engineers of his dream, the ones who put human faces, human minds, and bodies and loves and wishes up for sale. We told ourselves there would be no harm. We tasted the dragon's blood; we sang the lying song.

He was exhausted, but he didn't sleep well. And even when he finally dozed off, he awoke abruptly to find the sleeping Per bumping gently against him. After that, he lay awake for the rest of the cycle.

21

The next morning and after, the boy followed him around constantly. Rameau kept him on a leash, but it didn't seem to be necessary. He had expected Per to bolt at the first opportunity, but apparently the combination of big people and plenty of food was enough to keep him close.

Many of the noncritical wounded were ambulatory again, and needed only occasional monitoring. Rameau had shown them the rehabilitation exercises they needed. He still watched over the others, but he worked equally hard on biospherics and life support. Work served as an excuse to learn about the essential infrastructure. He was certain this station had been meant to provide self-contained, sophisticated life support and laboratories. Large areas remained unexplored, but the threatening presence of the sinué limited his searching. He wondered if Gunnarsson wanted it that way. So far, the Commander had made no move to eliminate the threat.

Rameau was thinking about this as he sorted through a newly discovered set of freeze-dried algae stocks. The cohorts had assembled another set of growth racks, and Rameau was trying to pick the best variant for incubation, all the while keeping Per from putting the spore packets in his mouth.

"What I really need is some seed grasses," Rameau said. "This much algae in the diet makes the cohorts fart like tunnel rats."

Per looked at him, astonished, then laughed. It was a surprisingly deep belly laugh to come from such a board-thin stomach. The boy paused to savor the joke, and laughed again.

I guess he hasn't heard many jokes in the last few years, either.

"Let's head back to the biosphere. It's time for morning rounds. We'll stop at the tanks and get another bag of glucose."

Rameau watched as Neb and Nor deftly replaced depleted drip bags of glucose solution, bending solicitously over their sib when they reached his resting place. Rameau noticed that they'd found a thermal wrap for Nuun, to protect him from drafts.

"How's he doing?" Rameau asked, out of habit. It was obvious that Nuun wasn't improving in any way.

Neb shrugged, a mannerism he seemed to have picked up from Rameau. "Nuun no ken this cohort here," he said. "This cohort think Commander recycle e soon."

Rameau bent to examine Nuun. "I won't let him—not as long as Nuun's still breathing."

Neb switched from ship jo into more formal speech. "He is the Commander," he said. "Neb and Rameau must obey."

"Don't be shocked," Rameau said. "I mean, I'll do what I can to change his mind. Is that better?"

He was distracted from his examination by Neb's evident distress.

"Why do you keep worrying about a nonfunctional cohort?" he said. "When the sinué ate that other cohort, his sibs just said 'Original Man is one,' and that was that. Doesn't Neb believe Original Man is one?"

"Yes, this cohort believe that," Neb said. "But . . . that cohort already terminate. Sibs no could do nothing. Neb still sees Nuun. Neb still wants Nuun to open eyes."

"Isn't it all the same, as long as you and Nor are alive? Doesn't Nuun continue in you?"

"This cohort know that is correct," Neb agreed. "But in here say not." He clenched his fist against his chest. "Disco wonder if maybe whole sib defective. Some have terminate, and others have this error inside. Maybe all should terminate. But Neb— Neb still want to continue, even if defective."

Rameau finished checking Nuun's vital signs. At the same time, he casually took a blood sample. "I don't think he can last much longer like this. Tell me, have you ever heard of a burned pilot being put in a stasis pod?"

Neb shook his head. "No. This cohort has seen pilot put in regeneration tank, but e no regenerate. Just stay always same until order come to terminate."

"Has any pilot ever recovered from being burned?"

"This cohort no ken. That never happen. They burn the pilot, e terminate."

Rameau looked at Nuun's slack face, and wondered what was going on behind that mask. Was the pilot's mind still operating, yet unable to connect? Or had his brain suffered a traumatic insult from which it never would recover?

If he'd had Nuun in a good hospital, with a brain scanner . . .

Crazy! I'm treating him as if he were a human being. He was created to be a pilot, and his usefulness has ended. He's a spare part. Not even "he," really.

But the cohorts looked so much like human beings.

Put eyes and a mouth on anything and we start to think of it as human. A dog, a stuffed toy, a rock, even. We project ourselves into the space behind the mask and imagine the other thing is just like us.

But they're not.

Still, it was possible that trying to help Nuun could pay off. Rameau had to motivate the Commander to eliminate the sinué, so he could return to Per's den and get access to the lab equipment there.

Otherwise, I'll have nothing to do but sit here and play with algae.

I have to get out into the station.

"There's a stasis pod in the room where I found Per," Rameau said. "It's not working, but there's no damage that I can see. I think it just needs to be resupplied and recalibrated. It might help Nuun, if we could fix it. Do you think you could handle that?"

"This cohort affiliate to medical, not—" Neb started to say. Then he paused, as if shifting gears. "This cohort affiliate to medical. Rameau is medical officer. If he order this cohort, fix pod, Neb will exert all possible effort. Ask permission, get Nor and tool kit."

"Permission granted. But don't go down there until I see the Commander, and get his permission to move Nuun and put him in stasis."

He could see the tension in them as they moved marginally closer to their sib's limp body. They feared for him. They did not believe the Commander would consider their sib worth preserving.

Rameau knew that he couldn't really protect Nuun. He might pretend defiance, but like the cohorts, he would ultimately do what he was told.

But before that happens, I'll use my baseline craftiness.

He ordered Neb to keep watch over Per, and left the dome alone, in spite of Per's protests. He crossed over into *Langstaff* to find the Commander.

I have to do this in person, so I'll be harder to get rid of. He can't just push a button and turn me off!

As he entered *Langstaff*, he was shocked to see how much remained to be done. He wondered if this twisted hulk would ever be flightworthy again. He passed cohort teams at work, but most of them didn't seem to be repairing the damaged decks and infrastructure. Instead, they were installing a thick, heavily shielded cable that stretched from deep in the core of *Langstaff* all the way through the docking bay and into Vega. They had to work without benefit of gravity. The artificial gravity field was still off-line, and *Langstaff* was still hard-docked to Vega and could not be spun.

The Rukh were everywhere on *Langstaff*, working on the heavy construction. That was why he hadn't seen any on the station. Rameau tried to avoid looking at them, or brushing past them too closely. It didn't help that the Rukh kept looking at him.

At first he thought it was just his own paranoid loathing of the creatures that made him think their eyes were following him. But then he found two of them hovering together. They turned as he went past, and he saw the dark gleam of their eyes, under the cavernous brows. They put their fingers to their lips—in unison, as if his presence had evoked some signal.

He was afraid they would move toward him. He felt choked, and tried to take a deep breath, but that was a mistake. It brought their thick, animal smell into his throat. He thought desperately of seizing a cohort weapon and firing at them. His heart finally beat wildly enough for the enabler to kick in and calm him. Then he moved on, and they didn't follow.

Gunnarsson was perched in the corridor outside the command nexus, overseeing the cable installation. He let Rameau wait for long, dragging minutes before speaking to him, without turning his head to look at him.

"Medical officer. State your request, and be brief. You interrupt a priority operation."

Good—maybe he'll say yes without thinking.

"It's a small thing. I'm sorry to bother you. I just want permission to move the burned pilot."

"To a regeneration tank?" Gunnarsson made a dismissive gesture. "Useless. Even if you've found one. The damage is in the mind, not the body. The pilot will not recover."

"No—not a regeneration tank. Neb thinks the stasis pod where the boy was hiding can be repaired. If so, I suggest placing the burned pilot in stasis to prolong his life.

"The cold will slow his metabolism, and the pod will monitor his body and tend it with nutrients. It's the only thing I can think of to try."

Gunnarsson paused and considered this.

"Permission to move him is granted," he said. "But not to the lab area. My personal hibernation pod is still functional. It will be installed in the pilot space, here on *Langstaff*. He can be placed there until our jump engines are working again. You and the remaining sibs must continue to monitor him."

"I thought you said he was useless and should be terminated." Frustrated and angry, Rameau spoke without forethought; he wanted to call back his words as soon as he heard them.

Damn it! Don't make him change his mind.

But the Commander appeared indifferent.

"He was useless in our former configuration. Conditions have changed. There is a possible use now."

Rameau scrambled to find some other way to get the access he wanted.

"But, sir, there are other reasons for returning to the space where the boy was found. It may contain useful equipment—facilities for performing a gene scan on the boy, for instance. You ordered me to do this, but it has been impossible because the sinué prevents safe access to the lab equipment."

"You will not refer to him as a 'boy,'" Gunnarsson stated flatly. "He is one of us—a juvenile, but still Original Man."

"How do you conclude that?" Rameau was startled enough to be distracted from his original goal. "He's phenotypically human. Where's the evidence that he's Original Man?"

Gunnarsson frowned. "This is not a question we discuss with baselines. You will accept my judgment."

Before Rameau could protest again, the Commander called out commands to the cable team, then moved Rameau out of the way with a brusque shove between the shoulder blades.

When he floated to a stop, Rameau persisted.

"You agreed to share data with me. You ordered me to examine this—what was it you called him? 'This very dirty little life-form'? Now you claim the dirty little life-form is Original Man. Why have you changed your mind?"

"I will attempt to explain it in terms a baseline can comprehend," Gunnarsson said stiffly. His voice held the usual thinly veiled contempt, but Rameau noticed that he was speaking more softly than usual, as if he didn't want their conversation to reach other ears.

He really doesn't *want to talk about this for some reason.* That was enough to make Rameau listen carefully.

"You baselines are divided between XY and XX forms, and therefore you reproduce at will, in random combinations, correct?"

"It was the last time I checked," Rameau said.

"Specific improvements made to Original Man no longer permit reproduction through random recombination. Occasionally an anomaly occurs, and genes from the Y chromosome that are normally suppressed in Original Man are expressed to such an extent that the resulting cohort reverts to baseline characteristics.

"We call them defectives, but they are Original Man nevertheless. It appears this juvenile is such an anomaly, though it gives me no pleasure to acknowledge the existence of a defective on Vega."

The explanation sounded convincing. Rameau felt disappointed. He had believed the child human. He'd wanted him to be human. Even though the boy was a nuisance, he made Rameau feel less alone.

But it's better this way. He's not human—that makes him their responsibility, not mine. One less thing to worry about.

"It is important that the juvenile should be recognized as Original Man," Gunnarsson said. "He is a singleton and a survivor of a failed crew. He requires the protection of Original Man to survive. If you designate him as a baseline, you jeopardize his survival."

His survival? Why is Gunnarsson so concerned about this?

Rameau couldn't resist baiting the Commander a little in an attempt to satisfy his curiosity.

"But I don't understand why the survival of an isolated individual matters one way or the other," he said. "Original Man is one, right? So this boy—this particular bundling of genes—isn't really significant. There are plenty more out there, somewhere."

Gunnarsson's gaze wavered slightly.

I am getting to him. I must be encroaching on some sensitive area.

"Did I not inform you that the Founder had a plan for Original Man that extended beyond his death?"

"You mentioned that possibility. But what does that have to do with this juvenile?"

"Try to use your mind!" Gunnarsson sounded genuinely frustrated. "As a baseline, you should understand this. Baselines tolerated Original Man only as long as we did not become too threatening. We were not self-replicating. Thus, in their view, we were controllable.

"The Founder, however, saw our inability to self-replicate as a defect. Before his death, it was rumored that he had been working on another metahuman variant. It is said that he had returned to working the baseline genome, in search of an improved variant that *would* be self-replicating. Many in the High Command questioned his purpose.

"Baselines are inferior. He was our Founder. He had no need to return to baseline engineering."

Rameau, to his surprise, heard bitterness in the Original Man's voice. *Like a child who wants to be his father's favorite, and suddenly suspects that he isn't.*

"At the time of his death, the Founder left us no information about these experiments. It was not known what he had done with his results. Then I received his final orders."

"He told you his experiments were taking place here, on Vega." Rameau dared to state it boldly, hoping to force an admission from the Commander.

But Gunnarsson was not so easily caught.

"It is not for you to know the content of the Founder's orders," he said. "But, yes, I learned this station existed, and I drew my own conclusions. Others in the High Command will have worked it out by now, especially since our flight. They will know that *Langstaff* would not have attempted escape without a destination."

"But what happened here?" Rameau said. "You can't have expected this—an empty station, nothing working, nobody here."

The pained look crossed Gunnarsson's face again.

"You promised me information," Rameau insisted. "Fulfill your agreement! What happened here?"

"It is not a simple explanation," Gunnarsson said. "Baselines are incepted for affiliation based on biological ties—is that not so?"

"Normally, humans are attached to their families," Rameau said. "If that's what you're trying to say."

"Yes, that and more. You bond with the larger group whose genes you share—a clan, a tribe, and so, in your past, states and nations gradually accreted."

"That's one theory," Rameau said.

"Original Man is also incepted for affiliation," Gunnarsson said. "Though our biological loyalties differ from yours. At the same time, we are trained for loyalty to a particular task. Based on tensions among these loyalties, factions form among groups.

This is a normal and logical stage in building a larger cohesion, just as baselines experienced tribal warfare as a stage in nation building. The Founder explained that it was so."

"Doubtless," Rameau murmured. Then he bit his tongue. He couldn't afford sarcasm now. He wanted Gunnarsson to continue unchecked. But the Commander missed the mockery.

"It seems clear that factional strife arose on this station. If it contained a mixed population of cohorts and other variants, the tension would have been extreme. Disagreements over the mission could have fractured consensus."

"I don't understand," Rameau said carefully. "What kind of conflict could cause disagreement among Original Man? Wouldn't the right answer have been obvious to their superior minds?"

Gunnarsson didn't seem to realize he was being played.

"A baseline might think so," he said. "But here, the mission involved fostering the improvement of a variant form. Some cohorts felt affiliation to this task. Others believed, like the High Command, that Original Man exists to foster Original Man— not to aid in his own possible replacement. I feel the conflict myself."

He stopped Rameau with a gesture, before he could ask another question.

"Enough. Factions exist. That is all you need to know to understand the importance of the juvenile's survival. He may represent a branch of work undertaken by the Founder. As such, his survival is necessary.

"However, he must be protected from factions who deny the validity of the Founder's legacy. Therefore, he is to be classified and spoken of as Original Man, however defective. Do you now understand?"

"I think so." Rameau thought he really did, this time.

Gunnarsson doesn't know if the boy is human or not. He suspects that he is one of the Founder's new engineered variants. But he needs me to pretend he's Original Man so the kid will be left alone and not draw unwanted, maybe dangerous attention.

"Then, by the terms of our agreement, you will now obey."

Rameau took a deep breath. He wasn't sure what would happen if he refused, but he had to.

"No, sir. It's not that simple. I need access to the lab area. If you can't give me a reason not to go there, I'm going to keep trying."

"Clearly, you have understood nothing." Gunnarsson's voice held tension and anger. "High Command will send a ship—a jumpfighter—to recapture this station. We must use all our efforts to escape that fate. Until then, we have no time to satisfy your curiosity. When we are safely in jump, we can discuss your questions.

"Until then, no cohort will assist you if you attempt to enter the unexplored area, and you are not to discuss this with any cohort. This is an order. Do you understand?"

Rameau lowered his gaze. "I understand that it's an order."

"If High Command reclaims us, you *will* understand," Gunnarsson said grimly. "You should hope that day never comes, baseline. Now bring the pilot here. And hurry."

"Yes, sir," Rameau muttered.

Time to appear to submit. Conciliate. But he had to ask one more question.

"Sir, I was just wondering about the cable. It goes right through the docking bay. You couldn't seal off the *Langstaff* without severing the cable. Isn't that dangerous?"

"Haven't you paid attention at all? We are moving *Langstaff* and the station, together. Vega has conventional engines, used to place it in orbit. We will use those to accelerate to jump speed. By the time we leave this system, *Langstaff*'s jump engines will be repaired. Vega will enter jump with us. The cable is necessary to synchronize the shipminds through the process."

Rameau was stunned. *I guess I* wasn't *paying attention,* he thought. *He said they were moving the station, but I had no idea how far.*

"Is that even possible?" he asked incredulously.

"Do not underestimate Original Man," Gunnarsson said. His face twitched in a brief, grim smile. "Baseline, you are dismissed."

22

Rameau sped back to Vega, passing the busy teams of cohorts. As he flew the corridors, he felt as if, once again, the ground had been pulled out from under him, and he'd been sent tumbling without a local vertical. Gunnarsson was playing on a scale that made humans seem irrelevant. Rameau was only one small piece in a game that wasn't his to win.

But I got part of what I wanted, he thought. *And I know what's coming. If Gunnarsson's right, sooner or later we'll clash with the High Command again.*

Yeah, and what am I going to do then? Fight on Gunnarsson's side? I have until then to find some way to strike a blow, and it sounds as if it won't be long.

Meanwhile, he still had to move Nuun without killing him. Neb and Nor guided Nuun's litter, carefully guarding him against jostling. Per followed along, pulling at a corner of Nuun's thermal wrap and copying all of the sibs' movements. Rameau watched the boy with a new eye after his talk with the Commander. He looked for any signs of unusual, engineered characteristics, but as far as he could see, Per was an ordinary human child. He was extraordinary only in the things he lacked.

When they reached the pilot space, Gunnarsson's team had installed the hibernation pod next to the old pilot gear. Neb and Nor lifted Nuun into the pod. Rameau checked his life signs. They were stable but faint, as they had been since the battle. Nuun had shown no sign of awareness as they moved him. Now he lay motionless, awaiting the influx of icy, nourishing gel.

To Rameau's surprise, Neb and Nor carefully replaced the hood and gauntlets on Nuun, working with a precision that approached reverence. They paused when they finished, and Rameau realized they were waiting for his approval.

"I can't tell you anything about cohort physiology," he said. "You're the experts here. I can only hope we've adjusted the life support system correctly."

"It is correct," Neb and Nor said together. "Pilot ken pilot."

"There's a small risk that thermal shock will kill him," Rameau said. "But if he survives the initial cooldown, he should be supported at that level almost indefinitely. But what is all this going to do?" He touched the input cables that led to the pilot helmet.

Neb and Nor looked at each other. "Close helmet on Nuun now," they said. "We show."

It bothered Rameau to close the featureless kemplex hood over Nuun's face and seal the lid of the stasis pod. It felt as if they were killing him and sealing his coffin. He watched the readings carefully as Nuun's temperature dropped and all the life signs slowed. The monitor showed no change in brain activity, however. Rameau might feel fear for him, but Nuun felt neither fear nor pain. He slept in a cold peace, in the twilight shallows of an eternal night.

The two sibs sighed in unison—relief.

"Commander think like this," Neb said. "Long as Nuun see no fear in pilot link, e go stay this way. Sleep, peace. If something come, Nuun go fear. E go try evade, even in sleep. Brain scan show activity; Commander know something come, got to evade."

"But how can he have any perceptions at all when he's like this?" Rameau asked.

"Find out, maybe," Neb said cautiously. "Commander order us, link with him."

Nor donned the link helmet and gloves, and Neb adjusted the inputs. Nor took a deep breath, and went limp.

For a moment, Rameau thought he was dead, and nearly sprang to tear the helmet from him. But then Nor's readouts joined Nuun's on the screen. His heart still beat, his breath still came and went. They settled slowly into a rhythm that subtly paced Nuun's. Nor's fingers danced briefly in their gauntlets.

Then they relaxed as well, and there was a deep silence in the crowded little room.

Neb pressed the nodes of Nor's kenner, and Rameau saw the brain waves shift again, into something more like wakefulness.

"What are you doing?" he said.

"This communicate with that cohort," he said. "And that cohort communicate with pilot. Link is . . . is . . ." He seemed to be searching for a word. "Thin," he finished. "Pilot and pilot jock no never see same thing. But pilot jock see enough to know where pilot go, what danger is there. And pilot jock can get kenner message from outside and show pilot where Commander say to go."

"I thought the pilot was the one who set the course," Rameau said. "I thought he was free to choose the path."

"No, pilot in too deep to choose," Neb said seriously. "Pilot see. E see too much. Someone else go decide. When pilot hold too many choices in mind, too many decisions at once, e burn. E no can hold all data."

"Can the pilot jock get burned, too?" Rameau asked.

"Possible," Neb said. "Almost Nor got burned, before. Leave link just in time. If Rameau stayed in that link, Rameau go burn mind for sure.

"Neb think Neb burn, too, if Neb try help. But e no can ken for sure. Neb could go back, help sibs, but e no got order. Neb then no got no story in mind, say cohort can disobey."

What is he saying? That he could have tried to help Nuun, but didn't? Is he actually suffering guilt and remorse?

Rameau looked more closely at Neb. The cohort's face seemed haunted, as if by some deep feeling. What it was, Rameau could not know.

No can ken for sure, as they would put it.

Neb looked back at him.

"Rameau made monster in Neb mind," he said. "In mind see many Nebs, many days. Each choose different. Sometimes Neb think e mind go burn, from stories."

His fingers played on Nor's kenner again.

"Time for Nor come back," he said. "This time e come back."

Nor stirred and swept his hands through the sim field in the "finish" gesture. His helmet parted, and he pulled off the gear. He seemed happy and refreshed, as if awakening from sleep.

"Nuun good," he said. "That cohort in sleep mode. Star field nominal. Just move slow, round and round."

"If ship come," Neb said, "feel like scream in quiet room. Like you drag sharp knife across hand. Spikes on monitor. You know it."

He held the helmet out to Rameau.

"Rameau try," he said.

Rameau was surprised by how much he wanted it. But—

"Isn't that dangerous?" he said. "You said yourself, I nearly got burned last time."

But if I could learn this—

Neb shrugged. "No problem with burn right now. Not in jump. No movement. Very quiet. Rameau see something last time. This cohort think e should look again. Be okay—Neb shut down if danger come."

It was stupid. It was too big a risk. But he reached for the helmet. The memory of those shifting planes of light was still seductive. He let Neb close the helmet over his head. Once again he was surprised by the feeling of being freed. He was in a big dark space. The air supplied to him was cool and refreshing.

Then he forgot the air. He began to feel himself as a point of light. Close to him, so close, almost overlapping, yet not the same, there was another. A silent point. All around them, mighty shapes were moving. The pattern of their motion seemed slow only because it was on such a vast scale.

As he focused on the masses closest to him, he suddenly realized he was not a motionless observer but a part of the movement. In an instant, he perceived himself hurtling, swinging out among forces great enough to crush him without thought. *He* was the slow one; they were furiously swift and dragged him in their train.

He gasped silently.

Then his vision ascended one more level, and there was no danger, no threat. For the pattern of motion harmonized perfectly. Each point, each line, each densely folded mass of moving particles, maintained a constant relation to all others. Their dance was a pattern eternally woven in place.

Like Nor, Rameau relaxed.

As his perceptions stretched out at ease with the pattern, he became aware again of the other point of light nearby. But it was no longer a point, as he was no longer a point. It was a pattern of its own—small and narrowly focused, compared to the great networks around him. He moved his own pattern closer to it, with a vague intention of creating an overlay like the overlays of matched DNA scans. Closer, closer . . .

Too close! He felt a shock like a jolt of electricity. All his senses buzzed painfully. He slipped momentarily out of sync with the great pattern, and felt his perceptions convulse as he tried to catch up and was yanked back into its spinning.

He left the other pattern alone and focused on relaxing again. He felt his heart pounding distantly, not as if it were a part of his body, but as if iron hammers clanged in his ears. Slowly that sensation eased. Then he approached the tiny pattern again. This time he kept space between them. Instead of closing on the little knot of brightness, he paced it as they swung through the mighty cycles together. He could sense it as it brightened, dimmed; brightened, dimmed . . .

Only then did he move his orbit gradually closer, until he felt something lock as their masses swung together around a common point. Rameau felt a deep inner satisfaction, a rightness in this touch.

He had forgotten that he was Rameau, or even that he was a single mind in a body of flesh. If he had been asked to translate his identity into words, he might have said, "We are one." But even the "we are" was fading, as the great worlds spinning on their journeys sang to him "one . . . one . . . one."

Then another sound entered his awareness. It was too loud—grating, disharmonious. It broke his concentration and tugged him back, away from his place in the dance. It rasped his perceptions like sandpaper on the skin, like bitter alum on the tongue. But it demanded his attention.

"Ra-meau. Ra-meau."

With deep dismay he remembered who he had been. An instant of memory was enough to hurl him out of the dance and send him falling back through planes of light that shattered against him like pale ice. He was thrown aside at tremendous speed, through stones and stars that hurtled toward and past him.

He came back gasping and convulsing as if he had dreamed of falling, and awakened as he hit the real, solid ground. Neb was opening the helmet that had enclosed him, and Nor lifted the gauntlets carefully away from his twitching hands.

Neb peered into his eyes. "Rameau okay?" He pulled Rameau out of the chair. Briefly, Rameau was paralyzed. The connection between mind and body seemed lost. Then it came back, and he struggled feebly.

"Let go. I'm fine." He fought to focus his eyes.

"Rameau did good, but maybe too far in," Neb said. "Rameau forgot name?"

"It was . . . intense," Rameau said. Already the memory was fading. He remembered the euphoric feeling, but he also remembered that he hadn't been in control, and that disturbed him.

To his surprise, Nuun's heart rate was up, and the cortical functions looked marginally more like sleep and less like coma.

"Rameau help Nuun," Neb said seriously. "Nuun getting better."

"Yeah . . . maybe. Watch him. If he comes up any further, you may have to drop his temperature a bit. The whole point of this was to maintain him in stasis, not raise his metabolic rate."

"Rameau must go back, help Nuun again," Neb said excitedly. "Maybe Nuun wakes up!" His eyes burned with determination. Rameau kicked himself backward, but ran into the wall. He was afraid that Neb would forcibly send him back. His experiment had worked too well.

"Listen," he said, "maybe you're right. Maybe contact will help Nuun recover. But not with me! I'm not the right person to work with him. He needs his sibs."

Neb hesitated.

"There's a story about that," Rameau said desperately, racking his memory for something appropriate as he spoke.

"Tell," Neb said instantly.

"Give me a minute!"

That story about the girl who eats poison fruit and falls asleep. No, the one who saved her was a prince from somewhere else. Neb might think that sounds too much like me. Uhh . . . The one about the girl who looks at her lover when he's sleeping and . . . too long and complicated.

Damn.

Neb looked impatient. Rameau feared he would abandon the whole idea and return to his original goal—putting Rameau back in the pilot interface.

I want to try again—but when I'm in control.

"Once a Commander and his first officer wanted to create a special pilot cohort," he said hastily. "They had seven different genedocs work on the embryo. Each one gave the cohort a special characteristic, and the cohort was just about perfect. Then a renegade genedoc showed up. He was angry because they hadn't hired him to work on the project. He got into the lab and gave the cohort one bad transformation.

"When the embryo grew to completion, it was taken out of the tank. Because it was an experiment, there was only one sib. They didn't clone a whole group. All the genedocs were there and announced the special characteristics of the new pilot sib. The renegade doc was there, too, and announced that no matter how wonderfully functional the new sib was, when he was locked into the pilot pod, he would die.

"Then the last and best of the genedocs came forward, and said he had noticed the anomaly in the embryo and had done his best to repair it. He couldn't fix it all the way, but he altered the genes so that when the sib went into the pod, he wouldn't die, but he would fall into a coma and never wake up."

"This true?" Neb interrupted. "Bad genedoc try to kill Nuun? Tell name; this cohort find e and terminate."

"No, no, this is a story," Rameau said. "Happened a long time ago, not to Nuun. I don't know the name of this genedoc, but he's probably been dead for a long time already."

Neb subsided, but an angry look remained on his face.

"The Commander decided to send the sib far away for training, to a place where he could never get into a pod, even by accident, while they tried to work out an answer to the problem. They gave him the persig Bri.

"He reached maturity, and was exploring some unused levels of the ship where he was training, when he found a pilot pod that wasn't being used. He was attracted to it, and he climbed in and put on the helmet."

"True," Neb said. "E pilot sib, e go want try pilot even if training not finished. This cohort see that happen. Pilot ken pilot."

"So . . . what do you think happened then?" Rameau asked.

"E go sleep like Nuun; e no never wake up," Neb said.

"That's right. Not only Bri, but all the cohorts on the ship went to sleep. The ship drifted away from its course. No one could find it. The plant forms in the biosphere grew and grew until they filled all the corridors and no one could have gone in, even if they had found the ship. In the middle of the wild bioforms, Bri and all the cohorts slept for a hundred years."

"Story come out bad," Neb said. "How this help Nuun?"

"Ah, well, wait a minute. In lots of stories, the worst part always comes just before things get better. While Bri had been training far away, the old Commander had another copy made from the Bri template. This time they locked the bad genedoc in the isolation cube so he couldn't interfere. So the new Bri sib came out just like the old one, but he could pilot without sleeping.

"The new sib went out to look for the old one, and because he was incepted as a great pilot, he was able to find the ship that had drifted for a hundred years. The plant forms from the ship were engineered to recognize Bri-sib genes, so they moved aside for the new Bri and let him through. He found the sleeping sib and—"

Now what? They don't kiss.

"Why stop? Tell!" Neb demanded.

"I have to think," Rameau said. "It's hard to translate. You see, baselines have a special kind of contact, called a 'kiss.' It's what a baseline would have done to wake the sib. But I don't know what Original Man would do.

"So I'm afraid I can't tell exactly what kind of contact it was. But I know that the new Bri-sib got into the pilot link and made contact with the Bri who was asleep. Then Bri woke up, and the whole ship woke up with him. There was a great celebration, and the sibs worked together to pilot the ship from then on."

Neb let out a long breath, as if he had been holding it the entire time.

"Story come out good. Okay, sibs try first, make contact with Nuun. Try find that kiss. Thank Rameau for idea."

23

Neb turned his attention back to Nuun, and Rameau felt like heaving a sigh of relief himself, but he saved it until he had left the pilot space. He felt that if he had gone back into the link so soon, he would have been in serious danger of losing his mind.

Like the sib in the story, he was attracted to the link in spite of the danger. Still, he knew that if he wanted to survive, he must resist that longing until he could gain control over his response.

Logic dictated that he resist his desire to return to the lab space, too. It seemed clear that Gunnarsson wanted the monster to remain on patrol until *Langstaff* was under way again. But knowing Gunnarsson had a secret only whetted Rameau's desire to explore the shipmind on his own. The sinué had never come far enough down Rat's Alley to be seen again. Rameau brooded over the danger.

It would be insane to go without protection. Yet Gunnarsson had forbidden cohorts to accompany him. He might persuade Neb to come along, but Neb alone was small protection.

There was an alternative. The Rukh.

No. Nothing is worth that.

But the thought nagged at him as he went about his tasks. He continued to monitor the surviving casualties, and each day he traveled to *Langstaff* to check on the pilot.

This has gone way beyond giving emergency assistance. You're working for Gunnarsson as if you were part of his crew. But you don't have the guts to find out what he's doing.

He couldn't put it off any longer. He approached Neb as they returned from a shift in the pilot space. The docking tube between *Langstaff* and Vega was the most private space available. Cohorts passed through; they didn't hang around and listen.

"Neb, suppose I needed a Rukh for a repair crew. How would I get it to obey me?"

"For combat, need control codes for collar. For work crew, just give order. Rameau is senior officer. He can command Rukh."

"Aren't they dangerous without the control codes?" Rameau asked.

"Sometime Rukh go bad, have to be terminated. But usually okay."

Neb glanced sideways at him. Even the cohorts had noticed that Rameau avoided the Rukh.

"Why Rameau need Rukh now?"

Rameau wasn't sure he could trust Neb—yet he needed the pilot to repair the stasis pod. It would be better to have Neb on his side.

"Here's what I'm thinking," he said. "I don't know how long the Commander will keep Nuun in stasis. He might order him unplugged from the pilot space when we go to jump. If we can fix the pod I found, we'd have a backup in case Nuun needs it."

"Rukh do construction," Neb said. "No ken pod diagnostics."

"Yes, that's what I was afraid of. For that, I'd need you. But you see, the Commander said no cohorts could escort me down the corridor where the sinué lives. I need the Rukh for protection."

"If Commander say no—" Neb began.

"He said 'no escorts,' Rameau broke in. "He didn't say you couldn't repair the pod."

Neb stopped himself in midflight to process this idea. At last he nodded.

"Rameau is right—no error," he said. "Disco get Rukh."

He turned back toward the ship.

Rameau continued into the biosphere, and pulled Per out of the vines where he was sleeping.

"We're going back to your old place," he said. "I want you to take us by the way you think is safest."

He no longer questioned Per's mental acuity. Certainly, Per knew Vega's layout better than any cohort.

Per looked scared, but did his best to negotiate.

"You give me a gun," he suggested hopefully.

"Guns are only for the cohorts," Rameau said, "but I'll give you a light. If you don't want to get eaten, make sure you lead us the right way."

Per tried to hide behind Rameau when Neb returned with a pair of armed Rukh. Rameau understood the feeling. He, too, had trouble standing his ground next to the massive transforms. But he hushed Per before the commotion could draw too much attention.

"Look how big they are," he said quickly. "They're monster-killers. They'll protect us. And if that doesn't work—well, the monster can eat them first! He'll be too full to want you and me, after that."

Per stopped struggling and gave a smothered laugh. Cautiously, Rameau loosed his grip on the boy, and removed his hand, unbitten.

The trip was shorter than it had seemed the first time. There was an ominous absence of rats, though, and the monster smell clung to the wider passages. Once Per made them huddle in an access tunnel until the boy's finely tuned senses confirmed that it was safe to continue. But they didn't see the sinué—or it didn't see them—and the Rukh never had to use their weapons.

With a sense of triumph, Rameau floated through the hatch and let it lock behind them. The cramped, dilapidated cube was unchanged since the last time he'd seen it. Per made a leap for the pod and huddled in it, hugging a comforting armful of his old rags. The smell hadn't faded much, either.

Rameau wished he could leave the Rukh outside. Their presence in the small room seemed to absorb all the space and air. But he feared that their scent in the corridor might actually attract the monster. He fought down his claustrophobia and tried to focus on his investigation.

First, he evicted Per from his nest and ordered Neb to start repairs. The cohort immersed himself immediately in the pod, only his long legs waving above it.

Rameau turned back to the kenner and screens. The ship-mind still responded to the identity he had created on his first visit. But the space was far too small and cramped to contain the sensing and analyzing panels he expected in any kind of auxiliary lab.

Whoever put Per here didn't pick the place at random, he thought. *They expected to monitor him. But if this is a lab, where are the scanners and sorters? Where's the sim tank?*

He opened or unfolded everything that had manual access, and found only conventional devices and empty storage. Then he combed the walls and lockers, flashing the "open" command with his kenner.

Nothing.

The walls were still coated with grime that held traces of everything that had ever happened here.

I could scan for cohort DNA. If the previous inhabitants had significant features in common with Original Man, the enabler should read the traces.

He swept his enabled hand back and forth across the curve of the wall. Immediately, he found a thick band of traces running around the walls roughly at the center line. That must be the route Per had used himself, hundreds of times.

He found a scattering of traces across the wall opposite the pod.

Probably just marks Per made in passing. He must have flown through here many times, hitting every flat surface with his hands and feet.

He moved slowly across the apparently blank wall behind the built-in kenner, and hit a motherlode of the traces he was searching for, so dense that his own little kenner screen glowed green with hundreds of hit points. The kenner built up a graph of the trace density for him. It was a spindle shape, like an oval with pointed ends. The most densely marked area formed a line down the middle.

As if there was an opening and those were its edges, where it was touched most often.

But the "open" command yielded no effect.

Rameau felt over the faintly curved surface with both hands. He thought he could feel a hairline seam in the smooth kemplex, too narrow to see with his naked eye. But there was no way to get a purchase on it, to pull it apart.

Okay, think like a cohort. Or try. A door with no console, no controls, no handles or studs to open it. What else do they use around here—or what else did they use, when the station was being built? Something a little old-fashioned maybe.

A blood key? But there's no sensor.

Maybe they used real blood.

He reset the enabler and swept his hand across the seam again. It registered old proteins, consistent with blood. He searched in Neb's kit for a tool that wasn't electronic, and was sharp enough to draw blood. He finally found a tiny nonlaser drill, and punctured his finger.

"Blood!" Per said in dismay, from the corner where he had curled up.

Rameau pushed back to the wall and ran the cut finger slowly along the invisible seam, where the old proteins were most dense. There was a clicking sound, and the wall folded back into itself, revealing a cube three times the size of Per's den. Neb emerged from the pod to watch curiously.

Light panels brightened at his presence. The cube wasn't really cubical; it was slightly wedge-shaped to fit the curve of the station's inner structure. The room was crammed with scanning panels, stacked consoles, and unfolding screens—a complete basic lab set condensed to fit neatly into this space.

Finally!

Faced with such riches, Rameau hardly knew where to start. There were so many questions he needed to answer.

Stick to the program. Find out what the boy is. All these things are here because of him; so find out why.

He wanted to compare Per's DNA to both Original Man and baseline genomes. He could use himself as one control, and his blood was already available. He placed his finger in the sample slot, and felt the quick sting and suction as it tasted him.

He would need a cohort for comparison, as well.

"Neb—come here. I need some of your blood."

Neb approached, though he looked apprehensive.

"Oh, relax. Just a drop. Well, maybe a couple of drops. But not a rat's worth. The machine takes one tiny little sip. It won't even hurt."

He made sure Per was watching. But even with Neb's stoic example, he had to chase Per around the room before he could get a blood sample. The boy fought back madly before Rameau managed to immobilize his hand and get one finger into the slot. Per nearly sampled Rameau, instead, as he tried repeatedly to bite.

Rameau heard the panel humming faintly as it sorted and scanned the components of the blood samples. While he waited for the complete analysis, he used the console to access the shipmind again. He searched for information about transforms. If Vega had been built as a haven, as Gunnarsson had claimed, the shipmind should contain records of the transforms' presence, and those files might be closely linked to the station's history and structure.

The first locus he opened was a treasure house. It revealed design parameters and techniques for a whole library of engineered entities. He unfolded the first design in the file—and then turned away from the screen for a minute. He didn't want to believe what he was seeing.

I must be reading this wrong. It's been too long since I've reviewed design schematics.

He tried running it in expanded form, as a hologram. That only made the conclusion more inescapable. This was the blueprint for creation of a sinué. The monster had been built—perhaps here, on Vega. Rameau searched desperately for markers indicating that it had been built from animal stocks, from a snake or a lizard. But, with increasing horror, he recognized the truth.

There was something in that eye that should have warned me.

The sinué was built from human stock. Very few of its genes were insertions. Most of the differences were based on tweaking of the homeobox. Without those interventions, it would have appeared no less human than the cohorts.

The structure of the brain had changed, as well, but it retained a cortex. In theory, it could think. It had no language, but it could hate. If it had a mind at all, it *must* hate. It would hate its creator, above all else.

The techniques that had been used were sophisticated and elegant. Rameau admired them, and that made him sick.

I could have done this myself. I would have done it pretty much like this. Oh, Kannon.

"What is that?" Per's voice said from behind his back.

Rameau's hand poised to slap the panel and make the vision disappear. But then he stopped.

What's the point? I can't make the monster go away.

"That shows how to build a sinué," he said.

Per peered into the holo tank.

"It looks like snakes," he said. "Two snakes. You make a sinué out of two snakes?"

"No. You make a sinué out of a human."

Per immediately pulled back, confused fear in his eyes.

"Not a boy like you. It's too late to twist you that far. You have to start when it's less than a baby, before the arms and legs have even begun. Those things aren't snakes. They're more like the nets we use for catching rats. You know the way the strings knot together to make the shape of a net?"

The boy nodded, his eyes still focused on the helix turning in the tank.

"This is like a net. It twists and ties these little strings inside you until you get the shape of a human. If you change the pattern, you get a different shape. Same thing with the sinué. Change the pattern just a little on the inside, and you get a big difference outside."

Per pinched his own thin arms, as if he might find a grotesque shape lurking under the flesh. Rameau reached out, trying to be reassuring. The boy dodged, kicked, and launched himself past the Rukh to cling to a bracket on the far wall. He glared angrily at Rameau.

"I don't like you here!" he yelled. "This is my place!"

Rameau saw the trapped look in the boy's eyes, and wished he could think of something comforting to say.

Alone for so long, and when people finally come, they bring more nightmares with them. He probably wonders if he's a monster, too.

"I don't like it here either," he said. "It's scary. But they can't do this to you, Per. You're not a monster, I promise. You're like me—look, I'll show you."

But Per refused to look at his scan, when Rameau put it on-screen with his own and Neb's. He was afraid to see.

For Rameau, it was a relief to turn away from the twisted vision to something closer to the human norm.

He expected to find clear indications to show whether the boy was an ordinary human child or an Original Man scion. But it wasn't that easy. Certain markers were found in all Original Man. Some, but not all of them, were present in Per's genome. Not enough for a cohort, but too many for a human. And many of the genes from the Y chromosome, inactivated in cohorts, were still expressed in Per—enough to make him look like a human male, perhaps enough to allow him to reproduce normally, when or if he reached puberty. That made him seem like a human. Yet, in certain areas where Neb's genes had definitely been tweaked, Per's were identical to the cohort's. Per and Neb had enough identical DNA to qualify them as relatives.

That isn't possible, unless they've both undergone the same transformations.

Rameau's own scan was even more perplexing. He didn't have the long identical stretches that marked the boy's genes and Neb's, but there were more matching loci than he would have expected to see. Most of them were found in areas that normally related to cortical function.

Kannon help me if I think like either of them.

His fingers itched for better equipment. This cube seemed to be equipped for keyboard access only. When he'd worked in the design lab on Varuna, he'd had direct access to the shipmind through a sim link that allowed him to visualize and manipulate VR genes at the molecular level. He turned his attention to searching for a better interface.

"Open, open, open," he flashed at the walls, patting them impatiently in search of another key.

The far corner of the wedge-shaped room held a promising bulge of kemplex—white, ovoid, about the size of a seated human being. But no matter what he did to it, he evoked no response.

Maybe it's just a structural feature after all.

He swept his hands across every surface. Everywhere he touched, his kenner registered traces of others who had been here before him. But nothing moved at his command.

Go on, bite me. Take another sample. Just open, damn it.

He twirled slowly, scanning all sides of the wedge-shaped space. Looking back at the console where he'd been working, he spotted two vertical slots, one on each side, like additional sampling slots.

He tried sticking a finger into one of them, but felt no contact. The slots were long enough to accept an entire hand. Warily, he slid his right hand into the right-hand opening. A dry but yielding surface brushed lightly against his palm, but nothing happened. Cautiously, he slid his enabled hand into the other slot. The fingers touched something that triggered a wild burst of response from his kenner. The light contact suddenly enclosed both hands tightly.

In reflexive fear, Rameau tried to snatch his hands back out of the slots, but the contact clung. Per, watching, whimpered in fear.

"Don't be afraid," Rameau said. "I'm just trying to get a better interface. So I can show you—"

He tugged harder, and his hands came free, tightly clad in gloves that seemed woven of hair-fine, glittering wire.

A new kind of sim gauntlet?

He swept his hands experimentally across the console, and a whole new set of function lights appeared. One light, at the front edge of the console, blinked yellow, and then steadied to green just above the twin notches of a double thumbblock.

It looks like a ready light.

In response, Rameau pressed his mesh-clad thumbs into the shallow depressions, and the console opened, presenting him with a semicircular band of hardware lined with the same micromesh that formed the gloves. It looked like sim gear, but lighter and more flexible than any he'd seen before—not a helmet, but a headband. He picked it up and slipped it on, a visor-shaped front end covering his eyes.

The walls and floor around him seemed to disappear. With the same jolt he'd felt when stepping out on the hull, he found himself surrounded by starry space—the same view he'd seen from *Langstaff*'s command nexus.

I'm in the shipmind. Kali Mat, what a beautiful interface.

He extended his right hand, palm outward, in the sim gesture that normally brought up a menu. Here, colored nodes and branching trees appeared, like a three-dimensional watershed of data gathering to an ever-greater stream. Each node he touched bloomed into another cluster of choices. He sifted the shipmind like a fisherman sweeping his net among bright fish. He stirred, beckoned, pointed, and the knowledge he summoned appeared in tangible forms.

Forgetting Per's genes in this waterfall of data, he followed the node he'd already opened, the one that led to the transforms. He found the command that would allow him to view their physical location.

At his order, the starry vastness misted and then cleared to show another open space, one Rameau had never seen before. The room was bigger than any other area he'd seen in the station, even the plant dome. Rows of glass-and-kemplex pods filled three-quarters of the wall space. Rameau fixed his eyes on those glistening ranks, and seemed to swoop through the empty volumes of air that lay between him and the pods.

Incredible luxury—so much cubic space, so much air and light, all wasted. Maybe they kept it pressurized in case some of them woke up. Whoever is sleeping here must have been important.

Rameau's heart beat so fast that the enabler kicked in, and he felt unnaturally calm as he brushed each pod with virtual fingers to request identification. Still some block seemed to prevent full access. He received only numerical codes that looked like cohort designations, and meant nothing to him.

Could all of these be only sleeping cohorts? Are they Per's "big people"—or Gunnarsson's youngest children?

He had to know. Heedless of danger now, he pressed on into the virtual heart of Vega.

There was one part of the room he hadn't checked on yet: the wall that seemed empty of pods. He touched the wall, and learned that it was made of thick transplex reinforced with metal mesh—an impenetrable barrier. But on the other side of the transplex lay a honeycomb of miniature storage cells. By their size and shape, he guessed they must hold frozen embryos—enough to plan a whole ecology.

Vega, he thought. Something about the name had nagged at him. Looking at this vault of unknown beings awaiting birth, he remembered that Noreuropan had been the Founder's first language, too. One of the old words—*Wiege*—would have been pronounced the same way: "vee-gah." But the meaning would be different. Not a bright star, but a cradle. Could the Commander have known this all along? Rameau extended his hand to point and unfold the files that would tell him what waited in the vault. But he couldn't grasp the node. It felt as if a wall of glass slid between the controls and his searching fingers.

Something is blocking access.

He was out of his depth; he'd never had any skill in penetrating security codes.

There must be some way to make it recognize me.

He pressed his palms against the virtual glass, and felt it give gently, as if his hands were sinking into the surface.

The wall became visible, and just beyond it, a figure appeared. But it wasn't anyone he'd wanted to see. It was Gunnarsson Prime.

He must have been using the shipmind at the same time, Rameau thought, trying desperately to free his hands from the smooth surface where they seemed embedded. *I must have done something that made me visible to him!*

It was too late. The Commander saw him. But he seemed more horrified than angry.

"What have you done?" he mouthed. *"What have you done?"*

Rameau tried to step back, out of the field, and close the shipmind behind him, but he couldn't move. As if in a nightmare, he felt a presence behind him, and could not turn around.

Then he heard the voices. The shipmind had been silent.
Now a confused, overlapping chorus, like the voices in blue
sleep, washed over him, bewildering and deafening. Someone
questioned him repeatedly. The insistent, demanding tones pen-
etrated his hearing, his mind, but he couldn't understand. He
couldn't answer. And still he was paralyzed, unable to flee.

Abruptly, the virtual field of the shipmind closed around
him, and he was back in the crowded cube, feeling the shock as
if he had fallen from a height. He swam weakly back to the console, and let the slots strip the mesh from his hands, leaving
them bare and vulnerable. He stowed the visor in its hiding
place.

He realized Neb and Per had been watching him the whole
time. As soon as the unfamiliar gear vanished, Per leapt across
the room and clung to him in fear.

"What Rameau see?" Neb said. "'E go deep in shipmind."

Rameau hung on to the console, breathing heavily. A sense
of dread still filled him like a dark tide, leaching away his
strength.

"I don't know," he said finally. "I felt as if I touched something in the shipmind. I woke it up. I don't know what it was,
but it was danger.

"We need to go back to the biosphere—now!"

For once, he outflew Neb, pursued by the fear that had
touched him in the shipmind. He feared Gunnarsson, too, but
he was driven by an overriding need to see the Commander and
find out what had happened.

They reached the lights of Rat's Alley, and everything
seemed normal.

Maybe it was nothing—all in my mind.

A few cohorts glanced toward them as they entered, but returned to their drill when they saw who it was. The baseline, the
extra juvenile, and the spare pilot apparently rated little notice.

Rameau slowed down. He felt foolish, yet the fear was still
with him. *Why?*

24

Then Gunnarsson emerged from the docking tube. Armed troops accompanied him, with a handful of Rukh in motley battle armor bringing up the rear. Rameau's stomach lurched as he flashed back to the attack on Varuna. He was ready to bolt into the darkness again.

No! he told himself, bracing to confront the Commander. *Face up to him. This is it. He's got to tell you what's happening—or shoot you,* he thought grimly.

But Gunnarsson seemed indifferent to his presence. He waved his troops off, with barked orders that Rameau could not understand. Only when they had scattered in all directions did he turn toward Rameau, and then his face was unreadable.

Before he could speak, a din of shouting and gunfire broke out from both ends of the corridor. By the time Rameau had turned to look, the Alley was already filling with more cohorts than he'd seen since Eyrie. Something was different about them, he thought confusedly. They wore clean, white uniforms adorned with medals and insignia, not the worn, grayish coveralls of *Langstaff.* They moved faster than his stumbling thoughts. Like all cohorts.

The din closed in, and now there was screaming in the same room with him. It came from Per, who now dangled upside down from a cohort's hand. He had just realized that when they seized him, too, in that hated, irresistible grip. Wrenching his arms behind his back, they turned him upside down as well. There wasn't enough weight for the position to be painful, but it was disorienting.

As he dangled like a chicken about to be plucked, he saw the

Langstaff crew drop their weapons and freeze in place with their hands raised high. It was surrender. But to whom?

"I'm an officer," he shouted.

Maybe that's a mistake, he thought too late. *Maybe they kill officers first.*

But he had to do something—try to save the boy, at least. One more try.

"I'm the medical officer! The boy is harmless—leave him alone."

That made them stop and rapidly consult. They spoke a ship jo, but not the kind he had learned to understand.

Out of the corner of his eye, he saw one of the *Langstaff* cohorts—Neb?—look up and start to turn toward him.

"Stay!" a deep, commanding voice barked. A shot sizzled neatly between Neb's head and his raised arm, missing each by inches, leaving a black mark on the tough wall behind him. Neb froze again, eyes down.

Another conference; then the cohorts holding Rameau bound his wrists and ankles painfully tight and floated him helplessly at the end of a tether. A body length away, he saw Per writhing in the same kind of binding, his face twisted with panic.

Several of the new, shiny cohorts took up guard positions. Others left the room, weapons ready. Rameau waited. Softly, he tried to reassure Per, but the boy seemed not to hear him, and when Rameau raised his voice a little, there was another shout of "Silence!" Per paid no attention; he kept screaming.

Please don't shoot him, Rameau willed at the guard. *Kannon, don't let them shoot him.*

Gradually, he realized that Per's raving had words in it, though they weren't immediately familiar.

Something about rats. No. Pirates. He's yelling "pirates"! He knows them. He's seen them before?

Upside down relative to his captors, he watched the new troops return, bringing the remnants of Gunnarsson's advance guard. The *Langstaff* cohorts who lived were bloodied and bound. Most were dead already. The new forces shoved their bodies aside in a lifeless tangle. Familiar scents filled the corridor again—scorched air, smoke, blood.

The Commander was one of the living—bound and carried upside down. Rameau thought he hated Gunnarsson. But when he saw the Commander as helpless as he was, he felt despair, as if some kind of protection had been removed.

Big lesson: things can get worse. Always. Things can always get worse.

One of the cohorts pointed his gun at Rameau.

"Is that the medical officer?" he asked. He spoke formally, though a little thickly.

"Yes," Gunnarsson said. "That is Rameau."

"Why do you call a baseline a medical officer?"

"We took losses in our last conflict. We have not been able to resupply with cohort personnel. And this baseline was recommended for salvage by the Founder himself. I attached him pursuant to the Founder's orders."

Gunnarsson managed to sound like an officer even when he was trussed up and inverted.

"I need to speak to your commander," he said.

"You will," the cohort replied. "Bring him, too." He gestured to Rameau.

Rameau's head spun as he was flipped over. Taking his cue from Gunnarsson, he tried to make his voice sound crisp and unafraid.

"Sir! Permission to speak!"

The cohort, as he had hoped, responded to his address and manner.

"Speak."

"The baseline suggests the officer place the juvenile with the other—"

What do I call them? Prisoners?

"With the other surrendered personnel. The noise will stop."

The cohort thought for two seconds. Then, with a gesture, he ordered Per to be cut loose and shoved to the side of the room with the other *Langstaff* prisoners. Per's outcries diminished to a breathless whimper.

The new cohorts had set up an impromptu command post at

the main communications node. They herded their captives there to join the rest of *Langstaff*'s crew under guard. Another perfect pale man perched above the console, wearing a uniform that matched the one Gunnarsson had been wearing when Rameau was dragged before him.

A certain lack of inventiveness to these situations.

He looked again, from the new cohort to Gunnarsson.

A certain lack of inventiveness there, too.

They looked remarkably alike, even more so than most cohorts. Rameau guessed they would have been identical except for the indefinable wear of a few additional years on Gunnarsson's face.

The new cohort seemed to have noticed it, too.

"You come from the Founder's lineage," he said.

"Gunnarsson Prime," the Commander said. He spoke proudly.

"I, too," the other said. "Gun Three, my persig." But he sounded more bored with it than anything else.

"There is no need for two Gunnarssons here, nor for two Commanders," he continued. "From now on, I will be addressed as Commander. You will use the persig Gunnarsson—if a persig is needed."

Even their names can be changed at will, Rameau thought. But Gunnarsson himself seemed to accept it without question.

"Permission to make a request?" Gunnarsson said.

"Speak."

"Will you allow me to issue orders for a general submission? I see that you have terminated several cohorts already. There is no need to further diminish Original Man. They will submit when ordered."

"Granted," the Commander said. "On condition they affiliate fully to my command."

"Accepted."

Gunnarsson floated to a point in front of and below the new Commander and issued rapid orders in ship jo. As one, the captured cohorts bowed to their captors. The guards lowered their weapons then, though they still kept them in the ready position.

The crew from *Langstaff* relaxed and were allowed to perch at ease. Last of all, Gunnarsson bowed to the Commander.

"May I ask the name of the new command?" he said.

For the first time, the Commander seemed less than perfectly self-assured.

"I command the Reunification Faction of this station," he said. "We were selected through conflict to command here."

What does that mean? "We fought and won"?

"This station was supplied with excessive numbers of experimental baselines. Reunification Faction determined it was in the interests of Original Man to return the baselines to control of the High Command."

"To whose control did the station affiliate before, if not High Command?" Gunnarsson said.

"You have no reason to know that," the Commander said. "And I remind you that you are now committed to further the interests of Reunification Faction, as defined by its Commander. Any contradictory actions would call into question the submission of your former crew."

"Yes, sir. This cohort obeys."

"Now let us discuss the question of your competencies and where you affiliate within my faction," Gun Three said.

His control isn't as good as Gunnarsson's. Or maybe he sees no need for it. He's arrogant, and it shows. Kannon, I would not have believed it possible to find anyone more arrogant than Gunnarsson.

"I am aware of preparations to move the station," the Commander said.

"We are now fully committed to the move," Gunnarsson said. "The station's position has already been altered."

"I have not countermanded your orders. We have awaited transportation home to Eyrie for many years. We won the conflict on Vega, but we were left without jump engines or pilots. We sent a message to High Command, then placed ourselves in stasis until certain parameters indicating presence of potential transportation were satisfied.

"Your entry into the shipmind awakened us. Now your ship will transport us back to Eyrie. Had you exercised more forethought, you might have deduced why a large force of cohorts was in stasis on the station, and taken steps to counteract our plan. Since you did not, you are unfit to command here."

"Yes, sir," Gunnarsson said. "Allow me to remind the Commander that *Langstaff* is still under repair, and that only two pilot sibs survive."

"Again, a lack of forethought," the Commander said, with obvious contempt. "You are unfit to command. There is no place for you in my crew. You are relieved of duty and placed in isolation, pending retraining when we reach Eyrie."

There was a perceptible pause before Gunnarsson answered. "Yes, sir." He looked as if he had been struck. "Will anyone . . . be assigned to me, sir?" he said in a low voice.

The Commander actually smiled.

"Yes. This baseline can attend you. He will suffer no danger of contamination."

He summoned a guard, and Gunnarsson was led away.

Finally Rameau understood what had happened.

"What have you done?" he said to me. I woke the cohorts. *Gunnarsson knew they were here. He knew why the station had been destroyed. That's why he wouldn't let me into the ship-mind. He was afraid they'd set a trap there. And I walked right into it.*

He felt naked now, a pawn in a game he'd once thought he could learn. He no longer had any idea what the rules were.

"You—baseline. You serve as medical officer?"

"Yes, sir." That seemed the safest response.

"We currently lack a medical officer. Until we resupply, you will serve ReUFac as medical officer. Inadequate performance will result in termination."

"Yes, sir."

"Now, baseline medical officer—I have seen damaged cohorts and transforms on my station, some too damaged to function, and others moving freely about the station. Explain the presence of defectives. Why were they not returned to full function, or terminated?"

"Quality medical care was unavailable. Some remain permanently damaged. But my former superior determined that they could be used even in less than full capacity. They perform basic tasks and free the fully functional for other missions. The medical officer respectfully suggests that this has worked well, and might be continued until resupply is possible. The medical officer monitors the damaged personnel."

Before Rameau even saw what was coming, the force of the blow had propelled him across the room to smash against the wall. The whole side of his face seemed on fire. Blood rushed into his mouth.

"Return to your position," the Commander said calmly.

Rameau tried to right his tumbling. He swallowed blood and tried not to be sick. He turned to face the Commander, as best he could.

O Compassionate One, help me. What did I do?

"Your suggestion is acceptable, baseline. But you referred to Gunnarsson Prime as your 'former superior.' Never forget that all Original Man are forever superior to you. There is no excuse for your lack of respect."

"Yes, sir," Rameau mumbled.

"Now, Medical Officer, I have a task for you."

He turned to one of the cohorts ranged at his side.

"This is my first officer. Persig Kir Ninety. Follow him and obey his orders. First Officer, return him to transform storage."

As he was towed again through the corridors, two guards fell in behind them. Rameau shook his head to cast off the tears that leaked from his bruised eye. He guessed why they were taking him back to the cold-storage bay.

There'll be more crying soon.

The impregnable mesh gate that had closed off the fourth wall stood open already when they reached it. Banks of frozen storage cubes had been pivoted aside to show another vault packed with pods, like a mortuary.

"You will supervise the revival of these transforms," the officer said. He touched a control stud, and one of the pods slid silently forward for examination. Rameau bent over it, but the lid was opaque and armor-sealed.

"There," the officer said. He indicated the controls on the side of the pod. Rameau touched the message panel, and the cube that recorded the pod's contents rose into visibility. An icy gel seemed to pulse through Rameau's veins, as if he had been put into a stasis pod himself.

The holo in the cube appeared harmless, at first glance. It was a child, of indeterminate sex, wearing a thin white shift. Its skin was pale, but not the healthy, flawless pallor of the cohorts. The child's skin had a livid tinge and was pocked with small, weeping sores. Thin, wispy hair imperfectly concealed the ugly scurf on its scalp. Its eyes were empty, its bluish lips drooped half-open.

"What is that?" Rameau whispered. But he knew. He had seen it before, on Varuna. The death child.

"This is a toxicant," the officer said. He seemed mildly surprised. "You are not familiar with that transform?"

"I've . . . seen it," Rameau said. Between horror and his swollen mouth, he could not raise his voice above a low rasp.

"You will revive twenty-four of these transforms," the officer said, "leaving the remaining twelve as a reserve. When you complete this task, you will revive additional bioweapons as required."

"I won't."

"Repeat," the cohort said, as if the words were so alien that he had not quite heard them.

Rameau had to take a couple of breaths before he could speak again.

"I won't. This transform is an abomination, and I will not revive it. I will have no part in its existence. I won't do it."

"The transforms are necessary for our defensive system," the officer said in a reasonable, explanatory voice. "In case we are attacked en route to Eyrie, all lines of defense must be fully functional. You must see the logic of this order."

"I can't," Rameau said. Even to himself, it sounded as if he were pleading. He knew what came next.

"You refuse a direct order?" The officer sounded as if he couldn't believe that was possible.

Rameau floated silent, head hanging. He had nothing more to say. He tried to stay in that moment as if it were his last, to savor the last few seconds of breathing, of seeing, of being without pain.

The officer sighed and pointed. The guards seized Rameau and ripped the sleeve off his coverall. Then they ripped the enabler from his arm. His skin tore like cloth. Blood splattered everywhere.

He screamed. He begged them incoherently to stop. He had no choice.

They beat him from head to foot, using all the special pressure points and fracture zones they'd been trained to recognize. They shattered him like an eggshell.

But they were inexperienced with baselines. They treated him as if he had the density and stamina of their own kind. They hit him too fast and too hard. His consciousness was shaken loose almost immediately, so that while he writhed and cried like a bloody animal, another part of himself saw it happening as if from a distant height. In the cohorts' merciless hands, his body was no more than a rat, a roach under someone's shoe.

But his distant soul grieved endlessly for the agony of all fragile flesh in the hands of its destroyers.

III
Ship of Monsters

I have never seen a greater monster or miracle in the world than myself.

> MICHEL EYQUEM DE MONTAIGNE,
> *Of Cripples*

What a chimera then is man! What a novelty! What a monster, what a chaos, what a contradiction, what a prodigy! Judge of all things, feeble worm of the earth, depository of truth, a sink of uncertainty and error, the glory and the shame of the universe.

> BLAISE PASCAL,
> *Pensées*, sect. VII, no. 434

25

He woke up as they were taking him out of a regeneration tank. He choked and spat nutrient gel. He had a vague feeling that it was blood, but when he blinked the thick fluid away, he saw that it was just more of the pinkish gel that covered his body, like amniotic fluid on a very large, late-term baby. *So they finally located the tanks*, he thought.

Suddenly he remembered why he had been in the tank, and who had put him there, and curled up, screaming once again, expecting the next blow to fall. His heart raced in terror, so hard it felt as if it would burst in his chest, and there was no enabler to quell it.

They hosed him down with cleansing spray. He floated, naked, in front of the new Commander. His body was perfect again. He felt the inside of his mouth with his newly healed tongue, and it was smooth again. One or two teeth seemed to be missing.

I suppose they didn't have time to regrow.

"You are ordered to revive the transforms," the Commander said.

They couldn't allow me even five minutes of peace in this body.

More cohorts were present, and some of them carried devices. He saw that out of the corner of his eye. He didn't want to look. The terror was back, and there was nothing but terror. His hands were clenched on his bare chest, pleading. But he managed to shake his head.

No.

The cohorts weren't stupid. They learned from failure and formed alternative hypotheses. They never beat him so hard again.

They tried burning; they tried cutting, flaying, electric shock, and smashing his kneecaps. He never had anything different to try. He screamed and screamed, and when they pushed his head into water he inhaled immediately.

But he always woke up on his way out of the tank. After he had been in the tank three or four times, he couldn't scream very loudly anymore.

The vocal cords need specific intervention. A general regen isn't enough to repair all the damage. Strange that everything else seems to work okay.

The first moment out of the tank was the worst, because he was fully conscious then, and that moment held the knowledge that it was all about to happen again. That it could stop. Having a choice was the worst agony he had ever suffered. Which was saying a great deal at that point.

He woke up again. It got worse every time. He didn't even bother to look, just closed his eyes immediately and crossed his arms over his face in vain defense. One of the cohorts pulled his arms down to his sides.

"Look at the Commander when he speaks," the cohort said.

"You must obey," the Commander said. "You cannot refuse. You understand that we can do this to you forever. With access to regeneration tanks, we can inflict painful but nonlethal damages indefinitely."

This is weakness in him. He's afraid of failure. Talking to me shows weakness.

Rameau found words.

"It won't work," he said. "You can keep my body going, but I'll lose my mind. Eventually I'll go crazy. Baselines are like that. I can feel it happening now."

There was a long pause. Rameau could feel himself trembling. He no longer had the strength to straighten his body completely from a fetal curl. Then he saw the last thing he had expected. Cohorts escorted Gunnarsson into the room.

"The baseline says that prolonged motivation will destroy his mental functionality," the Commander said. "Is this true?"

"To the best of my knowledge, it is, sir," Gunnarsson said cautiously. "Motivation is one of the problems encountered in working with baselines. Pain has an incalculable effect on them, one that goes beyond the physical trauma."

"You have experience with baselines," the Commander said. "You have one cycle to find an alternative motivation for this one. He must obey the order."

"Yes, sir," Gunnarsson said. "I will require the use of sick bay, and a couple of medtechs."

"Granted."

Rameau found himself back in the familiar surroundings of sick bay on *Langstaff*. He noted that the renovation was almost complete. But this time he was in the patient's position, strapped down on the portable litter. Gunnarsson had chosen Neb and Nor as his medtechs.

"Activate the recorder," Gunnarsson said. "Is it working properly?"

Of course it's working properly. Their equipment always works.

It seemed odd to Rameau that Gunnarsson would show any uncertainty. But the ex-Commander looked down at him with a strangely intense expression, as if he wished Rameau to gather some meaning from his words.

He wants me to know that we're on record. Why?

Gunnarsson didn't seem ready to begin immediately. He perched next to the head of the litter, looking down, as if he were thinking over his course of action.

"You feel strongly about this, it seems," Gunnarsson said. The comment was unexpected, but Rameau was willing to talk about anything if it would postpone the inevitable.

"Yes, I do. It is wrong to build beings from human genes and use them as tools."

"As if baselines haven't been doing that to each other all through their history! And you tended entertainment-class transforms on Varuna."

"That's how I know it was wrong."

"Typical baseline reasoning. It became wrong when you found it uncomfortable. We propose to change your mind by making it more uncomfortable to refuse."

"No! It was wrong. It was always wrong. I just didn't want to admit it."

Gunnarsson pushed himself from one wall to the other, the micro-g equivalent of pacing.

"If you no longer wish to employ your skills, we could arrange that, too. We can make your hands useless. Then you will feel no temptation to do anything that is 'wrong.' "

There was so much fear in Rameau now that he didn't think there was room for more, but it continued to grow. Fear creates its own words: "please" was the one that dashed frantically to and fro inside his head. But he wasn't going to let it out yet.

"I learned something about baselines while I was with the Founder," Gunnarsson said. "They reason only from particulars. Original Man is motivated by general principles, but baselines are motivated by specifics. If you can learn what one particular thing a baseline wants or fears, you control him. That is the difficulty, of course. Baselines are so irrational that they are hard to understand.

"But in this case, it is not so hard. Rameau affiliates to medical. The use of his skills is everything to him. In this, he is much like a cohort, and that is why I hope that we can still work with him. As a medical officer, he is aware that full rehabilitation of nerve tissue is problematic, and full restoration of fine motor skills can often be difficult. I believe Rameau would do a great deal to avoid the destruction of his hands."

He turned to Nor. "Cohort," the Commander said. "Show the medical officer what we can do to his hand. Left hand first."

Nor tightened the cuff that held Rameau's arm down until it was cutting into the blood supply. He attached a clamp that forced Rameau to extend his hand and would not permit him to curl the fingers in a protective fist.

"Neb," Rameau said, "don't let him do that. Neb, you affiliate to me. You're supposed to help cohorts, not cause injury." He tried to keep his voice level, but even to himself he sounded like a terrified child, after the Commander's calm, deep commands.

Neb's face twisted with apprehension, but he didn't move from his appointed station.

"Rameau is not a cohort," he said. "This cohort must obey the Commander."

Rameau was expecting cunningly cruel surgery. Instead, Neb braced his feet against a bracket and picked up a hammer.

The sheer shock of it froze Rameau for a moment. He was just opening his mouth to cry *"No!"* when the blow hit him, and the word turned into a scream. Even before the pain struck, he could feel all the little bones pop and the muscles tear from their moorings. Then Neb hit him again.

Rameau screamed and sobbed. There was no room for any thought of shame; there was no corner of his mind that wasn't exploding with pain. Pain wasn't new, but he never got used to it. And having this done to him by familiar faces made it worse, if anything could.

"Don't, don't, not again, no, no, no . . ."

Neb raised the hammer again.

"That's enough for now," Gunnarsson said. "Nor, elevate the hand and give the medical officer a good look."

Nor unlocked the clamp and raised Rameau's left arm, displaying what was left of his hand: a mess of splintered bones, yellow-and-white rags of skin and subcutaneous fat, all against a contrasting background of bright red blood pulsing everywhere.

Rameau had seen worse. But not at the end of his own arm.

"We can do this to your right hand, too," Gunnarsson said. "To your only original hand. Oh, don't worry. We can graft on another cloned hand. Perhaps, with practice, you will recover most of your skills." Nor stepped closer, ready for orders.

Rameau didn't know he was going to vomit until it happened. He just managed to turn his head to avoid choking.

Self-preservation. How mindlessly it works at the worst of times.

"Neb," Gunnarsson said. "Clean that up."

Neb handled his head gently, apologizing when he accidentally stuck his cheek with the suction tube.

It gave Rameau enough time to think. They could damage
his hands permanently. He knew that. An ordinary regen tank
couldn't cope with severe nerve damage, couldn't rebuild the
skill that had taken him years to learn. And the mere idea of losing his hands terrified him even more than another beating.

But if they destroyed his skill, they would lose, too. What
game was being played here?

Gunnarsson bent as if to examine the hand, turning his back
to the recorder.

"The recorder doesn't seem to be working now," he said, a
little too loudly. "Baseline!" he continued in a much softer
voice. "They'll use the boy against you if you don't submit now.
They saw that you were in charge of him. They will motivate
him for your benefit. I gave you a reason to submit before they
start on the boy. Take it. If you give in now, they'll think it was
the threat to your hands, and they won't think of using the boy."

He spoke swiftly, his lips hardly moving. Under cover of
Rameau's weeping, the words were almost inaudible.

O Kannon, O Compassionate One, oh, have mercy.

But there was no mercy. Rameau kept crying, to cover his
hesitation, but his despair had reached a depth that no outcry
could express.

*That's what he meant by all that garbage about specifics. He
meant that he knew I'd cave in for the boy, and if I didn't cave
now, for him, he'd tell the Faction Commander. Now he has his
own noose around my neck, and he can hand it to the others
whenever he wants to. He has a bargaining chip again.*

Rameau had never really believed that he had a soul, but he
could feel something inside him dying. He could feel himself
losing something that could never come back. If he gave in, he
would never be whole again.

But if he refused, he'd be sending a child to hell.

*Either way. That transform could have been a child, too. Ei-
ther way, I'm one of the devils now.*

He knew he had to surrender, but after resisting the words so long, he had trouble finding them again. Then a thought came to him that seemed to promise a solution to everything.

Give in now. You can kill yourself later.

"I—will obey," he gasped.

Gunnarsson was close enough that Rameau could see the tensed muscles relax in the cohort's arm. Gunnarsson turned to the other cohorts.

"Learn a further truth about baselines," he said. "They have imagination in place of certainty. Our certainties serve us well. Their imaginations can be turned against them."

He signed to Neb to put down the hammer.

"We are finished here," he said. "Get the bleeding under control and put him back in the tank. I want him ready to go to work as soon as possible."

"I hate you," Rameau whispered. "You and all your kind. I listened to you talk. I came to believe that maybe it wasn't your fault that all those people died on Varuna, on Garuda. That maybe you weren't involved, that you were different.

"I know better now. You're all killers. And I will find some way to bring you down. You and all your kind."

"I do not hate you, Medical Officer Rameau," Gunnarsson said calmly. "I only regret that we must take such extreme measures to induce you to do your duty."

This time they didn't keep him in the tank long. They wanted him to eat. His body was starving. The circulating nutrients in the tank hadn't had time to replace all the elements used up in producing new tissues. Under threat of an implant, he forced himself to choke down rations. And they gave him back his enabler.

It helped his hand to heal faster, but more important to Rameau, it smoothed out everything. It let him sleep, or just trance out, for long periods. He hoped his hand would never heal, and that he'd be able to stare at the wall forever.

But the cohorts were impatient. They came to get him long before he was completely well. They enclosed his hand in a cushioned splint, filled with healing gel and wired to send electrical pulses through the splintered bones to encourage their mending. In micro g, he could move about without jarring the hand unbearably, if he was careful.

They escorted him back to the cold-storage bay. The first officer was present again. Rameau understood. They had to recreate the whole scene and make sure he did it right this time. This was symbolic. The serious work would begin later.

When the order was given again, he said "Yes, sir," and moved to the pod's controls.

Reviving a toxicant was difficult for many reasons. He knew the problems, at least in theory. All genedocs had studied the basic weapon transforms; so many of the techniques were used in ordinary commercial transforms, as well. As a student, Rameau had never been able to resist an elegant solution.

My first bite of the poisoned fruit.

Virulent organisms lived symbiotically within the toxicants, and it was important not to let them regain vitality ahead of schedule. Restraining factors in the transform's metabolism had to work at equal strength, or the host body would be overcome by its inhabitants. And the tricky final warming had to be done in complete containment, with the transform remaining lightly sedated until it could be transferred to a sealed holding tank.

Rameau lost himself in the process, in the details, as he had always done. He tried to view the body that lay before him as an alien, possessing only a faint resemblance to a human being. Working with just one hand added difficulty to the problem, but his understanding of the shipmind helped. And he was grateful for the enabler. Without its feverish incitement to spur him on, he wouldn't have had the strength.

When it was finished, he had to cling to the edge of the litter as he accompanied his newest patient to the holding tank. The toxicant was cloaked in its airshroud, the inside beaded with condensation. All cohorts had been cleared from the route they followed, all hatches sealed, for fear of contamination.

And I will do this twenty-three more times.

Then he remembered.

No, I won't. I'll be dead soon.

The cohorts had been busy while he had been regenerating. They had prepared sealed holding tanks near the outer hull, enough for two dozen toxicants and numerous sinué, enough for other things, as well. They must have assumed he would give in.

Of course. They always win. They can't imagine a baseline standing in their way.

They transferred the toxicant through the lock. The air-shroud opened. The pale childlike figure stirred inside the shroud and struggled feebly free from its folds, like a white moth emerging from its cocoon. It propelled itself to the back of the tank and curled in the darkest corner, showing no curiosity about the humanoids who were staring at it. An air current sucked the shroud away for disposal. It would be converted immediately, at temperatures resembling the interior of the sun.

"Baseline, you have performed well," the first officer said. "You may return to your sleep cycle."

"This baseline usually sleeps in the plant dome, with the other damaged personnel," Rameau said. "If this is permitted."

"Granted," the officer said, waving them away. Rameau wobbled in the air as he followed the cohorts to the dome. He made it to the door and waited until they left before dragging himself inside.

He crept around the edges of the dome into the shadow side, pulling himself along, one-handed, through the vine stems. More cohorts were sleeping in the dome than he remembered. The moss and leaves under his nose smelled good—organic and green.

But another smell, a dark fur smell, moved toward him like a groping paw. It was the Rukh smell. It reminded him of the large-animal labs on Garuda, but without any mitigating trace of disinfectant. It was rich, layered, and full, like a dark cake of many spices. He could hear their sleeping breath, resonant and deep.

Their presence choked him. While he had been gone, the Rukh had invaded his refuge.

It doesn't matter. I'll be dead soon.

The nearest Rukh rolled toward him and opened one eye. Its large hand, thick-fingered, furred with ginger tufts above the knuckles, moved toward its mouth, and the breath modulated to a hum, a burr, as the fingers slowly crossed and pointed. The Rukh unfolded its arm with massive care, to show Per curled into the space next to its ribs.

Rameau's mind was so crammed with violence that he thought it was showing him Per's body. He was certain the boy was dead. A sick heat pierced his stomach. Had they saved the body to show him? Did they want to gloat over their kill?

Then the boy shifted slightly and whimpered, nuzzling deeper into fur.

They were just trying to comfort him. They wanted me to know he was all right.

Any act of kindness was more than he could fathom. He turned away, his heart full of bitterness.

I'm disappointed. Yes, truly. I hoped *for a moment that he was dead. Then my responsibility would have ended. That's what I've come to—wishing a child dead, to ease my mind.*

But it's all right. I'll be dead soon.

Something to look forward to.

It was the one thought that let him sleep.

26

He woke up with a jerk, thinking that he had just come out of the tank again. He had rolled himself reflexively into a ball before he remembered where he was. He uncurled cautiously, and was surprised to see that no guards were posted, either on him or on the room itself. It looked as if the station had returned to normal.

He saw a cohort watering a bank of amaranth nearby. A few others, farther off, were busy with other tasks. He didn't recognize any of them. Neb and Nor were absent, and that was good. He didn't want to see them. They had become familiar to him. He had started to think of them as companions, almost as friends. But they were no more his friends than a rock with a face painted on it. And in the right hands they were just as ready to hurt him.

A bell sounded, and the cohorts put down their tools and headed for the door. Rameau wondered vaguely where they were going. It didn't occur to him to follow, until one of them came back and reached for his sleeve. He recoiled violently. Surprised by his reaction, the cohort waited for him to uncurl from his defensive posture.

"Rameau must attend ceremony," he said.

"Oh, no. No. I'm not going anywhere."

"Rameau must come," the cohort insisted. "Transformation ceremony for cohorts who terminate. All must come."

Rameau looked around the dome and realized why it looked so clean and spacious. There were no more injured cohorts waiting to recuperate.

"Where are they?" he said. There must have been something frightening in his voice, for the cohort moved back.

"Functional cohorts return to duty."

"And the others?"

"Rameau, you come now."

And Rameau followed him. It was better than being dragged.

He found himself in the cold-storage bay again. The Faction Commander presided over rows of cohorts in clean uniforms. Rameau and his escort filled in the last row, where he recognized many of the *Langstaff* survivors. The Faction cohorts, unscarred, in their clean, undamaged uniforms, filled the front ranks. A line of shrink-wrapped cohort bodies floated front and center, between the rows.

Those were my patients.

Just below the Commander's perch lay a circular hole, like an open hatch. Rameau bobbed up to peer between the tall bodies blocking his view, and saw trash bots beginning to tow the bodies, with inanimate decorum, as the Commander came to the end of the speech he had been giving.

"Outside the will of Original Man there is no life," he intoned. It had the sound of a ritual. "Within the consensus of Original Man, there is no death. These members of the body have given their all for our common life.

"Now they go to be transformed in the purity of fire, to offer us life in another form. All power comes from Original Man. We are one."

"Original Man is one," the cohorts repeated.

The lead bot nudged the first body dead center into the waiting opening, like a projectile fired straight to the heart of the target. The bot veered away, making room for the next. Reflections gleamed fitfully on the edges of the opening, hinting at an energy source within. Then the bodies were gone, and the hole in the decking closed.

The Faction cohorts jetted away, still in perfect array. The *Langstaff* cohorts trailed behind in smaller groups.

"Work cycle now," Rameau's escort said.

And Rameau was left hanging alone. There were others in

the big room—his Faction assistants, waiting for him to get to work, a couple of Rukh performing routine maintenance—but he was alone with his memories of all the dead. Now that included a dozen cohorts whose pain he had known very well, but whose names he'd never heard. The Faction hadn't considered them worth healing.

Anyway it doesn't matter. I'll be dead soon.

The ceremony had given him an idea. The conversion chute looked like a simple exit. An elegant solution. The other trash hatches weren't big enough, but this one was cohort-sized and would easily accept him.

But as he worked through his shift, a less pleasant idea came to him. If he died like that, he'd be contributing his body mass to fuel Vega's return to High Command. In fact, if he died anywhere on the station, his fate would be the same.

It was the only way to remove himself from their control. To make sure they could never use him again. But it no longer seemed like enough.

He couldn't think what to do about it, though. Vega was invulnerable, like all the works of Original Man. Even cohort weapons couldn't scratch it. The station had already survived one combat between factions.

I'm a weapon maker, but I still know nothing about weapons.

Waiting for another toxicant to defrost, he stared numbly across the room, where the Rukh were slowly completing their task. The sharp smell of the kemplex patching compound they were using drifted toward him with the air currents. Two types of plastics had to be combined. The resulting mixture attained a high temperature, and had to be used before it cooled into its final shape. After that, it was stronger than steel. The fumes were toxic. That was probably why the Rukh were doing the job.

Mixing the compounds improperly could cause some ugly accidents—he'd dealt with the results. Generous amounts of energy were liberated—enough to sear flesh, but not enough to damage a structure like Vega.

But additions could be made that would render the kemplex a potent explosive.

He decided to live until his next shift, though it meant that he'd raise another toxicant into a travesty of life. Two packets of patching compound returned to the biosphere with him at the end of the cycle.

After that, he only had to go as far as the storage area adjacent to the food racks. On *Langstaff*, all the nutrient chemicals needed in the biosphere had been in permanent solution, in circulation.

But Vega could afford to keep backup supplies, in concentrated form. Rameau mixed what he needed and divided it neatly into packets. Then he cut up his sleep sack to make a vest, with the packets glued inside. The result fit easily under his oversized coverall.

None of his actions could escape notice in the biosphere.

"What are you making?" Per said.

"Something I need for work. Don't bother me."

Used to brusque dismissals from Rameau, Per wandered off to pester the Rukh.

He felt briefly guilty about Per, but his attempts to protect the boy had only highlighted him as a target.

When I'm gone, they won't have any special reason to hurt him. Gunnarsson won't be able to use him as a pawn anymore. He's better off with me out of the way.

When Per had gone, one of the cohorts came to watch him. That was the one thing he'd feared. Cohorts knew a great deal about weaponry. They might guess at his purpose. But this one said only, "Rameau be careful. That can hurt you."

When he had finished, he dressed again, feeling the weight of the vest on his shoulders. It might be better to wait until his next work cycle. Then his presence in the storage bay would be normal. On the other hand, during the off-cycle, his assistants wouldn't be there to interfere.

The boy is sleeping. Best to go now.

The one thing he didn't have was an ignition source. But he guessed that the conversion chamber applied flash heat at a very high temperature—probably enough to set the explosives off. He couldn't be sure he'd damage the station, even if he succeeded in blowing himself up. But he thought the chances were good that he'd make a hole in the conversion chute, even if he didn't damage the chamber itself. If he could slow them down, even a little, it would be an achievement. And if he couldn't . . . Well, he'd be past caring.

The big room seemed empty and quiet. He used his kenner to order the tube opened, and held on to the edge. The enabler sensed his agitation and made him feel very calm. He planned to pull himself in, then fire his thrusters.

Time to go.

He wondered how long it would take, and what it would feel like. *All I have to do is hit the thrusters, and the result is out of my hands.*

Still he hesitated. His body didn't want to give up. It begged for its life, this time from him. *I did my best for you,* it seemed to say. *I got well; I gave you back the power to think and to act.*

But he wouldn't listen. The only way to stop creating evil was to kill this body.

One jump. That's all.

No prayers. No thoughts. One jump.

He placed his fingers in position to press the studs, took a deep breath—

And flew. He hit something, hard, and it knocked the sense out of him.

What happened? Did I fire the thrusters too soon?

Am I dead?

I'm alive! O Kannon—

He hung against the wall of the cold-storage bay, pinned there by the heavy arm of one of the damaged Rukh.

"Let me go. Damn you! I order you—" He panted. It was all he could do just to take a breath.

I have to try again—just blast for it and jump—

But he couldn't move. The Rukh wouldn't even let him turn his head, let alone plunge to his death. Others had gathered in the room: another Rukh, more cohorts. Then the first officer, Kir Ninety, arrived.

"What's going on here?" the officer demanded.

"Nothing, sir—an accident—" Rameau panted. "Tell it to get off."

The Rukh couldn't speak. The officer looked from Rameau to the transform, then back to Rameau.

"Baseline, I did not see what you did, but I do not trust you.

"And you—Rukh—move away from the baseline."

At that, Rameau was turned loose. He drifted along the wall, found a handhold, and clung to it, rubbing his throat where the Rukh's hard forearm had cut into his windpipe.

The officer pointed his fist at the collar gleaming around the Rukh's neck.

"Whatever the baseline was doing, you should have prevented it earlier. This kind of disruption will not be tolerated."

He flashed the Rukh, and it convulsed with a deafening howl of pain. It flailed its massive fists as if it would charge the cohorts, but the pain prevented it. The cohorts laughed cheerfully. The officer shocked the Rukh again and again, until it tore at its own throat in agony.

Finally the cohorts had had enough. Kir Ninety lowered his arm.

"From now on, two Rukh will accompany the baseline at all times. Prevent him from deviating from his duties. Any failure will be punished."

The Rukh bowed its shaggy head to acknowledge the order, and the cohorts left. He was alone with the Rukh, and the other monsters still in storage. Two Rukh flanked him, towering over him, too close.

"Leave me alone," he pleaded, despairing. "I wanted to die. Why did you interfere?"

The one that had saved his life placed its hands together and bowed deeply—nothing like the perfunctory bob that signaled its obedience to the officer.

" 'A-'o," it rumbled, almost too deep to hear. " 'A-'o." As it mouthed the sounds, it put its fingers to its lips as if to shape the sounds to greater coherence. It tapped its chest with thick fingers, in a slow rhythm. Then it reached out and tapped Rameau. He tried to shrink away from it, but only bumped into the other one. Its hand rested on his chest for a minute, as if feeling for a pulse. Then it tapped again, in time to his pounding heart.

What could it mean?

" 'A-mo," it said. Again, massive fingers shaped precise signs next to its lips. " 'A-mo. Yiiv."

"Rameau"? Is that what it's trying to say? My name?

"Rameau," he repeated. " 'Rameau . . . live'?"

The creature nodded, all the while keeping its eyes fixed on him.

" 'Uh a shee'," it whispered. Again the fingers twitched beside the mouth.

" 'Uh," it reiterated, repeating the finger sign. It pointed to itself and its companion.

"Rukh," Rameau said.

God, it spoke to me. That finger gesture—it's some kind of sign, for the sounds they can't make. It said "Rukh . . . have—"

" 'Rukh have . . . speech.' "

"Ao." It was an affirmative, in a deep tone like the low notes of a bassoon.

The Rukh bent closer. " 'A-mo help Rukh," Rameau understood it to say. "Rukh help 'A-mo."

Then it said another word—Rameau struggled to understand, and finally made out "friend."

"No," he said helplessly. "No, never! Rukh killed her. You don't understand."

"Ao," the Rukh hummed again. It leaned closer until its deep-browed, lantern-jawed, misshapen face rose in front of Rameau's like a mountain range. It plucked at its collar, and he could see fresh burns from the shocks it had been given, and old scars radiating from the band of metal.

"Co'ar make . . . kill," the Rukh said, in a voice like a mountain speaking. "Rameau take off collar."

Already he understood its speech more clearly.

"Take off collar," it insisted. "Rameau will do it."

He could only shake his head, overwhelmed. "No. No, I can't. I wanted to die. You shouldn't have stopped me."

The Rukh leaned closer yet, and slowly extended one thick finger toward Rameau. It touched his forehead with the fingertip.

"Collar . . . in here," it said.

The Rukh straightened to its full height, looking down on him with an unfathomable expression. He thought there was pity in that look.

"Rukh . . . teach," it said, tapping its lips. And then it fell silent, as if it had never spoken, and led him out of the room.

Damn it, Rameau thought as he reentered the Dome and smelled the familiar scents of damp soil, fungicide, leaves, rat droppings, and Rukh. *I thought I'd left all this behind.*

The Rukh pushed him, not unkindly, into a convenient perch, and brought him a scoop of green, faintly spicy mush and a stack of protein crackers to eat it with. He needed the food, but he had to force himself to eat, like an old man who no longer savors the taste of life.

All his plans had crashed to a halt. He no longer harbored any hopes for the future, no matter how frail. At every turn, when he had confronted Original Man, he had failed.

They really are *superior—in strength, in weapons, in forethought; there's no way I can oppose them. They beat me every time.*

The Rukh who stood guard rumbled a deep warning that made him look up, toward the door. ReUFac cohorts, commanded by their first officer, herded a group of *Langstaff* crew members in plain coveralls into the dome. Rameau lost interest in his meal.

Kir Ninety found a perch from which he had a commanding view of the room, including Rameau.

"Baseline, I ordered you to return to your duties," he said. "Why are you not occupied in transform storage?"

"The officer can monitor my blood sugar levels if he wishes," Rameau said, extending his arm. "This baseline is not yet fully regenerated. I require frequent nourishment."

"Noted," the officer said. "An exception to the duty roster is granted. It is good that you are here. Your input is required.

"These are damaged cohorts from *Langstaff*'s complement," the officer continued. "They cannot work as combat troops, yet they remain ambulatory. Since the medical officer thinks they can be useful, it will be his mission to make use of them.

"If the effort is judged unsuccessful, they will be terminated, like the others."

He gestured to someone behind him, and Rameau turned to see. But his nose had already told him what was coming.

"These, too, are damaged." All the scarred Rukh had been gathered into one group, and they clustered at the door, their deep-set eyes looking about them warily, as if expecting a threat.

"No." He backed away. Seeing them all at once, blocking his escape, was too much.

The officer's arrogant face softened slightly, showing malicious pleasure at Rameau's discomfort.

"The Commander is aware of the baseline's dislike of the Rukh. But no cohort of Reunification Faction will work with defectives. If Rameau also refuses responsibility for them, he can choose to terminate them—and the dysfunctional cohorts as well. He may select assistants as needed, and perform the terminations himself."

Damn him. Damn him! Rameau thought. But by now he had learned enough to say nothing. *I wonder if Gunnarsson told him the best way to blackmail me.*

Kir Ninety beckoned to his guards, and turned to go.

"Wait—" Rameau croaked.

"No discussion. The decision is made. Your response is up to you."

He left Rameau facing the damaged cohorts, and the Rukh.

Rameau tried to convince himself that he could terminate them.

It would be justice, he argued. But he knew that these were not the Rukh who had destroyed Varuna. *Face it—they didn't kill her. You'll never find the ones who did.*

They're all the same, he protested silently. *These Rukh must have committed other atrocities, as bad or worse. They deserve to die.*

But he knew he couldn't do it. They were sentient beings, placed in his care. He couldn't harm them.

They spoke *to me. They asked me for help. Even in hell, I have to draw the line somewhere.*

With difficulty, he unclamped his fingers from the vine and moved toward the newcomers. He still couldn't look directly at the Rukh.

Kannon! I get sick just looking at them. But if I'm to prove they're useful, and keep them alive, I have to make them obey me.

He moved closer, staying above them so they'd have to look up, minimizing the height difference.

Cohorts first. At least they don't smell foul.

"I want your persigs," he said. He tried to bark it out authoritatively, but his voice broke.

Hopeless! There's no way I can impersonate a cohort. Not for a moment.

"Okay, let me try that again. I want to know your persigs. From now on, all cohorts will refer to each other by persig. You will call me Rameau. You affiliate to me. And to each other. We are all one team." ·

They gave him their persigs: short cohort barks, Mar and Tok and Den. Finally one cleared his throat, a hesitant sound unusual in a cohort.

"Rameau leader, team e name what?" he said.

Plant Men. Trash Bots. Tunnel Rats. How should I know what to call them?

"Remnants. Rameau's Reconstituted Remnants," he said, to his own surprise. As he looked at their patched and mended bodies, the words came to his lips without forethought.

"Recon . . . remat . . . ," the cohort said haltingly. "No ken say that."

"Just 'Remnants.' That's good enough. Now say it! Speak the name! *I can't hear you!*"

Soon he had them all shouting it. The Rukh watched silently.

"Now disco ken name," the cohort said. "Tell name e mean what?"

"Can mean the scraps, left-over junk," Rameau said. "Most likely, some think of us that way. But it also can mean what's left of the true. The core that gives birth to the new. A name is like a story—you have to decide what it means.

"Remember, this team is not named by function. We affiliate

to *all* functions. Anything on this station, we can do it. Understand?"

He felt a faint stirring of hope as he spoke.

It's true. With them I can cover the whole station.

He gestured to the waiting Rukh.

"They're part of our team, too," he said to the cohorts. "Transforms are not expendable. Got that? Not expendable."

Again he made them say it, made them repeat it until it looked as if they understood.

"You heard what the Commander said. They live; we live. No one's expendable."

That's not the idea the Commander was trying to get across. He was trying to back me into a corner. But if I can use it against him, I will.

Finally, he turned and addressed the Rukh directly. His mouth went dry, but he persisted.

"You have persigs?" No answer.

Idiot. Of course not.

"Rukh not have speech," said a cohort.

"Maybe not, but we do, and we have to be able to tell them apart."

He looked them over. With their patchwork of impromptu grafts and stitches, the Rukh were even more diverse than the damaged cohorts. The coat of hair that covered most of their bodies had grown back raggedly, bleached in splotches that patterned each one in a different way.

I guess I could call them Spot and Patches, and so on. But whatever they are, they're not animals. Monsters, maybe. But not pets.

He thought about naming them for famous monsters of old. Rakshasa. Typhon. Cerberus.

No. I have to call them something I can live with.

They seemed so huge, up close. He never got used to them. *Like towers walking around, like living monoliths.*

"Rukh are warriors, too," he said. "So I'm going to name you after the ancient cities of war."

He pointed to them each in turn.

"Stalingrad," he began. "Jericho. Nineveh, Uruk, Troy. Carthago,

Krak, Istanbul." He dredged up names from his memory for all the Rukh.

One of the cohorts muttered something.

"What? Speak up."

"Disco say, Rukh got better names. Longer. Better."

Now what am I going to do?

"Well . . . when we win a great victory together, then I'll let the cohorts pick their own names."

Now there's a promise I'll probably never have to keep.

To his surprise, the cohorts turned toward him almost as one, and there was a look in their eyes he'd never seen before in Original Man.

What is it?

Anticipation. They're thinking about the future.

"What mission?" a cohort said.

No—I have to stop thinking of them as "this cohort" or "that cohort." That one is . . . Tok.

I think.

"What mission e go first?" Tok said.

"Ah. Our first mission." There was too much to think about. Rameau needed time. He had been a leader of cohorts for less than half an hour. And half an hour before that, he'd been on his way to kill himself.

When in doubt . . . fake it.

"Your first mission is to hear and understand this story. Get comfortable. I mean, at ease."

One by one, they allowed themselves to drift into a relaxed curl, floating off at all angles.

Kali Mat! What should I tell them?

He didn't dare hesitate. He said the first thing that came into his mind.

"Okay. There were three sibs. The first two were sent on a special mission, but one after the other, they failed. And they were afraid to come back, afraid they'd be judged defective for not fulfilling their orders. So they went rogue."

There was a stir among the cohorts—looking at each other, punching each other's arms and legs.

I can never tell what's going to get them going. I guess it never occurred to them to avoid motivation. And it's not that easy to run away on a jumpship.

"When they didn't come back, the third sib went out to retrieve them, and complete the mission. But when he found them, they made fun of him, and said that if they couldn't fulfill the mission with all their training, then he could never succeed. Nonetheless, he wanted to try.

"Now, they were on a planet surface, so there were lots of natural life-forms around—not enhanced, just living wild. And the cohorts came to the nest of a colony organism—an anthill. Ants are this big." He showed them.

There were murmurs of disbelief.

"Dis ant e nanomachine?" another cohort asked—Ket, Rameau thought.

"No. They're self-organizing. Came before nano. Thousands of ants work together, to bring food and keep the anthill running. Like lots of cohorts working the ship, only smaller. It's a beautiful, organic system.

"But the rogue cohorts didn't care. The first sib wanted to crush the anthill with his foot, just to watch the ants try to run away. But the third sib, the one they thought was stupid, wouldn't let him.

" 'They are living things,' he said. 'I won't let you hurt them.' So they kept on going.

"After a while, they saw some ducks swimming in water. Ducks are birds—flying creatures, like the ones in the story about Sig. They taste good to eat—better than tunnel rats. By this time, the rogue sibs were hungry, so they wanted to kill the ducks and eat them.

"But again, the stupid sib wouldn't let them. 'They are living things,' he said. 'I won't let you kill them for food. You can eat some of my protein crackers instead.' "

"Sib e stupid for real," Ket said. "Rogue sibs right. Duty of Original Man is self-preservation. Other forms must serve."

"Well, that's what they thought," Rameau said. "But wait and see. The sibs kept traveling together, and they came to a beehive. Bees are like ants *and* like ducks. They're tiny, and form a collective organization, but they also can fly, and like ducks, they provide a food source. They manufacture a substance called honey that is very, very good to eat. It's sweet, like glucose solution, but tastes better. Bees are also like cohorts—they won't give up their resources without a fight. If someone tries to take their honey, they sting with poison and cause great pain.

"The rogue sibs wanted to take the honey. They thought they could build a fire underneath the bees' nest, and suffocate the bees with smoke. But the stupid sib wouldn't let them.

" 'Stop!' he said. 'They're living things. I won't let you kill them and rob them. You can drink my squeeze of glucose instead.' And so they continued on.

"Finally, they came to a big house. Have any of you ever seen a house?"

There was silence.

"Okay, it's a large structure, built on a planet surface. Humans live inside, like you live in the jumpship, or in this station. Some cohorts even live in houses. When he was a juvenile, the *Langstaff* Commander—Gunnarsson—lived in a house with the Founder."

Again there was a stir among the cohorts.

"Truth! He told me himself. But in this house, they found no human and no cohort. They looked in the ports, thinking they might see someone, or at least domestic animals like humans keep sometimes. And they did see animals, but these were made of stone. But that was all. No matter where they looked, they saw no other life-forms, until finally they found another one of those short, tricky transforms like in Sig's story—a dwarf.

"They knocked on the door—that means, they asked to come in—and the dwarf let them in and gave them food. They were tired, and he showed them where to sleep. Then, after their sleep cycle, he showed them what they would have to do to complete their mission.

"There were three specially designed metahumans, kept in stasis in a secret room. They were clones, and appeared identical, but through embryo surgery, each one had been given unique characteristics. The sibs had to choose the right one, wake it up, and bring it back to their ship.

"First, the sibs had to find the secret room. To do that, they needed a scanner built from one thousand microchips. But the scanner had been smashed and all the chips scattered. They were tiny, almost too small to see. The first sib set to work and tried to find all the chips, but at the end of the cycle, he had only found one hundred. That wasn't enough. He had failed. To discipline him for his failure, the dwarf used a transmutation device to turn him into stone.

"When the next cycle started, the second sib tried to find the chips. But it was so hard to see them and pick them up that he only found two hundred. That wasn't enough, and the dwarf turned him into stone.

"Now only the stupid sib was left. He tried to find the rest of the chips, but it was so hard that he knew he could never do it. He sat down and cried. Have any of you ever cried?"

"Disco no ken cry," Ket said.

"Extra liquid forms in your tear ducts. The tears are full of chemicals that aren't in the regular moisture of your eyes. The tears overflow and run down your face, and you make sad noises. It's an emotional reaction that helps balance your hormones, and sometimes elicits help from others. But baselines don't think about it in such a technical way. We just say we feel sad, and cry.

"Well, the stupid sib felt sad, and he cried. But while he sat there and cried, the Commander of the ants that he had saved heard him, and brought five thousand of his ant cohorts to help. The ants found all the microchips, and even put them together again so the scanner would work."

"Why e do that?" Tok asked.

"He was grateful. The sib helped him, so he wanted to help in return. To show that they were friends.

"So, now the stupid sib had a scanner. He searched the whole structure where the dwarf lived, and he found the hidden room where the metas they were looking for were kept. But the door was sealed.

"The second task was to find the coded transmitter that

would open the door. But the transmitter had fallen to the bottom of a deep tank of water—too deep to dive through without breathing gear. The stupid sib didn't have breathing gear. Still, he tried and tried, but he couldn't dive deep enough to get the transmitter.

"He was out in the middle of the water, gasping for air, when the ducks he had helped came swimming toward him. Ducks are good at diving, better than baselines or even cohorts. They dove down to the bottom of the tank, and brought back the transmitter.

"Then came the hardest part of the mission. The stupid sib opened the door, but when he did, the three metas inside looked exactly alike. The stupid sib had not been trained to perform a gene scan, so he didn't know how to identify the right meta.

"He knew just one thing about the metas: each of them had received a different nutritional supplement while they were in stasis. One was given plain nutrient gel, one was given glucose solution, and the one needed for the mission had been given honey. But the stupid sib didn't know which was which.

"Just then, the Commander of the bees flew to help him. Bees have very accurate senses. The Commander of the bees flew to the lips of each meta and tested them for chemical traces. He found the one that smelled like honey, and the stupid sib woke that one up.

"Then the meta ordered the dwarf to reverse the transmutation process and free all the beings who had been turned to stone. The stupid sib brought the prime meta back to his ship, where they combined their genetic material to create a whole new cohort group.

"So you see, the stupid sib's alliances with the flying and swimming life-forms enabled him to complete the mission. After that, they always called him the smart sib."

There was silence as the cohorts tried to wrap their minds around the story. Then the one called Den spoke.

"When Rameau tell story of Sig, e say story is like training tape. What is teaching in dis story?"

Rameau hedged. "One of the best things about stories is that each person can find a different teaching."

But the cohorts were too quick for him.

"What teaching Rameau see?"

Not to tell any more stories to cohorts, Rameau thought. But then he realized there was something he hadn't seen in this story before he told it in cohort language.

"Sometimes," he said slowly, "when one sib alone isn't strong enough, or smart enough, he can still win by working with a team. Small things can become great. This is a good thing for us to think about, because our team is still small.

"It also teaches that sleeping is a good thing! We should always sleep before we go on a mission."

While the cohorts scattered to their sleeping spots, Rameau pulled off his explosive vest and buried it under a layer of moss. It seemed a very long time since he'd put it on, sure that his troubles would soon be over.

When he curled up among the vines, he realized that Per wasn't next to him.

I guess he's used to sleeping with the Rukh now.

But when Rameau made a slow spin, searching for signs of the boy, he didn't see him.

"Has anyone seen Per?" he asked. But he was startled when one of the Rukh lifted a massive arm and pointed toward the zenith. He hadn't expected them to respond.

Up where the Rukh pointed, he saw toes sticking out from behind a sheaf of vines. The foot was hastily withdrawn, but a shaking in the leaves still revealed Per's hiding place.

Wearily, Rameau rummaged among the vines and fished Per out. The boy kicked, but halfheartedly.

"What's wrong? Why are you hiding? I want you where I can see you—with the rest of the team."

"I'm afraid of them!" Per wailed finally.

"What do you mean? You slept with the Rukh while I was away."

"The new ones. They're strange. They scare me."

Rameau looked down; the assembled group of scarred and hairy life-forms was frightening, he had to admit.

"The new Commander put me in charge of them," he said. "So you don't have to worry. None of them will hurt you now.

Anyone who looks messed up is going to be your friend. You only have to worry about the perfect ones."

But Rameau worried about the Remnants, far into the night cycle. His own words frightened him. He had named them, promised them a mission.

What the hell was I thinking? How will I carry out that promise?

Yet, when he finally slept, he dreamed of Dakini, for the first time in many nights. She danced in the deep void beyond the station. He tried to leap out to join her, but the Rukh wouldn't let him go, no matter how he fought or begged. He needed to explain to her why he'd turned down his chance to kill them for what they'd done to her. But he couldn't find the words.

It wasn't a nightmare, though. At the very end, just before he woke up, it seemed that she glanced back at him and smiled.

27

Morning brought him an answer to his question, in the form of a new problem. A squad of ReUFac guards arrived in the biosphere, and escorted him to the familiar hallway in front of the com node, which the Commander seemed to be using as a command nexus.

Or a throne room, Rameau thought sourly, summoning all his scorn as a barrier against the fear that rose in his throat as soon as he reached the spot where he'd been beaten so many times.

He had wanted above all to avoid bringing Per with him, but the boy had clenched his bony fists around Rameau's gear belt and hung on with grim determination. As a result, Per now hovered before the Faction Commander, too, though partially occulted by Rameau's body.

"The baseline Rameau has been designated as temporary chief of staff for biosupport and reproduction," the Commander said.

"That is correct," Rameau answered, in as neutral a voice as he could manage.

"He is now ordered to review holding tank accommodations and order any necessary additions for life support of a sinué. He must also calculate the dosage of anesthetic sufficient to subdue a large specimen without termination."

"Might the baseline inquire just which specimen we are discussing?" he said cautiously.

"The station holds an unusually large and valuable sinué. Acceleration would kill such a large specimen. Therefore, we must recapture it, for safekeeping, before the prejump burn."

"We," Rameau said. But his meaning was lost on the Commander, who merely waited for him to finish the sentence.

"What this baseline means to say is, when you—uh, when the Commander—says 'we,' does he include the medical officer?"

"Of course. You have seen and survived the sinué. You will provide guidance to determine the best way of trapping it. My cohorts have little experience with uncontrolled life-forms."

Now isn't that *the truth.*

"Kill it! Like the story!" Per shouted from his hiding place behind Rameau's back.

Rameau enjoyed the startled look that flashed across the Commander's face, but he quickly tried to hush Per. This was difficult, since the boy dodged back and forth, and couldn't be caught and quelled.

"No, we can't kill it," Rameau said. "Specifically not. The Commander has ordered it kept alive."

"Is it normal for the juvenile to speak without permission?" the Faction Commander said.

"As far as I recall, they are talkative," Rameau said. "They need to practice speaking. It is part of their training."

"Juvenile cohorts are trained to speak at specified times," the Commander said. "When receiving orders, they remain silent."

"Yet another superior feature," Rameau said gravely.

"I know how to kill it," Per insisted. "Like Sig. We can find where it comes to eat, and hide. And kill it."

The Commander looked directly at the boy, who promptly hid again.

"Medical Officer—determine the extent of the juvenile's knowledge, formulate a plan, and report to me. You will also select a team of your damaged personnel to work with you in capturing the sinué."

"Uh—the baseline obeys. But may I ask if my team will be issued weapons?"

He waited, trying to appear unconcerned about the reply. *If we had guns—*

"No. We cannot arm defectives."

"Then we need a squad of your cohorts to accompany us and

handle the weapons. As the expert on uncontrolled life-forms, I must advise you that, without weapons, our chances of success are very low."

And if you give me some armed cohorts, maybe I can at least find out where you keep the arms.

"No. My cohorts are not expendable. And I will not issue weapons to the capture team. If you found yourselves at risk, you would use them to save yourselves, and possibly sacrifice the specimen."

"And if we don't have weapons, my team might be sacrificed instead!" Rameau protested.

The Commander seemed surprised that Rameau would make such a pointless assertion.

"Of course. You are all expendable. That is why you have been given the assignment. If this team fails, another will be assigned. And so forth. But, at all costs, the sinué must be preserved. It is unusually large and has combat potential. I will order that you be issued tranquilizer guns and thrusters. No weapons."

When Rameau returned to the biosphere, cohorts had already delivered the equipment—a cargo net made of electroset mesh, full of tranquilizer guns and thruster packs. Rameau padded Per's thrusters, and tied them so they wouldn't slip off his skinny wrists and ankles. He also made the boy put on cohort chest armor, which covered him almost to his knees.

"You must not try to run away. If you do I'll take these things back."

Per practiced in the secure end of Rat's Alley under the lights. Before Rameau could stop him, he jetted toward the far end and disappeared into the darkness. Cursing him, Rameau took off to follow. He heard the boy's brief shriek of alarm. Then Per shot toward him out of the darkness. Apparently he had flipped into a turn without slowing.

"Slow down!" Rameau shouted, flexing his wrists to show the boy how to decelerate. Per turned to look, misaligned himself, and tumbled sideways into the wall. The thrusters cut off automatically, but his momentum carried him a long way before Rameau caught up with him and stopped him. He was shaken up but ecstatic.

"I like that!" he shouted. He seemed to take pleasure in saying everything as loudly as possible, now that he was no longer in hiding. "It's . . . it's—"

"Fun," Rameau suggested.

"Okay. Fun."

Once Per was used to the increased speed the thrusters gave him, he flew with easy skill. Rameau felt a twinge of envy, watching him dart through the corridors like a hummingbird. Rameau had been taught to fly by keeping his feet together and going in a straight line. Any turning motions were controlled with careful discipline. But Per flew naturally, using any of his four thrusters with equal ease. Even when he went in a straight line, he fired his foot thrusters alternately to create a zigzag, rocking motion—for no particular reason, just for fun.

Of course—he's been flying around this place for years. Flying is easy for him. Walking might be hard.

Rameau let Per continue to practice just outside the dome, while he called the Remnants to a strategy session inside.

Now I understand why the Faction Commander graciously gifted me with the "defectives." He had a mission for us that nobody else would want. He plans to use us up.

But Rameau wasn't going to let him win that easily. Surveying his cobbled-together Remnants, he was surprised to feel a kind of grim affection for them. He knew every inch of their skins—he'd put them back together piece by piece.

They're mine.

"Listen," he said, "the Commander has given us a mission he thinks no one can perform. He wants us to capture the monster and put it in a cage. He thinks we can't do it. I think we can.

"He won't give us weapons. But we have a secret weapon— our own Sig. He knows more about the monster than anyone."

He snagged Per on his next pass and hauled him inside for consultation.

The plan Rameau had in mind was simple: find the sinué, stun it with tranquilizer darts, and drag it into the holding tank. It sounded simple, but he knew the reality couldn't be that easy.

"This monster," he said to Per, "does it ever come out into the light?"

"Sometimes. But just to grab a rat, then go back."

"So it doesn't like bright lights."

"No," Per said. "That's why I like it here. Always light."

"So the only reason it would follow us would be to eat us, and only then if we turn off all the lights. I don't fancy that."

"Give him rats," Per said. "That's what he likes, when he can't get boy. He likes rats. When he's eating, you can sneak up on him."

"Where do we get rats?" Rameau said.

"I can show you."

"Good. First we'll have to decide who's going. Large numbers won't help with this mission. Stealth and speed will be more important."

Everyone volunteered. Rameau had to make a selection. He chose four Rukh: Stalingrad and Jericho, who were his own daily guardians, plus Nineveh and Carthago. He picked the cohorts who seemed the strongest and healthiest: Saf, Ket, Tok, and Jep.

Per led them far past Rat's Alley, down dark corridors where many cross-channels still stood open, and mazes of access tubes shrouded the larger tunnels. From a locker near one of the tunnel nodes, he retrieved a manually operated net made of electrical wire knotted together. He gathered it into a ball and flicked it out in a practice cast.

"Too small, e no catch monster," said Ket, who carried the heavy mesh cargo net on his back.

"I *know* that," Per said scornfully. "But I can catch plenty of rats. You'll see."

Per parked them near the node, in an access tunnel barely big enough for the small group, where they could perch on conduit cables and keep still.

"Be quiet," he breathed. "I usually see them here."

They waited for what felt like a long time, while Rameau's anxiety grew. What if the sinué found them first?

"You washed me too much," Per complained. "They can't smell me now. Do you have any food?"

Saf shamefacedly brought out a wad of meat-flavored algae cake he'd hoarded. To Rameau's nose, it didn't smell like meat, but it had a brown, salty scent strong enough to diffuse through the air. Per flitted down the corridor and crumbled the cake where the vent would blow its scent past them.

"If this doesn't work, we cut you and use *blood*," Per said in a ghoulish whisper.

It worked. In a few minutes they heard a faint chirping and rustling, a rattle of claws scratching walls as the tunnel rats bounced from edge to edge of the corridor in search of the tempting crumbs. Per activated a tiny hand light, giving just enough light to show the rats as silhouettes. He cast the net and gathered in a clump of half a dozen rats. Cursing, one of the cohorts trapped another one that had attached itself to his head. The rest scattered.

The cohort was cut, oozing a few drops of blood.

"That's good," Per whispered. "Now we'll get him for sure."

He took them farther into the maze, until Rameau was thoroughly lost. With his kenner and locator, he could have figured out his current position, but even so, it would have taken him a long time to find his way back to the secure parts of the station. Finally, they emerged into a wide, empty corridor where the ancient, evil smell was strong.

"Spread the net here," Per whispered. "He comes every day."

The cohorts rigged the net loosely around the corridor, close to the walls, leaving no obstacle to alert their prey. In midcorridor, they floated the squeaking net of rats.

"I used to do this every day," Per said. "I hunt rats down here; there are lots in the small tunnels where I can't go. When they come out—I get them. Most days *he* came along just when I finished up. That's when I used my trick. I'd let him have some rats, and while he was catching them, I'd get away."

"That's clever," Rameau said.

"Yes . . . but I don't know why he keeps coming here. At first I only saw him sometimes. But then he came every day almost, as if he knew I'm here. He can't know that, can he?"

"I don't know. Don't know if a sinué has a knowing mind or not."

While they waited, Rameau ran the scenario through his own imagination. This would be the most dangerous part, the open space where they passed through a corridor big enough to accommodate the monster.

Per would have to drag the rats ahead of the sinué, waiting until the last minute before he jerked his body into a turn and hurtled around the corner. At some point he would let go of the net. If he lost it too soon, he risked getting caught, trapped in the corridor, after the monster had vacuumed up the snacks he had provided.

Per fidgeted nervously.

"I have to go out there," he whispered. "Have to be in the right spot."

Rameau instinctively wanted to stop him. But the whole plan depended on the boy's being there at just the right time.

He knows the monster. I don't.

Per edged out into the darkness.

Kannon, that smell! Rameau thought. A moment later, with a rush, the huge body was upon them. At that moment he was certain the whole plan was stupid, lame, without a hope of success. Nothing could stand against a creature that size.

There was a muffled shriek from Per; the Remnants' portable beam lights flashed on, blinding Rameau as well as the sinué. He saw only one thing: one mad red eye looking sideways into his face, and the corner of the blood-smeared mouth. The monster's glance struck him like a bolt of electricity. It knew what he was; it hated him. If it could have reached him, it would have eaten him alive.

He heard its whistling scream as it hit the net. The Remnants triggered the mesh, sending an electrical pulse that snapped it tight around the thrashing body. More electricity sent the sinué into convulsive spasms, disrupting its nervous system as the Remnants fired stun bolts deep into its hide.

Rameau fired his tranquilizer gun just as the sinué's tail lashed sideways and slammed him against the corridor wall. The breath was crushed from his lungs.

He lost his hold on the gun and drifted helplessly forward along the sinué's flank. He struggled to move, to push himself away from the monster, but the blow from its tail had paralyzed him. The sinué rolled itself from side to side in the net, its jaws snapping. In seconds, Rameau would be within reach of those rows of teeth.

Then Ket launched himself in a dangerous trajectory from the opposite wall, just an arm's length from the gaping mouth. He collided with Rameau, and the momentum carried them tumbling back, out of harm's way.

But Nineveh had been clinging to the wall next to Ket. As the sinué thrashed in frustration, the side of its huge head caught him a glancing blow, just enough to knock him from his perch. He tried to catch himself, but failed, and Ket wasn't there to save him. Nineveh didn't have time to scream before the relentless maw gathered him in. It took him in two gulps, like a snake swallowing a frog. For a moment his legs were still visible; then they, too, disappeared.

The sinué was still swallowing when the tranquilizer finally took effect. It fell into a stupor with blood still drooling from its lips.

Rameau gasped. Finally air rushed back into his lungs. He gagged on the smell of slime and blood as Tok grasped his arm and pulled him away from the captured monster. The corridor smelled like a slaughterhouse. Per darted toward him, but did not cling to him as usual; Rameau's coverall was too slimed to touch.

"I got him!" Per exulted. "Did you see, Rameau? Did you see me? I'm Sig; I'm Sig!" He jaunted from side to side of the corridor, triumphing. "I just wish I had a long knife, though." He jabbed the air fiercely with his hand light.

Working quickly, the cohorts attached towing lines to the net. They pulled the stunned sinué back to the holding tank, thrusters on full. It took tricky maneuvering to get the monster through some of the narrower corridors. Though he felt shaky, Rameau took one of the ropes and pulled hard. He didn't want the Remnants to see his weakness.

Per led them. Whenever they hit a tunnel too narrow for their captive, he found a roundabout way that took them back in the right direction, until finally they burst out into the wide space in front of the holding tanks, under the astonished eyes of the Commander and two squads of ReUFac cohorts.

They pushed the sinué into the tank, peeled off the net, and closed the pressure door. It was a tight fit. They had underestimated the monster's size.

"Excellent," the Commander said. "The specimen is larger than anticipated. We'll enlarge the holding tank after jump." He looked at Rameau's stained coverall. "Any problems?"

"Ten of us went out, and only nine came back," Rameau said.

"You lost one of your defectives?"

Dark rage rose in Rameau, but he choked it back. Only the knowledge that others would suffer kept him from throwing himself on the Commander as he had once done to his predecessor.

"We lost one of our *team*," he said slowly. But the Commander didn't even notice.

"Was there any salvage?" he said.

Rameau shook his head, pointing to the beast and its stained mouth.

The Commander still seemed pleased. "One casualty is an acceptable price for this specimen."

Other, smaller sinué that Rameau had previously awakened from freezing thrashed angrily in their lesser tanks, striking the transplex with their tails. Rameau sympathized with them.

The Remnants reentered the dome as returning heroes. Though the Rukh were subdued by their loss, Rameau could see that the Remnant cohorts were inclined to move on without acknowledging it. Rukh had always been expendable.

If I let them keep thinking that way, it will split the group. I have to change that.

He called the group together. "You did well," he said. "Our first mission was a victory. We captured the sinué.

"But we lost something, too. Nineveh gave his life for us and the mission. Do you know what the ReUFac Commander said about him?"

He had their attention; all eyes were on him, cohorts as well as Rukh.

"He said, 'One casualty is an acceptable price.' Not to me it isn't. Not to *us*. Not one of us is expendable. There are no cohorts here, no Rukh, no baseline. Only the Remnants. And we stand by one another, the way Ket stood by me and saved me from getting eaten. Ket is a hero of our first mission. So is Nineveh. Remember Nineveh. He was the first to give his life for the Remnants. We honor him for that. And we will honor him by sticking together and staying alive."

He wished he could think of something he could do to ease the sting of death. He had no childhood memories of any soothing words or rituals to use now. His parents had treated innumerable poor and sick patients. When any of them died, the relatives had floated marigolds and candles in the river, burned incense, made offerings, chanted prayers. None of that would work here.

He could hear his mother's calm voice repeating, "All life is suffering, Piers. Causes are set in motion that we do not understand, and the result is suffering. We must bear it patiently, understanding that this, too, is illusion. This, too, will pass."

But I don't believe that; I can't believe it, he thought. *Nineveh wasn't an illusion. Nor was he a soulless thing with no more value than a toy. He was part of my team. It matters that he died. It matters.*

"We get new names now?" Saf asked tentatively. It shook Rameau out of his trance.

"No," he said. "Not yet. This was just our first mission. And it was something we did because the Faction ordered it. One day soon we'll have a *big* mission. One that's just for us. If we win then, you'll get new names. You'll know when that day comes."

He looked around the dome once more.

There must be something we could do. Carve his name, or—

He saw the newly generated plant forms, waiting to be planted in the spots he would carefully choose for them, and he knew what to do.

"For Nineveh, we're going to plant a tree," he said. "We'll tend it carefully, and it will give us oxygen. And whenever we see it, we'll remember him and give thanks. There are seedlings in the tray. Someone who was Nineveh's friend, choose the tree."

Troy bent over the tray and brought Rameau the seedling, cradling the delicate stem carefully in his powerful hands.

"Good choice," Rameau said. "This is a Meruvian broca tree. On a planet surface, it would grow higher than the top of this dome. Here, it can't get that big, but it will grow tall enough to give us sweet-tasting fruit. It's a good tree for him."

The cohorts had already built up a series of terraces, where the moss-grown substrate had taken hold. Once the carefully stunted trees were planted there, it would look almost like a real grove on a real hill. A place of refuge. Rameau scooped out a hollow in the rich growth mixture, added measured drops from the hose, tucked in the tree as if he folded a blanket around a sleeping friend.

He tried again to think of suitable words, but none were needed. The Rukh hovered, legs crossed, and began to hum. The first notes were almost too deep for human hearing. As each Rukh joined, harmonics and chords formed. Rameau could feel his own bones humming.

The cohorts did not join in. It was too soon for that. But they listened.

Rameau had created this moment, but he couldn't take part in it. The killing had shaken him. He could see over and over again the moment when Nineveh had fallen.

If Ket hadn't jumped to save me, Nineveh would have been all right. Ket would have caught him.

I took them out on that mission. I don't know what the hell I'm doing. I'm not qualified to lead monkeys on a string—certainly not a cohort squad.

He'd been responsible for Dakini's death, and now for Nineveh's. Yet he'd accepted the responsibility for all of them, and he saw no way to get out of it.

He had no group to calm his mind. He focused fiercely on the young plants instead. At least he could work with trees without causing pain. Their green silence gave him a measure of peace. The small adjustments and observations as he cared for them occupied his mind and gave the rest of him a little breathing space.

Nothing broke his calm until he felt the familiar nudge against his back. Per tugged his arm just as he was about to clip a yellowed leaf. The unexpected pressure nearly caused him to chop off a whole branch. He restrained himself from cursing the boy, and let go of the clippers, instead. "Why don't you go to sleep?" he asked.

"Can't sleep. Not tired."

"Then why don't you go sit with the Rukh?"

"I sat already. It's spooky—that sound they make."

He picked nervously at the tree roots. His hands were dirty, and they were trembling.

Of course he's upset. He just saw blood all over the corridor again.

"Why didn't they kill the monster?" Per said fiercely. "Son of bitches! I want him dead."

"Don't call them that," Rameau said. "You can get in big trouble for calling the Faction cohorts names."

"I see him coming out of the cage," Per muttered. "All the time, I see him. He's still hungry."

He stopped scrabbling in the dirt and clutched Rameau's arm with both hands.

"Rameau, tell a story. Come on, tell something. With a boy in it. But not with killing. Not with monsters."

Rameau groaned. *Veterinarian, rat catcher, baby-sitter. Why did I ever start this?* But he saw some of the cohorts glancing his way, too. They might even have sent Per over on purpose. They all wanted a story—something with a boy in it, and no monsters.

"Okay . . . This is the story about the luck child. That means a young sib with a story that always comes out good. There was this old genedoctor who had been trying all his life to create a special kind of cohort with special abilities. He hadn't been able to clone a whole cohort group; just one embryo survived and came out of the incubator okay. But he could tell from some special gene markers that this sib was incepted to be lucky. To have things come out good, no matter what happened.

"A cohort commander had docked his ship at the facility where the genedoctor worked. He heard people talking about the luck child. They said this sib was so lucky that they'd done a statistical extrapolation about his life and decided that he was going to take the Commander's ship from him when he achieved maturity.

"The Commander didn't like that idea at all. He wasn't going to give up his command to anybody. But he knew he couldn't just take the sib and terminate him, because there was baseline law on the facility and the baselines would have made trouble for him.

"So he went to the genedoctor's lab and offered him a huge sum of money for the immature luck child. He said he wanted to train the child himself. The genedoctor had spent all his money to equip the lab, and he thought it would be a good deal for the luck child to get officer training, so he took the money and gave the child to the Commander.

"And what do you think happened? Was that a good deal for the luck child?"

"Sure, sound good. E go be officer," Tok said.

"No!" Per said fiercely. "The Commander was going to terminate him!"

"Per is correct. The Commander decided to terminate the luck child so he'd never get the ship. He put him in a hibernation pod, stuck it in an escape vessel, and shot it off into space. And he thought that was the last he'd ever see of the luck child."

"Like me!" Per exclaimed. "They stuck me in a pod, too. And they never came back. Son of—"

"Shut up!" Rameau said hastily. "Anyway, it so happened that some asteroid catchers were passing by, and they grabbed the escape vessel along with the asteroids. They saw there was a well-formed juvenile in it, and they warmed him up and raised him to work on their ship.

"He had just reached maturity when the asteroid catchers docked at a facility where the Commander happened to have stopped to buy mass. His ship was orbiting near the facility, and he and his officers had come down to do some trading. The asteroid catchers sold some mass to the Commander, and he saw the luck child working with them.

" 'Where did you get that worker?' he asked. 'He looks like a meta.'

"They told him the whole story, and he realized this was the same luck child he'd tried to get rid of. So this time he asked if they would hire the luck child out to him to pilot a supply shuttle up to his ship. He said he had an important packet to send up. But what he really put in the sealed packet was a message cube addressed to his crew that said, 'Terminate him as soon as you see this.'

"The luck child started out in the shuttle, but his course computer failed, and he got lost. He set his beacon, and a pirate picked it up and took him on board the pirate vessel. They thought the sealed packet must be valuable, so they waited until the luck child was asleep, then ripped it open and found the message.

"They laughed and thought it was a big joke, but they didn't like cohorts or officers, so they decided to make a joke of their own. They put a different message cube inside and sealed the packet up again. In the morning they fixed the luck child's course computer and let him go.

"As soon as he got up to the ship, the Commander's officers opened the packet, and they found the message. But now it said, "As soon as he comes aboard, turn over command of the ship to him." So the luck child became Commander of the ship, just as it was predicted in the beginning. However many times the Commander tried to make the story come out bad, it always came out good."

"Always come out good," Per repeated, as if it were an incantation. He had stopped trembling.

"Can't come out good," Tok said. "Commander e go be mad, e find some way terminate that luck child."

"Well, he was mad," Rameau said. "And he tried again to make trouble for the luck child, but that's a story for another time. That part of the story has a monster in it. Sort of."

"What kind of a monster?" Per said.

"The devil and his grandmother."

"What kind of monster is that?" Per said.

"The devil in this story looked kind of like the Rukh, I guess. He had bushy hair and a beard. And a bad temper."

"Tell," Per nagged.

"No, not tonight. No monsters, remember?"

"But it came out good, right? Even with the devil?"

"Yes. Even with the devil. The luck child couldn't lose."

"Good story," Per said dreamily.

"Yeah, now you go to sleep. Let me get back to my trees."

This started with one story, Rameau thought. *Now it's out of control. They look to me for orders, answers, comfort. This is wrong. I never meant to be a weapon maker; I was not incepted for command. What am I going to do?*

As he shaped and trimmed the trees, leaf by leaf, the answer came to him through his fingers. Each tree had evolved for a different environment. They were never meant to grow here, in this steel island. But Rameau was shaping them to make life possible, even here. The broca tree would never tower into blue skies, but it would thrive and bear fruit where he planted it.

Change them, Rameau thought. *I can't get into their genes. But I can change how they're expressed. Transplant them out of Original Man. Subvert, contaminate, seduce.*

28

The Faction cohorts worked on repairing *Langstaff* and prepared for the burn that would take the joined ships out of orbit
into their jump trajectory. Rameau kept the Remnants at work
in the biosphere. He wanted to keep them together, away from
the others, and build in them an unspoken sense that they were
different.

*They're sense-deprived. They know nothing of other life-
forms: plants, animals, even bugs. That's why it's so easy for
them to feel superior. "Other forms must serve," indeed.*

He gave them nicknames and allowed them space to hoard
and stash food and small treasures.

Subvert, contaminate, seduce.

He put them to work culturing out as many types of plant genetic material as possible from all that was stored on Vega, from
plankton to Meruvian broca trees. With the Remnants to work
construction, he began to convert the plant dome into an inten-
sive garden where every inch of space was fertile. He included
open water storage for humidity, equipped with containment
membranes to allow vapor to disperse into the room while
keeping liquid inside. In the renovated space, the bare kemplex
or metal surfaces would be covered by living things, layered
and terraced into multilevel environments.

"We lay down this substrate-impregnated webbing," he explained to the Remnants who worked with him, "and then we'll
turn the bacteria and the thread-fungi loose on it. They'll create
a mat that can hold soil particles and nutrients and that will be
cohesive enough that the air won't be full of fragments.

"Before the bacteria polish off the original substrate, we put in a mixture of lichen, moss, and various tweaked cover plants with roots that spread out tenaciously. Most of these varieties can actually be eaten after some pretreatment with enzymes, although they're not very tasty."

He paused to help tug the heavy sheet of webbing across the wall. Per scrambled ahead of them, happily squeezing adhesive on the surface.

"After that comes the tricky part. I have to access the ship-mind to model the results I get, depending on which species I introduce first. The order makes a difference."

"Not same plants, same garden?" Tok said.

"No. They're not interchangeable. The order counts. Web comes out different, depending on which knot you tie first. It's the same with us, really. Much of what makes you and me different is in the relationships between genes, not in specific different genes. That's why the basic human set can make anything from Rukh to sinué with so little tweaking."

The Rukh lifted the webbing and pressed it into place while Rameau stopped to catch his breath.

"Maybe we'll try some competing mini-ecologies and see which one takes over. Anyway, we'll have to build some racks and terraces. That will be hard work. But after that comes the fun part, where we use grasses, shrubs, and even some trees. And to go with that, we're going to try some heterotrophic life-forms. Beings that eat plants, or even other animals. Small ones at first—worms, beetles, maybe even some ants."

"Like in the story," Per said. "Will they make me a scanner?"

"First we have to find out if they can thrive in micro g. Then we'll see."

"Why so much work?" Ket said, wiping off the sweat that clustered unpleasantly on his brow. "We eat algae and protein supplement. No eat trees, worms."

"Do you plan to stay in a ship always?" Rameau said. "Don't you ever want to see a planet surface? You've been living in a cage. You should know something about ecologies."

The construction kept them busy while Rameau was away at his work with the transforms. It made them seem necessary. More to the point, in Rameau's plan, it gave them plenty of excuses to be seen traveling the station corridors, carrying fertilizers and construction tools and heavy rolls of webbing. When he figured out what else he wanted them to carry, and where, the cohorts might have stopped noticing.

He worked through cycle after cycle in the storage bay and the holding tanks, creating nightmares. He worked feverishly in the dome afterward, on the twilight edge of the dark cycle, coaxing plant genes back to life, as if they could leach from the air the horror he'd brought into it in the waking hours. He spun stories for the Remnants whenever he was with them—anything to take their minds, and his, from the prisons that confined them.

He kept Per physically with him most of the time, to keep him out of trouble. But he let the ReUFac cohorts think that he had made a slave of the boy. He gave Per orders, made him work, kept him at arm's length. The ReUFac cohorts did not interfere with the affairs of baselines and defectives. He sometimes thought they found it amusing, as if he were a mongrel who, when kicked, took it out on a smaller cur.

Per seemed to believe this cover story, too, and to regard Rameau with more fear than affection. Sometimes Rameau felt a twinge of regret when the boy flinched from him. But it was best that way. The faintest hint that the human had any care for the lone juvenile could be fatal. And most of the time, Rameau was more than happy to turn aside from any contact.

In the daytime, he maintained a low profile while considering his next move. Along with the Remnants, the Commander had unwittingly given Rameau another gift. At last the sinué was gone, and the path to the lab in Per's den was clear. The Rukh would be the perfect escorts, because they'd never tell anyone what he'd been doing. He could solve two problems at once. It was time to speak to the Rukh.

Once he'd reached this decision, he asked the cohort who supervised him for permission to go the lab area to research a problem with the latest transform.

"The *Langstaff* commander allowed it," he said.

"The Rukh go with you," the cohort ordered.

The Rukh moved closer, as if threatening, and Rameau lowered his eyes humbly.

"Of course, sir."

Once that was established, the cohort seemed uninterested in what the baseline did during his off-cycle. He waved them off.

Safely out of earshot, Rameau turned to Stalingrad.

"I want to learn Rukh speech," he said.

Stalingrad bowed, rumbling a phrase Rameau finally understood as "Teach Rameau."

Rukh speech was surprisingly simple for something that had been kept secret for so long. The Rukh used the same words as the cohorts, but lowered in pitch until they were almost too deep for human ears to hear. They could form vowels and a few consonants. They used inconspicuous finger signs to symbolize the sounds they couldn't make.

Their communication with each other was fluid and swift, the finger signs sketchy and near-invisible. Rameau caught only fragments of what they said to each other. But after an hour's practice, he knew enough for a halting exchange of thoughts, if the Rukh spoke slowly. He could understand them well enough to ask the question that gnawed at him.

"Why did you save my life?"

Stalingrad ran a finger along the edge of his collar, as if it was too tight.

"Omo control collar," he said. "Collar make the Rukh kill. Can't fight it. Can't say no. Rukh dream—someday one comes to take off collar. Rameau is the one."

Rameau backed away, his hands raised in denial.

"No. I've seen the Rukh kill. I'll never turn that loose on the world. I am not that man."

"We didn't kill her," Stalingrad said. "Not kill the dancer."

"But you killed others. Many others. You have speech—but you're still monsters."

"Monsters?" Jericho repeated softly, interrogatively. Stalingrad burred and rumbled to him. Rameau had time to reflect on how tired he was of conversations that did not include him. Then Jericho seemed to understand, and turned away from Rameau, as if the word had hurt him.

"Monsters," Stalingrad said. "Yes. We are monsters. Maybe Rameau needs monsters to help save Vega from Omo."

"I don't want to save Vega," Rameau said bitterly. "I want to destroy it, and everything on it. So they'll never use what's here to hurt anyone else. That's what I was trying to do, when you stopped me. Thanks for nothing."

"Rameau, better see what's here first," Stalingrad said.

"I already know. Weapons. Monsters. Creatures of death."

"Rameau, please—you look first. Then decide."

That was what he'd meant to do when he came to the lab— finish the exploration that had been interrupted by the arrival of the Faction cohorts.

Suddenly he frowned at the transform.

"Why do you want this so badly?" he asked. "What do you know about what's here?"

"Rukh work everywhere," Stalingrad said, "Rukh have eyes and ears. Watch cohorts in storage bay."

"Then why don't you just tell me what you know?" Rameau said.

But Stalingrad refused to explain. "You look," he insisted.

"I plan to look," Rameau said. "But it won't change my mind."

He opened the shipmind, slipped into that space as a welcome haven from his current reality. With ease, he found the bright streams of data and followed them back to the storage vault.

There were more empty pods now. He'd raised toxicants and juvenile sinué. More of those waited for him. And behind them—the specifics were compressed into Original Man code. He worried at it briefly. Something like sinué—he stopped, appalled. These were full-gravity organisms, and they weren't just tweaked, they were cyborged. They still fed organically, though. In fact, they'd eat anything. Turned loose on a planet, they'd ravage the landscape, and leave behind droppings that would poison land and water for years.

Why are they stored with the toxicants?

He had a sudden, sickening vision of toxicants mounted on these creatures, spreading through a countryside, or a world, with horrifying speed and efficiency. It looked as if these were slated for revival next, as soon as he finished with the toxicants.

No wonder the Rukh wouldn't try to describe this. It's beyond words. I've seen enough. I'd go back to killing myself now, but I have a ship to kill first. A ship full of death.

Kalidurga, what's this? There's more?

He found another set of pods, separated from the rest. Each was specially calibrated, indicating unique organisms.

Information on that group wasn't coded. In fact, the record contained standard pop-ups of the kind Rameau was used to in medical facilities. Each held a visual, as well as genetic and physical data.

He reached out to the first touchpoint.

Mist swirled and cleared, forming the image of what lay within the pod—a humanoid shape, long, lean, dark-skinned. It turned a proud, silent face toward the onlooker. Its eyes, dark and clear as obsidian, flashed as if cut in facets.

The shape began to dance.

"No," Rameau choked. But he couldn't look away. The dancer wasn't like Dakini. He danced with weight, proudly fending off the mass of a whole planet with his slender arms and legs. And yet, he was like her. His dance, too, held strength and grace beyond human ken. For a moment, Rameau tried to imagine a world where this dancer and Dakini could have coexisted—a world of impossible beauty, made real.

In the real world, the dancers coexisted with the creatures in the next bay—those who would consume all life and leave nothing but poison behind.

He couldn't look any longer. He stabbed at the image until the file closed and it vanished.

He couldn't look at the visuals for the other pods, either. He only scanned their descriptions. Here were athletes, musicians, pattern-building minds—each one specialized and perfected in a way baseline humans had never seen.

So there was a place for transforms. The Founder told the truth. Maybe she could have come here and survived.

And if I destroy this place, I'll be sending people like her to the same kind of death she died.

And if I let the Faction take it, I'll be condemning them to the same life she had to live.

And if I do nothing . . . the monsters live and reign.

Too overwhelmed to continue, Rameau closed the interface, and found himself in the cramped little room again, with the Rukh.

"Rameau see," Stalingrad said. "Rameau, listen. Rukh are monsters, yes. Rukh never have choice. Take off collar, and see."

He touched Rameau's forehead again, very lightly, and repeated the words he'd said when he pulled Rameau from the conversion chute.

"Take off collar in mind. Before you say 'monster.' "

Rameau had believed that he no longer cared about anything—all that had been beaten out of him by the fists of Original Man, by Gunnarsson and his hammer.

Now he knew that wasn't true.

He felt a deep, undying rage fanned to life within him. There was no longer any choice.

I will not let this happen.

He held out his open palm to the Rukh. Stalingrad closed his massive fist over it—this time, not as an enemy.

"Okay, we're going to stop them," he said. "But I have to tell you, I don't know how. I don't know enough about cohorts. What's their plan? What will they do next?"

"Know one, might help us," Stalingrad said. "Old Commander."

Gunnarsson! Rameau had blocked the Commander from his thoughts for many days. Phantom pain shot through his cloned hand at the mention of the name. *But they're right. I need to see him.*

"Where is he?"

"In isolation," Stalingrad said. "Commander say Rameau should attend him, but Rameau is . . . busy. So Rukh take care. Nineveh's job. Nineveh gone now. Rameau can take him food—Omo think okay."

"All right. Next meal break, we'll go there."

The isolation cube wasn't completely isolated. It was located close enough to the central com node to be kept under observation. As Rameau approached, he saw occasional cohorts in the neighboring corridor, but no guards posted in front of the closed door. He flashed the door, and it opened to his kenner.

Gunnarsson floated, cross-legged, inside. He was reading from a small flatscreen. The cube contained wall fittings for wastes and water, and nothing else.

Kali! He looks terrible.

Gunnarsson couldn't have become paler than he already was, but he had lost a lot of weight. He looked shrunken inside his dirty coverall. Dark marks had appeared under his eyes.

"Medical Officer," he said, struggling to straighten up.

"Are you allowed to come out—sir?" Rameau said.

"Yes. Provided you're here with guards. I can perch in the corridor. I could perform calisthenics if you were willing to guard me during that time, but I must not be approached by any cohort who might become contaminated, pending my retraining."

"I brought your food," Rameau said, brusquely shoving the rations in his direction.

The ex-Commander took the dish and began wolfing down the paste it contained. Suddenly he seemed to remember something, and slowed down.

Probably trying to keep me here as long as possible.

Rameau looked up and down to make sure no officer was nearby to punish his disrespect before he spoke.

"A 'thank you' would be good, from the—can I call you a person?—who had my hand smashed with a hammer and caused me to sell my soul into hell."

Gunnarsson looked up, impassive as always. "Thank you? It is not a custom of Original Man. Duty is duty. There is no need for expression of sentiments about the outcome."

He, too, checked for the presence of ReUFac before speaking again.

"I did you a favor. In the interests of efficiency, of course. It is well known that baselines are protective of juveniles. I knew that, sooner or later, they would think of pressuring you through the juvenile.

"They would not have hesitated to deconstruct the boy for your motivation. Probably he would not have been rendered permanently dead, but I wished to spare you feelings I knew would be painful to you, given your baseline psychology."

He looked up from the meal.

"You would have given in. Even a baseline must acknowledge this as truth. One alone cannot oppose them."

He expects me to thank him. He thinks I should be grateful.

Infuriated, Rameau wanted to leave immediately.

Wait. He said "One alone cannot oppose them." Is he trying to tell me something? Could that be an offer of alliance?

"How many would it take, to oppose a victorious faction?" he said.

Gunnarsson pinned him with that disconcerting, ice-blue stare.

"Perhaps only a few, if they were the right ones."

Is the Commander using him to spy on me? Will he repeat what I say? Or is he hoping to use me to get back at them? How far did his surrender to the Reunification Faction actually go?

Rameau switched tactics, trying to provoke some revealing reaction from Gunnarsson. It was easy to let his bitterness show.

"The right ones? I'm sure that doesn't include a baseline like me. This has never been about the Founder's wishes, has it? It's all about which of your factions will replace humanity, and how violent the struggle will be.

"I know now why Vega was so important to you!"

He saw a flash of interest in Gunnarsson's guarded eyes.

"I've had a good look at this precious cargo—nothing but death. We carry enough toxicants to wipe out whole systems. Is that what you meant when you said you'd share information that would make me want to help you?"

Gunnarsson seemed to relax a bit, as if he'd lost interest.

This isn't news to him.

Rameau lowered his voice, leaning closer.

"The others, too," he said. "I know about the transforms. The ones we're not reviving."

Ah! That's hooked him.

"Who told you?" Gunnarsson demanded.

"*You* should have told me," Rameau said. "You should have explained to me what we were looking for. You should have trusted me."

"Told you? Trusted you?" Gunnarsson dismissed the idea with an impatient gesture. "You disobeyed me and opposed me at every turn. I told you to stay out of the shipmind. You didn't listen. Your rash action woke the Faction cohorts, to our destruction."

"If you'd trusted me in the first place, if you'd kept your agreement to share data, that never would have happened," Rameau protested.

"Baseline, recall that I saved your life twice, at the cost of my command," Gunnarsson said coldly. "Yet your sole objective was to destroy yourself. How could I trust a dysfunctional baseline whose only goal in life was to die?

"Even now, when you think you know so much, you have not yet begun to guess what is truly at stake here."

A contingent of cohorts headed in their direction. Gunnarsson glanced at them, then handed the bowl to Rameau as a signal that the conversation had ended.

"A baseline and a disgraced officer have little to talk about," he said. "Visit me again when you can speak with more understanding."

Is he warning me that we shouldn't seem to be conversing too intently?

The cohorts were nearly upon them.

Seething with frustration and anger, Rameau tried to speak in a neutral tone.

"The baseline seeks instruction," he said stiffly. "Please help me."

"When strife is imminent," Gunnarsson informed him, "the wise faction will conceal necessary resources for later use. Seek to understand what is hidden in plain sight."

As the cohorts passed them, Gunnarsson withdrew into the cubicle. Rameau turned away, carrying the empty dish.

Consider me just another unimportant life-form on another

unimportant little mission, Rameau thought, hugging the wall to allow the swift, confident Omo the right of way.

Once they were gone, he kicked the wall to speed himself toward the holding tanks.

Even in an isolation cell, he tries to seize command, he thought furiously. *He won't let me know where he stands until he's sure I understand the situation—on his terms. Until then, he won't trust me. And he made sure to let me know it was my fault.*

But he knew Gunnarsson's accusation wouldn't have stung so much if it hadn't been partly true.

He did save my life—whatever his motive. And it's true—all I've done since is try to get myself killed. I should have died with Dakini.

But if I can't save the transforms in storage here, it will be like letting it happen all over again.

He'd been flying along, blind to his surroundings.

"Orders, Rameau?" Stalingrad finally rumbled.

What could still be hidden here? Why is he playing these games with me?

He still hadn't given Stalingrad any orders.

"I'm due at the holding tanks to check on the sinué. After that—since Gunnarsson hasn't been much help—we need to cross over into *Langstaff* and see if we can find out when they're going to start burn. It's time I had a look at Nuun, anyway."

In fact, he hoped he wouldn't have to go as far as pilot space. The possibility of seeing Neb again still filled him with sickening, baffled anger.

Viewing the sinué was almost as bad. The creature was so ugly he could hardly bear to look at it, yet he had to use the waldos built into the holding tank to take a blood sample and make sure its body chemistry had returned to normal. The Commander had recently ordered it anesthetized for implantation of a control collar, like those the Rukh wore.

Revived, the sinué hurled itself against the transparent wall of the tank until the corridor shuddered under the impact.

The Commander flashed control codes from his kenner to

test the collar. The sinué writhed to a halt, and floated motionless. Shudders passed through its hide, and it stretched its mouth grotesquely wide in protest. But the Commander's control held. Rameau wondered if the Commander had ever looked into the monster's eyes.

While the Commander toyed with the sinué, Rameau finished analyzing its body fluids.

"It's as well as can be expected," he said. "I'll send you a detailed report from the lab."

The Faction Commander continued to experiment with the control device, maneuvering the monster within the narrow confines of the tank. Rameau turned away from the sight, toward an equally distasteful task—his daily evaluation of the toxicants.

He was startled and displeased to find Per clinging to a handhold next to the toxicant tank, with Troy perched in the background, keeping an eye on him.

While Rameau argued with the cohort supervisor over the proper balance of the bioweapons' nutrient mix, he was aware of Per behind him, gesturing and mouthing silently to the toxicants. Rameau knew the boy had made up a kind of game to play with them. Per had even given some of them names. One that most closely resembled a girl child was his special favorite. He called her "Embla." He thought she was his friend.

Rameau shifted his position to cover the boy from sight. He didn't want the cohorts to take note of his odd behavior.

It's sad that he'd seek companionship in a toxicant, Rameau thought. *But his life is pretty sad in general—it can't be fun to spend his days being towed behind me on a leash, or hiding out in the plant dome.* Rameau ended the discussion with the officer quickly.

Nose to the window, Per was marking on the transplex with his fingers, as if the creatures inside could understand his secret writing. The toxicant closest to the window was Embla, Rameau observed.

"That's enough," he said, tugging the boy away from the window. "You know it doesn't really understand what you say."

He had explained to Per many times that the toxicants were

not real humans; they were only human-shaped carriers for populations of deadly viruses, bacteria, and fungi. But all attempts at reasoning only evoked tantrums from Per.

Rameau felt brutal, especially when Per, flushed with anger, told him that he was "evil"—a word the boy must have picked up somewhere else, since it certainly didn't occur in the vocabulary of Original Man. But there was no kind way to tell a juvenile that his only playmate was a genocide weapon.

"Someday I'm going to get her out of there," Per said defiantly, loud enough that the cohort guards might have heard him if they'd been listening.

"Shut up," Rameau said. He slapped Per lightly across the head to emphasize the admonition. The boy seemed determined to get himself noticed and motivated.

"You must not say such things," Rameau said. "If the Original Man took you seriously, I don't know what they'd do. And you must not even think such things. If you ever tried to take a toxicant out of the sealed tank, you'd die a horrible death in seconds. I've seen it."

"I could. I could become a genedoctor like you, and then I'd find a way to fix them. *You* could, if you wanted to. But you won't. Because you're like *them*. You help them. You're *evil*."

He said the word with lingering satisfaction. Rameau issued no punishments for insults to himself.

What can I say? He's right.

"You can think what you like about me. But you will obey. Now are you coming with us, or must I order Troy to carry you?"

"I'm coming, I'm coming. Where are we going?"

"We're going back to *Langstaff* to get some information."

"See Neb!" Per shouted happily.

"No. Not see Neb. Not if I can help it. And your job is to keep quiet and stay in line, or I'll tell Troy to hog-tie you and send you back to the dome on automatic pilot."

"Neb is my sib," Per muttered mutinously. "I want to be a pilot, too."

"Neb is not your sib. You don't have a sib. Now be quiet."

Langstaff seemed packed with big, healthy, fast-moving cohorts. After living in the comparative quiet and space of Vega for so long, the tight quarters made Rameau unbearably jumpy. He felt constantly as if he were about to be run over.

He searched for a drop tube that would take him from *Langstaff*'s outer ring straight to the core. It would be faster to traverse the ship through its central axis than to thread his way through the rings to the pilot space. And he'd be away from the cohorts. The Rukh were a tight fit in the drop tube, but they managed.

Once there, Rameau realized that he should have brought some biosample boxes. The core looked homogeneous and dull compared to the garden they'd created in Vega, but it contained a few useful species that Rameau hadn't seen in the biodome. While he tasted leaves with his enabler and collected a few clippings, the Rukh stood by with massive patience, and Per foraged around and beneath the racks.

"Look! Rameau, I found a machine. What is it?"

Annoyed, Rameau turned reluctantly from his preoccupation and looked. But for once, Per had made a productive discovery.

"My bot!" A smile spread over Rameau's face as if he had rediscovered an old friend. He even felt a little guilty that he had temporarily forgotten the machine's existence. The trash bot had never turned on him. It had never tried to amputate his hand with a blunt object.

"It's Dentley," he said, beaming. Per smiled uncertainly in response, and Rameau quickly assumed a straight face again.

"It's just a trash bot," he explained. "Giving it a persig was only a joke. But it helped me out several times. I programmed it to respond only to me. So I guess it's been waiting here for me to come back and take notice."

He felt an absurd impulse to apologize to the bot. Though currently in powered-down mode, it winked at intervals to show that it was ready for service.

"Come here," he said to Per. "Bot, accept additional command code, reference juvenile Per." The bot woke up.

"Recognizing Rameau," it said. "Accepting command code, unclassified juvenile Per."

"It said my name!" The boy was delighted.

"You don't have a kenner, but the bot will accept your commands now, if you figure out how to program them in manually."

Rameau felt pleased. One small thing had gone right. This would be a new toy for Per, and if he learned to manually program simple commands, that at least would teach him a useful skill. And it was always good to have an inconspicuous helper.

"Like the pet animals in the stories," Per said, as if echoing his thought.

Rameau turned back to the plant trays, to finish the job and move on, but Per shouted again.

"Look, Neb's coming! Neb!"

Rameau's throat constricted. He turned and saw the pilot sib flying down the axis of the room, perilously close to the light bar. Neb looked distraught. The last time he'd looked that way, the ship had been in danger. But Rameau bent over the plant trays, pretending an indifference he didn't feel.

"Go away. I'm busy." He forced the words out.

Neb still possessed that astonishing cohort swiftness. He lunged and turned a somersault that brought him up facing Rameau. His hand shot out as if to seize Rameau, but stopped a fraction of an inch from his arm, as Rameau flinched. Neb's eyes were wild. Even the thought of being manhandled again made Rameau feel as if he were about to choke on his own heart.

Things can always get worse.

But he had the Rukh with him now. Stalingrad rumbled deep in his throat, and drifted over them like a dark cloud. He put one massive hand on Neb's chest and pushed him back. He made even the cohort look small.

"Thank you, Grad," Rameau said. His knees buckled. Deep inside, he despised himself for his weakness.

Neb snarled, and his hand flew back, clenched into a fist. Then he stopped, lowered his hands, and floated with his arms drifting out helplessly.

"Rameau, this cohort ken e come out bad," he said. "But Rameau got to go help Nuun. Neb hear new Commander say e go terminate Nuun. Rameau promise. E promise help. Please."

"Oh, *shit.*"

I promised. I did promise. I can't let them dump Nuun in the converter. Oh, Kali Mat. If I try to stop them—what are they going to do to me? Not back in the tank again, oh no, please . . .

Neb and Stalingrad were both staring at him now. He took a deep breath.

Pull yourself together, you jackass! he thought. *What's the worst that could happen? You'd die!*

The thought was no longer as consoling as it had once been, but it helped.

"Okay, Neb, tell me what's happening," he said.

"Come quick, please! Fly and tell," Neb said. He reached back to tow Rameau, as he had done so many times before, but Stalingrad was there first. Jericho and Troy closed up behind them, pulling Per along with them. As they flashed through the corridors, Neb panted out his story.

"Neb and Nor in pilot space with Nuun like always, and new Commander e come in with guards, e say 'Move burned pilot out, go convert e. Need pod for that one.' And e point Nor. And guard e give Nor shot, e go down, e no can do nothing."

"Wait, wait," Rameau said. "They shot Nor?"

"No, not gun," Neb said. "E shoot skin, *tsss.*" He mimed an injection, poking his finger into his own neck.

"E start disconnect Nuun, and Neb e say no, not that way, but cohort no listen. Cohort look like e come shoot Neb, and Neb think, Neb and Nor both go sleep cold, and who go help Nuun? So e fly. E think, Rameau e no Neb's friend no more, but maybe e still help Nuun."

Rameau thought furiously, even while Neb was talking. He was sure already that he couldn't talk them into leaving Nuun in the pod. He'd never dealt with catastrophic rewarming. He didn't know if he could save Nuun. But he knew that he had to get him back to his lab.

"Neb—you remember the pod you fixed?"

"Yes. Remember."

"You remember where it was? No—don't say it. We don't want anyone to know. We have to hide Nuun there."

"Understand. This cohort obey."

"And stay outside the cube. We don't want them to grab you again."

"Per!" Rameau pulled on the boy's foot to get his attention. "Don't say anything. Just keep quiet. If you have to speak, say 'I don't know.' Understand?"

Per kicked at him, but muttered, "Okay, okay."

When they reached the pilot space, Nuun had already been pulled out of the pod; he floated to one side, arms and legs askew, while the cohorts flushed the pod and plugged Nor into it.

Rameau saw at a glance that Kir Ninety, the first officer, was present, supervising the two cohorts at work on Nor. He couldn't use his first plan, which had been to yell "Stop!" and pull rank. Instead he braked hard, to kill his own momentum and slow the others.

"Sir!" he panted. He wanted to salute, or do something to appease the officer, but he couldn't recall the right suck-up moves.

"Excuse the interruption—uh—I was told that the burned pilot was scheduled for termination. Perhaps you weren't aware that I had orders to perform tests before the body was disposed of. I brought Rukh to carry the body. Oh, good—I see you have a litter ready.

"Rukh! Prepare the body for transportation."

Stalingrad could only fit half his body through the doorway. He reached one long arm between the cohorts to grasp Nuun by the wrist and drag him out of the pilot space. He and Jericho strapped Nuun to the litter. Rameau dared not stop even to see if Nuun was still breathing.

"I'll return to monitor the condition of this one after you complete the installation," he said.

Kir Ninety wore a faintly puzzled expression, as if he felt something was wrong, but couldn't figure out what it was. Yet it seemed in order to let the medical officer take charge of an unneeded body. Kir Ninety's face cleared, and he turned back to the more important task, installing Nor in the hibernation pod.

"Dismissed," he said to Rameau, over his shoulder.

As soon as they emerged into a corridor where they could fly, Neb pushed the Rukh aside and took charge of his sib. His chest heaved. He looked as if he would cry if he only knew how. But all he could do was push his speed to the maximum. Even the Rukh had a hard time keeping up.

The cohorts had become accustomed to seeing Rameau come and go with his odd companions. No one questioned their passage out of *Langstaff* into Vega. Soon they were safe in the empty corridors, headed for Per's den.

"I hope you actually fixed this," Rameau said as he activated the pod where Per had once been hidden. Without a word, Neb pushed him aside and began adjusting the controls.

Rameau turned to Nuun's flaccid body. At least he wasn't permanently dead—yet. The body still twitched. Rameau passed his enabled hand across it. Nuun's temperature was already spiking at a dangerous level. An hour ago it had been close to the freezing point.

"He's going into hyperthermal shock," Rameau said.

"Five minutes," Neb said.

A spasm passed through Nuun, shaking the litter. He gasped in a hard, irregular rhythm, then stopped breathing. Rameau waited for another breath, but it didn't come. He swiftly tapped his kenner, asking the enabler for a stimulant. But then he stopped. He didn't know the proper procedures for treating a cohort in thermal shock.

I can still use the old-fashioned emergency methods.

He bent over the cohort and started breathing for him.

Awkward in micro g.

It couldn't matter too much how many breaths per minute a cohort normally took. If Nuun took even one more, it would be a success. It was hard to make Nuun's chest rise; it took so much breath to fill cohort lungs—more than Rameau had. He tried to compress the chest, but there was nothing to brace Nuun against. He stopped to take a quick breath for himself. And Nuun gulped in air on his own.

"I've got him breathing again. For the mercy of the Compassionate One, don't you have that thing on-line yet?"

"E go here." Neb took the feet, and Rameau slid Nuun's

head and shoulders into the pod, which was already filling with cooled liquid. He let Neb connect the life support tubes and sensors. But Neb didn't finish the job; he didn't close up the pod.

He unwrapped a length of connector cable from its place of concealment under his belt. Then he reached into the front of his coverall and extracted sim headgear.

"Rameau open shipmind," he said.

He jacked one end of the cable into the pod's monitor port, plugged the other into the headgear, and slid the device over Nuun's head. He tapped inputs on the band a couple of times, watched while lights whose meaning Rameau did not know changed color, and then, seeming satisfied, closed up the pod just before the gel that was filling it reached overflow level.

He looked up and saw Rameau still staring at him.

"Neb take things without asking," he said. "Like Sig take weapons from dragon." He gestured impatiently. "Rameau! Open shipmind!"

Wincing, Rameau cut his finger again, and opened the wall. But he didn't know how to make the connection Neb wanted. With the startling speed of a cohort in overdrive, Neb moved before Rameau could comprehend and comply. He found components Rameau didn't even recognize, hooked up links, then tested with his kenner, and apparently found the work satisfactory.

"Hurry," he said. "Get shipmind remote. Nuun not have time."

"What do you—"

Neb moved Rameau aside with a touch, too fast for the Rukh to interfere. He slid his own hands into the console, and when he pulled them out again, they were clad in silver mesh. Neb showed no surprise; he seemed familiar with the process. The console offered him the headband, and he snatched it.

"What are you doing with that?" Rameau demanded.

"Remote link to shipmind," Neb said. "Nuun sees through shipmind now.

"Link to Nuun. He need pilot jock with him, same now like always."

"No!" Rameau said. "I need that equipment. I promised I'd save his life. I didn't promise to baby-sit him for the rest of the trip."

"Listen, Rameau," Neb pleaded. "Life signs go bad for Nuun. Cohorts think e terminate. But Neb think signs go bad because Nuun see something. E see bad thing, go in fear, need sib."

"What is it you think he saw?" Rameau said.

"Ship," Neb breathed. "This cohort think Nuun see ship coming."

It was the one thing he could have said to make Rameau stop and listen.

"All right," Rameau said grudgingly. "Use the gear. We'll see."

Neb slipped on the headband. His gloved fingers danced briefly, and then he floated free. He looked naked, unsupported, without a pilot chair or monitor. He didn't even have a tether to keep him from drifting into the walls while he was caught up in his interior experience.

His fingers moved constantly. He trembled and twitched. Even his legs jerked, as if he dreamed that he was running away.

Rameau had no access to what was happening inside the pilot's mind. He could only see the physical facts reported on the monitors. Jagged spikes showed in Nuun's life-sign readings. His body lay motionless, but frantic action was taking place in his brain.

Neb's readings paralleled Nuun's, in a complex harmonic relationship. The peaks were closer together, moving faster, but still in synchrony.

How can Nuun register that much activity in hibernation?

Rameau still didn't know the correct protocol for closing down the pilot jock's input, especially with improvised equipment. He slowly turned down the inputs on the sim gear until Neb no longer received data from the pilot's senses. Neb gasped and struggled as his scans fell out of sync with the pilot's. His heart rate and brain waves floundered wildly, and then steadied into a waking rhythm. Rameau swept his hands through the sim field to signal "finish," and carefully removed the inactivated headband.

Neb regained control slowly. At last he was able to rotate to face Rameau, keeping one hand braced against the pod to hold him in position. Rameau moved toward the pod's controls, to calm Nuun by lowering his temperature and adding sedatives, but Neb stopped him.

"Nuun need contact, not meds."

"What did you see?" Rameau demanded.

"Nuun feels fear. Ship is coming."

But Rameau couldn't trust Neb's report.

I have to see this for myself.

"Put the gloves back."

When Neb complied, Rameau placed his hands in the console to be gloved.

Amazing how they fit themselves to any hands.

Rameau was surprised by how little he missed the support of chair and hood. The link was all he really wanted. At the first view of the static star maps that formed the basic matrix of the sim interface, he felt free again. He breathed easily.

In those initial moments, he sensed no incoming data from Nuun. All remained dark and quiet. Deliberately, he took long, calming breaths, and waited. Then he started to feel another rhythm—but slow, so slow. He tried to match himself to it.

He lowered his threshold of perception, slowed himself. It was like sinking into dark, cold water, deeper and deeper. He had a fleeting memory of the story he had told—the cohort who couldn't reach the bottom of the pool.

No ducks to help me here.

Slower. Slower. He could feel himself hovering on the edge of trance. Briefly, he hoped Neb was watching his life signs, and would have the sense to pull him out if he got into trouble. Finally he felt Nuun's pattern close enough to mesh with his own overlay. There was a shifting, unstable sensation as he found a balance. It had to be counterpoint, not synchrony. Nuun was still too far out of normal rhythm for Rameau to move simultaneously with him. But Rameau danced around him, like a rapid moon orbiting a slow, majestic planet. And at last the data that Nuun received directly flooded through the interface, and into Rameau.

The star patterns locked into that place in his mind that had been unsatisfied since the last time he'd been in the link. First came the representations of visible light; then the hushed surf of radiation, the rain-sounds of particles fleeting past. Finally, he yielded to the perception of mass and movement. At first with a shimmer of vertigo, then with the pilot's unique sense of security and freedom combined, he was cradled and arrowed into time.

All his perceptions slowed because Nuun's consciousness was sunk so deep. But the data that he received seemed no less sharp and clear. He wondered if Nuun's mind could still be intact. Perhaps it was only the link between mind and body that had been damaged. But if there was a way to touch Nuun's consciousness, Rameau couldn't find it.

Reluctantly, he moved back, seeking to swing his focus around, to find the giant planet they would pass on their way out of the system. He wanted to see it, and he'd had no chance from inside the station. Cradled in Nuun's senses, he watched the giant rush toward them with stately yet inexorable force. He couldn't see its colors with his eyes, but he could sense the swirl of magnetism and the changing bands of temperature variation. They weren't colors, but they were beautiful.

And then, with equal clarity, he felt the touch of the incoming ship.

It wasn't the shriek of agony it must have been in the pilot's mind, but it ached like an old wound. It dulled his vision like a flash of blinding light that leaves a green haze behind. Even in the brief time he'd been in the link, he sensed it moving closer.

Then he perceived something like a shrill, two-toned beeping, at such a high frequency that he felt rather than heard it.

An alarm? But more musical . . . my name! Someone is calling me.

And as the thought formed in his mind, he seemed to surge up out of the depths with tremendous speed, like a whale breaching from the deepest gulf of the ocean. Faster, faster—he flung his hands out to save himself from the crash he expected.

And then light that seemed blastingly bright streamed into his eyes, and he found himself curled in the air above the pod. Neb was just dragging the gear off his head.

"So fast," he said indistinctly. "But you're right. Felt . . . a ship."

But how far away? How much time do we have?

"Rameau," Neb said, "why you have pilot chair, and not use?"

Rameau, still groggy, righted himself and tried to understand.

"What?" he said, sounding stupid even to himself.

Neb pointed to the white, ovoid object whose function Rameau hadn't been able to figure out.

"Blood key," Neb said. "Open like this." He flew into the corner and ran a finger along a groove in the object. It unfolded silently, separating into seat and hood.

"Can I do that?" Rameau asked. Per flew across the room before Rameau could move, and pulled himself into the seat.

"Out," Rameau ordered, pulling him aside. "Fold it up."

Neb touched another groove, and the chair closed up like a puzzle box. Rameau slid his finger into the groove, in turn, and felt the brief sting of the lock tasting him. Did it hesitate for an instant longer before accepting him? He couldn't be sure—but it unfolded once again.

Did Neb stare at him an instant longer than normal? Again, he couldn't be sure. When he looked up, Neb was checking his kenner.

"This cohort has work cycle now," Neb said. "If this cohort not come back—Rameau watch out for Nuun. Please."

Neb left before Rameau could answer, as if he realized that his continued presence could only make Rameau more likely to refuse.

Rameau heard a throat-clearing from Stalingrad—the Rukh must think it was time to go. But something nagged at Rameau, and wouldn't let him leave the room. Per fidgeted around the room, and poked and prodded at the folded chair, trying to open it.

"Leave that," Rameau said. But Per ignored him. The boy ran his finger down the same groove Neb had touched, then recoiled with a whimper when the lock stung him. A moment later, the sting forgotten, he spun happily in the air as the chair unfolded.

"Look what I did," Per said gleefully. "Look! It works for me! I'm a pilot, too!"

"Quiet," Rameau said. This time, sensing that he was serious, Stalingrad gathered the boy in with one big paw and kept him out of the way.

Gunnarsson said, "Find what's hidden in plain sight."

The chair had been hidden in plain sight. But Gunnarsson couldn't have been thinking of a piece of equipment.

He meant something integral to his mission. What else is hidden in plain sight?

The boy.

Gunnarsson implied he could be a survivor of the Founder's experiment.

But if Per was the only one left, wouldn't it make more sense for Gunnarsson to protect him above all? Instead, Gunnarsson still cared about Vega. Or something on it.

Stupid! He thought. *Gunnarsson's right about me. I'm an idiot.*

But he didn't have time to kick himself.

"Grad, I know we're due back at work," he said. "But there's something I have to look at first. Keep Per out of trouble, will you?"

This time he entered the shipmind, not Nuun's cold dreams. With easy speed, he returned to the nodes that concerned cold storage. What he wanted to know was harder to find than the transforms had been. But every session in the interface brought him greater skill in following the patterns of information.

"Give it to me," he muttered as his fingers danced and streams of bright data flowed through his hands. At last he grasped it—a densely packed matrix like a golden cube. It unraveled into chains—no, helixes.

He couldn't look at them all. There were hundreds, maybe thousands. But he pulled out a few at random and lined them up.

Not Original Man. They're too different. But not a random

sample of humans, either. They're different, yet so similar—as if they're all related. And in these key regions—

The shipmind highlighted the areas he wanted to compare. Then he called up his own scan, Neb's, and Per's. Per's was a perfect match, Neb's nearly as good. Rameau's showed dots of light in an imperfect pattern.

In some way, we are all similar. And the blood key in this room isn't interested in whether we're cohorts. It looks for that similarity.

He needed to check one more thing—was the matrix a record of something that existed physically on board Vega?

Yes.

The genomes he examined weren't abstractions or simulations. They were enfleshed in living beings, stored on Vega. Behind the transforms, behind the bioweapons, the Founder's dream lived on—the dream and the nightmare together.

Rameau closed the window and stepped out of the shipmind.

There's one more thing I have to know.

"Per, I've changed my mind. I want you to try this."

Per's face lit up as he shot across the room and fitted himself into the chair.

I'm endangering him, Rameau thought. *This could destroy his mind. But unless I know what he really is, I don't have any hope of protecting him. I can't remain blind.*

He remembered how Neb had told him that those born to be pilots were drawn to the interface, no matter how dangerous it seemed, and he found some hope in that.

He returned briefly to the shipmind. Whoever had placed Per in such close proximity to this equipment must have intended to monitor him carefully—not to fling him rashly into a situation he couldn't control. It seemed logical that the shipmind would contain a test pattern of some kind, a simulation. His logic was rewarded. He found a simple check program for the pilot's hood.

"I'm going to put the hood on you now. Don't worry—this isn't going to hurt.

"But you can't go off to look for Nuun yet. You have to practice first. I'm going to show you a pattern. Try to re-create it on your own."

Per didn't show gross symptoms of distress. His life signs stayed within acceptable bounds. Rameau let him have five minutes before pulling him out.

The boy looked dazed, his pupils widely dilated. Nevertheless, he complained about being taken out of the interface so soon.

"I told you," he boasted. "I *told* you! I'm a real pilot. Neb is my sib!"

Rameau snagged his foot just in time to keep him from crashing into the wall.

"Whoa," Rameau said. "If you're so good at piloting, watch where you're going."

He reeled the jubilant child in and looked him in the eyes.

"You can tell anyone you like about this," he said. "*But*—do you know what will happen if you do? You'll never get to come here again. They'll make sure of that."

Per sobered immediately. "Never tell," he said.

29

Rameau was already weary, but he still had to revisit Nor—and see Gunnarsson. He sent Per back to the dome with Troy.

"And don't let him out of your sight," he ordered the Rukh.

As he dragged himself back to work, Rameau wondered if it really made any sense to feel pity for Nuun.

He'll never come out of the pod. But within his narrow cell, he travels in infinite space. Meanwhile, I fly through infinite space, but within it, I live in a cell. Moreover, I have bad dreams.

He took a large meal to Gunnarsson, hoping to provide extra time to talk. Most of the Faction cohorts who worked on Vega had finished their work cycles. The corridor was deserted, except for a guard or two who drifted back and forth at regular intervals. The Rukh placed themselves to hide the conversation from the guards' view, as much as possible.

"You asked me to come again when I had found what was hidden," Rameau said.

"And have you done so?" Gunnarsson leaned forward, ignoring the meal.

"I begin to understand what's at stake for you," Rameau said cautiously. "Yet I wonder if it's wise to discuss that here, where all the cohorts have surrendered to the new faction."

I won't expose my position until he makes a commitment, too.

Gunnarsson looked up and down the corridor again.

"Not all," he said very softly. "Some were in the regeneration tank. They were never asked for surrender, and they never gave it. And some never surrendered the original mission."

322

That's as much of a clue as I'm going to get. It's now or never.

"There are no cohorts within hearing," Rameau said. "You will tell me where your affiliation lies, or the conversation ends here."

Gunnarsson's mouth tightened as it always did when he felt forced to reveal some shortcoming or dissension within Original Man to a mere baseline.

"If you cannot say," Rameau said, "then I will assume that you affiliate to the Reunification Faction now, and that you were sincere in your surrender to them. I will leave here and let them decide what to do with you. You can go back to High Command and be retrained, or starve to death first. It will no longer be my concern."

"Your conclusion is a logical one," Gunnarsson said. There was no contempt for the stupid baseline in his voice now. "I have not surrendered my mission. I still believe that following the Founder's orders will be for the ultimate benefit of Original Man. The only way I can continue to pursue my mission is by affiliating to those who remain from *Langstaff*'s crew, in the biodome."

Rameau took a deep breath.

"You no longer command these cohorts and Rukh," he said. "I am their officer now. Whatever we discuss, know this: I will not return command to you."

Gunnarsson looked startled.

"A baseline cannot command cohorts," he said.

"You dumped those cohorts on me," Rameau said. "I have salvaged them, and they are now my responsibility. I didn't want them. I had no desire to command them. But I am in charge of them. I cannot return that responsibility to one who has declared them worthless."

"Again your conclusion is logical," Gunnarsson said.

"But I cannot command a ship," Rameau said. "I don't know where we are, and I don't know where to find safety. I need your knowledge. An alliance is possible."

"Agreed," Gunnarsson said.

Rameau motioned to the food. "Have a cracker. You're supposed to be eating."

Gunnarsson stuck a cracker in his mouth without looking, and chewed.

"While you eat, I'll tell you what I know, and what I need to know," Rameau said. "This time, I expect you to honor the agreement to share data. Nothing hidden."

"You've found what was hidden," Gunnarsson said.

"Not entirely. I know that what's most valuable to you is still present on Vega. No need to specify, right now. But I don't understand the boy's place in this, and mine."

Gunnarsson swallowed, and took another bite without speaking.

Even now, he doesn't want to tell me.

"No alliance without truth," Rameau said. "I know they're self-reproducing, and I know the boy is one of them."

Gunnarsson cleared his throat.

"Not just self-reproduction," he said hoarsely. "That was never the most important thing for the Founder."

"Then what?"

"That they should be *better*. Better than us. He wanted them to have freedom. So he gave them the pilot genes."

He made them all *pilots? That can't be. The pilot complex is too unstable.*

"Not like our pilots," Gunnarsson whispered, as if hearing Rameau's thoughts. "A stable variant that can pass to the next generation without technical intervention. The whole clan would have pilot capacity. Freedom of movement. No more cohorts who give their lives to the pilot pod because pilots are so few. That was the Founder's dream."

Once again, Rameau had believed he knew the situation. Once again, he was thrown off balance, stunned.

Not just self-reproducing Omo, but self-reproducing pilots. No limitations on their journeys!

He felt a pang of envy. *To be one of them—to be free . . .*

Yet when he looked back at Gunnarsson, the *Langstaff* Commander seemed to be looking at *him* with envy.

"The pilot genes are the greatest treasure mined from the

human genome," Gunnarsson said. This time he spoke without hesitation, as if stating a truth that couldn't provoke any opposition.

"Pilot mind includes so much more than guiding the ship through jump. It is seeing the path ahead. Understanding the pattern. The Founder gathered all these scattered gifts out of the baseline genome and linked them together."

"And what does that have to do with me?" Rameau asked resentfully. He was in no mood to be lectured on the wonders of Original Man.

"You are so blind, in light of what you are," Gunnarsson said. "Don't you see? The original genes were born within humanity. In people like you. From time to time, a baseline is born carrying some fragments of the complete pattern. The Founder recognized such people. You were one of them.

"Not fully—not enough to be a pilot—but enough to shape so many other things. Yet bearing this gift within you, your only desire was to throw it away. Can you wonder that I thought you mentally defective?"

"Your opinion of me is irrelevant," Rameau said. "What about the boy? If he's one of them, why have you treated him with such contempt?"

Gunnarsson looked surprised. "Conceal valuable resources," he said. "This is the first rule of action when factional strife is expected. If the *Langstaff* crew had known his value, they would have revealed it to their new Commander. They must believe him worthless."

He gulped a spoonful of mush.

"But he's not worthless," Rameau said. "Is that what you're telling me? That he has this capacity?"

Gunnarsson shrugged. "It lies within him. Without training, he'll never achieve it. Find a way to train him, and you will have secured a precious resource. Yet one that is still useless to us in our current condition."

"Agreed," Rameau said. "Talk of pilots is useless if we have no ship. To remove Vega from their control, we have to find a way to take back *Langstaff*."

Gunnarsson gave a brief snort that might have been laughter. "I see you've expanded your view of what is possible."

"Yes. I need to know when they'll initiate burn, and when they expect the final prejump burn. Any kind of plan depends on that knowledge."

Again Gunnarsson looked surprised. "Find out from the shipmind. Surely there's a record of available reaction mass."

"I don't affiliate to navigation, as the cohorts are so fond of pointing out. I wouldn't know how to find what I need. You're still one of them. Listen to what they say. Find out. I expect useful information when I return."

Rameau decided not to tell Gunnarsson what he'd learned from Nuun.

Not until he gives me something definite. Something that demonstrates commitment.

"Time to go," he said abruptly. "I promised to visit pilot space and check on Nor. They've put him in stasis. Does that tell you anything about their plans?"

Gunnarsson hastily cleaned up the rest of the meal, as if conversation with Rameau had restored his appetite.

"Standard procedure for this situation," he said. "Only two pilots left. The ReUFac Commander seeks to ensure that at least one pilot is under his control at all times. Stasis is safe; the pilot cannot be harmed, accidentally or otherwise."

"Is that what happened with the boy?"

"Probably. Those who placed him in stasis must have expected to retrieve him, after securing the station. But their faction was defeated. They must have died before telling the victors where to find him."

Gunnarsson clattered the dishes together and shoved them toward Rameau, scattering eddies of crumbs.

"We have talked long enough for now. I will seek the information you need. Return quickly."

Rameau hurried back to *Langstaff* to check on Nor. As far as he could tell without interfacing, Nor was successfully installed in hibernation. His signs were steady and on a higher level of activity and responsiveness than Nuun's had been.

There's really no point to this examination, but I need to make them think I'm essential, and keep them accustomed to seeing me move through the ship.

Rameau let Stalingrad tow him on the final return trip. He could feel, again, the hot buzz of too many enabler drugs.

He was finally catching a nap in the shaded half of the Dome when he heard the leaves rustle, and looked across to see a familiar outline. It had to be Neb, because Neb was the only one left.

"What do you want?" he said. "Nuun is still okay. Nor is okay, too."

"Neb wanted to disobey," the cohort said. If he'd been human, Rameau would have thought he was about to cry. "When Rameau got motivated. E wanted to, but e no ken how. Cohort not incepted to be alone. 'Outside the will of Original Man there is no life.'

"Nuun okay. But e sleep. E no look Neb, e no say nothing no more. Nor e sleep too. Only Neb awake. Neb has no sib now. Soon be Neb's turn to pilot. Neb no never come back, no speak again. Till then . . . e want stay here with you."

This would be the moment to say no, Rameau thought. This would be the moment to savor the sweetness of denial. He had begged Neb for help. And Neb had denied his plea. Now it was time for Neb to find out what it was like when you only had one place to turn and that appeal was denied to you.

All he had to do was say no. No to this smug superman. To this child of no parent. To this perfect creature born to die alone, as an emaciated catatonic carrying other people to worlds he would never see.

Neb was trembling with the same drug-supported weariness that pulsed through Rameau. He remained silent—of course. He was a well-trained cohort; he would not speak again until Rameau responded. He was well disciplined. If Rameau ordered him to go, he would go at once.

Rameau realized that he had not yet said anything. And yet, Neb was still waiting. Apparently it was not enough to say nothing. Apparently it was necessary for him to say something.

"Okay," he said. "You can stay."

. . .

When the next cycle started, Neb left early, to report to work on *Langstaff*.

Rameau ordered the door closed behind him, shutting all others out.

"My friends," he said. "My fellow Remnants. The time has come for us to be the heroes of our own story."

They gave him their wholehearted attention.

"Do you remember when I said we would have a great mission one day, one that was just for us? That day is coming soon. You know the Reunification Faction is working to return Vega to the control of High Command. Once we've finished the repairs they demand, once they take the joined ships back into jump, our usefulness to them will be ended. I believe they'll terminate us then. We can't let that happen. The Remnants are not expendable.

"The only way for us to survive is to take back the *Langstaff*—not for any faction or commander, but for us. The old *Langstaff* Commander has affiliated to us, but he will no longer command. We command ourselves. We decide what to fight for. So I ask each one of you to decide now. If you will fight with us to reclaim the ship and defeat the Reunification Faction, come to my side. If you don't want to stand with us, you can seek a hibernation pod and stay there, and take your chances. No one fights unwillingly. But all who affiliate to the Remnants, come forward now."

For a minute he thought they weren't moving. Then he saw they'd all moved at once, pressing forward in a tightening circle.

"I can't tell you the mission plan, because I don't have a plan yet. I had to know first if you'd fight. Now that I know you're with me, I'll figure out what to do. But there is one more thing I have to ask you."

They waited in complete silence.

"We might give it everything we have, and still lose."

A mutter and rumble from cohorts and Rukh alike denied this possibility.

"It's something we have to consider. They're Original Man.

They're strong. And I know that the custom among Omo is to surrender when the fight seems hopeless. But—speaking for myself—I've had enough surrender. I will not surrender. I won't be taken back to Eyrie in a cage, no matter what happens.

"I say that if the fight goes against us, we should blow the cable between ships and retreat to Vega—if we can. If we do this, we may die, but we will deny them their prize. They'll never take us back.

"But I can't make that decision for all of you. I ask you to vote. It's how baselines decide important questions. All who agree with me, extend your hands, like this."

Not one of them hung back. All hands stretched toward him.

"No more surrender," Tok said. The cohorts shouted it, and the Rukh boomed deep in their chests.

"We have agreement, then," Rameau said.

He looked over at Stalingrad. "Permission to speak?" he said.

The Rukh hesitated for a long moment. Then he nodded, and hummed a long note of assent. "Ao."

"Our Rukh teammates are ready to share their secret with us," Rameau said. "The Rukh have speech. They can teach you to understand them. Never communicate when the Faction is present—but know that our bond is closer than they realize. We'll share a language that's hidden from them. We share our stories, and we share a hope of freedom they can never know."

He paused to let them cheer again.

"Okay, now we get to work. My job is to get the information we need to plan the time and the way we strike. You'll keep working on your Faction-assigned tasks. But slow down any nonessential repairs. Drag them out. Don't give them any excuse to think they're already through with us.

"Meanwhile, look around on every job for tools that could serve as weapons. Don't bring them here—we don't want to make them suspicious—but try to stash them around the station, where we can get them later. Mark the location of any materials we could use for emergency acceleration padding. They may not be planning to take care of us when they burn. We have to be ready to take care of ourselves.

"Go to it. And remember—no surrender."

After the speech, Rameau unearthed his homemade explosive vest, and showed it to the Rukh.

"Do you think this would have actually worked?" he asked.

"No—couldn't blow hole in conversion chamber," Carthago said. He examined the material, sniffed it, rubbed a little cautiously between his fingers.

"Good idea, though. Can use same sources, mix it better. Get ignition caps. Got caps for construction work—no danger by themselves, too small. But add to this, can blow big."

"Big enough to sever the cable?" Rameau asked.

Carthago nodded. "Can do that."

"Good," Rameau said. "Collect materials in small quantities. Bring them in here and build me the charges. Bury them in the substrate. When the Faction pulls back from Vega, that will be your priority—packing the cable with explosives."

Rameau headed for the storage bay, his mind roiling with plans, contingencies, the need for haste. *Maybe if I think of this as a delicate operation with a dozen assisting surgeons, I can keep everything in order.*

His first priority was a quick meeting with Gunnarsson, to see if he'd secured more data on the timing of the coming burn. But he and his Rukh escort had just reached the end of the corridor that led to the isolation cell when Per collided with them—traveling at top speed, his face distorted by panic. Troy was close behind him, trying to regain control of his charge.

Per clutched Rameau's coverall. Rameau noticed in passing how much he'd grown already. His legs were too long to let him cling like a monkey. And his hands were stronger. It was harder to break his grip.

"Rameau! You have to do something! They're taking them away."

Why is it that everyone starts out "Rameau, you have to do something"?

"Who?" he said. But he had a sinking feeling that he already knew.

"They're moving the transforms! They're taking them to the

ship. Embla and the others. They pumped gas into the tank and stunned them. Then they waldoed them into the airshrouds. Now they're taking them to the ship. I wanted to do something, but they're all dressed in suits. I couldn't get at them to cut them."

"Kali Mat!" Rameau swore. "That means there are toxicants coming through this corridor! No wonder they wanted to move all their people out. Shit!"

The Rukh didn't wait for Rameau's order to move. They shot away in the opposite direction. Troy had Per by the back of his coveralls. Even Per couldn't wriggle out of that grip, but he protested as they flew.

"No, the other way! We have to go back. You don't understand. They can't do that. They're going to put them to sleep, and I'll never see her again."

He finally gave up and cried, the angry, desperate weeping of a child who knows he's helpless in the face of a catastrophe, and that the adults are not going to listen.

"Whoa, wait," Rameau said. "I'm going to find out what's going on. But you have to calm down."

He turned to the Rukh.

"Troy, take the boy back to the dome. Seal the pressure door against contamination. Tell them the cohorts are moving the toxicants, and they should stay inside till I come back."

"Grad, Jeri, I'm afraid you'll have to come with me. I have to check this out."

It made his skin crawl to think about breathing air that had passed over the toxicants' pods.

But I brought them back to life. I have to know what's happening to them.

He couldn't hide as long as the Rukh were with him. He found himself flattened against the wall near the command post as the procession passed by. It looked like a funeral, with the cohorts hooded in their protective suits, and the toxicants sealed in double airshrouds. Four cohorts guided each shrouded figure on a litter. Evidently they weren't taking any chances of unbalancing or losing control of the pods.

Rameau counted two dozen—the full complement of toxicants he had reawakened.

Behind the toxicants came two columns of cohorts carrying a cylindrical object sealed in a flexible tube of fabric. It looked something like a huge sausage done up in cheesecloth.

The sinué! They're moving those, too. What in heaven's name are they going to do with those on board Langstaff?

Are they moving them all? Kali! The sinué will be crushed like beached whales when they begin burn.

Even before the cohorts had turned into the next corridor, Rameau flew toward the emptied holding tanks.

They might have let the tanks leak. We could still be contaminated.

"What's going on?" he demanded of the guard on duty. "Why wasn't I informed?"

"Rameau was late for work cycle," the cohort replied, unperturbed.

One of the cohort supervisors appeared at the other end of the tank array. He'd been checking the pressure seals, Rameau saw.

"Where are they taking the transforms?" Rameau asked.

"To *Langstaff*," the Omo said. "Ship approaching jump requires full complement of bioweapons."

"Will my presence be required to monitor the transforms on *Langstaff*?" Rameau said.

"No. Cohort specialists will supervise. The baseline is not required on board."

"But if you're going to burn soon, the sinué especially will need special care. The shock of acceleration can kill them."

"No need for concern," the cohort said. "Holding tank will be pumped full of medical gel. Sinué inhales, pressure equalizes, weight is cushioned. Seventy-five percent survival rate."

Rameau felt relieved.

What's the matter with me? That thing is an abomination. It should be killed. It would be better off dead.

But somehow, the thought of killing it deliberately and in a reasonably painless way seemed different from imagining the creature left to suffocate, crushed under its own weight.

Anyway, it's out of my hands now.

"Does this mean my work here is finished?"

The cohort seemed indifferent to him.

"Postburn, there may be more duties for you. For now, you attend the damaged cohorts. Make sure they are fit to finish the repair work."

He turned back to the routine of closing down the holding tanks. Rameau was familiar with the process, but didn't offer to help. He retreated toward the isolation cell. It wasn't mealtime yet, but he decided to take a chance. He needed to see Gunnarsson.

"Grad, get me some rations," he said. "Anything—whatever you can find quickly."

The Rukh returned with a tray and a couple of nutrient bars, sliced up to resemble a meal. Rameau didn't see anyone left in the corridor; even the guards had withdrawn. He hurried to speak to Gunnarsson while they were still unobserved.

Gunnarsson emerged from his cell and looked curiously up and down the corridor.

"I see they've begun stripping the station," he commented. "They plan to retreat into *Langstaff* during the burn. Good. That will make our mission easier."

"So you've learned something of their plans."

"No precise data. But I know they now have sufficient mass to begin the deorbit burn. That is why they're stripping useful materials and loading the transforms onto *Langstaff*. A ship under way must be equipped for any emergency—including combat requiring bioweapons.

"It is my impression that the Faction does not intend to provide for our well-being once burn commences. No one on this station will be considered essential after that. Only Vega's cargo has value."

"I figured that out already," Rameau said. "But thanks for the confirmation."

He hesitated. Was it safe to reveal Nuun's existence?

I have to tell him, if I want his best guess about what the Faction will do.

He leaned closer, even though he saw no one nearby.

"The burned pilot is still alive," he said softly. "And he's on Vega. I salvaged him."

Gunnarsson's eyes gleamed. He almost smiled.

"Then we have a chance," he said.

"But Neb says his reactions have registered an incoming ship," Rameau continued. "My observations confirm that. What do you know of this ship?"

"Nothing definite," Gunnarsson said. He stuffed the scraps of ration bar into his mouth, as if fueling himself for anticipated exertions. "It hasn't been discussed in my presence. But I believe we can assume it's the Original Man ship the Faction summoned, when they first seized power on Vega.

"If they act as I would—and remember, Original Man is one—the incoming ship will not leave jump. Instead, *Langstaff* will enter jump, then dock with the other ship. They will transfer cohorts to *Langstaff* to complete the crew, including backup pilots. Then the other ship will escort *Langstaff* and Vega back to Eyrie."

"This is what I don't understand," Rameau said. "And it's a critical point. Why would Gun Three take the risk of entering jump with only two pilots on board, when he could simply wait for the other ship to arrive, complete his crew, and then go home in safety?"

"It is a question of status," Gunnarsson said. "Once Gun Three enters jump, he is the commander of a functional ship. If he waits in orbit for the arrival of the rescue ship, then primary credit for recovery of Vega will go to the captain of that ship. Vega is a valuable prize. To bring it home under his command would increase the status of the Faction Commander considerably—if he had the training or intellect to succeed."

Contempt was audible in Gunnarsson's voice. He no longer seemed to be speaking from his normally objective viewpoint.

"I don't like him either," Rameau said, amused.

"It is not a question of emotion," Gunnarsson said. "His persig is Gun Three. He is not even a secondary. A mere tertiary variant. His arrogance in believing he could subvert this mission has been extreme. I am Gunnarsson Prime, of the Founder's own lineage."

"Then you believe we actually have a chance to take Vega away from them?" Rameau asked.

"Yes. Their decision to jump provides a window of opportunity—*if* we can utilize the burned pilot. We must act before they can be reinforced by the new ship. It will require precise timing."

"That's what I need to know. When do we time our action?"

"They will commence burn in the next cycle. Once that happens, the burn schedule will be accessible in the shipmind—even to you. Acceleration will increase gradually, to a standard one g, which will be maintained until we reach the giant planet. This is standard procedure. The crucial period will begin when they fly by the outermost planet, and acceleration increases radically. That is the point at which we will need acceleration support.

"Immediately thereafter, when we've cleared the system, acceleration will end. There will be a brief period of weightlessness as they prepare for jump. The crucial moment will come when they enter jump and approach the incoming ship, to attempt docking.

"We cannot save ourselves through combat. We have no weapons to oppose a jumpfighter. We must seize control of the jump field as the Faction attempts to dock, and exclude the incoming ship from the field. The other ship will fall out of jump.

"That will deprive the Faction of reinforcements. Most of the crew will still be in semistasis. That will be our moment to recapture control of *Langstaff*."

Gunnarsson's supreme arrogance amazed Rameau, as always.

But he's on our side this time.

"Why not seize *Langstaff* first, then perform the maneuver? Wouldn't it be easier to do from a secure command with a functional pilot space?"

"Of course," Gunnarsson said scornfully. "If I had a functional cohort force, that would be my choice. But even if your Remnants could defeat the Faction forces, they could not operate in a manner that would deceive the Commander of the incoming ship. He would perceive an anomaly and approach in hostile mode. We would have no opportunity to take him by surprise—and *Langstaff* is still unfit to fight. We must eliminate the threat of the new ship first, then retake *Langstaff*."

If only it were that easy.

"This maneuver is the same one that burned Nuun on our outbound journey, isn't it?" he said. "What makes you think we'll succeed this time, when he's already in a coma?"

"Nuun is not our only asset," Gunnarsson said. "We have the juvenile as well. He affiliates to you. I thought it was mere baseline foolishness in you, to promote such an attachment. Now I see it was a part of that craftiness I admire in you. He'll obey you.

"You have a few days, a week perhaps, for emergency training. Get him accustomed to linking with the pilot. When we enter jump, you will be with him, monitoring him, as you did with the *Langstaff* pilots. Only one maneuver is necessary. With you to command him, I believe it will be possible to complete a single configuration."

Rameau could see, as clearly as if he read the Commander's mind, that Gunnarsson did not expect Nuun or Per to survive that "single maneuver." He considered them expendable.

Could I really do that? Gunnarsson's right—Per would joyfully obey me. He wants to be a pilot. He doesn't know it could destroy him.

"And what if you're wrong?" he said.

Gunnarsson shrugged. "Then the rest of the plan will fail. You can surrender. Your cohorts will be terminated, but your life will be spared, at least until you reach Eyrie."

"No. I will not surrender. Not again. No matter what happens, we'll keep fighting." Rameau met Gunnarsson's eyes, and this time the Original Man was the first to look down.

"Baselines are strange," Gunnarsson said. "And yet—when other options fail . . ." He bowed his head slightly. "Perhaps it has not occurred to you that *I* have not been transferred to *Langstaff*. I am unsure of their plans for me."

"You think they're going to leave you here?"

"Often, incorrigible retrainees are abandoned in place. 'Permanent isolation,' they call it. It is not cruel treatment. There is water to drink. Often a drug is added to the water supply. I do not believe I would survive retraining in any case."

"Why would they treat you so harshly?" Rameau asked.

"I am the leader of a failed faction. My fate must serve as an example, to encourage solidarity among the others. It is the way of Original Man. Yet, I find I would prefer to survive."

His eyes met Rameau's again—pleading, not demanding.

"When the Faction cohorts have retreated to *Langstaff* for the burn, I ask that the medical officer salvage me. I am Original Man, and I am durable, but I believe I would sustain injury from experiencing full burn on the floor of this cube."

Rameau laughed out loud, incredulous.

Now he wants me to salvage him. Maybe karma exists after all!

"Granted," he said. "The Commander will be salvaged."

"I accept your command," Gunnarsson said. "In this situation, you have shown yourself the superior commander. And I accept your no-surrender protocol, unorthodox though it may be. My affiliation will remain with you, no matter what the outcome."

"Noted and accepted," Rameau said, trying not to show his amazement. "And now you must excuse me. I have a lot to take care of. I'll send for you as soon as the Faction cohorts have left the station."

"I shall await your return with some eagerness," Gunnarsson said drily.

Rameau left him without informing him of the backup plan. He couldn't trust Gunnarsson's apparent change of loyalty quite that much.

Not yet. He's willing to risk his own life now—but if he knew that I'll risk destroying Vega and everything on it before I'll let them have it, he might change his mind.

If none of this works, I'll still blow that cable. If High Command possessed unlimited pilots, and Vega's bioweapons, no human world would be safe from them.

He reached the sealed hatch of the biodome, and flashed it. They opened the door for him. They seized his arms eagerly and pulled him in, muttering his name. They needed him; they'd waited for him. For the first time in many days, he didn't shrink from the touch of hands.

"You can leave the door open," he reassured them as soon as he was inside. "There's no danger from toxicant contamination. They've all been moved to *Langstaff*."

Per cried out in anguish, struggling to get away from Troy.

"Be quiet," Rameau said sternly. "We have a plan to get them back. We're going to win it all back—*Langstaff* and everything. But it's going to take hard work and precise timing. Everyone has to listen, and do their jobs perfectly. That includes you."

Per choked back his sobs, and the Remnants gathered close as Rameau went over the plan.

"And now we have to move fast. Stage one is preparing to survive burn. Someone tell me, because I don't know—how do Rukh stand up to high g?"

"Designed for it, Rameau," Stalingrad said. "Our bones are very strong."

"Okay. Then, here's my plan. Just before the final burn, I'm going to send most of the cohorts down to the hibernation pods in the storage bay. There are plenty of empty ones, left when the Faction cohorts woke up. Set them for semihibernation, as you would for jump. That way, you'll revive quickly and be ready for action.

"As for the Rukh—since the pods aren't sized for you, we have to create some kind of acceleration pads here. I'm thinking the cohorts may have left shock-absorbing mats in place in their exercise room. We can collect those. Get cables. Don't go to the docking bay; they're still loading things through there. But check other equipment storage areas to see if the cohorts left any of those expandable nets behind. Hang them like hammocks and secure the mats on top. Two layers if we have enough. We don't know exactly which direction the weight will come from, so we need to fix them to swing freely and not dump us off.

"And scour the hibernation area for jump meds. There's always an emergency supply stashed near the pods.

"Remember, don't let the Faction cohorts see you doing any

of this. Go about your regular duties—slowly—while they're looking. Then work like hell as soon as their backs are turned."

He counted off the crews leaving to work on each task.

"I'll be spending a lot of time with Nuun. We'll need him when we seize control of the *Langstaff*. So I'm putting Tok and Uruk in charge of building the acceleration pads. Mat and Carthago, you're in charge of finding or creating weapons. Per, you stay with me.

"Set up teams, and make sure everyone gets a four-hour sleep cycle. Now—let's go!"

As the first feather touch of acceleration nudged the giant structure, all loose items drifted toward the surface that would serve as a floor. Rukh and cohorts adjusted their work patterns to the slowly returning gravity.

As Rameau had guessed, Per wasn't used to gravity. He wobbled slowly and uncertainly down the corridors where he'd once flown. If possible, he clung to Troy's back and let the Rukh carry him, or perched on the bot as it trundled along.

If Rameau had let him, he would have spent all his time in the comforting embrace of the pilot chair, his mind free in space. He took to the pilot training with such enthusiasm that there was no longer any doubt he'd been born for it. Yet Rameau still feared for him. True jump was far different from the drifting peace of Nuun's slow dream. And though Per might be a pilot child, he was still a child.

Neb came occasionally to visit his sib. Most of the time, he was occupied on *Langstaff*, and could rarely escape his duties for more than a few minutes. Per nearly burst with pride on those infrequent occasions.

"Neb! Look, look what I can do! I'm really a pilot now, huh, Neb? Can I be your sib now?"

Neb watched silently.

He must know that we're planning something. Yet he says nothing. Will he report us?

The day acceleration reached one g, and held steady, Neb was waiting in the biosphere when Rameau and Per returned from visiting Nuun. He beckoned to Rameau.

"Rameau," he said softly, "maybe I don't see you again."

He's learning to use pronouns, Rameau thought.

"Rameau bring Nuun back twice," Neb continued. "Please, you help one more time."

He bent over Rameau. In gravity, with their feet fixed to a common floor, he seemed taller than ever. But Rameau no longer felt intimidated.

"Rameau not tell anyone where Nuun is," he said. "Never tell. Neb can't help his sib no more. So let Nuun sleep until . . ." His voice trailed off. "Until." He finished.

"I'll do the best I can," Rameau said.

Neb hesitated for just a moment, as if hoping for something more, some assurance Rameau couldn't give.

"Okay," he said finally. Then he was gone.

But Rameau did see him again.

Rameau had just flashed the shipmind to check the burn time. They'd been pushing steadily outward at one g as the countdown for prejump burn ticked away. Now they had one hour and twenty-four minutes left until the final sweep around the giant planet.

Seeing the numbers made Rameau's heart pound faster. It hadn't been real until then. Now he knew that he was about to begin the final effort that would end in freedom or death.

The last bustle of Faction cohorts transporting gear out of Vega had given way to an eerie stillness and emptiness in the station. While the Remnants in the biosphere worked feverishly to complete the installation of acceleration mats, Rameau made a final dash to the storage bay to make sure the cohorts were safely stowed in the pods. Stalingrad and Jericho were with him, as always. Troy followed them, with Per riding his shoulders. Rameau wouldn't let the boy out of his sight.

Halfway back to the Dome, Stalingrad suddenly tapped his ear, signaling that he heard something. A cohort appeared, running toward them at full speed. It was Neb. He slid to a halt just before crashing into them.

"Rameau," he panted. "You have to—"

But he never got to complete the sentence. A squad of Faction cohorts, in close pursuit, hurtled toward them and flung

Neb to the ground. They immobilized him—carefully, to avoid damaging him, but with such efficiency that he couldn't struggle or speak.

Per shrieked with fury and tried to hurl himself on the cohorts.

"Troy, *stop* him," Rameau said under his breath. "Don't move. Nobody move."

Troy clasped one large hand over Per's mouth, but the boy still fought to get free.

The cohort in charge of the squad turned his attention toward them, and Rameau recognized him as Kir Ninety.

"Secure the juvenile," he ordered. Two cohorts who were not involved in subduing Neb reached out to take Per from Troy's grasp.

The Rukh roared and struck out at them, flinging them ten feet down the corridor with one blow.

Kir Ninety pointed his kenner-clad fist at the Rukh, and Troy fell to the ground, bellowing in pain. Even on his knees, he struggled forward, clawing at the collar, as the cohorts seized Per and dragged him away, screaming.

Kir Ninety continued the punishment until Troy sprawled on his back. The cohort's fingers danced across the kenner nodes, and Troy raised one fist. Briefly, the fist trembled in the air, and then, with a cry, Troy bludgeoned his own face again and again. When he groveled on the floor, bloody and choking, Kir Ninety finally lowered his hand.

The cohort grinned at Rameau.

"Did the baseline think he could mislead us?" he said. "We are aware of the juvenile's potential. He'll be returned to High Command for proper training."

Moving swiftly, and perfectly in step, the cohort squad bore its captives back to *Langstaff*. Rameau tried to run after them, but the rear guard menaced him with their weapons, and Stalingrad pulled him back. Jericho helped his battered comrade to his feet.

Oh, Kannon, we've lost him, we've lost him!

At first Rameau could think of nothing else. He realized that he was repeating the words out loud when Stalingrad shook his shoulder gently. The Rukh was trying to say something Rameau couldn't understand at first.

"Luck child," Stalingrad repeated. "Remember luck child. Story come out good."

Rameau just shook his head. *You're done for. You can't beat them.*

He looked at Troy's bleeding face, eyes swollen almost shut. Yet Troy was still looking at Rameau, as if he could find some hope in him.

No! Rameau thought. *I told Gunnarsson I'd go on fighting. No matter what.*

"Take me to the Commander," he ordered. "Quickly!"

Stalingrad picked him up and ran with him.

When Rameau flashed the cell door open, he found Gunnarsson splayed on the floor like a starfish, trying to brace himself against the walls with outspread arms and legs.

"Ah, Medical Officer," Gunnarsson greeted him. "Or should I now call you Captain? We have less than half an hour to burn, according to my chronometry."

"Out!" Rameau ordered. "Give me control codes for the Rukh—now!"

Gunnarsson glanced at Troy's battered condition, but didn't question it.

"A good thought," he said. "You will need to control them for battle."

Rameau waited impatiently as his kenner absorbed the codes, though it took only a few seconds.

Pointing his noded fist toward each Rukh in turn, he flashed, "Delete . . . delete . . . delete."

"What are you doing?" Gunnarsson protested, in shock. "Uncontrolled Rukh—you can't—"

"Cease to inform me what I can and cannot do," Rameau quoted grimly. "Time to go. Grad, Jeri—move us, please."

The Rukh swung Rameau and Gunnarsson to their shoulders and stampeded down the corridor. They crowded into the biosphere, and Rameau ordered the door shut behind them.

Mats and nets hung from every available support. Every mat seemed covered from edge to edge with reclining Rukh.

"Rameau, hurry, save you space," Carthago called from the far side of the room. The pad held a single unoccupied space.

"Commander!" *Shit, I have to get over calling him that.* "Get up on the mat!"

"There is room for only one," Gunnarsson said.

"What I said. Get up there."

"No. You are a baseline. You are fragile. And you will be needed."

Stalingrad grasped Rameau and laid him atop the mat.

"Do not struggle," Gunnarsson said. "You will disturb others."

"But what about you and Grad?"

"We are durable," Gunnarsson said. He and the Rukh found places where the moss on the deck curved in depressions that would support their backs.

"You might not be facing the right way when the weight comes on," Rameau protested. "You could fall and be crushed!"

"I have estimated the direction of burn with some accuracy," Gunnarsson said. He sounded smug, but for once Rameau didn't want him to be proven wrong.

I hope our weight doesn't tear out those bolts, Rameau thought. *Every one of those pallets is going to be tremendously heavy in a few minutes.*

Then a hammer of force slammed his entire body.

The double aerogel mats beneath him suddenly turned to slabs of steel. He felt like a tunnel rat being pressed flat between two metal plates—the surface below and the invisible force above. The suspended mats swung slightly as they assumed a new horizontal.

The smallest twinge of movement made him feel that he was about to slide from the mat, to be crushed beneath his own weight. His eyes had been open before the burn, and now he couldn't blink. Even his eyelids seemed as heavy as blocks of stone.

His vision darkened, reddened. He couldn't get his breath.

He heard the cohort beside him grunting in explosive rhythm. He remembered dimly that the technique was supposed to help. He tried to tighten his abdominal muscles, but they hurt so much already that he wasn't sure if he had succeeded. "Huunnhh . . ." He tried to mimic the larger form beside him. As a cry of pain, it was effective. And he was able to suck in a trickle of air after each exhalation. He imagined himself getting flatter . . . flatter . . . *I'll be a slab of pressed meat when this is over.*

And then he stopped thinking and could no longer believe it would ever end.

He must have lost consciousness at some point. When he came to, he was rotating gently, somewhere off the side of the mats. A little string of blood went past his face every time he turned around. He put his hand to his face, groaning with pain when he bent the elbow, and felt blood trickling from his nose. He reached out for a handful of moss and pressed it to his face.

Slowly, he searched himself for other injuries. His chest was sore, but without the stabbing pain of broken ribs. His left arm and side were turning dark blue. *Hematoma. I must have been too close to the cohort and got bruised by his weight.*

But he was essentially functional.

"Report injuries to me," he called, and turned to look for Stalingrad and Gunnarsson. The Rukh was just trying to sit up, groaning. Gunnarsson was his usual imperturbable self. Under the Rukh's thick mat of hair, it was hard to see the damage, but he seemed to have bruises over most of his back. Gunnarsson had a bruised wrist, and some capillaries had burst near one eye, making him look as if he wore a purple eyepatch, but he was otherwise undamaged.

Other injuries were mostly bloody noses, black eyes, and occasional bruises. A cracked rib seemed to be the worst damage sustained.

Gunnarsson looked around and frowned. "Where is the boy?"

Rameau quickly signaled Stalingrad for silence. He knew the other Rukh would follow Grad's lead.

"His location doesn't concern you," he said. "Everything is proceeding according to plan. That's all you need to know."

"Ah." Gunnarsson nodded as if he understood. "Hide essential resources. Good. You're learning well."

He held out his bruised arm. "And—while I speak of hiding—my locator must be removed. If they come looking for me, I don't want them to find me. Cut it."

He pointed to the forearm. "There—approximately two inches down, I would say. Cut directly from the top to avoid major nerves."

Kali. More surgery without anesthetics. Well—if I have to do it to someone, I'm glad it's him. This should be a real pleasure.

"Istanbul, Krak—hold his arm steady," Rameau said.

"That will not be necessary," Gunnarsson said disdainfully.

"I'm the officer in charge, and I deem it necessary," Rameau said. He borrowed a knife from one of the cohorts. Then he felt Gunnarsson's arm, probing for the locator. Amid the tough masses of muscle, it was hard to find the small lump.

"This isn't a sophisticated tool here," he warned. "The blade is pretty large and will make a correspondingly big wound."

"I am in no danger," Gunnarsson said. "Cut."

Rameau wished that his anxiety for Per could be forgotten for a few minutes. He would have liked to fully savor the moment. For the first time in his surgical career, he really enjoyed the process. Gunnarsson's stoic manner added to his pleasure, because he didn't have to pity the patient.

He found the locator disk with the first cut, and twisted the knife slightly, to loosen the disk. He plunged finger and thumb of his opposite hand into the incision, seized the blood-slippery object, and pulled it loose.

"You are a precise surgeon," Gunnarsson said calmly. "I recommend you dispose of that in the first converter chute you come to."

"I can't provide a dressing for that right now," Rameau said, wiping his hands at the hose nozzle and watching the pink-tinged bubbles float away. "Get someone to give you an antiseptic wipe, and then pack it with moss to stop the bleeding. Mar will show you which moss. Then get in the plant shed and hide there."

Swiftly, he reviewed his orders for the next, crucial hour.

"Carthago is passing out jump medications. You will line up to receive medications, then pass in front of me, and I'll delete your command codes. Then strap down and wait until we enter jump. Gunnarsson, you will wait here with the rest.

"As soon as we enter jump, you will all proceed to the storage bay. Gunnarsson, you will supervise revival of the Remnant cohorts. You will await my signal, and then assault the *Langstaff*. Drive for the command nexus. Attempt to salvage the pilots. Tok will be in charge of the assault; Gunnarsson, you will serve him as first officer. I rely on your strategic experience.

"Stalingrad, you're with me. You know where we must go. Grad and I will join you as soon as our job is done. All clear? Then go, Remnants! No surrender!"

30

Compassionate One, keep Per alive, he thought as he flew toward the lab and the pilot chair. *Help us get him back.*

Stalingrad interrupted his worrying.

"Rameau—what will you do?" the Rukh said.

"The only thing I can do—take the jump myself."

Half his mind protested.

This is crazy. Per was our only chance, not you. You might be able to pilot with Nuun's help, if it was an easy course, a normal jump. But you can't perform this maneuver and you know it. What do you think will happen to all of them if you fail?

But at the core, he stubbornly believed that he could do it. At least, that he had to try.

I've got Nuun to feed me the data. Together, we make two half pilots. And at least I have the judgment of an adult.

As he strapped himself into the pilot chair, he knew he had always planned this. He had never intended to put the child in the link for this jump.

"It's okay, Grad," he reassured the Rukh. "I wanted it this way. But promise me one thing. If I don't come back, it's up to you. If they're losing, if all hope is lost, you have to blow that cable. Try to pull the Remnants back to Vega first—but whatever happens, don't let the Faction recapture us."

Stalingrad nodded. "Yes. Rameau kept his promise. Rukh keep ours. Don't worry."

Rameau felt the massive clasp of the Rukh's hand.

Then he stretched out in the chair, at ease. He pulled on the helmet and gloves.

All systems operational. Nobody to pull me out before my time. O Compassionate One, I ask no mercy for these bones. Just let me dump that ship before I go.

Then the heavens spread out around him, and he stopped worrying. He breathed, and let the turning of the stars pour into him.

There was Nuun. He slowed down to meet him. Nuun seemed like an old friend now—one who didn't speak much, but was always there. They were going much faster this time. And there was no planet in the way, nothing to hinder them from speeding onward. It was a wonderful and dangerous sensation, like sailing a foam-torn sea with no land in sight.

There was another presence, too. He was startled at first, but then he remembered the station was still linked to *Langstaff*. He needed to hold back and let *Langstaff*'s pilot pull them into jump. He held Nuun back, braking, hiding, to keep their presence invisible until *Langstaff* made its move.

It was hard to hold back. The other pilot was skillful and daring. He felt the quick perceptions almost catching him. He wanted to match the other move for move, racing side by side. They were going almost fast enough now, as if they rode a wave that was nearly ready to crest, to curl over in a thunder of speed and foam as they soared along its curve.

He knew that what he saw in the link wasn't the full truth that Nuun experienced. But it was hard to remember that. This seemed more gloriously real than any perception he'd had in that tiny and crowded other world.

Faster, oh faster! He swung out, flung by the dancing masses, as they became visible to the other pilot, like a bright star rising over the horizon. He felt the field gather and brighten around him, shaped by the other pilot's subtlety. It tingled in his senses like snow, like salt spray. It blazed like starlight seen from Outside.

For a single instant, he crested the wave, plunged down the mountainside in a shower of crystals, then soared into starfire and was consumed.

Then he had come through it, and hung in the timeless space where he could see everything at once. He could move toward any point by redirecting his focus—or Nuun's focus, though they were the same. But there was no reason to move or change. The dance was perfect as it was. Suns flared and died, planets formed and shone, and melted away, brief as snowflakes. The pattern was ever-changing and always perfect.

No . . . that was Nuun, and not him. *He* was Rameau, and he had a job to do. It was painful to pull himself away from this perfect moment. But that was good. Pain helped him remember.

They were in jump now. He had to seize the moment and reshape their field to exclude the other ship. The enemy would fall from this space, back into chaos.

They would continue on alone. Unmolested.

He began to gather the field into his own consciousness, pulling away from the other pilot. This time it was Rameau who suffered, not Nuun. Nuun felt the ghost of long-past agony, like heat on an old burn, and twisted away. But Rameau had to do the work, and it was hard. He felt the oncoming ship like a needle through his brain, like a hot knife in his heart. Burning lines of force crossed in his mind. He tried to hold them together and force them into a different pattern. They tore at him. If he lost control, he would be rent into a million shards, each one on fire. He could feel cold brightness blasting him as he pulled the forces closer to him, closer . . .

The brightness wasn't a joy now but a consuming agony. Still, he pressed onward. He couldn't take his eyes from it. He had to go there. To the place where the pain glowed most brightly.

Just before it closed over him, the moment seemed to slow into timelessness again. He tried to move forward, toward his fate, but something held him back, like a restraining arm.

The Rukh? They wouldn't let me go . . .

Not Rukh. But it was a familiar pattern. Glowing symbols flared and faded like sparks. Fireflies? No—bees, one of them momentarily crowned by a golden circle.

While he watched the sparks flicker, entranced, the other presence gathered up the forces that had so bitten him with agony. It wrapped them easily around itself, as if the field were light as floating silk. The intruder faltered within that folded space, and was gone, like a snowflake touched by the sun.

Rameau and Nuun were one again. Their vessel soared on in peace, accompanied only by the starry dancers. Within Rameau's mind, the lost one soared with them, golden and beautiful, and Rameau watched her, finally in peace. Finally he understood.

Original Man is one. We're all one. Or will be, one day. If they don't know it now, they will.

You understand now, Nuun's presence murmured, sleeping yet alert, like a mind alive inside a dream.

So why can't I stay here, where peace has already come? I can wait here for the day. Now that I know it's coming.

It was not Nuun's sleeping mind that answered him, but his own.

The day will come. But someone has to bring the day. The job is waiting for someone who can do it.

Why does it have to be me?

Why not? "Sentient beings are numberless . . ." Maybe you can't save them all. Start with one or two. An ant, perhaps, or a bee.

Rameau knew where he'd heard of those things before. He remembered who he was. And he knew the sounds that called to him. He didn't want to answer. He hung there, perfectly poised between two worlds. But he heard them calling, and turned back.

This time it was like falling from an endless sky, until he crash-landed in his body again.

"Ah—god. Have mercy. Water—please."

They held the squeeze to his lips, and he managed to swallow. They moved him, and he managed not to throw the water up again. He could feel his body, most acutely, but he couldn't seem to move.

He struggled. Even his eyeballs jerked randomly, out of control. Finally he was able to focus. Stalingrad was there, which made sense, but so was Gunnarsson, and that seemed wrong.

"Uh. Where are we? Did we jump? Did we shake them?"

"The screens show no trace of the cohort ship," Gunnarsson said. "We came through jump transition, still docked with *Langstaff*, but the second ship is gone. It was hard to awaken you. You were in very deep."

Stalingrad pulled Rameau out of the chair and rubbed his arms and legs. It hurt, but he found that he could move again.

"What did you think you were doing?" Gunnarsson said. "The boy was to act as pilot. How did this happen? You risked all our lives."

Rameau was feeling good. "Yeah. And it worked, too, didn't it?" he said. In spite of the grime that still coated him, he felt clean and strong.

"The Faction took Per, just before burn. I didn't tell you that, because I didn't want you to lose focus. But now we have to go get him. Come on! What are we waiting for?"

"We know where he is," Gunnarsson said grimly. "After the jump transition, we found this."

Oh, Kannon, don't let them say he's dead.

"Watch this," Gunnarsson said. He leveled his kenner at the wallscreen and transferred data. The screen showed a patchy, hesitant transmission. Per's face, in close-up, bent over a kenner that seemed to be attached to someone else's hand.

"Rameau," said his thin, childish voice, "you told that story about the luck child. When the cohorts came, you let them have me, just like that stupid old genedoc in the story. They thought they could lock me up, but I'm not going to let the story come out like that. I called the bot and told it to take me to Neb. He needs me. I'm going to link with Neb now until I'm ready to be a pilot myself. You think I can't, but you're wrong."

The boy in the picture glanced sharply upward, and the transmission ended.

"Kannon! We're wasting time." Rameau tried to leap into action, and nearly cracked his head on the ceiling.

I thought they'd stash him somewhere safe. Away from trouble. He got as far as the pilot pod. Where is he now?

Stalingrad caught him and steadied him.

"Luck child come out good," he rumbled.

Gunnarsson stared. Rameau wasn't sure the *Langstaff*

Commander could actually understand the Rukh, but Stalingrad's speech was certainly comprehensible enough to make clear that it *was* speech.

"The Rukh has speech," Gunnarsson said.

"Indeed. One more thing Omo didn't notice," Rameau said. "Now, move—that's an order!" he added.

31

Rameau had not imagined what would result from this simple command. Stalingrad took him under one arm, and they flew down the corridor at combat speed. The rest of the Remnants surged toward them in a dark wave as they neared the biosphere. They wore protective work vests and goggles, blackened by soot and wear. They carried weapons of every shape and size—laser tools with the safety features disabled, projectile weapons built from metal tubing, and more that Rameau couldn't recognize. They'd cobbled the weapons together from every kind of scrap and spare part.

They can build anything, once they get the idea.

Rameau hated weapons. Yet perversely, undeniably, he was proud of them.

They swept down the corridor in formation, carrying Rameau along, so he had no need to use his own frail strength to navigate. He found himself in the center of the group, protected on all sides, yet somehow separate from this perfectly coordinated machine of many parts. He couldn't command them; he didn't speak that language. Gunnarsson barked out ship jo, and the group turned all at once like a school of fish.

Someone put a weapon into Rameau's hands. In micro g, it wasn't heavy, but he could feel how massive it was and how clumsy in his hands.

I handle small tools. Laser scalpels, microtomes. Not this.

He was afraid even to shift his grip, lest he push the wrong stud and kill someone.

And yet, in a strange, unexpected way, it was glorious and exhilarating to be part of this fast-moving, irresistible unit.

Original Man is one. And now I know what that's like, for one brief glimpse.

He had been trying to break them loose from that unity. But he'd never realized how good it felt.

They were closing on the corner where the holding tanks stood. Rameau couldn't remember ever covering that route so fast. *Too fast.* Because now it was time for him to know what to do, yet he didn't.

They were flying. He caught brief glimpses of the gleaming coppery cable overhead as they passed through the docking bay. Darker patches, like insulation wrap, showed where Carthago had packed his charges against the cable. A sudden change in the wall color and the smell of the air showed they'd reached *Langstaff*. Then there were armed Faction cohorts all around them. The Remnants' swift, unified column broke up into a yelling, chaotic horde as they chased the Faction fighters helter-skelter through the once familiar rings and tubes of their old ship.

"To the core!" Gunnarsson shouted. "Don't chase them! Drive for control! We take the nexus!"

Gunnarsson fired a blast to clear the way, and explosive shells rang against the kemplex wall in a clangorous tattoo, deafening Rameau so that the scene unfolded for him in an eerily muted tone. Faction cohorts appeared in front of him, their weapons pointed toward him. He swung his own weapon up, and pressed what he hoped was the firing stud.

He heard the tearing-fabric *sssssshhhHHHH* of hot gases, and a fist-sized ball of yellow-white fire shot from the muzzle. The cohorts before him scattered—but when the blue-and-green dots stopped dancing in his dazzled eyes, more enemies had taken their places.

One of the Rukh shoved him backward, and he slammed against the wall. When he stopped bouncing, he was behind a conduit casing that gave him a slender margin of cover.

They gave this gun to the wrong person. But I have to try to do something with it, since I've got it.

Peering from behind the conduit, he pointed the gun into the mass of opposing cohorts and pressed the stud again. Again the tearing sound, and the crack of impact, this time so close in time that the sounds piled into his ears on top of each other. Still, he saw no effect. The Faction troops crowded in as thickly as ever.

He pressed the stud twice more, and finally hit some vulnerable spot. Fire flashed from a support pack on one cohort's back, and the reaction sent that cohort spinning across the corridor. Rameau couldn't see what damage he'd caused, but he heard the cry of agony before a better marksman crushed the flailing body into limp silence.

All around him there were screams and cries, the hiss and thud of fire and impact, the growling of the Rukh. One of the Rukh plunged across the corridor, its fur afire, howling. It caught an armored cohort by an arm and a leg and tore him in half. The armor remained in place, but a severed limb drifted slowly away, trailing a bright flag of blood. The Rukh was hit again, convulsed, and then drifted away with its prey, entangled in the spreading net of red liquid.

Rameau wanted to drop his weapon and speed to aid the wounded.

Not incepted for combat, not *incepted for combat . . .*

The Faction cohorts had no Rukh, but they were better armed and stronger. They pushed the Remnants back a few meters, into a bottleneck where there was little room to maneuver.

I have to use this thing, help them . . .

It was harder now to aim without hitting his own people. A Rukh—Stalingrad?—seized Rameau and dragged him backward. One of the Faction cohorts had his gun up, pointed straight into Rameau's face. The Rukh's huge fist shot out like a hammer. It couldn't crush the face mask on the armor, but Rameau heard the dull smashing sound inside the helmet. The cohort crumpled up, his weapon flying wild. Rameau could hear Gunnarsson shouting orders, but couldn't understand him.

The Remnants pushed forward again, still firing, still fighting. Each time one of them went limp, it tore at Rameau. He didn't know who they were. He could only guess which ones were falling. Desperately he hoped that certain cohorts hadn't been the first to go, and then felt ashamed.

No one is expendable.

He fired whenever he had a clear view. It seemed as if a life-time had passed since his first shot. At the same time, it seemed like only a few confused seconds—not long enough for lives to disappear forever.

Then, behind them, he heard a sound more terrifying than any weapon—the shriek of the sinué, an endless whistling cry like something being scalded.

They've unleashed the monster, to hunt us down like rats! And if it eats a few of the Faction, too—I guess they're expend-able.

Still they were being forced back. They'd be in the jaws of the monster in moments. He fought to turn around, to point his gun toward the threat behind them.

Then he let the useless weapon fly from his hand.

You can't beat them with their own weapons. You've never won that way. Think!

"Out of the way!" he screamed. "Let the monster through! Let it go!"

Pulling at Stalingrad's arm had no effect; he had to punch the Rukh in the back of the head to get his attention. But Grad finally understood, and dived for a cross-corridor, away from the worst danger—that the sinué might catch them in the bot-tleneck, leaving them nowhere to go.

Stalingrad bellowed like rolling thunder. The Rukh heard and scattered in all directions, dragging the cohort Remnants with them, just as a wedge of flying Faction cohorts came at them. The Faction cohorts arced over them, but before they could turn and fire, the sinué was on them.

The Faction fighters scattered in reflexive terror from the snapping, bloodstained jaws. The monster tore into them, biting one in half, shaking another to bloody rags, not pausing to swallow in its thirst for blood. Shots fired at it singed the hide and blew smoking holes in its flesh, but did not slow it down.

It seemed mad with joy to have one final chance at vengeance. The Faction crew who escaped its jaws ran into withering fire from Remnants crouched in the cross-corridors, waiting to pick them off.

The creature's madness served the Remnants now, as it moved ahead of them, slaughtering their enemies.

Rameau found the control commands with his blood-smeared kenner. He couldn't attempt any complex orders, but he jammed down the flash node, firing one simple command: "Forward—forward—go—*go!*" The sinué lashed its tail, driving its body onward. The Remnants closed in behind it.

Where are we? Almost to the inner ring! A few meters farther—

One Faction cohort held his ground, dodging with expert thruster burns, yet always aiming steadily as the monster clashed its jaws and shook its head. Rameau used his own thrusters, rose above the plane of the main conflict for a better view, and recognized Gun Three, the Faction Commander.

He's trying to take out the sinué—looking for a clear shot down its throat.

Gun Three fired again and again, searing the creature's hide without apparent effect. Then he launched himself across its path, firing at its eyes. It roared in agony, half blinded. Gun Three let his weapon float on its tether and pointed his unarmed fist at the creature's head.

No, not its head—he's aiming for the collar. He's not trying to kill it—he's trying to turn it back against us.

Rameau raised his own fist and sent a countervailing command. *"No—forward—forward!"*

The sinué thrashed and flailed. It flung its head first one way, then the other, clashing its bloody jaws at each tormentor in turn.

But Rameau's mastery of the control unit was limited. Convulsively, the sinué coiled sideways. Soon it would turn to tear the Remnants apart as easily as it had destroyed the Faction troops. Rameau could not match Gun Three's command of the monster.

He screamed to the Remnant fighters behind him to pull back.

If I can't control it, I can let it go. Let it choose for itself which one of us it hates the most.

He flashed a final command: "Delete . . . delete . . . delete."

The sinué was wild again, beyond any control. Bleeding, coated in slime, it turned and gaped at Rameau. He saw the red eyes, glaring with hate, the jaws stretched open till he could see all the way down its reeking gullet.

He flung his arms wide, in search of a weapon, but found none. He faced the monster alone.

But it writhed once more, howling in agony, or in mad triumph. It flung Rameau aside with a stunning blow from its tail, and turned back toward the Faction Commander.

Gun Three fired explosive shells in one last desperate burst.

Too late—the massive jaws closed over his head. As if in slow motion, the monster's scarred sides swelled and distended; then ragged holes tore open, spilling the monster and its last meal in one burst of ruin.

It convulsed once more. Its bulk still tumbled toward them, like a pilotless shuttle, but there was no longer any intent behind the movement. It was dead.

Stalingrad caught Rameau and lifted him away, into less contaminated air. Rameau's breath labored against his aching ribs. He choked on the stench he inhaled with every gasp. The Remnants were a grotesque sight, drenched with their own blood and that of their enemies.

He turned his eyes away from the monstrous fragments that filled the air around him.

Keep fighting . . . no matter what . . .

"Grad—get me a gun," he gasped.

But all around him, the few Faction cohorts who remained let their weapons drift away. They bowed and extended both arms above their heads in the gesture of surrender. Combat had decided the issue. The Remnants had won. The Faction submitted to their vindication by victory.

Rameau felt himself slipping into the burn of drugged exhaustion once again, his enabler redlining, unable to cope with the stress of jump, of the monster, of memory grinding him again on its harsh wheel. He had a nightmare feeling that he was back in the Dome on Varuna where it had all started, again the only living man in a storm of corpses.

He found the strength to grasp for Stalingrad's arm.

"Grad," he whispered. "Take me—have to see—"

Stalingrad understood. The Rukh lifted him and flew with him to the pilot space, used Rameau's kenner to flash it open. Inside he found them, miraculously untouched by the carnage outside. Neb and Nor. And Per perched beside them, safe, absorbed in the link.

Rameau hadn't been able to do more than watch as Gunnarsson himself had pulled the dazed Per out of the link. Neb and Nor could not be awakened. They still steered the joined ships as they fled through jump space. But Rameau had seen their life signs, before his weariness had taken him down. No pilots had burned, not on this journey.

"It was Neb," Rameau mumbled. "He helped me."

"What?" the helpful voices around him asked. He couldn't explain it to them, but he knew, and the knowledge stayed with him as consciousness dropped away.

I would have burned myself on that maneuver. I couldn't have handled it. Neb dropped the other Faction ship out of jump, to save my life.

Commander of the bees. Mercy for the small things, help in return for help. He must have heard the story, after all.

They'd let him sleep for a long time, while the worst of the damage was cleared away, and the Faction cohorts were disarmed and confined. The Remnants had posted guards on *Langstaff* as Gunnarsson had demanded, but a core group had insisted on carrying Rameau back to Vega, to the dome they now considered their home.

Now, hours after his awakening, Rameau was again weary. There had been casualties to tend in the aftermath, as always. There would be time, later, to complete repairs, time to face their losses, and mourn them. But this moment was a rare chance for what was left of the Remants to relax together, recall what had passed, and dream of the future.

"Where will we go now?" Rameau asked Gunnarsson. "What course shall we set?"

They've lost their past, he thought. *They need something to look forward to.*

"I believe a planet would be our best choice," Gunnarsson said. His usual self-possession had returned. Only an occasional gleam in his eye revealed his satisfaction with their victory.

"I will work with the shipmind to find some alternative destinations. We need an untouched world, far from danger, where we can risk awakening the new clan. A place that will support life."

The thought of a planet to explore caused nudges and excited murmurs among the Remnants.

"We will be hunted by humans and Original Man alike," Gunnarsson said repressively. "We must hold to our identity as warriors. We must continue to fight for the Founder's last command."

"Don't think of it that way," Rameau said. "Say, instead, we must hold to the Founder's dream—a dream meant for all of us. I think I've come to understand it better."

Gunnarsson held his peace, startled by talk of the Founder from Rameau.

"I don't think the Founder ever intended his creation to cause destruction. He wanted Original Man to survive, yes—but not at the price of genocidal war. When he saw that humans and Original Man were locked into a collision course, he built Vega as his atonement. This was how he hoped to return to humankind the gifts he stole from our genome.

"The lives that Vega holds must have a chance to grow in peace—not as the tools of any warring faction, human or Omo. They are the Founder's hope of preserving what was best in us. They're his hope of someday reuniting both groups in a shared humanity. That should be our hope, too. It's a big mission."

He spoke more to Gunnarsson than to the others. He wasn't sure they'd understand him, yet. But they'd picked up one word, at least.

"Rameau, we complete mission," Ket said. "What about names?"

It took Rameau a minute to remember what Ket meant. The day he'd founded the Remnants seemed very far away.

"Rameau said, when cohorts perform great mission, we choose names."

"Yes, I did, didn't I? Well, you've certainly earned them. There are many to choose from—great names, heroes' names. The shipmind has a complete selection. Or you could wait until you hear a few more stories."

"What stories?" another cohort asked, instantly intrigued.

"Stories of heroes. Red-maned Thor, strong as a Rukh, who battled giant transforms armed with fire and ice. Commander Arthur—his warriors were remnants, too—and his great ship called Avalon, the ship that can never die."

"Tell!"

"Tell!" The call echoed from all over the dome.

"No, not tonight," Rameau put them off softly. "Tonight, the story of the *Langstaff* Remnants is the greatest story of all. Tonight we rest. Tomorrow we begin a new story."

The off-duty cohorts exchanged opinions and bandied about names as they drifted off to sleep.

Rameau made the rounds of the newly wounded. He missed Neb and Nor at his side. All three pilot sibs were together tonight, he thought, and wished them well.

By the time he'd finished, most of the others were asleep. Rameau stayed up long enough to retrieve his message cube from its hiding place and set it carefully in the grove of little trees. He pressed the stud and watched Dakini dance, light as a golden leaf in a green forest.

Stalingrad came to his side, moving very quietly for such a large being, and watched her with him. For the first time, Rameau shared the vision without a sense of intrusion.

And for the first time, he was able to watch her without tears.

"You said once that nothing you did would ever matter," he said. He spoke to her image, but for the Rukh's ears as well.

"That's not true now," he continued. "You've changed the

future. Everything that has happened here, happened because of you.

"I don't know exactly what we'll do next. I haven't seen everything that's in the frozen storage, or the hibernation pods. But I know that all of them deserve compassion and freedom. I know that because of you.

"Most of the genes that made us—and I mean you as well as me—began as invaders and then made us their home. Maybe this ship, and others like it, could act as viruses in the bloodstream of human history. We'll invade them—humans and Original Man alike. Viruses aren't picky. We can work our way into the genomes of both species, until the day they look at each other and realize they're one again.

"That's a long way from now. But there are other things that matter.

"I can take off the collar—on the neck, or in the mind.

"I can look for a way to heal the toxicants.

"I can say 'No one's expendable' and mean it.

"I think I can do those things, because it matters to me now. It all matters."

The dance ended, and Rameau fell silent. He wondered how *Langstaff* looked now, to the dreamer still sleeping in its core.

A ship of hopeful monsters, speeding through the starry distances, toward a future imagined only in dreams.

"Sentient beings are numberless," Rameau thought. He remembered the next line. He had never been able to say it.

Humans say impossible things because we want to make them true.

"I vow to save them all."

Visit www.delreydigital.com— the portal to all the information and resources available from Del Rey Online.

- Read sample chapters of every new book, special features on selected authors and books, news and announcements, readers' reviews, browse Del Rey's complete online catalog, and more.

- Sign up for the Del Rey Internet Newsletter (DRIN), a free monthly publication e-mailed to subscribers, featuring descriptions of new and upcoming books, essays and interviews with authors and editors, announcements and news, special promotional offers, signing/convention calendar for our authors and editors, and much more.

To subscribe to the DRIN: send a blank e-mail to join-ibd-dist@list.randomhouse.com or sign up at www.delreydigital.com

The DRIN is also available at no charge for your PDA devices—go to www.randomhouse.com/partners/avantgo for more information, or visit www.avantgo.com and search for the Books@Random channel.

Questions? E-mail us at delrey@randomhouse.com

 www.delreydigital.com